The Mutation

Book Three of the Virus Series

Damien Lee

Edited by Linda Nagle

Cover art designed by Matt Seff Barnes

Part One

1

Zielinski jerked his head, trying to penetrate the encompassing darkness. He feared he had gone blind, unable to tell whether his eyes were open or closed. He tried to reach up, but felt resistance from his bound wrists. Deprived of his sight, he had no other choice than to make use of his other senses.

A heart monitor beeped rapidly in time with his escalating pulse. A ventilator wheezed nearby, and then Zielinski heard the hollow sound of his breathing. A mask covered his nose and mouth, forcing oxygen into his lungs. He twisted his head, grinding his face against the firm mattress beneath, and pushed the elasticated mask aside.

With his face liberated, he took a deep breath, and gagged. The stench of rotten flesh and decay burned the inside of his nose and coated the back of his throat in a film of bile. He tried to rise, thwarted again, this time by bindings across his chest and legs. He blinked, his eyelids scraping against a blindfold.

Where the fuck am I?

Then: footsteps. They sounded distant, but gradually drew closer, echoes growing louder with each rhythmic step.

Fuck. Fuck. Fuck!

Zielinski longed to cry out, but as he opened his mouth, all he could muster was an incoherent garble.

"Ah, you're awake."

Although the voice was unfamiliar, the soft, well-spoken accent lent itself to a distinguished gentleman. Zielinski tried to reply, but words failed him. "Don't speak," the man said, his footsteps getting louder. *Closer.* "Rest. The sedative will wear off soon."

"Seda... tive?"

"Your memory will return, too. Although, one could argue that in the current climate, ignorance is a blessing."

The footsteps stopped beside him. Zielinski could sense the man looming above his face, accompanied by an aroma of chemicals and disinfectant. The cloying smell displaced the odour of death as Zielinski felt the face mask cover his mouth.

"Keep that on. Your respiratory system will appreciate it."

The man started interacting with one of the machines, which bleeped in response. Zielinski surrendered to the life-giving oxygen, relaxing into the firm surface beneath him. The man's words floated around his brain. *In the current climate, ignorance is a blessing. What does that mean? Where the hell am I? How did I get here?* He struggled to pull his snippets of memory together into a meaningful timeline. Everything felt jumbled. He recalled an army base, yet had no recollection of having served in the military. Then: prison—something about a prison. More of his memories seemed to originate there. He remembered the inmates, the guards. Then the zombies.

Zombies? What the fuck?

Zielinski tried to lurch upright, ignoring the frenzied beeping of the heart monitor as he fought against his restraints.

"Whoa, calm down."

Zielinski ignored the man and twisted his head to the side, mashing his face into the mattress, successful at undoing the mask once again. This time the blindfold rode up, offering him a glimpse of his surroundings.

Bright fluorescent lights illuminated what looked to be a medical ward. Several unoccupied gurneys, similar to the one he was lying on, ran along the wall beside him. Medical charts adorned the other walls, with glass partitions separating different rooms.

"You need to relax."

Zielinski turned to look at the man, who now loomed over him. His tufty white hair matched the lab coat draped over his slim frame. He stood with an air of authority, yet his eyes offered a surprising kindness. His unshaven face seemed like an addition the man had not become accustomed to. He scratched the silver whiskers and offered a polite smile.

"Who are you?" Zielinski asked, without reciprocating the man's warm demeanour.

"My name is Doctor Armstrong. And you are Mr... Zielinski, right?"

Zielinski didn't respond, but his expression gave him away.

"I thought so. Although it was hard to distinguish, what with all the colourful names your friends call you."

Zielinski frowned, picturing his fellow inmates. For a second, he considered the possibility he was at the prison, but the whitewashed walls and glass partitions were alien to him. He looked down at the restraints binding him to the gurney. He tried to move, but knew his efforts would be futile.

"Where am I? How did I get here, and why the fuck am I strapped down?"

The doctor's smile faltered and he rubbed his brow in exasperation. "So many questions, all with such trivial answers. You've failed to ask the most important one."

Zielinski scowled, waiting for the doctor to continue.

"*Why* are you here?"

The smile returned to Armstrong's face, and he pulled back a curtain that had been concealing the next bed. Zielinski's stomach lurched when he saw the occupant— the source of the rotting stench. The decomposing corpse stared back, its lifeless eyes peering through him.

"Don't worry. He's dead," Armstrong muttered. "And I mean *dead*-dead, not the *undead* type you've had to deal with."

Words failed him, and all Zielinski could do was stare at the corpse.

"He became infected a week ago. We thought we had made a breakthrough, but we were wrong."

"Wh—I don't—"

"You don't understand," Armstrong said, pulling the curtain closed. "But you will."

He leaned over the rail so he was directly above Zielinski's face.

"I intend to save the world, Mr Zielinski. And you're going to help me do it."

2

Frank hissed in pain, squirming as Lisa peeled the bandage away from his side.

"You're enjoying this, aren't you?" he grumbled.

"On the contrary, my dear. I hate seeing you in so much pain."

"Bullshit."

Lisa threw the blood-soaked bandage into the bin and poured a cup of boiled water. Whilst the Eden Spa Hotel offered countless amenities, including fresh water, food, power, and safety, it was severely lacking in the first-aid department. With a handful of bandages, and no sterile solution at all, Lisa had to adapt. She soaked a cotton ball in the hot water and dabbed it against Frank's wound, prompting a further outburst.

"Ow! Not so hard."

"I need to keep it clean. Bullet wounds don't heal overnight, you know."

"You could be a bit gentler."

"Pussy." Lisa smirked.

"You *are* enjoying this."

Lisa placed a gauze pad over the bullet wound and settled behind him. "Here, hold this while I do your back."

She repeated the procedure, peeling the bandage from the exit wound, cleaning it, and redressing. Once finished, she wrapped a bandage all the way around Frank's torso.

"There," she said. "Happy?"

"I'd be happier once we've started barricading this hotel." Frank rose from the bed, grabbing his t-shirt from the back of the chair. "Where's Kara?"

"Where d'ya think?"

"Still on the roof?" Frank eased the t-shirt over his head, careful not to strain his side as he pulled it down.

"Yup. Been up there for hours."

"You ought to go and check she hasn't jumped. We need her to look after this place when we head out."

"She'll be fine. She just needs space."

They moved onto the corridor, illuminated by the rays of the morning sun. The bedroom they had chosen was the largest in the hotel. Not only did it boast a fully stocked minibar, a standalone bathtub big enough for two, and a king-size bed, but it also had an incredible view over the moors—an ideal vantage point to keep on the lookout for trespassers.

So far, they hadn't encountered anybody, but with this being their first night in the hotel, Frank wasn't going to allow optimism to cloud his judgement. He slung the shotgun over his back, wincing as a fresh wave of pain pulsed through his body.

"You know you could leave that in the bedroom, right?" Lisa said, as they made their way downstairs.

"I could, but what if this place comes under attack?"

"Then we've got these." She tapped the handgun holster on her hip.

"And what if there's loads of them?"

"Then don't miss." Lisa cast a smirk in his direction, but her remark reminded him they were running low on ammo. Their assault on the prison had consumed a vast number of bullets. Yet, Frank couldn't dispel his suspicion that Amy's party had taken the rest, especially the cop and his wife. He couldn't be sure, but when he and Lisa had gone to gather the rest of the ammunition before leaving the base, there was only a handful of bullets left.

"What's up?" Lisa asked.

"Just thinking about that baldy bastard who took our shit."

"We don't know it was him."

"We know how much was there *before* that lot appeared."

"And we also know we'd be dead if they hadn't come along. Even if they did take our stuff, it's a small price to pay."

Frank eyed the bruises covering her face and neck and felt the familiar flicker of anger.

"Maybe. But if I ever see them again, we're not playing happy families. At least not while that pork scratching is with them."

"I doubt we'll see them again, to be honest." Lisa ducked behind the reception desk and produced the notepad and pen she had been working with the previous night.

"I hope so. At least we managed to recover our lorry."

After escaping from the prison, it had been the last thing on his mind. But upon leaving the military base and discovering their ammo had been plundered, they had rushed back to Doxley, finding the lorry and its contents untouched.

Once they had unloaded box after box of food at the hotel, they went on to discover a fully stocked kitchen. Food and water had instantly become a distant concern. Frank's stomach growled at the thought of the overflowing shelves and cupboards, but he paid it no heed, instead focusing on Lisa and her pen darting back and forth across the page.

"What are you doing?"

"Finishing off our inventory," she said. "Once we've worked out what we've got, we'll have a better idea of what we need."

"What we need is a way of securing this place." Frank cast a glare at the glass entrance. The windows were clear, but it didn't stop him visualising a wave of the undead smashing through. It was unlikely, given Kara's self-designated role as lookout, but that wouldn't mean much if she'd taken a nosedive off the roof.

"Does Kara still have the rifle?" he asked, leaning against the desk.

"Yeah, why?"

"We might have to take it with us, too."

Lisa finally looked up from her pad. "What?"

"Between me and you, we have nine bullets left. Her rifle has at least six. We're going to need all the firepower we've got."

"And what about Kara?"

"What about her?"

"We can't leave her without a gun."

Frank huffed. "She can't shoot for shit. We'll need every bullet if we're going to be up against zombies *and* survivors out there."

"And what if this place comes under attack?"

Frank rapped the butt of the shotgun at his side. "Then let's hope she's got a good baseball swing."

"She won't be able to kill them with brute force."

"Well, she's going to have to learn. We all will. As soon as the ammo's gone, we're gonna have to go old-school. That's why we need to concentrate on finding more bullets."

Lisa tore off the sheet and passed it across the counter. "Is there anything I've missed off?"

Frank read through the inventory: a dwindling first-aid kit, minimal weapons, and two vehicles. Having roamed the floors and checked every room twice over, he knew she was right, but it didn't leave him feeling any less deflated.

"Nope. That's everything. You had to waste paper and ink on this? I could've told you that last night."

"It's not just that. I'm writing a list of what we need, too."

Frank rounded the desk and read the second list over her shoulder.

"What's this 'cables and conductors' with all the question marks after it?"

"To electrify the fence surrounding us," Lisa replied. "We'll have to see what we can find."

"You think it'll work on zombies?"

"Dunno. At the very least, it'll push them back. Besides, it'll work on any survivors who touch it."

"Not if they choose to ram it in a van."

"That's why we need one of these," she said, tapping the bottom of the list.

"A digger?" Frank laughed. "You're taking the piss. Where the hell are we going to find a digger?"

"There'll be one somewhere."

"So what do you want to do, dig a moat? Jesus Christ, I know I said old-school, but I didn't mean medieval!"

"Not a moat, dickhead. We need a ditch or something to go all the way around. It's the only thing that'll stop them driving through the fence."

"We need *bullets*. Something to keep us alive, not all this *Home Alone* shite."

"This is *England*. We don't sell guns and groceries in the same shop! I'm not saying we don't need them, but it'd be foolish to go out there solely hoping to find them."

Frank sighed, running a hand over his short hair.

"Here." Lisa ripped the page off the notepad. "This is what we need. We might not get it all in one go, but it's what we need to consider."

Frank read the rest, which primarily listed hardware and medical supplies, with bullets and weapons appearing at the end.

"We should've gone through the army base one more time before we left. There might've been more guns, or bullets, or something."

"Add it to the list. We can head over that way while we're out."

"Okay, I'll get the van. If we're lucky, we'll be able to fill it. Although we might have to hitch your digger to another trailer."

Lisa cuffed him on the shoulder as he passed. "I'll tell Kara we're heading out. Hopefully, you'll have stopped being a smartarse by then."

"I wouldn't bet on it." Frank smirked. "And don't forget the rifle."

"I know, I know. We need *every* bullet."

Almost on cue, a gunshot echoed overhead. They both snapped their gaze to the ceiling, as another followed.

"Kara!"

They sprinted up the stairs, heading for the rooftop as a third shot resounded.

3

Tilting his head, Ben closed his left eye, staring down his outstretched arm and over the sight of the handgun in his wavering grip.

He fired again.

The bullet whizzed through the bushes, way off his intended target. The zombie snarled at him, fighting against the bindings pinning it to a tree.

"Concentrate," Kev said from his perch on the police car's bonnet. "Remember, exhale before you shoot. It'll steady your aim."

Ben raised the gun again, aiming at the zombie standing a mere twenty yards away. He fired, this time striking the tree above the snarling corpse's head.

"Take your time."

"I am!" he snapped. "I just can't steady my shot anymore." He glared at his injured left hand. Amy had dressed it an hour before, yet blood had already begun to seep through the bandage. He stared at the space where his fingers used to be, feeling as if the pulsing ache was still radiating through them. He flexed his remaining digits, unable to process the bizarre sensation of only having three left.

Kev slid off the bonnet, drawing his handgun. "It'll take some time to adjust," he said. "You've suffered a traumatic injury; nobody is expecting you to recover straight away."

"Then why bring me out here? Why go to all this trouble to get me shooting again?"

"Because it's important to get back on the horse. I've seen it before, skilled marksmen losing their confidence because they left it too long. You were a pretty decent shot, considering you've had no training. We need you at your best."

Ben sighed, staring up through the canopy of leaves above them.

"Come on." Kev nudged him, motioning to the bound zombie. "Again."

Ben raised the gun for a third time, trying to line up the shot, but the longer he waited, the harder it was to keep his arm still.

Kev laughed. "It's not a duelling pistol! Why are you aiming like that?"

"I thought it was obvious?" Ben raised his injured hand. "I can't hold it with two hands anymore."

"You don't need to. You're right-handed, so you should use your left as a platform to hold your gun steady. If you can't do that, then rest it on your forearm like this."

Kev brought his arm across his body, his gun sat atop it, his unwavering aim fixed on their captive. Ben followed suit, noticing immediately that his hand was a lot steadier. He fired, puncturing the zombie's cheek.

"Not bad," Kev said. "Try again."

Ben fired twice more, the first bullet hitting bark, the second striking the centre of the zombie's forehead. Its frenzied protests ceased as it fell limp against its confines.

"There, y'see," Kev said, beaming, "nothing to it."

He made his way through the undergrowth towards the zombie, but froze at the sound of rustling bushes.

"Company," he muttered, taking a step back.

Ben aimed in the direction of the noise as it intensified. He could see the bushes moving. Something was almost upon them.

As soon as the first snarl reached their ears, the duo fired, retreating as more and more animalistic screeches surrounded them. Finally, a zombie lunged through the undergrowth, barely managing a couple of steps before crumpling to the ground.

"I'm out," Ben announced. Whilst the noise had abated somewhat, they could still hear growls deeper in the woods.

"Yeah, I'm running low, too. C'mon, let's split."

They jumped in the police car and backed out of the forest. The undergrowth ahead of them parted, and a trio of undead men and women scrambled after them.

"I told you we'd fix your aim," Kev said coolly, ignoring the encroaching zombies. He swung the car around once they reached the road, and retraced their route back to the cottage.

"Maybe next time I'll be able to save more bullets." Ben grabbed the box of rounds from the glove compartment and started thumbing them into the handgun magazine.

"Your aim has improved massively. All that worrying for nothing."

"I wouldn't say that. I missed a hell of a lot."

"Nothing a bit more target practice won't fix. We can come out again tomorrow if you like? Whatever you need to build your confidence up."

"Thanks, Kev. I appreciate it."

"Don't thank me. It was Amy's idea. I just found us a suitable spot."

"Yeah."

While Amy had been treating his wound earlier that morning, he had confided in her and expressed his concerns. It was she who had offered encouragement and suggested he practice with Kev.

"She really cares about you, that one."

"Huh?"

"Amy." Kev chortled. "I reckon we'll be hearing wedding bells before the year's out."

"Why? Is that what we're shooting at next?"

"Don't try to pretend you're not interested. I've seen how you look at her. It's clear as day. And, FYI, I do a great best man speech. I always start out with the joke about the nun and the—"

Kev slammed on the brakes, swerving towards the treeline as a car cut across their path. He pulled down hard on the steering wheel, avoiding the trees before slamming into a ditch. The impact threw them into the dashboard.

"Fuck!" Kev snapped, rubbing his forehead. "You all right?"

Ben couldn't answer. The impact had blasted the air out of his chest. He tried to nod, gasping for breath. Car doors slammed behind them.

"Shit," Kev said. "Leave this to me."

Two men advanced, one brandishing a crowbar, the other with a baseball bat slung over his shoulder. When Kev got out of the car, they stopped in the road to appraise him.

"Well, well, look who we've got here," one of them said, with a sinister laugh. Before the man's companion could utter a retort, Kev shot him in the face, his crowbar clattering to the ground. Ben jumped out of the car as the other man held his hands up, a look of astonishment briefly registering on his face before a bullet struck him in the chest.

"Kev!" Ben wheezed, finally finding his voice. "What the fuck are you doing?"

"They were armed."

"With blunt weapons. They weren't a threat."

"I wasn't going to take the chance. They ran us off the road."

Kev approached the pair, scanning the surrounding woodland, but there was nobody in sight, the only sound coming from their attackers' idling engine. He rolled the first man over, patting down his pockets, before moving onto the next.

"Let's hope they've at least got some supplies," Ben said, walking towards the car. He stopped when he saw movement through the tinted windows. It was slight, but enough for him to draw his weapon. The movement came again as the engine roared, and the car squealed around, racing off down the road.

"Shit! Get in the car, now!" Kev snapped. He ran back to the police car with a perplexing urgency, one which Ben couldn't leave unchallenged as he jumped in beside him.

"What's up?"

Kev didn't reply. Instead, he veered back onto the road in pursuit of the other vehicle. Ben fumbled for his seatbelt as the car drifted around the sharp bends, narrowly missing a stone wall. He had never been in a police pursuit, but he imagined the only components missing were the static-filled radio and the siren.

"What the fuck are you doing?"

"He's getting away!" Kev snapped, having lost his usual composure.

"So? Leave him!"

They reached the pinnacle of a bank, briefly soaring through the air before the wheels hit the downward slope of the other side. Ben bounced in his seat, yelping when his injured hand hit the door handle.

"He's just beyond this next hill. We'll get him."

"We don't *need* to get him. What's the matter with you?"

Kev ignored the query, pushing the car harder than ever as they raced up another bank, the top of which revealed a crossroads. There was no sign of any vehicles.

"Fuck!" He punched the wheel and threw himself back in his seat.

"You wanna tell me what that was all about?"

Kev dragged his fingers through his beard, eyes darting along every route. "That car could've had supplies—food, water, anything."

"And? It's not worth risking our lives over."

Kev shrugged off Ben's concerns and adopted his customary joviality. "You're right. C'mon, let's get back. The ladies might be worried."

He turned the car around and retraced their route, driving at a more conventional speed. When they reached the site of their confrontation, they rolled to a stop. The man with the crowbar remained motionless, his dead eyes staring skyward, with a circular red hole in the middle of his forehead. His companion, however, was gone.

"Shit." Kev pried his handgun from its holster as he climbed out of the car.

"Now what are we doing?" Ben asked, trying to keep the frustration out of his voice. "He can't have gone far."

"He could if he was wearing a vest."

Kev bent down, examining the foliage by the side of the road, before stepping through and into the undergrowth.

"There's blood here," Ben called after him, "and you hit him square in the chest. If he's not dead yet, he will be soon."

"I want to make sure."

Ben groaned, trudging after Kev through the makeshift trail he had created. He wished Amy was with them. She'd confirm he wasn't imagining Kev's strange behaviour, which was becoming more and more unsettling. He pushed through a thicket of brambles, grunting in pain—a sound that was dwarfed by the blast of a handgun in front of him.

He rushed into a clearing, where Kev stood over a body lying prone in the dirt. A single bullet wound in the back of its head shimmered under strands of light breaking through the overhead canopy.

"What—was he a zombie?" Ben managed, trying to process the scene.

"No. But these woods are crawling with them. I figured I'd put him out of his misery."

"You followed him all the way out here so he wouldn't be eaten?"

"Exactly. It's important not to lose empathy in times like these. Just because others would let us die a slow, horrible death doesn't mean we have to stoop to their level."

"Empathy?" Ben scoffed. "You shot him for carrying a baseball bat."

"Which he would've used to smash our heads in."

"I dunno, Kev. This feels… personal."

"Personal?" He slid the handgun back into his holster. "You think I knew those lads?"

"Well, why go to such lengths to kill them?"

"They attacked *us*, remember? We just happened to have the better weapons. What do you think their intentions were, ramming us off the road like that?"

Ben fell silent as a gentle breeze caressed his arms. While it was a welcome change from the heat, it brought with it a sense of unease as it rustled the surrounding foliage.

"We've got to do things like this to survive," Kev continued. "If somebody displays hostility, they need to be neutralised."

The rustling came again, but Ben was more disturbed by Kev's line of thinking. "And what constitutes hostility?"

"I'd argue smashing into us with their car and brandishing weapons is constitution enough."

"And what about the guy trying to flee? You pursued him like a madman."

"Where do you think he's going? What if he's part of a group that comes after us now, looking for revenge? The cottage isn't far from here. And if they clock my police car parked out front, we could have a full-scale assault to deal with! You need to get this into your thick skull—treat everyone like an enemy until you know otherwise!"

Before Ben could protest further, the breeze-induced composition became an orchestra of sound. Twigs snapped, foliage rustled, fallen leaves crunched... and zombies roared as they sprinted towards them.

Ben drew his gun, realising that their route back to the car was compromised—a fact confirmed when the first zombie darted into the clearing.

4

Frank was the first to reach the roof, with Lisa close at his heels. Another shot directed them to Kara. She stared down the rifle scope, resting it on top of the railing encircling the rooftop.

"What's out there?" Frank snapped, drawing his handgun as he rushed to her side.

"Huh?" Kara turned, looking at them both in confusion.

"What are you firing at?"

"The tree. Figured I needed the target practice."

"The tree?" Frank spat. "Are you fucking mad?"

"Frank." Lisa gripped his arm, but he shrugged her off.

"We've hardly got any bullets left, and you're wasting them on a fucking tree!"

"How else do I learn how to shoot?" Kara crossed her arms, staring back at him defiantly.

"You can start learning how to swing a bat, because that's all you'll be using from now on."

He snatched the rifle from her and turned to leave.

"Where are you going?"

"To get more supplies." He examined the remaining rifle bullets, finding two left. "If we don't make it back, you know why."

"You're leaving me here?"

"You're no good to us out *there*."

"What he means is we need someone to stay here and protect this place," Lisa said. "We can't risk somebody else taking over while we're away."

"What kind of threat am I going to be without a gun?"

"The same kind you'd be *with* one," Frank said.

"Here." Lisa removed the magazine from her handgun, flicking the bullets into her palm before passing it to Kara.

"An empty gun? Thanks."

"The only ones likely to come across this place are living people. People who are more likely to listen to someone holding a gun. You get to be a threat, and," she gave the bullets to Frank, "you get more ammo. Everyone's a winner."

"And what do I do if they have guns *with* bullets?" Kara asked.

"Hide. Besides, we shouldn't be too long."

"Yeah, we're probably gonna find a digger in the first town we come across."

Frank sidestepped Lisa's swipe as he loaded the bullets into his magazine. He slid it into the handgun with a click before returning it to its holster.

"C'mon, then, let's get this done."

The pair headed back into the hotel, leaving Kara alone on the rooftop.

"Here," Frank said, handing Lisa the rifle once they had reached the third floor.

"I'm still not happy leaving her without protection."

"There are plenty of things she can use to protect herself."

"Like what?"

"Like that." Frank pointed to a wall-mounted fire extinguisher.

"Oh yeah, if this place catches fire, she'll be sorted."

"It can also smash zombie heads in. She'll be fine."

They reached the foyer and headed towards the entrance. The warm air encircled them the minute they pushed open the glass doors. They shielded their eyes as they strode toward the side of the building where they had parked the LGV.

"We should've left her some ammo," Lisa said.

"You're the one who gave her an empty gun."

"Because you insisted on taking the bullets!"

"What good would they have done? Unless this place comes under attack from a bunch of trees, I think she'd be fucked either way."

"Let's hope it doesn't come under attack at all—"

"Hey there, got any vacancies?"

At the sound of the unfamiliar voice, Frank swung the shotgun off his shoulder, ignoring the agony in his side as a figure emerged from behind the LGV.

"Get down!" Frank yelled, dashing towards him.

The man raised his hands. "Whoa, I'm unarmed. I—"

"Down!"

"Hey, I don't want any—"

"Get the fuck down!"

Frank booted the man in the gut, shoving him to the ground when he doubled over. He stood on the back of his neck, grinding the man's face into the gravel. The man's yelps ceased when he felt the shotgun muzzle against his cheek.

"Who the fuck are you?"

"Someone who clearly made a mistake coming here," the man gasped. Lisa stooped down next to him, examining his grazed face.

"What's your name?"

"Jay. Jay Cowan."

"And what the fuck are you doing here?"

"Hoping to rent a room," he said. He cried out when Frank dug his boot in harder. "Okay, okay. I saw the hotel and thought I'd check if there was anything to eat or drink here."

"You thought wrong."

Frank yanked the man's arm up behind his back and dragged him to his feet. Before he could protest, he slammed him into the wall.

"Do you have anything on you?"

Not waiting for a response, Frank patted down his pockets, finding a packet of cigarettes and a lighter in one, and a couple of energy bars in the other.

"No, I'm unarmed."

"You weren't," Lisa said, retrieving a machete from behind the van. She held it up to his face.

"Oh, come on. You can't walk around here without a weapon. You guys know that."

"What I do know is you're a liar," Frank growled. "Now, move!"

He dragged the man away from the wall and shoved him towards the strangely lopsided LGV.

"You've gotta be shitting me."

Frank massaged his forehead as Lisa inspected the deflated tyre.

"Did you do this?" he snapped, aiming the shotgun at the man once again.

"What? No!"

"There's no obvious damage," Lisa added. She ran her fingers over the tyre, pushing the malleable rubber. "Must've been a slow puncture."

"The prison van it is," Frank said. "Come on, dickhead."

He shoved their captive towards the back of the hotel. Jay kept his arms raised, careful not to stumble in the uneven dirt.

"How did you get in here?" Frank asked.

Jay motioned toward the metal barrier.

"You climbed the fence?"

"Yeah."

Lisa cast Frank a knowing glance. She was right—if they were going to keep their haven secure, they would need to electrify the fence.

"Where did you come from?"

"Charbridge."

"What's it like there?"

"Overrun. I made it to Bealsdon, but that's just as bad, so I figured my best option was somewhere rural."

"So you came here?"

"No." He stopped beside the prison van. "First, I went to Blackstones—the place with the farmers' market and the restaurant."

Frank shrugged, and from the look on Lisa's face, she hadn't heard of the place either.

"It's about ten miles east of here," Jay continued. "It's ransacked, but there was nobody there, so I managed to hole up for a couple of days with the bits and pieces that were left. Then, when the bottles of water ran out, I had to leave. Now I'm here."

"Not for long. Get in the back." Frank opened the side door and gestured for him to enter. Jay glanced in, hesitant to comply until Frank took the choice from him. He pushed him inside, dragging him by the collar to the first open cell.

"No. Wait."

Frank ignored the plea and shoved Jay inside. In the confined space, his body contorted awkwardly, just like Frank had done when he had been captured the day before.

At least he doesn't have cuffs on. Frank slammed the door, ignoring the muffled protests as he joined Lisa at the front of the van.

"What are we gonna do with him?" she asked.

"We're going to take him far away from here and put a bullet in his head."

"Wow."

"What do you mean, *wow*? He knows about this place. We can't risk him joining up with others and coming back to take it by force. We have to get rid of him."

"Oh, I agree. I'm more surprised you're willing to use a precious bullet when we've got *this*." She brandished the machete, examining the smears of blood on the blade.

"Clearly has no qualms using it," Lisa said. She climbed into the passenger seat, placing the machete on the dashboard.

"Should we give it to Kara?" Frank suggested, jumping in beside her. "It might serve her better than an empty gun."

Lisa shook her head. "That guy tried to hide the machete as soon as he saw we had guns. If that's what she's up against, she should be fine."

"Unless he dropped it because we outnumbered him. One-on-one with her might've been a different story."

He started the van and drove around to the front of the hotel. The road and neighbouring fields were clear, but with Jay Cowan's arrival, they couldn't afford to be complacent. Frank scanned the area for any sign of movement. He could hear the muffled complaints of their captive, but there was nothing to suggest there were any threats nearby. With a cautious sense of reassurance, he rolled the van down the dirt trail and veered left onto the road.

"Y'know, Kara's tougher than you think," Lisa said. "I bet she can hold her own when the shit hits the fan."

Frank thought back to their time in Doxley—the zombies pursuing them, his scuffle with the one that overpowered him, and Kara's headshot that had saved his life.

"I know," he replied. "She can handle herself."

He fixated on a distant movement at the side of the road. Something low to the ground, bent over. *Zombies this close? Fuck, if it reaches Kara, she's dead.* As they approached, the undead woman's head snapped up, discarding the eviscerated rodent she had been feasting on, focusing on the bigger prey. She shrieked as the van bore down on her—a sound cut short when Frank swerved into her, striking her head-on. The woman's corpse bounced off the bumper, sailing aside until a tree stopped her with a crushing impact.

He could feel Lisa's sardonic gaze.

"She *can* handle herself," he said. "But I don't want to take any chances. That's one less zombie she has to worry about."

"You don't fool me," Lisa mocked. "Beneath the macho façade, there's a caring, thoughtful man, waiting to get out. You've been released from your prison. Why not release him from his?"

Frank scoffed. "Cool your jets, sensei. I'm trying to make sure the place is still in one piece when we get back. That's all."

He eased off the accelerator as they reached a junction. A left turn would take them through miles of countryside, passing through Witton Village, but not much else. A right turn would take them back to Doxley. They slowed to a halt as Frank deliberated over the options.

"Doxley again?" Lisa suggested.

Frank drummed his fingers on the steering wheel. "Well, I don't know if we'll find a *digger* there, but there's likely to be a lot more resources. Only…"

"More likely to find trouble as well?"

Frank nodded, chewing his lip in contemplation.

"Why don't we take the stealthy approach for once?"

"You mean we haven't been doing that all along?"

"Are you kidding?" Lisa laughed. "Every town we've driven to, you've barged in there like a virgin on a promise."

"Hey, I opted for the stealthy approach last time. It was the trigger-happy cop that fucked things up."

A banging sound echoed from the rear of the van.

"And the quicker we get rid of this noisy bastard, the better."

Frank veered onto the road leading to Doxley—a desolate stretch of asphalt, cutting through dense woodland. After a couple of miles, he slowed to a crawl as a congregation of undead sauntered into view ahead of them.

"Christ, we're in the sticks! Why are there so many?"

"Ran out of food in the towns," Lisa said, holding on to the door handle as Frank accelerated. "Only natural they'd start looking further afield."

They struck the closest zombie, who went barrelling into the others, knocking them down like bowling pins. Frank eased off the accelerator, watching them in his side mirror as they scrambled to their feet.

"What are you doing?" Lisa asked.

"Waiting."

"For?"

"For them to start chasing. We can't kill them all, but we can lead them further away from the hotel. I don't like the idea of them being this close."

He pushed the van on as the horde sprinted after them. The sharp acceleration prompted another tirade from the cells in the back.

"I'm half tempted to leave the prick here," Frank growled.

"You're not that callous."

"Callous? I thought you were up for getting rid of him?"

"I am. I don't trust him. But I was thinking of a more humane, mercy killing. He doesn't deserve to be ripped apart."

The banging continued.

"Are you sure?" Frank whistled indignantly through his teeth. "If we weren't so close to the hotel, he'd be out on his arse."

He checked his mirror, making sure the horde was still following. They had fallen behind, but their ragged determination was still clear. Up ahead, a time-ravaged sign proclaimed Doxley to be seven miles away.

"Are you gonna play this cat-and-mouse game all the way to Doxley?" Lisa asked.

Frank shrugged. "Either that, or until they lose interest. Although, I've never seen them give up on a potential meal yet, have you?"

"Only when an easier option becomes available."

They came across a two-car collision which occupied most of the narrow lane. Frank eased off the accelerator, guiding the van towards the parallel treeline. Low-hanging branches scraped against the windshield, snapping and rustling as they went. The occupants of the first car were missing, their former presence marked as a void amidst the blood spatter and fleshy pulp. Those in the second car, though, were still there. As the van drew level, the elderly couple inside lunged through the broken passenger window, arms flailing, eyes wide, their feral roars matching those of the pursuing undead. They scrabbled against each other, pushing their torsos out as far as they could, but a tangle of seatbelts kept them in place. They fought against the restraints, their efforts futile as the van picked up speed.

"Seems like all the easy options are gone," Frank muttered. "I thought seatbelts were meant to save your life."

"Not in a zombie apocalypse, they don't."

The road opened up into a clearing, where a derelict building occupied a plot. Its walls were strewn with graffiti, which, judging by the '2k0' tag, had adorned it for some time. A charred pair of beams stretched skyward—a shrine to the roof that had since collapsed inside. A faded petrol sign dangled from a resolute chain—a solitary indication of the building's purpose, given that the fuel dispensers had long since vanished.

The van slowed.

"What are you doing?" Lisa asked. "There won't be anything in here."

"I know."

"And the zombies are right behind us. Quit fucking about."

THE MUTATION

"I'm not!" Frank couldn't control the tremor in his voice as he stomped on the accelerator, over and over. But the van offered no compliance. They rolled to a stop, both staring at the empty fuel gauge as the roaring undead sprinted closer.

5

Zielinski struggled against the straps, groaning with exertion. The doctor didn't seem to notice, his attention monopolised by the visual display of his microscope. Excitable mutterings drifted out of the man, but they were beyond Zielinski's comprehension. He turned his attention to the leather bindings enveloping his wrists and the metal bars they clung to. If he could muster enough strength, he was certain he could bend them. He was unsure how it would help his predicament, but lying back and accepting his fate wasn't an option.

He balled his fist and pulled against the restraint, the leather digging into his flesh. His arm trembled, his muscles tightened, and his circulatory system throbbed beneath his waxy skin. The plump, pulsing veins regurgitated memories Zielinski longed to forget. Dirty bedsits, dark alleys, stolen cars, and places he used to shoot up bobbed through his mind like crackheads on a dinghy. Drugs had always been his downfall, but now he needed a hit more than ever.

THE MUTATION

He stared at the pit of his elbow, at the countless pocks adorning the thin veil of flesh, all defunct entry holes that once permitted the sweet brown nectar into his body. He glanced at the crook of his other arm, expecting the same minute craters, but saw only a cotton swab taped to his skin.

Did I start using again? He scoured his memories for an answer, but came up short, recollection hidden deep within the darkest recesses of his grey matter.

Footsteps echoed around the ward, prompting Dr Armstrong to look up.

"Ah, Martin. I was wondering when you'd be joining us." Armstrong held out his arm as if introducing a celebrity. "Mr Zielinski, I'd like to introduce you to my colleague, Dr Scrivener."

The man stepped into view, wearing the same garb as the other doctor. But that was where the similarities ended. Martin Scrivener was a tall, wiry man with a thin pencil moustache. His tempered, calculating stare exuded a coldness which put Zielinski on the back foot. Scrivener's unblinking gaze darted between the two men.

"Armstrong." His voice was low, with a hint of annoyance. "I told you to inform me when the subject regained consciousness."

"He's not going anywhere, Martin." Armstrong chuckled.

"But the tests—"

"The tests can wait, check this out." He ushered his colleague over with the urgency of a child showing their parent a newly acquired skill. Scrivener sauntered over to the microscope, his gaze flitting back to Zielinski before peering through the lens.

"What's this?"

"T-19. I'm introducing a sample from the patient."

Armstrong reached for a row of test tubes by his side. Zielinski watched as he drew a pipette of blood out of a vial. *His* blood.

For a moment, Zielinski could see a monitor which mirrored the microscopic lens. A dark blob swam lazily through a clear sea, a sea which turned crimson when Armstrong introduced a drop of blood. Immediately, the blob came to life, rolling and darting in a frenzy. But Zielinski didn't get to see the outcome. The doctor's bulk blocked the screen once more as he hunched over the lens. Seconds passed, with Armstrong becoming more and more excited, rocking on the balls of his feet, until his colleague finally stepped away.

"His lymphocytes are—"

Scrivener stared at Zielinski. The calculating appraisal had all but vanished, replaced with a look of wonderment.

"He's immune?"

Armstrong's smile faded. "Not yet. Those aren't his natural antibodies. I infected the sample with T-12."

"You went into my lab?!"

"I had a theory. I needed—"

"You had no right to go in there!"

Armstrong took a step back, rubbing the silver whiskers on his cheek. "I'm sorry, Martin. You were asleep. I didn't want to wake you. But don't you realise? This is a breakthrough. If we can isolate the—"

"You're not touching that virus, Armstrong," Scrivener spat. "*I* created T-12. *I'll* modify it."

"But it's—"

Armstrong stumbled to the side as Scrivener snatched a test tube from the worktop. He turned on his heel and marched out of the ward as Armstrong watched, waiting for his footsteps to fade before addressing Zielinski.

"He's emotional," he said. "I guess we all are. But make no mistake, Mr Zielinski, we *will* save the world."

"Why do you need me?" Zielinski asked, half-heartedly pulling against his restraints. "Why am I here?"

"We needed a living sample. I can't tell you how much of our own blood, sweat and tears we've poured into this project... literally! We were growing weak. And with you and your friends right above us, we saw it as the perfect opportunity."

Zielinski stared up at the foam ceiling panels, trying to process the doctor's words. "Above us? You mean the army base? We're underground?"

"Yes, yes, and yes." Armstrong beamed. "We have a live feed set up." He turned one of the desktop monitors around to face Zielinski. A five-by-five grid filled the screen, with each square showing a different part of the army base—all currently unoccupied.

"You were watching us?"

"Absolutely. You were the first living people we had seen in almost a week. We knew we had to get one of you down."

"And you chose me? Why?"

"Your self-imposed exile was the perfect opportunity. When we saw you break away from the group, we took our chance."

"But… how? I don't—don't remember."

"Naturally, on account of the sedative. We had to get you here somehow, and I'm sorry to say we opted for the forceful approach. A blitz attack, I believe it's called."

"You snuck up on me?"

"We had no choice. We couldn't risk our operation being compromised, and it was unlikely you'd cooperate, given the colourful demeanour we've witnessed over the past few days. We injected you with a sedative, held you until you lost consciousness, then brought you here."

Zielinski closed his eyes, trying to quell the rage coursing through his body.

"But that's beside the point," Armstrong continued. "You're here now. Safe from harm. And making a difference."

"How?"

"We're going to engineer an antidote."

6

Amy strode through the field with Donna at her heel. She adjusted the apple-laden basket in her arms as they reached the next tree.

"This place is straight out of a survival handbook," Donna mused, placing her own basket on the ground and picking up a loose apple. "We've got food, a freshwater well, and a secure building."

"Yep." Amy looked back at their cottage in the next field. Despite the boarded windows, it still held a serene beauty, complementing the tranquil aesthetic of the countryside.

"And I've not seen a single zombie since we got here."

"They're around, trust me."

"Maybe. Until the boys find them, that is."

Amy smiled: a polite gesture, but one that belied her inner turmoil. It had been at least an hour since Ben and Kev had left for their expedition, and as the seconds turned into minutes, she grew more and more concerned.

"I wouldn't worry," Donna said, placing a hand on her shoulder. "Kev won't let anything happen to him."

"I know. And I think you're right. Ben needs to rebuild his confidence. Thanks for talking me into it."

"Hey, it always sounds better coming from you. You're the only one he listens to."

Amy smiled again, a genuine gesture this time. "Oh, I don't know about that."

"Yes, you do," Donna said playfully. "He's head over heels for you."

"You think?"

"It's clear as day."

Amy looked back at the cottage and the snaking road beyond. She longed to see the police SUV driving into view. Her gut had told her it was a bad idea for Ben to go out, despite Donna's insistence he would be safe. But, after her perseverance, Amy convinced herself it would be good for him, something she then relayed back to him.

He can still shoot, she told herself. *And he seemed in good spirits.*

Yet, her pep talk did little to alleviate the growing knot in her stomach. She placed her basket beneath the tree, catching the handgun holstered at her side. Its presence reminded her of its purpose, and she scanned the field for movement. She and Donna were the only ones there.

"Do you think we'll have enough after this lot?" Donna asked.

"I think so. Let's get these last few and head back."

She reached up through the low-hanging branches, staggering on tip-toes until she clasped an apple. She yanked it down, bringing with it a thumping rain of fruit. Donna gasped and leapt back, laughing as she covered her head.

"That's one way to get them."

Amy chuckled, but the humour was short-lived when a growl came from the bordering woods.

"Time to go." Donna collected her basket, but Amy remained still, hand hovering over her gun.

"Amy, grab your basket. Let's go."

"Wait."

Amy raised a hand as she tried to locate the source of a new sound. It was a quiet, crunching noise, with an intermittent skitter. The sound gravel might make underfoot. But the only gravelled area was the driveway. And as more footsteps began grinding the pebbles, Amy had heard enough.

"Run!"

She took her handgun from its holster and fled back toward the house, vaguely aware of a distant shriek coming from the woodland behind her. She paid it no heed, focusing instead on the bodies rounding the building, getting closer and closer.

"Oh, fuck," Donna cried. She raised her gun and fired, each bullet missing their mark, as the zombies started to close in.

"Wait!" Amy yelled, but the cacophony of roars and gunshots drowned out her voice. She had no idea how many bullets Donna had fired. What she did know was that the twelve bullets in her handgun might not be enough. She raised her weapon, confident she could hit the closest undead man.

The bullet missed.

But her second attempt struck him above the left brow, causing his body to crumple. She fired at the next, striking him square in the chest. The impact caused him to slow, but did not diffuse his unwavering determination as he collided with the fence. Amy ushered Donna farther down the field as more of the undead hit the heavy wooden border. Some bounced back, whilst others flipped over the top, courtesy of their momentum.

"There," Amy wheezed, pointing to the metal gate separating the two fields. She cast a glance behind her. The zombies that had stopped before the fence were now running parallel with those who had toppled over.

Amy fired again as Donna vaulted the gate. She half expected her to flee towards the house, but instead, she unloaded the rest of her weapon at the encroaching horde. Her gun clicked empty as Amy jumped beside her.

"Go!"

The pair ran toward the house, faced with the zombies remaining on their side of the fence, who now ran on a diagonal course of interception. The back door of the cottage loomed ever closer—their original exit which led to the field, and which she hoped would now be their entrance to sanctuary.

Donna shouldered open the door. Amy leapt after her, stumbling into the kitchen before Donna slammed the door shut behind her. A second passed before the wave of flesh and bone crashed against it.

"What are you doing?" Amy gasped. "Reload!"

She holstered her handgun and pinned herself against the wooden door. She could feel the timber behind her shuddering with every strike. The zombies wailed in anger, joined by more on the other side of the house. Amy began to shake when more of the undead hammered on the boarded windows opposite her. The relentless banging surrounded them, with disconcerting cracks as the doorframe started to give.

"They're getting in!" Donna cried.

Amy's anguish turned to frustration when she realised Donna's handgun was empty. Before she could reprimand her, a fist burst through the wood panelling above Amy's head. She yelped in alarm as the arm swung across, pinning her chest, pincer-like fingers grasping her shoulder.

Her breath caught in her throat. She wanted to plead for help, longed for Ben and Kev to return. But her only hope now was Donna, who no longer wielded an empty handgun. She darted away from an open drawer, brandishing a kitchen knife. Amy was trying to prise the undead fingers off her shoulder when Donna lunged forward, plunging the knife deep into the zombie's forearm, severing flesh, muscle, and tendons. It released its grip, allowing Amy to slide away.

"Run!"

Amy's words merged with the sound of cracking wood. The door behind her crashed open, bringing with it a surge of zombies. The pair made for the stairs, their pursuers at their heels.

"Come on!" Donna urged. She reached the top, and turned, stretching out a hand: a perplexing gesture, given that Amy was only four steps behind her, but one which quickly made sense when she felt a hand grasp her ankle.

Amy cried out and reached for the lifeline as her feet gave way. She felt another hand grab her leg, and her shoe coming loose, as Donna heaved her up the remaining steps. Yet, the strength of the undead prevailed. Amy felt herself being dragged back, with Donna's two-handed grip beginning to waver. She felt another hand on her calf as she blindly groped at her holster. Her fingers found purchase on the handgun, and she twisted round, coming face to face with a mutilated man.

She fired, freeing herself from the horde as the dead man tumbled back. She fired again for good measure, the bullet striking the chest of another. She ran with Donna to one of the bedrooms, slamming the door shut behind them, as Donna darted over to the wardrobe that was up against the same wall.

"Help me," she gasped.

Together, they heaved the wardrobe over the door. The relentless onslaught started again, this time muffled by the additional barricade. Next, a chest of drawers. The solid oak proved heavier than they had expected, but with Donna's help, Amy was able to shove it up against the wardrobe. The pair leaned against it, breathless and trembling. The furniture shuddered, but withheld the undead assault.

"Are you okay?" Donna asked.

Amy, still unable to form words, nodded in response. She could still feel the cold, dead grip on her legs and the savage fingernails on her shoulder.

"That was too close." With her back against the chest of drawers, Donna slid herself down to the floor, pulling her knees up to her chest. "What are we going to do?"

Amy swallowed hard, trying to control her ragged breathing. She rubbed the gooseflesh from her arms as she joined Donna on the floor.

"I don't know," she said. Ordinarily, the zombies would lose interest after a while. They may move away from the door, but they wouldn't go far.

"How many do you think there were?" she asked.

"Eight? Ten? There were at least five of them behind you on the stairs."

"Sounds like there's more than five out there now." Amy tried to ignore the commotion behind the door: the sounds of scrabbling; pounding; and yearning, hungry groans. Even if the zombies ceased their assault, even if they moved away from the door and dispersed, the pair couldn't risk leaving the room, not without a sufficient amount of ammo. They were trapped.

"We could try the window," Donna said.

Amy shook her head. "It's too high. If we so much as sprained an ankle, we'd be dead within seconds."

"I guess we'll have to wait until... Oh my god."

"What?"

"The boys! They don't know. If they come in the house, they'll..."

Realisation brought with it a greater anxiety, and Amy instinctively rose to her feet.

"We have to do something."

"But what?"

"I don't know. But we need to do it now."

7

Frank leapt from the van, slinging the shotgun strap over his neck. The ravenous crowd pursued them with an even greater urgency.

"Let's go!" he snapped, but Lisa dashed to the side of the van. "What're you doing?"

She leapt into the back and yanked open the cell door.

"Out. Now!"

Before Jay could respond, she grabbed him by his collar and dragged him out of the van.

"Wait—What—" Jay sputtered as he hit the ground.

"Run!"

Lisa didn't wait to see if he'd got the message, sprinting with Frank to the dilapidated building. The extent of the fire damage quickly became apparent. It was nothing more than a shell, a skeletal structure which wouldn't even afford them sanctuary from the blistering heat, let alone a wave of the undead. A one-storey outbuilding stood to the side, seemingly untouched by the flames that had gutted the rest of the petrol station.

"There!" Frank doubted they would find an entry to the small structure, but the roof would at least provide them a reprieve from the pursuit. They ran over, trailed by screeches and roars as the undead passed their abandoned van.

"Here." Lisa stooped down against the structure, interlocking her fingers to boost Frank up. There wasn't time to argue. He stepped into her palms and dragged himself onto the roof. Lisa leapt after him, her fingers clasping the ledge. Frank hurled his shotgun aside, seized her by the wrists and heaved her onto the roof. They fell back into a heap, the surge of bodies crashing against the structure below them.

"Fuck… that was close," Frank panted. He staggered to his feet, looking out at the prison van. There was no sign of their captive, nor his mutilated corpse.

"What the hell were you thinking?" he asked.

Lisa stayed prone on the roof, resting her head on her arm, her feet draping over the edge.

"You should've left him in there. He could've been a distraction."

"He doesn't deserve that," Lisa said. "Nobody does. Being ripped to pieces isn't a way for anybody to die."

"Those things can't break through metal." Frank looked down at the horde encircling them. Their clawing hands were scrabbling with one another, trying to reach their elusive prey. "He would've been safe."

"Not if we die, he wouldn't." Lisa shielded her eyes from the sun as she regarded Frank. "I had to let him out."

"Well, he's legged it. Let's hope he doesn't direct others to the hotel."

"Why don't we focus on *us* getting back first?"

Frank knew she was right, but he couldn't envisage any possible way of them getting back. They were at a stalemate. The surrounding zombies couldn't reach them, but they sure as hell weren't leaving. And, unlike the living, they didn't seem reliant on the same fundamental needs. They didn't drink, they didn't sleep, and they sure as hell didn't stop.

Frank began to ponder how it was even possible to manufacture such a virus, when a zombie caught his eye. It had been amongst the stragglers near the van and now joined the crowd around the building. Only this one seemed... different. Sure, they all had differing levels of mutilation (this one in particular had lost part of its scalp and a huge portion of its left cheek) but they all shared the same hungry stare and wicked grin.

Not this one.

After it spotted the pair on the rooftop, it looked away, its head darting back and forth, as if searching for an easier meal... or another way up.

Frank tried to dispel the unsettling notion. The dead didn't think like that. The dead didn't think *at all.* They were driven by relentless hunger, reverting to a primal state. They weren't capable of critical thinking or problem solving. Hell, they couldn't even open a door. Yet this one seemed to be perusing the scene with a calculating gaze. Then, something on the rooftop caught its eye, and that evil grin—the distinct characteristic of the undead—stretched across its face.

It was the same as the others. It had to be. Frank tried to breathe a sigh of relief, but he couldn't help but monitor its rapid perambulation through the crowd. It shoved its way through, like a die-hard fan trying to reach the barrier at a rock concert.

Then it jumped.

It happened in the blink of an eye. Frank gasped. Lisa shrieked. And the zombie seizing her foot yanked her down.

Frank lunged forward, grabbing her wrists as she was pulled over the edge. He held on tight, trying desperately to heave her back up as she bucked and writhed in his grip. He could feel his footing start to give way under the bitumen roof; despite digging his heels, he skidded closer to the edge.

He expected to hear Lisa's scream as the zombies tore into her flesh. The death knell. The swish of the guillotine. The sound marking her demise. Even if he were to get her back up, one bite and she was already dead. He pulled harder, desperate not to hear her scream.

What would he do? Would he let her go? *Being ripped to pieces isn't a way for anyone to die*—Those were Lisa's words. But if he dragged her up, he would have to kill her—something he couldn't even begin to contemplate.

The weight of his thoughts lifted the second Lisa did. She broke free from the zombies' grasp, allowing Frank to heave her back onto the roof.

"Are you alright? Did they bite you?"

"No, I'm fine… what the fuck was that?"

Frank tried to find the words. *It's not possible. They can jump. They've never jumped.* Weeks of being subjected to the animated corpses had desensitised him to the horror, the fear. But now, he was ashamed to acknowledge he was genuinely afraid. *If they can jump, what else can they do?*

When fingers clasped the side of the roof, Frank froze. Both physically and mentally. He was a statue. A landmark. Incapable of kinetic or physiological energy. Like a deer in headlights, all he could do was wait, and watch.

The zombie emerged into view, with its frenzied eyes and sinister grin.

"Frank!"

The name meant nothing to him, but the accompanying gunshot broke his trance. He flinched when the zombie's head snapped back, its grip lost, before it disappeared into the raging sea of corpses below.

Lisa staggered to her feet, the rifle cradled in her arms.

"Did you see that?" Frank asked. The world came back into focus, but the fear persisted.

"Of course I did."

Lisa looked back over the edge. Whether it was for confirmation the zombie was dead, or to see if any others were scrambling up, Frank couldn't tell. His gaze drifted, along with his thoughts. What the hell was it?

"What's up?" she asked.

"Nothing. I'm good. It just… caught me off-guard. It fucking *jumped*, Lise. It *climbed!*"

"I know, I was there."

"But *how?*"

"I dunno. I'm not a scientist. We need to be more alert, that's all. Providing they don't start sprouting wings, we should be okay."

The zombies continued to grapple, but none of them seemed inclined to try the acrobatic approach of their fallen companion. Despite this, Frank ushered Lisa over to the centre of the roof. There was no telling how many more might try to climb.

"What do we do now?"

Frank shook his head, unable to find an answer. They didn't have enough bullets to kill them all, and the gunshot might attract even more. They were sitting ducks surrounded by a skulk of hungry foxes.

A subtle movement beside the prison van caught his attention. The passenger door opened.

"Look." He nudged Lisa as Jay Cowan came into view.

"He's alive?"

"The stupid fuck never left."

Jay grabbed his machete from the dashboard and looked out at the horde surrounding the building. None of them saw him, their attention focused on their elevated meal.

"What's he doing?" Lisa asked, as Jay retrieved the keys from the ignition. He eased the door shut and retreated to the bordering woodland, locking the van with the key fob as he went.

"I have no idea," Frank admitted.

Jay didn't disappear entirely. He stayed at the edge of the woods, scouring the carpet of woodchip, twigs and foliage. He stooped down occasionally, but he was too far away for them to identify what he was retrieving.

"Looks like he's foraging," Frank sneered. "Why isn't the daft sod legging it?"

"Because he's helping us."

Jay collected another piece of debris from the forest floor. He stopped between a pair of trees, and hurled what appeared to be a large stone. It skittered beside the van, bouncing into the undergrowth beyond. He threw another. This time, it struck the windshield, prompting an ear-splitting wail from the van's alarm. At once, Jay dropped the rest of the stones and sprinted deep into the woods, as the swarm of undead darted over to the prison van.

"He helped us," Frank said. "He actually helped us."

"I've told you before, not everyone is out to get you. Come on, let's climb down this side and head for the woods."

Lisa led the way to the other side of the roof. After peering down and finding no threat, she lowered herself off the edge, with Frank close behind her. A stretch of woodland lay ahead, with no indication of what was beyond. With no means of navigation, they could end up lost, condemned to wander through the trees until they succumbed to dehydration or zombie choppers. It was difficult to tell which would happen first. More and more of the undead were materialising, and with a dwindling supply of ammo, their chances of survival were diminishing.

8

"Why?" Zielinski followed Armstrong's progress around the room. He collected glass vials, petri dishes, and a ring binder.

"Why? Why what?"

"The antidote. Why bother?"

A look of bewilderment creased Armstrong's face. He set the equipment down, arranging it in an orderly manner.

"What an outlandish thing to say. I know you're of poor social standing, but do you have no regard for your fellow man?"

"I know if I'd had my guts ripped out and my legs torn off, I wouldn't want you to bring me back. Why bother? They'll die again, anyway."

Armstrong gave him a knowing smile. "Ah, yes. I know what you mean. No, Mr Zielinski, I'm not referring to the second wave of infection, although if we could save anybody from that, it would be a bonus."

He strode across the room to Zielinski's side.

"I'm referring to the primary infection, those who ingested the pathogen. They are predominantly intact, and, dare I say, potentially able to make a full recovery. Those who succumbed to the second wave—the more violent means of transmission—they'd be unlikely to survive, depending on the varying degrees of trauma they sustained."

Zielinski's confusion must have reached his face, as Armstrong continued.

"You've already discovered how the virus breached the facility. I heard your conversation on our security feed."

"Yeah, Gus Razor's men attacked the army convoy."

"It wasn't a convoy, Mr Zielinski. It was a single truck. Perhaps it was naïve of us to task such an important mission to a pair of soldiers, but we figured a single unit would be less conspicuous. Besides, it's not an airborne pathogen; none of our samples were. It proved too dangerous. The virions spread through bodily fluid—the contained specimens merely needed to be incinerated."

Armstrong pushed his glasses up his nose.

"Anyway, I digress." He chuckled. "You also discovered the questionable integrity of the men tasked with disposing of the samples. Whilst they professed to have destroyed all the bodies, they were not all accounted for."

"So, a zombie got free and started attacking people?"

"Not at all. That would have been wholly negligent on our part. No, every specimen was euthanised prior to disposal. I saw to it personally."

Zielinski's lungs seized. His heart rate doubled as the doctor's words gave credence to his wandering thoughts. *Is that what I am? A specimen? A guinea pig? What if I die? What if they kill me?* The straps suddenly felt tighter across his chest. He readjusted himself as best he could under their crushing weight.

"We can only surmise an animal became infected after feeding on the corpse. Then we learned of the primary outbreak," Armstrong went on. "Our colleagues in other areas of the country reported symptoms similar to those our test subjects experienced. We traced the source back to a slaughterhouse a few miles away. But, by that point, it was too late. It was an ember to kindling, as it were. The infection was spreading like wildfire, and we had no choice but to seal ourselves inside the medical facility until we discovered an antidote."

"And you've discovered one?"

"Nearly. I'm so close to a breakthrough, I can feel it."

He turned to the corpse occupying the next bed. The curtain had been pulled aside, but now a sheet covered it. Yet Zielinski could still envisage the blank, staring eyes which had bored a hole in his mind. And the smell. It was a stench he knew he could never get used to, one which intensified as the doctor pulled the sheet back once more. The cloying smell filled the air like an invisible plume. Zielinski longed for the oxygen mask which had previously covered his face. He tried breathing through his mouth, but his saliva became tainted with the thick scent, causing him to gag.

"Justin was a lab assistant," Armstrong said, "helping me with my research. He became infected. I still don't know how, but there was no visible trauma. I can only surmise he ingested it somehow. Justin is an example of primary infection. His organs remain intact, his vital functions were still in operation. So, I tried to save him. I gave him the antidote we had been working on, but unfortunately, it proved fatal."

Zielinski stared at the doctor in horror. He wanted to plead, beg, shout, and protest, all at once. But all he managed was a whimper—quiet and pathetic.

"Rest assured," Armstrong said, "it will go through rigorous tests before we trial it on the infected. If successful, there's a strong chance we can save millions of people."

He covered Justin's corpse and went back to his work area.

"Is that why I'm here?" Zielinski asked. He didn't want to hear the answer, but not knowing was even worse. "You're going to test it on me?"

Armstrong chuckled again, his attention still fixed on his work.

"Don't let the savagery of your arrival taint your perception of us, Mr Zielinski. We're scientists, and not the Frankenstein ilk. Despite the temperamental nature of the world, we're still bound by a code of ethics. We have our morals. No harm will come to you while you're under our care."

Zielinski tried to heed the man's words, but he didn't trust him. Not by a long shot.

"Here."

Armstrong turned one of the monitors to face Zielinski. With a few taps of the keyboard, a video filled the screen, showing a number of mice scurrying around a small holding pen.

"These are our subjects. They were infected with T-19 soon after the initial outbreak; that's the virus which caused all this. Once I have the antidote ready, we can try it on—"

Armstrong's words faded to a whisper as he watched the screen. The mice meandered around each other, going from one wall to the next, seemingly inspecting it, before moving on. Armstrong raised a trembling hand to the monitor, pressing a button to zoom in on the sprightly creatures. From his limited vantage point, Zielinski was unsure of the man's sudden trepidation. The mice were moving in a peculiar manner, almost snake-like, their bodies bending every which way as they pushed past each other. But their actions were far from alarming.

Armstrong appeared to disagree, bolting out of the lab.

"Martin! Martin!"

His voice reverberated after him as he disappeared into a corridor, his rapid footfalls fading as he went.

Zielinski focused on the monitor. The mice didn't appear unnatural. They were all snow white, some with shiny black eyes, others with glowing red ones—but that wasn't uncommon, was it? The more he studied the screen, the more curiosities the video presented. The scrabbling feet knocked aside a small white tuft in the corner, which he had initially mistaken for another mouse.

Fur? Do mice shed their fur?

Perhaps that was what had alarmed Armstrong. But still, nothing too abnormal. Maybe the mice had been fighting, and the ball of fur was the aftermath.

What appeared to be a worm lay motionless at the side of the pen. Zielinski squinted, realising it was a tail.

Not a big deal. It probably came off when they were fighting.

When one mouse ran up the wall, Zielinski felt his mouth fall open. He stared, unable to grasp what he was witnessing. The mouse dashed along the smooth plastic in a gravity-defying feat, reminiscent of Spider-Man. It reached the corner, at which point it plunged back into the white throng of its brethren.

Zielinski waited. Watching. Trying to pick the nimble rodent out of the crowd. It was one of those with black eyes, but that was the only discerning feature amongst the rolling white cloud. The mice continued their expedition around the enclosure, going from wall to wall, scanning, appraising, searching for a way out.

Before Zielinski could process it, he heard rushed footsteps enter the lab once more.

"This better be good," Scrivener's voice droned.

"It's remarkable. You've definitely not touched them?"

"They're *your* subjects, Armstrong."

The pair strode into view, neither bothering to even glance at Zielinski as they made their way to the monitor.

"*I* don't make a habit of snooping around your lab and interfering with your research," Scrivener continued.

Armstrong ignored the jibe, instead spinning the monitor around. "Here!"

A moment of silence followed while the two men analysed the screen.

"They're the T-19 subjects," Armstrong said. "Seven or eight days' gestation."

"T-19? Nothing else?"

"No."

"Are you *sure*?"

"Yes, I'm sure!" Armstrong threw his arms out, accidentally knocking a pot of ballpoint pens off the table. They skittered across the floor, but nobody seemed to notice. "It's T-19."

Scrivener smoothed his moustache with his thumb and forefinger.

"So the pathogen doesn't just reanimate dead cells when it hits the pituitary gland," he muttered, more to himself than his colleague. "In fact, it acts as a catalyst."

Armstrong nodded. "Triggering mutation."

9

Amy searched the room for inspiration. Besides the bed, and the furniture barricading the door, the room was practically empty. Whilst the barricade continued to hold up against the undead assault, there was still no way of alerting Ben and Kev. Even the window proved insufficient, with views of the field behind the house—the opposite direction to the route the pair would take on their return.

"I guess we're gonna have to climb down," Amy said, chewing the inside of her lip.

"But you said it's too high. If we sprain an ankle, we're dead."

"I know, but one of us could lower the other down and limit the impact." Amy thought back to how she and Ben had escaped the hospital, using that same tactic in the lift carriage.

"But how would the other one get out?"

Amy struggled for an answer, but it wasn't forthcoming.

"I think it'd be best to stick together. If anything happens out there…"

"We could try tying the sheet to the bedframe, climb out that way." She threw the window wide, but felt her stomach sink. It wasn't the drop that unsettled her, it was the two zombies looking back. They ran to the wall, reaching up as far as they could, their yearning cries accompanying those of their brethren in the hallway.

"There's no way out." Amy moved aside, staring up at the dark ceiling beam.

"What are we gonna do?"

"We can get up into the loft." She dashed back to the window and yanked the wooden curtain pole down.

"The loft?"

"Yeah." She freed the pole of its curtain rings and pointed to the wardrobe. "We climb up there, put a hole in the ceiling, get into the loft, and that will give us access to the roof. We can warn Ben and Kev before they come inside."

"But how do we—"

Amy brushed past and aimed the curtain pole towards the ceiling. With quick stabbing motions, she cracked the plasterboard above the wardrobe. After a few strikes, the ceiling crumbled, exposing the faded yellow bowels of the loft space. The insulating wool tumbled down, leaving a dark void within. Once the space was wide enough, she gave the pole to Donna.

"Here, I'll go first. Pass that up after me."

Amy scrambled onto the chest of drawers and then shimmied on top of the wardrobe. There wasn't much room, forcing her to shuffle on her back until she reached the hole. Warm, clammy air and a musty smell greeted her as she manoeuvred up into the loft space, insulation and cobwebs caressing her arms as she blindly clambered through the darkness.

"Okay, pass it up," she said, having managed to grab hold of a wooden beam.

Donna obeyed, raising the curtain pole through the hole, where Amy guided it flat against her side. She shifted along the beam, allowing space for Donna to follow her up, all the while trying to keep hold of the curtain pole, which dragged along the plasterboard ceiling above the hallway. Amy froze as the persistent moans and roars of the zombies faded. There was no movement. They had to still be at the door. But why the sudden lull?

Donna clambered up into the loft. The gloom concealed her, but Amy caught a brief glimpse of her face. She shared her look of apprehension. Why the sudden silence?

Amy struggled to think of an explanation, all the while trying to dispel the unsettling notion that the zombies were listening. They lacked intelligence. She had grown accustomed to that over the weeks, but they had never fallen silent before. Certainly not when there was a potential meal on the other side of the door.

Only now there wasn't.

Did the zombies know? Had they heard them scrambling across the beam? Or had they heard something else?

The distant rumble of an engine spurred Amy into action. She didn't care if the zombies knew she was above them. She had to warn the others. Adjusting her position on the beam, she slammed the pole into the slate tiles above, repeating the same stabbing motion over and over. The zombies came to life once more, no longer focused on the door but the space above them. Amy could hear their feet dashing back and forth across the hallway, trying to find a way up to her. But she ignored them.

After a couple of strikes, the slate tiles cracked. Daylight flooded the attic as the broken tiles skittered off the rooftop.

The rumbling engine was getting closer.

The gap she'd created wasn't big enough to fit through, and she couldn't guarantee the men would see the curtain pole jutting out of the roof. She hit more of the tiles as the wailing of the undead grew louder.

"Hurry," Donna hissed.

The car pulled up outside the house.

Any second, Ben and Kev would enter and be set upon by the zombies. The gap was still too small, but they would be able to hear her. She scrambled to her feet, balancing on the beam, and leaned forward, her outstretched hands pressed against the roof tiles, her face close to the gap.

"Ben!" she screamed. "Don't—"

The tile under one hand gave way, pitching her forward into the rest. Amy tried to regain her footing, but with nothing beneath her except a thin layer of plaster, her foot crashed through the ceiling.

"Amy!"

Donna scrambled closer to help, but it was all Amy could do to cling onto a thin beam opposite her. She tried to drag her leg back up, a task which became arduous when she felt a hand clasp her foot, dragging her down through the ceiling.

***

Ben and Kev drove in silence, the car meandering casually along the uneven road. Ben stared down at the handgun cradled in his arm: empty and slick with blood. Having run out of bullets, he had resorted to using the gun as a club, beating the final zombie to the ground, smashing the barrel against its skull, until Kev dispatched it with a well-aimed bullet.

Kev drummed his fingers against the wheel, permeating the silence, as he sought the correct structure for his next sentence.

"Okay, I'm sorry for what I said back there." He pushed the words out in a single exhalation, gripping the wheel tighter.

"Don't worry, it doesn't matter."

"No, it *does* matter. I let emotion take over. Do you think I went too far?"

"With those lads?"

Kev nodded.

"What does it matter? What's done is done."

"It's important to reflect on your actions after a conflict. Discuss what went well, and what could be improved next time."

"Fucking hell, Kev, this isn't a school project. It's life and death we're talking about here."

"Which is why we need to keep improving in order to *stay* alive. I'm not perfect. I'll be the first to admit it. But I'm not sure how else I could've handled that. If I'd allowed those two lads to get within striking distance, I'd be fucked if they'd attacked me."

Ben stared at his handgun, trying to formulate a response.

"One of the first things we were taught whenever we attended firearm incidents is split-second decision-making. You don't have time to contemplate options, or rationalise choices. You react, or you die."

"Fair enough. You didn't need to chase the guy in the car, though."

Kev combed his beard with his fingers. "I know. I already explained why I did it, but I admit it may have been a bit excessive."

"Only a bit?" Ben laughed. "He was fleeing. He wasn't a threat to us. And then going into the woods to finish off the guy you'd shot. You almost got us killed."

"I know. I'm sorry. I guess my compassion got in the way of common sense. I didn't want the poor cock to be left at their mercy, especially because of my actions. We all have our bad days, right?"

"Yeah, true. Just try to keep your composure from now on. We need you. It's going to be a while before I can shoot properly again."

"Practice makes perfect."

"I think I've had enough practice today," Ben snorted.

"Don't be so sure." Kev's voice adopted an airy quality as he looked toward the cottage ahead of them.

Ben followed his gaze, concerned about his sudden change in demeanour.

"Have you reloaded yet?"

"Yeah." Ben released the handgun's magazine to confirm, and slotted it back into place.

"Good."

Kev accelerated hard to the end of the road and onto the gravel leading up to the cottage. Ben held the door handle, still unsure what the sudden urgency was for. Before he could seek clarification, the car lurched to a halt, and Kev scrambled out. Ben swung open his door and followed, stepping on a slate tile which snapped beneath his feet. He looked up to the roof, where a section of tiles had been displaced. It was then he heard Amy's voice from within, calling his name.

"Amy!"

A dull crash came from inside the house, coupled with muffled squeals of excitement.

"Fuck!" He lurched towards the front door, but the barricade was still in place on the other side. He slammed his shoulder against it, as screams came from inside.

"The back door!" Kev yelled, racing around the side of the cottage. Ben sprinted after him, losing his footing on the loose gravel before regaining his composure. Twin gunshots rang out from the back of the building and Ben rushed onwards, finding two corpses by the open back door. He bounded inside after Kev as the crack of a handgun sounded again.

"Amy!" Ben yelled. He reached the foot of the stairs, greeted by a rotting, stinking corpse bouncing down toward him. He leapt aside, allowing the dead body to roll past, blood splashing from the bullet hole in its head.

He made his way up the staircase, where Kev continued to fire halfway up. His bulk blocked most of the view, only granting Ben a glimpse of the carnage when he turned sideways to allow another corpse to bounce down the stairs. This time, Ben heaved himself up by the banister, letting the body pass under his feet. It was reminiscent of childhood video games, leaping over Donkey Kong's barrels. Although, as the next cadaver rolled towards him, it became apparent Mario was better at it than he was. The body hit him square in the chest, causing him to stagger back. He caught the banister with his injured hand, sending shockwaves up his arm.

The stairway was clear, but the gunshots continued as Ben made his way to the top. He tried to take in the scene quickly: a carpet of corpses at his feet, a hole in the ceiling, and a leg dangling through it. Kev fired into one of the bedrooms. The shot earned a screech from the occupant before a second bullet silenced them.

"That's the lot," Kev wheezed.

"Amy, can you move?" Donna's muffled voice came from above them.

"I—I'm stuck."

Ben dashed over to her swinging leg, praying there were no injuries. She had lost her shoe, and there was a large tear down the side of her leggings, but no blood, as far as he could tell.

"I've got you," he called. Supporting her foot, he pushed her leg up. "Is there something you can use to pull yourself up?"

"No, I—"

An almighty crash followed as Amy ploughed through the ceiling in a cloud of dust and debris. Ben caught her, but the sudden weight caused him to collapse in a heap.

"Shit."

Kev's voice found its way through the grey plume, his boots scrunching through the remains of the ceiling.

"Are you alright?"

"Yeah." Amy coughed. She took his hand and let herself be hoisted up, freeing Ben from beneath her. As the dust settled, the piercing heat radiated up his arm once more. Staggering to his feet, he grit his teeth. Fresh blood trickled out of his finger stumps, the saturated bandage now buried beneath the rubble.

"Thank you," Amy gushed, before noticing his cradled hand. "Oh my god. We need to get this treated!"

"It's fine."

"No, it's not. Get it raised above your head. There's more bandages downstairs. C'mon."

She made to usher Ben off the landing.

"Hang on," Kev said. "It's not secure. Let's reload and all go down." He stepped toward the hole in the ceiling. "Donna? Are you climbing down, love?"

"Yeah."

With Kev guiding her, Donna lowered herself through the gap, her descent proving a lot more graceful than Amy's.

Donna gasped, placing a reassuring hand on Amy's arm. "Did they—I mean, are you…"

"No, it's a scratch."

"Oh, thank god, I thought—"

"Don't worry about me, I'm fine. C'mon, I need to treat Ben."

"How many bullets do you have?" Kev asked.

"Not many."

"Okay, I'll lead. Get behind me and stay close."

The stairs protested under their weight as they descended single file. The scattered corpses at the foot of the stairs remained still, surrounded by the broken furniture they had crashed into.

"How did they get in? Just the back door?" Kev whispered as they reached the foot of the stairs.

"I think so," Amy replied. "But they were everywhere."

"Okay. You lot take the left. I'll secure the door."

The quartet parted. Ben led the way into the living room, his gun braced on his forearm, as Kev had shown him. He could feel blood dripping from his hand, but he stayed focused on the dimly-lit living room. Whilst it made zombie detection a lot harder, he was grateful for the gloom; it showed the windows were still boarded.

"It's clear. C'mon, let's go and help Kev."

They moved back into the hallway, appraising the grisly obstructions.

"We're going to have to get rid of these as well." Ben kicked the nearest dead body, the jolt causing its head to loll to the side, blood and brain matter oozing from the bullet hole in its head.

"Let's make sure there aren't any more first," Amy muttered, stepping past them and into the next room.

The kitchen was empty.

The back door stood ajar.

Kev was gone.

10

The midday sun pierced the canopy above them, warming the air until it felt as though they were in a greenhouse. Frank wiped his forehead, trudging on through the undergrowth.

"You'd think these trees would offer some shade," he huffed, leaning against the coarse bark.

"Stuff the shade. I'd take fresh air and water over that right now." Lisa stopped next to him, glaring accusingly at the patches of sunlight.

"How long have we been walking?"

"Half hour? Maybe more."

"How far do these woods go?"

"What am I, a tourist guide?"

Frank eyed Lisa's worn camo trousers and dishevelled blonde hair. "No, you look like Action Barbie."

"I'll take that," she said, flicking strands of hair out of her face. "But I still don't know how far they go."

"We don't even know if they lead *anywhere*. For all we know, we could be walking round in circles."

"It's a distinct possibility. Some of these trees are very familiar, all wooden, and bark-like."

Frank grunted. "You really think you're funny, don't you?"

"I'm hilarious, dear."

"It's a shame your comedy can't get us out of here."

Lisa paused, searching for inspiration. With the temporary reprieve, Frank took a deep breath in, gulping the thick, cloying air. His lungs felt hot, as if he were taking a drag of a cigarette. He exhaled, half expecting a plume of smoke to rise from his mouth.

"Well, I don't know which is the best way," Lisa said. "But we gotta keep moving."

"What's the point?"

Lisa frowned. "Look up there. What do you see?"

Frank glanced up at the trees. "A zombie trying to piss on me?"

"Huh?"

"The old Chak-a-Willie song, do you remember?"

"What?"

"You know, 'I was walking through a forest with a gun in my hand, shouting hey, you fucking zombies, I'm the king of this land'."

Lisa snorted. "Those aren't the lyrics."

"Yeah, well, I've adapted it."

"Alright, Fresh Prince of Bellend. Look beyond the trees. The sun isn't going away any time soon. If we don't get out of here, we'll end up Kentucky Fried Dead."

Frank scowled. "That the best you've got?"

"What?"

"Kentucky Fried Dead? It doesn't even make sense."

"I'm hot, okay? And you get the sentiment."

"I'm just saying, there's loads of puns you could've used." Frank raised his hands defensively. "Y'know… ones that actually make sense."

"Shut up."

"You could've even said *KFZ* if the zombies get us."

Frank's smirk disappeared behind Lisa's palm.

"I said shut up." She tilted her head, listening to something Frank hadn't heard.

He gripped his handgun, trying to hear what it was that had caught her attention. He knew even the slightest rustle in the trees could mean danger. What once would've been attributed to wildlife, well, those same creatures were now as deadly as their human counterparts. He was about to ask Lisa what she had heard, but before he could, she strode away through the undergrowth.

"Lise," he said.

He followed the makeshift trail she made through the foliage, unhindered by the interweaving vines, branches, and leaves. She walked with urgency; not something he would associate with having detected a threat, more of an allure, having heard something enticing. He didn't bother calling after her again. Instead, he stayed close, until the sound reached him, too.

"Is that water?"

"Yep."

They pushed through a thicket of brambles, which concealed a small brook, gently trickling over a bed of rock.

"Oh, thank fuck for that."

They splashed their arms and faces, savouring the cool, refreshing touch. Frank cupped the water and brought it to his lips.

"I wouldn't do that if I were you."

He leapt to his feet, gun trained on the topless man emerging through the bushes in front of them.

"Whoa, hold up!" Jay gasped. He raised both hands: one tightly wrapped in his shirt, the other holding a machete, which sported a fresh coat of blood and a few slivers of flesh.

"Get down!" Frank yelled.

"Come on. We've done this before, remember? I'm not a threat."

"Down!"

"Alright." Jay dropped to one knee, keeping his arms raised.

"Drop the machete."

"Are you kidding? Those freaks are everywhere."

"Drop it!"

With a hefty sigh, Jay released the weapon. Frank and Lisa jumped over the stream, the shotgun still aimed at his face.

"Can I get up now?"

"No. What are you doing here?"

"What do you think I'm doing? I'm trying to survive. Seriously, we've done this before, remember? You roughed me up, threw me in the back of the prison van, left me for dead."

"We released you," Lisa said. "Hardly left for dead."

"Which is why I saved your arse back there. Come on. Surely I've proven myself by now?"

Frank and Lisa locked stares, resorting to the wordless communication they had perfected over the weeks.

Finally, Frank groaned. "Fine. Get up."

Jay rose to his feet, dusting down his knees and retrieving his machete.

"How did you find us?"

"Sound travels."

"Bullshit." Frank moved forward, pressing the barrel into Jay's sternum.

"I followed the stream. Any time you're lost, you find a water source and then you trace it out to sea. Everyone knows that. Then I heard you two bickering... again. Seriously, you'd think you had a death wish. Don't you know how many of those freaks are in these woods?"

"Looks like you encountered some," Lisa said, motioning to the grisly remains on the blade. Jay tilted it, allowing the sunlight to reflect in the blood.

"Yeah. One of them caught up to me."

"And did they do that?" Frank pointed to the bloodstained shirt wrapping his left hand.

"No. I fell."

"That's an awful lot of blood to come from a fall."

"I fell *hard*."

"Hmm. I'm not convinced."

He raised the shotgun at Jay's face, causing him to flinch.

"What are you doing?" he gasped.

"A single bite from these guys is all it takes to turn."

"I told you, I fell!"

"Prove it!"

"Hey, gobshites. Keep it down," Lisa snapped. But her warning came too late. Snarls and growls drifted through the foliage. A crowd of undead rushed toward them.

"Let's move."

The trio ran upstream, leaping and dodging the natural obstacles presented by the forest. The outbursts behind them didn't belong solely to humans. There was a concoction of snorts, grunts, and roars as the undead wildlife joined the pursuit, some proving faster than the bipedal zombies.

A mutilated doe ploughed through the thicket, sprinting after them. With no time to aim, Frank brought his shotgun up and fired. The blast snapped the doe's legs from under it, causing it to crash into the ground amidst a plume of blood, dirt, and leaves. Despite the additional disfigurements, the animal tried to continue its pursuit.

Frank sprinted after the others, who dodged and weaved through the trees and bushes. Eventually, they slowed to a halt, emerging into a clearing.

"Did we lose them?" Jay clasped his knees as he sucked air into his lungs.

"I don't know."

There was no movement or sound from any pursuers.

"Cardio isn't my strong point," Jay wheezed, leaning against a tree.

"Well, it better improve," Lisa said. "You fall behind, you die. We gotta keep running."

"Can't we climb one of these? We can catch our breath up there."

"No, they might find us."

"So? They're thick as pig shit. It's not as if they'd be able to reach us."

"But they'd be sure to hang around until we come down," Frank said. "Besides, some of them might climb."

"What?"

Frank thought back to the zombie that had run and jumped for Lisa's foot. The alert, calculating gaze, the tactical mindset. It sent a chill through his body, one which even the scorching sun failed to thaw.

"They're getting smarter," he said, wiping sweat from his brow. "They're learning. Adapting. We need to box clever if we're going to survive."

"What do you mean 'getting smarter'?"

"It means exactly what you think it means! They're running, they're jumping, they're using their surroundings. It means you can't climb up a fucking tree and expect them to pass you by."

Jay blinked hard, glancing around the clearing uneasily. Frank couldn't tell if he was trying to process what he'd said, or thinking of a retort. Either way, he didn't care. He walked over to the stream, which now trickled along ankle-deep. He splashed his face again.

"I meant it when I said I wouldn't drink the water," Jay said.

"Why?"

"Because it's more than likely contaminated. There aren't many streams you can drink from, not unless you want to be spewing up your ring for the next couple of days."

"It's flowing," Lisa said. "I thought you could drink that?"

"No, that's a common misconception. There are all kinds of bacteria in streams like this. You need to boil it, at the very least. Trust me."

"Trust you?" Frank sneered. "You're having a laugh. Go on then, is this where you tell us you used to be a water filtration expert before all this shit kicked off?"

"No, I'm an energy consultant, but I've been a scout leader for the past eight years. I know how to survive in the wilderness, and drinking water from a stream, this close to habitation, is a bad idea."

"Well, I'm thirsty, so I'll risk it." Frank slurped some water from his cupped hands. It had an earthy taste, and a grit-like texture, but he wasn't going to show that to the others. He took another sip.

"You risk vomiting and diarrhoea," Jay continued, shaking his head. "Which, in this heat, can prove fatal."

"Aaah." Frank smacked his lips, motioning for Lisa to join him. "You want some?"

"I think I'll stick with Bear Grylls on this one," she said, walking over to Jay. "So do you know a way out of here?"

"Follow the water." Jay shrugged. "More often than not, where there's water, there's habitation. There'll be a town somewhere nearby."

"Yeah, and zombies to greet us," Frank said, wiping his mouth.

"You seem to know what you're talking about, Cowan," Lisa said, shifting the rifle on her back. "You get us out of here, and we *might* consider letting you join our party. Providing you pull your weight, of course."

"Of course," Jay said, beaming. "I'll lead the way. Just make sure you two keep us in one piece."

"We'll do our best." Lisa met Frank's wide, astounded gaze.

Once again, her face told him everything her lack of words didn't—*Trust me, I know what I'm doing.* But the problem was, he didn't know what she was doing. How do you trust a man you've just met? What qualities could Jay potentially bring to their party, which would outweigh every guaranteed hindrance? Frank was unsure. And, as they set off through the woods once more, he knew he would be keeping one eye on the relentless zombie threat, and the other on Jay Cowan.

11

Five hundred and nine, five hundred and ten, five hundred and eleven, five hundred and twelve. The foam ceiling tiles above Zielinski offered an infinite assortment of tiny holes, and endless ways of occupying himself. Having already counted the number of tiles (eighty-nine) within his limited line of vision, he had resorted to counting the decorative holes adorning each one. And, with each tile offering a bespoke medley of minute divots and pits, the excitement was almost overwhelming.

He guessed it had been a couple of hours since Armstrong had retreated to his quarters. Having dozed off more than once at his work bench—lurching awake when his body threatened to topple from the chair—he had admitted defeat and left to rest. Zielinski was alone, with only the rhythmic beeping of the heart monitor and the hum of the medical equipment by his side. After a fruitless attempt at freeing himself from the restraints, he lay back and sought other means of stimulating his mind.

He had reached seven hundred and seventy-nine before he heard footsteps in the lab. They weren't the sluggish, faltering steps produced by Dr Armstrong hours before. They were rhythmic, confident—a stride with purpose: Scrivener.

The doctor strode into view, making his way over to Armstrong's research. He picked up a binder, skimming through the contents with purpose. With an indignant grunt, he dropped the file and produced a steel hipflask from an inside pocket. Watching the doctor swig the contents gave Zielinski an idea.

"I'm thirsty."

Scrivener sifted through a wad of papers as if he were unaware of anybody else in the room.

Zielinski cleared his throat. "I said, I'm thirsty. I'm going to die of dehydration down here."

"I sincerely doubt that, Mr Zielinski," Scrivener droned, without looking up. "You're hooked up to a saline drip. I'd wager you're more hydrated now than you have been over the past few weeks."

He turned his attention to a clipboard Armstrong had left on the desk.

"What are you doing?"

"Minding my own business. I suggest you do the same."

"It doesn't look like it. Get me a drink or I'll tell Armstrong you've been snooping.

Scrivener scoffed. "Oh? The lab rat's resorted to blackmail, has he? Make no mistake, you're in no position to make demands. I don't care what tale Armstrong has spun for you, you're nothing more than a specimen, a vessel, a test subject for my vaccine."

Zielinski's breath caught in his chest. He tried to keep his voice calm, despite his thumping heart.

"Vaccine? Armstrong said it's an antidote?"

Scrivener laughed again—a mocking, derisive laugh. "And I'll tell you the same thing I've told him on countless occasions: you cannot bring back the dead. He'll find out soon enough."

Zielinski felt the tightness in his chest begin to ease. If there was no rush to create an antidote, there'd be no rush to start experimenting on him.

"So it's not as urgent as Armstrong makes out?"

"Oh, it's time-critical," Scrivener said, "but not for the reason Armstrong thinks. The infected *are* mutating, but that's only an exacerbating factor. The vaccine will aid whichever survivors are left, but these mutations will impact the number."

"What do you mean?"

Scrivener hung his head, his palms against the work surface. "Evolution, Mr Zielinski. Or, in this case, *forced* evolution. Armstrong's genome doesn't just reanimate the dead, it mutates them."

He began prising open a set of metal drawers, muttering to himself.

"The fool's obsessed with reptilian splicing. There's no knowing what effect this will have out there. But the sooner we stop transmission, the sooner we start to save lives."

He slammed the last drawer and moved over to one of the bookcases. Black lever arch files packed each shelf, all labelled, but from Zielinski's vantage point, indiscernible.

"Reptilian what?"

Scrivener went back to ignoring Zielinski. Eventually, his roaming hand stopped on one of the binders.

"How does mutation affect survivors?" Zielinski demanded, leaning as far forward as his restraints would allow. Scrivener tucked the folder under his arm.

"What do you know about the infected?" he asked.

Zielinski lay back against the mattress. While his memory had returned, the scenes in his head felt distorted, as if he were lending them from horror movies to better comprehend his experiences.

"They're zombies. You become one when they bite you. They have that horrible grin, and they can run. We shot them, but they kept coming. The only way to kill them is to shoot them in the head."

"Yes, yes," Scrivener replied, not bothering to hide the impatience in his voice. "Do you feel your friends have grown accustomed to the mannerisms and characteristics of these *zombies?*"

"They're not my friends."

"Trivial, and meaningless to the point I'm making. Do you feel the *people* in your party have become accustomed to zombies? Grown used to them, perhaps?"

"I guess."

"Now, imagine those zombies develop a titanium skull, impenetrable and nigh-on indestructible. Imagine they can run on all fours, at twice the speed of the average man.

Imagine they can climb. Imagine they can fly. Imagine if everything you know about the infected suddenly changes. *That's* how mutation affects survivors, Mr Zielinski. It catches them unawares, and before they can adapt again, they are slaughtered. *That's* why it is time-critical."

He turned away and marched back towards his lab.

Zielinski gasped. "Wait. Is that what's happening out there?"

"Who knows?" Scrivener called over his shoulder, without breaking rhythm. "Mutation affects everyone differently. But time will tell."

Zielinski looked up at the ceiling again, but the holes in the tiles now felt superfluous, given the new information. An imagination he had never called on before now conjured visions of monsters prowling the streets. Humanoid creatures that could sprint on all limbs, pursuing their prey and ripping them to pieces. Intelligent creatures that could plan, strategize, and execute. Whilst his situation in the lab was bleak, the situation the rest of the world was about to face was more horrifying than he could ever imagine.

12

"Kev?"

Donna rushed toward the open door.

"Donna, wait!" Ben urged. He followed her outside, scanning the area all around them, until he saw Kev standing beside the large gas tank that supplied the property, sliding a hand over his bald head.

"What's up?" Ben asked, only granting half his attention to Kev, using the other half to continue searching the bordering fields for signs of movement.

"They've fucked with the gas," Kev said.

It was enough to warrant Ben's full attention.

"What?" he gasped.

"There was a strong smell of gas, so I came out here to inspect it. And, sure enough…"

Kev stepped aside, allowing Ben a closer look. The supply pipe was bent at an angle, with a faint hiss escaping from it—along with the distinctive smell of gas.

"Shit." Ben covered his nose.

"The valve's broken," Kev said, pointing to the bent handle.

"How could that happen?" Amy came closer to inspect the damage.

"There's gotta be somebody else here," Kev replied.

The four scanned the open fields and the bordering woodland, going full circle to the open kitchen door.

"Was it the zombies?" Donna suggested.

Kev shook his head. "They're not that smart. This is sabotage."

"Sabotage?" Amy said. "But why?"

The two men exchanged a knowing glance. It was only slight, but enough to tell Amy they had an idea of who was responsible.

"It couldn't have been them," Ben said. "They wouldn't have got here so fast."

"Who?"

"Let's get inside," Kev said, ignoring Amy's query. "We need to secure this place and find a way of turning the gas off."

"Will the valve not turn at all?" Ben asked.

"No. It's knackered," said Kev. "We need a spanner."

"There's a toolbox in the cupboard under the stairs."

"I'll go with you," Amy said, following Ben into the kitchen, and towards the stairs beyond.

"Who were you talking about?" she asked, once they were out of earshot of the others.

Ben opened the cupboard door and dropped to his knees. They had inspected the space on their first day in the cottage, but hadn't needed to explore it further until now.

Besides the toolbox and a folded ironing board, the space housed mainly cobwebs and an assortment of junk. He dragged the hefty toolbox closer, inspecting the various tools within.

"We—uh, we had a bit of bother while we were out."

"What happened?"

"A car almost ran us off the road. Two guys got out and approached us, and Kev... he lost it. He shot them both before they said anything."

"Were they armed?"

"They had a crowbar and a bat. He explained why he did it; he saw them as a threat. The whole 'kill or be killed' mantra, which is fair enough."

"Did they survive?"

"No. But there was somebody else in the car. He drove off when he saw what had happened. We went after him, but he got away."

"Do you think it was him?"

"Kev thinks he could be part of a larger group who might seek revenge. But I doubt they would've found us so fast. I tell you what, though, he really lost it out there."

"What do you mean?"

Footsteps from the kitchen halted their discussion. Kev appeared in the doorway, a weary guise replacing his usual jovial smile.

"Any luck?"

"Yeah." Ben chose a large, rusted spanner before shoving the toolbox back into the cupboard.

"Ah, that'll do. I need you both to cover me," Kev said, as Ben passed him the spanner. "We need eyes on both sides of the house if it's zombies *and* the living we're dealing with."

Amy went to walk back through the kitchen, but Kev remained in the doorway.

"And be careful where you use that," he said, nodding towards her handgun. "We start a gunfight next to the gas tank, and we'll end up in the next field."

He stepped aside, allowing the pair to pass before following them through the kitchen and back outside. Donna stood beside the house, her eyes moist and her cheeks flushed.

"What's up?" Amy asked.

"Nothing," she sniffed, taking a deep breath of air, composing herself. "The sooner we get this done, the better, right?"

"Right." Kev inspected the damage to the gas tank before setting to work on the valve.

"I'll take this side," Amy said. "Ben, you cover the other side. Donna, did you reload your gun?"

Donna nodded sheepishly.

"Good, but make sure you stand far enough away and watch those trees. If there *is* someone out here, we don't want them getting a shot at the tank."

Amy didn't think that was likely. If somebody wanted to blow them up, they could've fired at the gas tank. Instead, they had damaged it. *Why?*

She eased around the corner of the cottage. There was no movement from the driveway or the road beyond. Amy knew she had to stay alert, but couldn't stop her mind from wandering.

Why focus on the gas supply? If it was to get them outside, it was working. There was no chance of using their guns around it, without the risk of being blown up. If the zombies attacked, they'd have to retreat, or use blunt weapons. *Is that the plan?*

She didn't even want to entertain the idea of the zombies being that intelligent. She recalled their time in the hospital when Terry, the maintenance man, had hidden inside the lift. The zombies had slammed against it, none of them having the basic understanding to press the button to open the doors.

No, it can't be them.

But then, earlier, the zombies had stopped banging against the door when they realised nobody was there anymore. They'd worked out she had escaped. They knew she was in the ceiling above them. They thought. They processed. They deduced.

Amy shook the unsettling notion from her head, trying to seek logic within the cloud of speculation.

It's gotta be people. The zombies aren't clever enough to plan this.

But who would have sabotaged their gas supply? The person escaping from Ben and Kev would be a prime suspect. If he wanted revenge, it was plausible he'd come after them. But how could he find them? And why the gas?

An icy grip seized Amy's chest. *For the same reason.* They were forced out into the open. Forced to split up to cover all bases. Forced to abandon the use of their guns. And if the driver was limited to the same resources as his dead companions, it meant he'd only have access to melee weapons.

Levelling the playing field.

The prospect stole the saliva from her mouth. It caused her hands to shake, her aim to waver. Amy suddenly felt more vulnerable from behind than from any potential threat presented in front. Before she could voice her concerns to the others, she saw movement in the road ahead. It was only slight, but it was enough to keep her rooted to the spot.

She stood. Waiting. Watching.

The movement came again, this time revealing a slow-moving corpse from behind a thicket of bushes in front of the house. Its head lolled back as it examined the sky, a strange expression adorning its mangled face. Was it awe? Or a trick of the light?

A clang from behind the house snapped the zombie's head in her direction. Amy swung back, out of sight, pressing her back to the wall. The clang came again as Kev tried to turn the warped valve. His arms trembled under the exertion, but the spanner slowly began to move.

"There," he said, dusting his hands triumphantly.

"Is it off?" Donna asked.

Amy clicked her fingers to silence them. Satisfied the message had been received, she looked back around the corner. But instead of the side of the house, she saw only bloodshot eyes, a mangled face, and broken teeth. The zombie lunged for her, dragging her to the ground. She crashed against the paving slabs, her gun skittering across the gravel, the zombie's face inches from her own. She seized the creature by the throat and shoulder, her fingers seeping through its torn, pulpy muscle, and closing around its clavicle. She heaved it up as best she could, but the zombie fought back, straining against her hands, desperate to reach her flesh.

"Shit!"

Kev's boots came crunching across the gravel before one of them met the side of the zombie's head. It connected with the force of a freight train, snapping it aside, sending the zombie rolling away across the ground. Kev grasped Amy's hand and pulled her to her feet. The impact might have killed her attacker, but she was sure she saw movement out of the corner of her eye as Kev ushered her back inside.

"Amy?" Ben clasped the sides of her arms. The action caused him to wince, and he withdrew his injured hand.

"I'm fine," Amy replied breathlessly. "But you're not. We're dressing your wound. Now."

She led him over to the table while Kev secured the door. She gathered the bandages, the gauze, and the sterile water she had used to treat Ben's wound earlier that morning. The finger stumps were red raw, and caked in dirt and debris. Whilst the thick, gritty paste served as a poultice to stem the blood flow, the chance of infection had significantly increased.

"Donna, we need you at the back," Kev said, taking up position at the boarded front window. "Look for any sign of movement. If they come back, let me know."

"Okay." Donna scrambled onto one of the worktops, peering through a small gap between the boards—a view which covered most of the field behind them.

"It wasn't the zombies that damaged the tank," Amy said. She doused a cotton ball in the saline solution and tenderly dabbed Ben's stumps. He groaned, slamming a fist against the table.

"Zombie, human, I don't care," Kev said. "Somebody's messing with us, and I'll be damned if it happens again, not on my watch."

With the grime washed away, the blood flowed freely, oozing out onto the hardwood table. But it wasn't the blood that concerned her, it was the red hue around the stumps. While it was still too early to attribute it to infection, Amy couldn't quash the sinking feeling in her gut. She pressed the gauze and wrapped his hand in a bandage.

"How's the little piggies?" Kev asked, a jesting glint in his eyes.

Ben smirked. "That's rich coming from you, plod."

"Have they grown back yet?"

"Not quite."

"Well, if anybody can bring them wee-weeing home, it's our favourite nurse."

Amy smiled. It was good to see the banter was back, but the prospect of infection still concerned her. They needed antibiotics. Sooner rather than later.

"I told you," Kev continued, "wedding bells before the year's up."

Ben snorted. "And where am I supposed to wear a ring?" He raised his injured hand to showcase his point.

"Wedding bells?" Amy asked.

"It doesn't matter. It's just Kev being a dick, as usual."

"Oh." She smiled again, but the disappointment lay heavy on her chest. Her imagination ventured to a dreamscape, torturing her with post-apocalyptic wedding scenes, Ben in a scavenged suit, while she wore a foraged white gown. They held each other close, slow-dancing around a silent ballroom. Wedding rings—plundered from a derelict jewellery shop—glistening under makeshift lights; a token of their commitment to one another, of undying love.

"You've got eight other piggies, haven't you?" Kev said. "Improvise. It'll hardly be an orthodox ceremony anyway, what with me being the best man *and* officiating. I'll tell you what, though, Donna can be your wedding singer. She's got an amazing voice, haven't you, love?"

Confused, Donna turned around and blinked, as if torn from her own reverie.

"No," she said after a couple of seconds, once Kev's question had registered. She shot him a reprimanding glare before returning her attention to the field outside.

"Bet she could knock up a cracking wedding cake as well," Kev said, seemingly unperturbed by the reproach.

"She won't be knocking anything up without a gas supply." Amy's dousing input extinguished the upbeat atmosphere. "It's all well and good talking about imaginary scenarios. But what we need to do is focus on what's real. Someone has tampered with our gas supply, and worse still, we don't know who. We don't know where they are.

We don't know what they're going to do next. We need to be alert. And we need to be ready."

Ben placed his hand on hers, a gesture that would ordinarily have soothed her, but not this time. She knew she had to stop letting affection distort her judgement. She pulled her hand away and motioned to the corpses at the foot of the stairs.

"We need to get rid of the bodies as well. This place has to be clean. Ben's hand is—"

She caught the last word between her lips, not daring to utter it lest it become true. There was no way of knowing for sure it was infected, and the last thing she wanted to do was cause more panic.

"She's right," Kev said. "Let's get back on the clock. Ben, take over from me. I'll get rid of the corpses. Make sure the guns are loaded. We need to be ready for whatever comes next."

13

Frank stumbled along, exhausted, weary, his vision beginning to blur. The relentless heat seemed to permeate every pore, expelling drop after drop of sweat. His feet felt as though they were encased in cement, every step proving more and more difficult to take. Lisa walked in front of him, with Jay leading a path through the thicket. Neither of them seemed to be struggling as much as Frank was.

Gotta be the heat. He'd be damned if his bout of lethargy was to do with drinking tainted water. But, despite not having eaten, a wave of nausea was rising. He shook his head clear, trying to focus.

"You sure you know where you're going, Cowan?" he called, hoping a line of questioning would slow the pace.

"Not entirely," Jay replied. "But if we keep following the stream, we'll find somewhere soon."

Frank grumbled. It wasn't the answer he was hoping for.

"Do you want me to carry you?" Lisa shot a mischievous glance over her shoulder.

"Oh, har har. Didn't take long to start with the comedy again."

"Helps pass the time."

"For you."

Jay laughed at the exchange. "How long have you two been together?"

"Two weeks," Lisa replied.

"*Two weeks?*"

"Yep. It's been a whirlwind romance."

"Whirlwind?" Frank scoffed. "More like a fucking hurricane."

"Now who's being funny?"

"Shit. You two are like an old married couple." Jay laughed again, batting aside a low-hanging branch, which immediately shot upwards. The piece of rope tied to the end of it burst from the ground amidst a shower of leaves, twigs, and forest debris. The rope flailed back down until its looped end snagged on a tree.

Lisa gasped. "What the fuck was that?"

"It was a trap." Jay stood rooted to the spot. "Don't move."

"A trap?"

"A snare trap."

He stooped down, scattering the leaves concealing a wooden pole that had been speared into the ground.

"It's used to catch animals. If I'd have stepped in the noose, I'd have gone up with it."

"Well, looks like you were wrong, Lise," Frank muttered. "He's certainly not Bear Grylls."

"I didn't think there'd be traps," Jay retorted. "But this is a good sign: it means there's people nearby."

"Or zombies."

Jay raised an eyebrow. "You think zombies did this?"

"I don't know. But after what I saw earlier, I wouldn't take it for granted."

"Climbing onto a roof is a far cry from building traps," Lisa said. "It'll be survivors. For all we know, it might've been set before all this shit started."

"Yeah, well, either way, I'm not risking it." Frank took a step forward, brushing past Jay. "I'll take the lead. We're following the stream, right?"

"Right." Jay looked as though he wanted to protest, or at least offer an alternative, but he stayed silent.

Traps, Frank pondered, treading carefully over the embedded stick. *Why would survivors build traps out here? Anything they catch would probably be infected. It can't be for food... Unless it wasn't survivors who set them.* Frank felt the tickle of fear caressing his spine once again. He imagined zombies planning attacks, digging pits, sharpening sticks, ready to impale, snare, and capture anyone unlucky enough to encounter them.

No. Lisa's right. They're not that clever. It's gotta be survivors. But the prospect was far from comforting. Humans were harder to fight. They *could* plan, strategize, and use weapons to their advantage.

He tried to stay focused. But the forest continued to move beyond his steps. He blinked hard, reaching for a tree to support his cumbersome legs. His eyelids felt heavy, but he pushed on, desperate to get out into the open. He heard

Lisa's voice behind him, but didn't process what she was saying. Everything sounded muffled, as if the thick, cloying heat had settled in his eardrums.

"Frank!"

This time he heard her, but didn't turn. Instead, he focused on moving one foot at a time, trying to maintain his balance while his body threatened to topple.

He saw the glint of a trip wire, but it was too late. The clank of metal rang all around them as Frank pitched forward. He hit the ground hard, thankful there wasn't a pit of spikes waiting to break his fall. The clatter continued, only now accompanied by dull thuds. Frank flinched when an old cast iron pan landed nearby.

He staggered to his feet, tentatively looking skyward, as a second pot fell from the rope above them. The linear formation of pots and pans was tied to a pair of trees either side of their route.

"Another trap," Jay said.

"No shit."

The clunk and clamour began to subside, as the suspended kitchenware swayed to a stop.

"We've gotta be close to a camp. Somebody must be within earshot."

"You're not filling me with confidence." Frank aimed his shotgun and breathed deeply, trying to steady his trembling hands. The greenery of the forest blurred. He felt himself stagger, as the innumerable shades of green and brown surrounded him. He tried to focus, to separate them in his mind's eye.

He managed to distinguish the trees from the foliage, and then from the fervent zombie, which ploughed through the undergrowth toward him.

Frank fired, striking a tree, casting an explosion of bark over the mutilated man as he lunged towards him. He aimed again, only this time he was beaten to it by Lisa's rifle. The clap echoed through the trees, sending the undead man pirouetting to the ground, his disintegrated skull oozing brain matter over the bed of the forest.

Lisa took Frank by the waist as he swayed again. He lowered his shotgun, confused when she recoiled her hand. She yanked his shirt up, exposing the sodden bandage over his wound.

"Frank!" She gasped. "How long have you been bleeding?"

"I didn't know I was."

Jay stepped closer. "Holy shit! Look at all that blood. Is it a bite?!"

"No," Frank muttered, trying to control the tremor in his legs.

"After you grilled me about my hand!"

"It's *not* a bite!" Lisa snapped. "He was shot."

"Shot? By who?"

Frank couldn't have replied, even if he'd wanted to. His faltering kneecaps could no longer carry his dead weight. He fell to the ground, aided by Lisa, who guided him onto his side. The woodchips beneath his face blurred in and out of focus, and he could no longer decipher the audible commotion above him. A single beetle scurried into view, hesitant which way to travel, with all the disorder around it.

Frank watched it retreat under a leaf, contemplating the susceptibility of insects to the virus.

If they were prone to infection, there would be no hope for humanity at all. It was hard enough keeping zombie humans and animals at bay, but infectious insects? They'd be as good as dead.

Lisa's knee came down, crushing the beetle and its hiding place as she crouched beside him. He could only laugh at the allegorical nature of its demise. They had survived so far. Even if the bugs *could* transmit infection, they'd survive those, too. With a newfound drive, he tried to sit up, but Lisa's hand kept him at bay.

"Hang on," she urged. "Rest."

Frank wanted to protest, but the way his sight and hearing betrayed him, he couldn't trust his speech would be any more efficient. He closed his eyes, trying to hone his other senses.

It sounded like there was a multitude of footsteps all around him. The crack of twigs, the rustle of leaves, and the sound of scraping boots were everywhere. Yet, there didn't seem to be any tension in Lisa's grip on his shoulder, no urgency in her voice as she spoke indecipherable words.

Frank strained his ears.

"Has he been bitten?"

I've already told that prick I haven't. But the voice didn't seem familiar. Jay Cowan had more of a non-descript accent. This voice sounded older, with a distinct Yorkshire dialect.

"No, he was shot." Lisa squeezed his shoulder. "Do you have any medical supplies?"

"We have some. But I'm a bit apprehensive about bringing guns into our flock."

"We mean you no harm, I promise."

Frank tried to see who she was talking to, but the piercing light was like acid in his eyes. He closed them again, resting his head on the forest floor.

"I'll put my faith in you. Let's get him up."

Frank suddenly felt weightless, as a number of hands hooked different parts of his body: his shoulders, his arms, his legs. He winced when a hand clapped his side.

"Careful!"

He felt a disturbance in his euphoric elevation before another hand gently pressed his wound.

"I'll do it."

Lisa's voice sounded close, but he lacked the energy to check. All he could do was allow himself to float through the forest on a bed of hands, unaware of how many people carried him, or who they even were. He felt himself being lowered onto a hard metal surface. Heat radiated through his clothes as footsteps clanged around him.

"We good?" a voice asked.

"Yeah, let's go."

With a rumble of an engine, they began to move. Frank tried to sit up, but it was no use. The blanketing rays from the sun kept him pinned to the back of what he suspected was the flatbed of a pickup truck. It rolled over the uneven ground, sending a burst of fire in his side with every bump and shudder. He tried not to show his discomfort, but

Lisa's hand on his shoulder told him he was doing a bad job disguising it.

"How far?" Lisa asked.

"Literally three or four minutes," came the reply from the Yorkshireman. "Don't worry, it's safe. We've got a community."

A community? Frank thought. *Where are they taking us, an old folks' home? Fighting the undead alongside the not-quite-dead?* It was a peculiar choice of word, one which formed an even more peculiar sense of foreboding. Frank was unsure why, but the term made him feel uneasy.

"We have some supplies," the man continued. "We've scavenged food, and we use the stream back there as our water supply."

"Have you encountered many zombies?" Lisa asked.

"A few, mainly in towns, but we're seeing more and more out here."

"What about survivors?"

"Oh yes, we actively search for others. Our community is growing larger every day."

That was it. That was the prompt he needed. He had heard those words recently from the couple they had encountered in Doxley. They had sounded as though they were on a recruitment drive; they had said a similar thing— *a community with more survivors joining every day.*

Frank tried to stay awake, to stay alert, to at least warn Lisa before the lure of unconsciousness claimed him.

But it was too late. The voices had already faded. The jolts from the vehicle numbed, and Frank was no longer aware if they were even moving. He didn't feel his body being pulled out of the pickup, or smell the stale, musty odour of a centuries-old building. He didn't hear the whispers and murmurs of the congregation as he was carried through the church. He didn't see the room he was placed in, at least not for another couple of hours, when he would lurch awake at the sound of gunshots.

14

Zielinski opened his eyes, immediately fixing on Armstrong, who paced back and forth. With no windows or clock, he had no perception of how long he had slept. Minutes felt like hours, and hours had become incomprehensible. He guessed it had been at least a day, possibly two, since Scrivener had entered the lab. As soon as Armstrong returned, Zielinski had informed him of the stolen folder and blood vials. The doctor had merely shrugged it off with a chuckle and said no more on the subject. He had, however, provided Zielinski with sips of water. Compassion seemed to be a trait inherent in only one of the scientists. Now, seeing the doctor so agitated, Zielinski was filled with dread.

"What's up?" he asked.

Armstrong didn't answer. He resumed his pacing, glancing occasionally at the different monitors angled around the room. Zielinski clenched his fists. He was sick of being ignored. He wanted answers.

"It's the mutation, isn't it?"

Without breaking his stride, Armstrong shook his head and laughed.

"Tell me!"

"With all due respect, Mr Zielinski, I fear this is way beyond your comprehension."

"Try me."

Armstrong shrugged and walked over to the monitor, which had caused him so much anxiety the last time he had viewed it. He spun the screen round, offering Zielinski another view of the mice, only this time, the holding pen appeared different. Half the mice scurried around the bottom of the screen. The others dashed across the sides, running up and down the wall as if gravity were an afterthought.

"How?"

"Have you ever heard of the van der Waals force?" Armstrong asked, a smugness replacing the cheerful glint in his eye.

Zielinski shook his head.

"No, of course not. Like I said, way beyond your comprehension."

The doctor spoke with a finality, as if the conversation was over, but Zielinski wasn't going to allow silence to envelop them once more.

"It looks like it's way beyond yours, too, *Doctor.*"

"Please, I'm trying to work."

"You're out of your league."

"Don't talk about things you know nothing about."

"It seems easy for you to destroy the world, but you don't have a hope of saving it."

"That's enough!" Any fragment of composure Armstrong had had left faded with the echo of his fist slamming against the worktop.

Zielinski watched, waiting, satisfied he had broken the man, who now started to weep. But he knew broken men could be dangerous, unpredictable. And all at once, Zielinski was reminded of his vulnerability, strapped to a bed, at the mercy of the man who now turned towards him.

"I never wanted to work here. I had no interest in bioweapons." Armstrong squeezed both fists against his eyes, wiping the tears away with a renewed passion. "I have a PhD in genetics, and a Master's in biology. I wanted to change the world, but not like this." He gestured towards the corpse in the next bed. "This catastrophe." He turned to the monitor. "This *abomination*."

The mice continued to scurry along the walls. Most were missing their tails, which lay discarded around the pen like dead earthworms trampled underfoot.

"I never meant for any of this."

"Didn't you know what you were creating?"

Armstrong's anguish reverted to annoyance. "Oh, I knew. There was no smoke and mirrors. I was headhunted for this team, and the objectives were clear. They tasked us with creating a bioweapon—a last defence against any would-be invaders. It was never supposed to be used as part of a warfare campaign. Purely defensive... at least, that's what they told us. They called it the Trojan project. You've heard of the Trojan horse, yes?"

Zielinski nodded, grateful to reveal some degree of intellect.

"It was intended to be the same kind of concept, except we wouldn't be killing them, they'd be killing each other. The virus would spread, they'd be forced to contain the issue, and in doing so, would obliterate their numbers."

"Spread through spit and blood, I know."

Armstrong smiled. "Indeed. You found the documentation I planted for you."

Zielinski gasped. "*You* left it there?"

"Naturally. You didn't think classified material would be left scattered over a table in a military base, did you?"

Zielinski shifted uncomfortably. He *had* thought that, but he wasn't about to admit it.

"When we retrieved you from the base—"

"Abducted," Zielinski corrected.

"—that wasn't the first time we ventured there. I left the documentation out so you would find it. You could read up on what you were dealing with, to better survive."

"Wait, first time? How many times did you come up?"

Now it was Armstrong's turn to shift uncomfortably. "A couple. Our supplies were dwindling, so we borrowed some of your rations. We figured you were in a better position than us to replenish stock."

Zielinski snorted. So, it hadn't been Gus Razor that was responsible for eating all the food. It was the eggheads in the lab below. Thinking of the rations caused his stomach to grumble. What he wouldn't give to taste the bland, crunchy pasta and processed meat again. Even the scurrying mice started to look appetising. He watched their frenzied dash along the walls. Some fell now and then, but ran straight back up. Those in the centre of the enclosure continued to slither back and forth, their unnatural movements more comparable to a snake or a lizard.

"Scrivener said you're obsessed with reptilian slicing."

"Reptilian *splicing*," Armstrong corrected. "How much has he told you?"

"Not much. He said the sooner you stop transmission, the sooner you save lives."

"Well, that's one thing we can agree on, at least."

"Is that why they're doing… that?"

Zielinski motioned to the gravity-defying mice.

"It looks like it. I won't go into specifics—far too complex—but the virus that caused all this is the nineteenth variant. I spliced gecko genes into the T-19 genome, as well as smallpox RNA to make it highly contagious."

Zielinski stared at him blankly, already lost in the maze of technical terms.

"Basically, it's a self-replicating microbe. It makes copies of itself inside your body, and it's engineered to target the brain. Once there, well, to cut a long story short, you die. But the virus reanimates the corpse, which was our intention. What we weren't expecting was for the virus to continue to mutate. This is leading to transformations which—" he pointed to the mice "—is clearly evident."

"So the zombies are going to start climbing walls?"

Armstrong screwed up his face. "Again, I'm not going to confuse you with my thesis and scientific jargon. But the simple answer is yes, it's possible… Only amongst the smaller ones, you understand. With the correct morphological changes, the body mass of say… a toddler, or young child, especially in a malnourished, or incomplete state, could potentially allow for it to scale walls like these mice."

"But adults won't?"

"No. Their bodies would have to mutate dramatically. They would need at least eighty per cent adhesion to any surface. That level of morphological change has not been demonstrated so far."

"So dead kids could be more dangerous. But what's the issue?"

"The possibilities are endless." Armstrong scratched his stubbly chin in contemplation. "These mice are showing increased intellectual capacity. The infected people out there could be the same. Not to mention the extensive variants involved. Think of all the animals that have succumbed to infection, the different anatomical structures. Anything could happen."

Scrivener's words sauntered through Zielinski's head. *Titanium skull, run on all fours, climb, fly.* Those were just some of the possibilities he'd suggested. But whilst Scrivener seemed almost in awe at the possibilities, Armstrong looked terrified.

Zielinski swallowed, a task proving more laborious than usual with his sandpaper mouth. He didn't know how long it had been since moisture had passed his lips, but he doubted Armstrong would be any more accommodating than Scrivener, not while he was hellbent on curing the dead.

"If this starts happening out there," Zielinski said, pushing the words through his gravelly throat, "will your antidote still work?"

Armstrong hung his head.

"I guess not," Zielinski responded.

"As you've already stated, they would die anyway if we brought them back. The virus requires only the basic anatomical functions to survive. It infects the brain, the brain controls the outer extremities, the host becomes operational. It doesn't matter if there's a gaping hole in the abdomen, or they are missing arms or legs, the virus doesn't require that. But living people do. If we cured them, after the horrific mutilations their bodies could have been subjected to, they would die in agony all over again."

"Is that why only headshots kill these things? Because it's in the brain?"

"Yes. You destroy the brain, you destroy the host."

"But I thought brains needed blood and oxygen and shit?" It was enough to impress Armstrong. He seemed keen to share his work with somebody—*anybody*—other than Scrivener.

"They do, but we engineered the virus to take over the brain and keep it alive. It will continue to fire neurons to every part of the body, even if those parts are incapacitated. The infected don't feel pain. They can struggle along on broken limbs, as I'm sure you've witnessed. However, without an effective respiratory or circulatory system, their limbs will soon become inadequate. The virus slows the decomposition process, but doesn't eradicate it entirely. Over time, the infected will cease to become a threat. Or, at least, that's what we thought, until these mutations started."

"So the mutations will prevent that?"

"Who knows? Evolution is a means of adapting to changing environmental factors. But this. This is—"

"Forced evolution?" Zielinski said, recalling Scrivener's rant.

Armstrong scowled. "Indeed," he said after a couple of seconds. It had become clear Zielinski was reciting terms he had heard from Scrivener.

"You know, Martin has an exaggerated sense of self-worth. He's a brilliant scientist, don't get me wrong. But he will always be reliant on others. And his methods..." Armstrong's gaze drifted to the covered corpse. It was only fleeting, but it told Zielinski everything he needed to know. "Well, they leave a lot to be desired, at times."

Zielinski longed to broach the subject. Armstrong knew more than he was letting on. He had tried to save the lab assistant, but did that mean Scrivener had infected him? And with no other guinea pigs left, would that mean *he* would be the next test subject? The worries tumbled through his mind like balls in a bingo machine. And before he could pick one to dwell on, an even greater fear took over, as the power cut out.

The lights went off.

The machines stopped beeping.

The entire lab fell into darkness.

15

Amy bent down and grabbed the final corpse's legs. She waited for Kev to hoist the torso up before shuffling with him towards the foot of the stairs. With a quick back-and-forth swing, they released the body on top of the others, which they had assembled onto the mock Persian rug in the hallway.

"That's them all," Kev said. "How we looking, Ben?"

"Haven't seen any movement," Ben replied from his perch at the kitchen window, leading out to the front of the house. Kev nodded and heaved the large chest of drawers—their makeshift barricade—away from the door.

"We'll have a quick check to make sure it's clear, then we'll get these intruders out on their arse."

"Okay," Amy said. "I'll grab the rifle."

"Handgun," Kev insisted, shaking his head. "It's got a better rate of fire, which is what we need in close combat situations."

Amy wanted to ask how it would be close combat with their being outdoors, but decided against it. Given the choice, she would have preferred the rifle. It was easier to hold, and she was more accurate with it than the sidearm. But so far, Kev had regularly demonstrated his tactical prowess when it came to open warfare. Even if she didn't fully understand his reasoning, it was easier to agree.

The front of the house was eerily quiet. A slight breeze disturbed the foliage opposite, but aside from that, the only sound came from the crunch of gravel beneath their feet. They walked to the end of the driveway, guns poised, alert to every leaf and branch the wind toyed with. The road was empty, as far as they could see.

"Let's do this," Kev said.

They marched back to the house, both happy with their assigned roles. Kev was in the doorway, heaving the bottom of the rug, while Amy stood guard outside. Once the carpet of bodies had crossed the threshold, she abandoned her sentry duty and assisted him with transportation.

"How far shall we drag them?" The fabric trembled beneath her hands, her knuckles white.

"Far enough so the smell doesn't reach us. This heat is gonna have them smelling real ripe, real quick."

Amy scrunched up her nose. The smell of decomposition had already permeated her nostrils. There was no knowing how long they had been walking corpses. She intended to keep tugging toward the road, but Kev was veering over to a row of juniper shrubs.

"We can't leave them out in the open," he said, his efforts straining his voice. "We don't want anyone driving past and seeing the bodies outside."

Amy couldn't argue with that logic. She tugged her corner over so she was back in line with him, and continued on. Beads of sweat overlapped her brows and trickled into her eyes. She squeezed them shut and pulled harder until the backs of her legs scraped against the shrubs.

"There," Kev wheezed, sweeping a film of sweat back over his head. "Now we just need to get antibiotics."

"What?"

"Come on, you've seen his hand. And you know better than I do the signs of infection."

Amy glanced at the boarded windows. She couldn't see him, but she knew Ben was on the other side, keeping watch through the narrow gaps. She didn't want to believe the wound was anything more than inflammation, but hearing the words from somebody else only gave greater credence to her fear.

"He needs antibiotics," Kev continued. "Hell, we could do with them anyway, to be on the safe side."

"I know." Amy started to make her way back to the house, but soon realised Kev wasn't following her. "What is it?" she asked, turning around.

"It's… it's Donna. I'm worried about her. She seems… distant."

Kev stroked his beard, choosing his words carefully.

"She's tearful quite a lot of the time. I try to cheer her up, but nothing's working anymore. What do you think?"

Although Amy wasn't a mental health professional, it sounded like depression. And while she hadn't picked up on any noticeable changes in Donna's behaviour, there was no denying that her husband would be the best judge.

"You've gone through a lot," Amy whispered. "We all have. And it can be hard to see light at the end of the tunnel in circumstances like these. You just have to be there for her. Make sure she knows she's not alone."

"I don't know how. I'm not good with stuff like this. Maybe…" Kev glanced around. Whether he was searching for threats or the right wording, Amy was unsure. "Maybe you could have a chat with her?"

"Oh, I dunno."

"I don't handle emotion very well. I never know what to say and try to fix things all the time. But this is something I'm not sure I can fix. I need your help. Please?"

Amy didn't know what kind of comfort she'd be able to offer. She wasn't a mother, and couldn't begin to imagine the despair of losing a child. But Kev's imploring look was one she recognised. It was somebody desperate to help their loved one. Amy knew how that felt. She would have done anything to save her family. To save her mother from her grisly fate.

"Okay," she whispered.

Kev's face slackened with relief. "Thank you. Me and Ben can get the antibiotics. Will you and Donna be okay alone?"

Amy clenched her teeth. She knew he meant well, but his notion of chivalry was wearing thin.

"Of course we'll be alright," she said. "They only got in because they spotted us outside. If we lie low and stay alert, we'll be fine."

"Yeah, and we won't be gone long, either."

Back at the house, Amy helped him pull the barricade in front of the door, her thoughts returning to the Ben and the poison potentially spreading up his hand. Gangrenous blood oozing through his veins. While she knew it would be nowhere near that advanced, even if his wound *was* infected, the thoughts alone were enough to spur her into action.

"How's it looking out the back, Donna?" Kev asked, striding into the kitchen.

"Fine, there's nobody out there."

"Good, come and have a sit down. We've got things to discuss."

They each took a chair around the table, eyes flitting between Kev and Amy.

"We need to head out," Amy said. "We need more supplies."

"Supplies?" Ben repeated. "What do you mean? We've got loads left."

He motioned to the row of cupboards, all of which concealed the stacks of tins and packets they had salvaged from the lorry.

"I'm not talking about food or water. We need medical supplies. Your hand…"

She took his bandaged hand in hers, picturing the grisly, swollen stumps beneath the cloth.

"This kind of wound can easily get infected. And with limited resources, if infection *does* set in, you can be in trouble."

"What kind of trouble?"

"Put it this way," Kev said, "my new nickname for you will be Captain Hook." He chuckled, but the humour was lost on everyone else.

"If sepsis kicks in, you could die," Amy said. "I'm not saying that's going to happen, but it's a risk we can't afford to take. We need antibiotics."

"Okay, so where shall we go?"

"I don't know. We need to think of somewhere that hasn't been ransacked."

Amy thought back to Sunnymoor hospital. There would be a ready supply of antibiotics there, but with the amount of time that had passed, there was no knowing what state the facility would be in. And they had barely escaped from there last time. The idea of returning was not one she favoured. It would be easier to find a pharmacy.

"We could go to Sunnymoor," Donna suggested, as if reading Amy's thoughts, calling out her apprehension. "You'd know where they're stored, so we wouldn't have to be there long."

"No," Kev said, saving Amy from the turmoil. "It's overrun. It'd be too risky."

"And quite far," Ben added. "We could try Bealsdon again. Me and Amy went there when we were with the others. There might be a pharmacy."

"That might be a good call."

"Okay, so when do we leave?" Donna asked.

Kev twisted his face in discomfort. "Uh—Donna, can I have a word?"

Kev led her out of the room and up the stairs. Once they were out of earshot, Ben leaned in to Amy.

"What's that about?" he whispered.

"He's worried about her. He thinks she's depressed and needs someone to talk to."

"Really?"

She nodded. "They lost their son. I don't think there's any coming back from that. But I think he's telling her to wait here."

"On her own?"

Amy took a deep breath. "No. With me. He wants me to have a chat with her, alone."

"What? Are you sure it's wise to split up?"

"I don't know. Do you think you'll be able to manage without me?"

Ben shifted uncomfortably in his seat. "Well—I mean—yeah. We should be fine."

"And we'll be fine here. I know it's not the best solution, but he's really concerned about her."

"Okay. Well, if that's what you want."

"What I want is for all of us to be content, and managing okay. We're a team. If one of us falls, we need to be there to pick them up."

Ben raised his bandaged hand. He didn't need to say anything. Amy knew what he was thinking. He thought of himself as a liability. It was why he had agreed to venture out with Kev, why he was disturbed that he could no longer shoot. He sought to prove that he was still reliable. Yet, the only one who thought otherwise was him.

Amy reached out and gently rested her hand on his.

"We're a team," she repeated. "We adapt. We overcome. We survive."

Ben smirked. "You've been spending too much time with Kev."

"Well, now you can spend more time with him. But be careful. We don't know what state Bealsdon is in."

"Can't be any worse than the last time we were there. Plus, the company will be better. I won't have to put up with Frank's bullshit."

"Nope. Just Kev's rubbish banter."

They snickered, falling silent when they heard footsteps on the stairs.

Kev and Donna entered the kitchen, neither of them speaking, and sat back at the table.

"Is everything okay?" Amy asked.

Kev's jovial grin returned, but she couldn't place Donna's emotion. Subdued? Relief? But there was a dubiousness that didn't seem to match her thin smile.

"Yeah, we're good. I was just telling Donna I think it's best for me and Ben to go alone. It'll be easier to sneak in and out if it's only the two of us."

Donna nodded, but the acceptance didn't reach her eyes. It was obvious she knew he was lying. But she didn't challenge him.

"So once we find a pharmacy, what exactly are we looking for?" Kev asked.

"As many antibiotics as you can find," Amy said. "Anything that ends in 'illin' or 'ycin' will be your best bet."

"Okay, 'illin' or 'ycin'," Kev muttered. "Got it."

"Grab whatever you can. Bandages, painkillers, vitamins. We can use it all."

"Noted. C'mon then, Starsky." Kev nudged Ben's shoulder.

"Why am I Starsky?"

"Because Hutch is the handsome one. And, well…" Kev swept a hand over his physique.

"Bollocks. You can be Starsky, I'll be Hutch."

"You're more like Bert and Ernie," Amy called after them as they strode into the hallway.

She heard a chortle from Kev as the pair shoved the chest of drawers aside. A conflict of emotions surfaced as the two men moved outside. Anxiety reared its head as she considered the danger the pair would face, but it was quickly usurped by guilt. It was her concerns that had led the two to venture out in the first place, and if anything were to happen to them, she'd never forgive herself. Apprehension was the final emotion, more overwhelming than any of its predecessors. The reason she wasn't with them. The cause for all her other emotions. She turned to Donna, not knowing what to say or do. Knowing only that if she had the choice, she'd much rather be venturing to Bealsdon, danger be damned.

16

"I'm still not sure I should leave him," Lisa said, glancing back into the room where Frank lay. Candlelight pierced the gloom—an alternate measure given the boarded windows blocking the natural light.

"Relax," said the Yorkshireman. "Theresa will monitor him."

"Who's Theresa?"

"I am." A short, stocky woman came over, carrying a container of water and a roll of bandages pinned under her arm. Her dark hair was plaited with an array of colourful bands, matching the vivid colours of her long, flowing dress.

"Nice to meet you, Theresa. I'm Lisa."

The woman smiled politely, expecting her to move aside, but Lisa remained rooted to the spot in front of the door.

"So what are you? A doctor? A nurse?"

Theresa faltered. "No. I used to be a vet."

"A vet? He's not a fucking dog." Lisa turned to the man, expecting a rebuttal, or justification, but all she got was a shrug.

"She's the best we've got, given the circumstances," he said. "And Theresa knows what she's doing. Please, let her tend to your friend."

Lisa stared at the woman, unsure how much human biology you needed to know in order to practise on animals. But, as the man had said, she was the best option they had. The only option, really. Begrudgingly, Lisa stepped aside, allowing the woman into the room.

"Shall we?" The man indicated down the corridor.

"I'd rather not leave him, if it's all the same."

"With all due respect, what good are you to him in this state?"

Lisa frowned. "With no respect due whatsoever, I don't know you, Theresa, or anyone else in your camp. I don't even know your name."

The man smiled. It was a warm, friendly smile that seemed to make his eyes sparkle beneath his thick-rimmed glasses. "My name is Michael Keller. But everyone calls me Mike."

"Well, it's nice to meet you, Mike. But you can understand my concern, given the state of the world right now."

Mike's smile faded. "Yes, of course. These are indeed trying times. But we cannot let the sins of the few count for the many. We must show compassion in the face of adversity."

"Ah, the whole 'love thy neighbour' line?"

"Leviticus 19:18."

"Actually, I was going for Matthew 22:39."

Mike beamed. "You know your scripture."

"Indeed." Lisa made sure her look of contempt didn't go unnoticed before she glanced back into the room. Theresa was crouched by Frank's side, applying a fresh bandage to his wound.

"Well, rest assured, we are all children of God," Mike said, a wary tone creeping in to his upbeat demeanour. "And, as you know the Bible, logic would dictate we'd bear no ill-will towards you or any of your party."

Lisa cast the man a patronising smirk. "Oh, of course not. Nobody who preaches the Bible would ever inflict harm on anybody else."

Mike nodded gravely. "There are bad apples in all walks of life. It only takes one," he said. "But if logic doesn't put you at ease, I'm sure your impressive arsenal can?"

Lisa studied her reflection in the mirror on the opposite wall. Her rifle occupied one side, with Frank's shotgun and handgun, which she had recovered as soon as he'd fallen, occupying the other.

"We possess only the most primitive weapons as a form of defence," Mike continued. "You could massacre our entire camp with ease. But I have faith. I believe you're a good person."

Lisa was still unsure whether she could trust the man, but she had a feeling he was telling the truth. Since their arrival at the camp, she had not seen a single firearm. And the fact the entire congregation had eyed her guns warily as she passed only supported this theory.

"Come on. I want to show you something."

Mike didn't wait for an answer. He made his way down the hall, hands clasped behind his back. He passed a boarded-up door—one which Lisa assumed led outside—disappearing down the gloomy corridor.

Back in the room, Theresa had finished dressing Frank's wound and was now applying a cool flannel to his forehead. He was still unconscious, but the gradual rise and fall of his chest gave Lisa comfort. With a parting glance, she walked after Mike.

They left the vestry and entered the main church. Despite its age, it wasn't a particularly large building, unlike the countless churches she had seen in her youth. She estimated it could have housed up to one hundred parishioners in its heyday. But, given the isolated location, with minimal housing for miles, she guessed those times were long gone even before the pandemic hit.

Their footsteps echoed through the hall as they made their way past the rows of pews. In between lay sleeping bags and various keepsakes.

"So what are you, a priest?" Lisa asked, keeping her voice low.

"Good heavens, no. I was a lector for many years. Father Thomas was our designated priest, but he... passed when all this first started." Mike followed his declaration with a sign of the cross. "My wife Marie and I have been running the church for the past few weeks."

They made their way outside, where a gathering of people went about their tasks. Some carried fence posts and wire, while others unloaded large containers of water from the back of a pickup truck. Three men congregated around a map on the bonnet of a car, gesturing to different parts of the landscape.

"And this is your flock?" Lisa asked.

"In a manner of speaking. Not everyone is from our original community. We've adopted a number of survivors, with more arriving every day."

Lisa nodded. The similarities between Mike and Kara's accounts had not gone unnoticed. *They were looking for people.* Kara's trembling words were still fresh in her mind.

"And you said earlier that you actively look for them?"

"In a manner of speaking. We send out patrols. Primarily for supplies, but also to bring back anybody who needs refuge."

"Like post-apocalyptic Jehovah's Witnesses?"

Mike sighed in annoyance. "There are only a handful of us practicing religion. The vast majority of the people here do not have any religious affiliation. And that's fine. We would never impose our views on others. We respect that everyone is entitled to their beliefs and expect the same courtesy in return."

"And these people you bring back—do they have a choice?"

"Of course they have a choice. We wouldn't dream of taking anybody against their will. What kind of people do you think we are?"

"That remains to be seen."

Mike closed his eyes, as if trying to repress indignation. "Lisa, I don't know what groups you've encountered so far, or what past experiences have led to you distrusting our faith. But rest assured, we're good people here. You're under no obligation to stay, and can leave any time you want. But we would very much like to welcome you and your group to stay with us."

"You said you don't have access to any guns?"

Mike gestured to the men and women around them. "What you see is what we have. I don't believe anybody here has even held a gun before, let alone knows where to find one."

"Makes sense why you want us to stay."

"We are pacifists. We don't ever condone violence. The fact you're harbouring firearms isn't an advantage for us. Quite the opposite, in fact. Yet, we'd still welcome you despite this."

Lisa scoffed.

"Everyone is welcome," Mike continued, "regardless of their belongings, experience or skill set. We're all equal, and in that respect, everyone contributes equally."

"You're painting a beautiful picture here, Mike. But I have to say, I'm not convinced. How have you survived so far? What's the church's stance on these zombies? Thou shalt not kill, remember?"

"Exodus 20:13. I remember it well. But one could also argue how do you kill that which is already dead?"

"Ah, religious loopholes. God knows there's plenty of those."

"Merely an interpretation."

"And what about survivors who want to kill you? They're not dead."

A wariness clouded the sparkle in Mike's eyes. "Fortunately, we haven't encountered any of those yet. We're a peaceful community. We bear ill will to nobody."

"Trust me, that's not going to put you in good stead if the wrong people come calling." Remnants of her ordeal in the prison came back to torment her. The brutality of mankind seemed to know no bounds, and was only countered by another evil when the zombies had infiltrated the prison. While she didn't know the fate of the men residing there, she was sure there were plenty of survivors. They would have a field day if they stumbled across the religious camp.

"Which is why I hope you'll stay," Mike said. "At least for a little while. I'm eager to hear of your experiences out there, of what terrors are lurking."

"Trust me, they're not stories you want to share round a campfire, roasting marshmallows."

"How about round a table with a cup of tea and a slice of cake?"

Cake?

Lisa wasn't sure whether Mike was being sardonic or genuinely meant it. But she didn't have time to ask, as he walked away toward a small outbuilding beside the church. She followed, feeling the curious gaze of the others tracking her. Whilst it seemed like an idyllic setup, she was sure there was something Mike was hiding. There had to be. How had they survived with only basic weapons? There was a variable missing, and she was determined to find it. She smiled politely at Mike as he held the door open for her.

The large room appeared to have undergone a recent layout change. Rows of pews were stacked up against the windows, blocking out most of the light, and any would-be trespassers. An array of tables and chairs—a mismatch of furniture which resembled the stock of a car boot sale—occupied the centre. A man looked up from one of the tables as Lisa entered.

"Hey, I was wondering where you'd got to!" Jay rose from his chair, chewing on a slab of bread. Despite not really knowing the man, the small notion of familiarity amidst a field of strangers helped put Lisa at ease.

"Nice threads," she said, eyeing his new white shirt, which had 'Team Jesus' emblazoned across the front.

"Thanks, my other one was covered in blood. And look." He raised his hand, showing a neatly wrapped bandage which had replaced his makeshift one. He sat back down, washing down the bread with a glass of wine.

"I see you're happy."

"Of course I'm happy," he replied. "We've struck gold here. Forget about anywhere else. *This* is Eden."

Lisa glared at him as he took another bite of bread. Whilst she would be able to offload him onto the religious freaks, she couldn't risk him telling them about their hotel. She adopted a pleasant smile, directed at Mike.

"You know what? I would *love* a cup of tea. And if you weren't taking the piss with the offer of cake, I'd love that even more."

Mike grinned. "Of course, and I would never lie about something as profound as cake. I'll be right back."

As soon as Mike closed the door behind him, Lisa vaulted the table and grabbed Jay by his shirt.

"What the hell?" Jay spat, spraying flecks of bread as she dragged him to his feet.

"You really *have* struck gold here, haven't you? But make no mistake, if you so much as utter the words *Eden*, *hotel*, or *jacuzzi* to these religious freaks, I'll rip your balls off. Do I make myself clear?"

"Wait, you have a jacuzzi in there?"

Lisa twisted his shirt, clasping part of his flesh between her fingers as she dragged him closer. "Do I make myself clear?"

"Ow! Yes," Jay gasped. He staggered away, clutching his neck and rubbing his chest. "Jesus Christ."

"Don't use the Lord's name in vain," Lisa warned, taking a seat opposite him. "This lot will have you crucified."

"I don't know what your problem is," he muttered, tentatively returning to his seat. "They seem like good people."

"I've known 'good people' before."

"Well, they're patching up your boyfriend. You should be grateful."

Lisa snatched the last piece of bread from him and crushed it in her fist.

"And *you* should be grateful I didn't let Frank kill you."

She hurled the crumbs at his face and leaned back in the folding chair. Jay dusted his shirt and swept the remaining crumbs off the table.

"So, you're not staying long, then?" Before leaning back in his seat, he picked up his glass of wine, a precautionary measure so Lisa couldn't swipe that from him, too.

"As soon as Frank's fit, we're going."

"What happened to him? That was a lot of blood."

"We ran into some bad people. And if they come across this camp, you're as good as dead."

"Dead?" Jay scoffed. "I doubt it. I might not look tough, but I can hold my own."

"Where's your blade?"

Jay retrieved the machete from the neighbouring chair, watching Lisa uncertainly.

"Killed many zombies with it?"

"A few."

"Reckon you can kill survivors as well?"

Jay shrugged. "If I have to."

"Okay." Lisa brandished the handgun and aimed it at his face. "Think you can kill me before I pull the trigger?"

The uncertainty warped into alarm. Jay's eyebrows arched, as if being lifted with invisible hooks. He didn't reply.

"Well?" Lisa persisted. "You've got your machete. Think you're faster than a bullet?"

"No."

"No, you're not. Those men are armed. They're dangerous. And they wouldn't think twice about shooting a cocky bastard like you—"

"Okay, I've got tea and cake." Mike eased open the door, stopping in his tracks when he saw the tense exchange.

Lisa holstered her gun and rose from the table.

"You're a star," she said, beaming. "And is that Christmas cake?"

"Uh—yes," said Mike, clutching the tray firmly as Lisa took the cup and plate balanced on top. "It's Marie's recipe. She bakes loads of them for the church's Christmas fete. She usually makes them this time of year, then feeds them with brandy every month until December."

Lisa took a huge bite, catching loose raisins and crumbs on the plate as she chewed. The sweet concoction of fruit and cinnamon brought with it a dopamine hit of merriment and festivities. For a moment, she was back in her kitchen as a child, helping her mum bake a Christmas cake. She would occasionally sneak some of the dried fruit into her mouth, while her mum pretended not to notice. The snow settled outside, bringing with it the promise of snowmen and sledging. An annual tradition, one she had repressed into the deepest recesses of her memory.

A solitary tear escaped the pool forming in her eyes. She turned away, and made for the pews up against the window.

"How is it?" Mike asked.

Lisa nodded, quickly composing herself as she swallowed the sweet morsel and the heartbreak it had brought with it.

"Good," she said, covertly wiping her face as she feigned an itch above her eyebrow. "Marie is one hell of a baker."

"Isn't she?" The cement shoes seemed to loosen as Mike finally stepped forward. "Jay, would you like a slice?"

"Does the pope shit in the woods?" As soon as the words left his lips, Jay's mouth fell agape. "Sorry. I mean—uh—yes, please."

Mike placed a plate in front of him before taking the seat opposite. "I trust you haven't changed your mind? About staying, I mean."

"Mmm, mmm," he mumbled, with a mouthful of cake, shaking his head.

"Good. If you speak to Luke outside, he'll assign you a role."

"Fnks." Jay covered his mouth, offering a thumbs-up to Mike, before stepping outside.

"And what about you?" Mike asked Lisa. "Can I convince you to stay a while?"

Lisa took a sip of tea, watching him over the rim of her cup. If the group didn't have any guns, she held a significant advantage over them. There would be no roles being allocated to her, for a start. And with such an unsecure setup, she knew it was only a matter of time before they fell victim to a horde of undead, or a swathe of rapists and murderers. But, at the same time, she knew it would be easier all round if she kept Mike sweet. At least until Frank was well enough to leave.

"I'll hang around for a while. You can show me what kind of ship you're running out here."

"Great. And perhaps we can share some stories while we're at it?"

"Oh, I've got plenty of stories to tell. Trust me."

17

"What's happening?"

Zielinski's voice rose higher as he tried to adjust to the impenetrable darkness. He looked around, desperate to see a pinhole of light somewhere. Anywhere. But the black void was all-encompassing. He blinked hard, as he had done when he was blindfolded. Only this time, his lashes didn't brush against any fabric. His chest felt tight under the restraints. The windowless room, countless metres underground, suddenly felt claustrophobic.

"What's happened to the lights?" Zielinski called again, more to ensure he wasn't alone than anything else. But still, there was no response. If Armstrong was still in the lab, he wasn't making himself known. As far as Zielinski knew, he was on his own.

No. That wasn't exactly right. The corpse in the next bed still was still there. The notion made his skin crawl, and despite the cloying heat of the lab, a cold sweat started to form on his brow.

He froze, certain he'd heard a noise nearby.

He imagined the corpse rising, the draped sheet sliding to the ground as it turned to face him. It wouldn't see anything, but it would definitely hear him.

He held his breath, trying to tune out the relentless thumping in his ears. His heart pounded against his ribcage, betraying his location to the reanimated corpse.

No. It's not alive. It hasn't moved. Armstrong said it was dead.

Yet, despite his attempt at reassurances, Zielinski was sure he could hear a shuffling across the lab floor. He tried to suppress a whimper, but the noise escaped as the lights burst to life once more, caustic luminescence scorching his retinas. The machines hummed and beeped beside him, resuming their rhythmic monitoring of his health.

Armstrong remained unmoved, his face a picture of calm contemplation. He resumed his poring over documents at the workbench, almost as if nothing had happened. In the next bed, the corpse was still there, concealed by the sheet, its reanimation a figment of Zielinski's terrified imagination. Nothing more.

He exhaled, trying to stop his hands from trembling.

"Well, that's it." Scrivener's footsteps accompanied his echoic voice as he strode into the lab. "We're on to the last generator. How goes your search for a cure, Armstrong?"

"I… need more time," the doctor replied, massaging his forehead. He didn't look up from his work, not even when Scrivener stopped beside him, a vial of red liquid in his hand.

"Pity. Time is a luxury you're running out of. Fortunately, I've done it for you."

"What?"

"Yes. I don't deal with ifs or buts. I deliver."

"How?"

"I've altered the genetic makeup of T-14. Your little experiment with the subject's blood inspired me."

He glanced towards Zielinski as an afterthought.

"T-14?" Armstrong gasped. "But that's the gator specimen."

"Indeed. And it was more receptive to human DNA than the T-12 you stole."

"But it was more *volatile*. All traces of T-14 were supposed to have been destroyed."

"They were. Well… most of them."

"Martin." Armstrong rose from his chair, an unmistakable quiver in his voice. "You know it's too dangerous. The mutations—"

"—Were a freak anomaly. Look!" He shoved the vial of red liquid toward Armstrong. "If blood infected with T-12 could stop T-19 multiplying, *this* will eradicate it completely."

"And mutate the host into a creature ten times worse!"

"Not if we administer *this* soon after."

Scrivener reached into his pocket and produced a vial of transparent liquid. Armstrong stared at the formula, scratching his chin in thought.

"Ah," Scrivener said. "You forgot I manufactured an antidote to T-14, didn't you? You preach about ethics and codes of conduct, yet I'm the only one who considers fail-safes to my experiments."

"T-14 was discarded for a reason, Martin. You can't use it."

"Bullshit. You're just irked because you didn't think of it first. Don't worry, Armstrong, I'll give you due credit. Should the history books ever continue, that is."

With a look of acceptance, Armstrong raised both hands and took a step back.

"Okay, I trust you're going to test your hypothesis?"

"Naturally."

Zielinski held his breath. He expected the two men to turn towards him, ready to inject the crimson concoction, which would cause a slow, agonising death.

His fears were about to become reality.

Scrivener approached the bed with a crooked smile.

"What are you doing?" Armstrong demanded.

"Testing my hypothesis."

Armstrong dashed ahead, blocking Scrivener's path. "On the infected *mice*. You're not gambling our only human resource on a hunch."

"It's not a hunch, Armstrong. I deal with facts. It *will* eradicate the T-19 infection."

He tried to step forward, but Armstrong stood firm.

"You saw what it did to the previous samples. How is that a cure?"

"As I've said, I've altered it, and already devised a three-step test."

"Which is?"

"Step one: we inject the subject with T-19 and wait for the virus to take hold. Step two: we administer T-14, monitoring the incubation period and vital signs. Once T-

19 is eradicated, we move on to step three: administering the T-14 antidote. Thereafter, we monitor vital signs and run periodic tests."

Armstrong sighed dejectedly. "Okay."

The word alone felt like a detonation in Zielinski's heart. He thrashed against his bindings, desperate to free himself from the mad scientists.

"But," Armstrong continued, raising his voice over Zielinski's struggling outbursts. "You test it on the mice first. They're already infected with T-19, which eliminates the need for your first step."

"We don't have time, Armstrong."

"If it's going to work, it'll work on any specimen."

"I couldn't care less about curing mice. Human survival is our sole focus."

"Which is all the more reason to test it on the mice first!"

The two men locked stares, both waiting for the other to back down. All Zielinski could do was watch the tense standoff. His wrists were raw from struggling against the straps, and he could feel welts beneath the bindings across his chest. The only way he would be set free would be if either of the two men were to release him. But, based on their current argument, it was impossible to tell what state he would be in if that ever happened.

After what felt like an eternity, a wry smile formed on Scrivener's stony face.

"Okay. I'll test it on your mice. Then we'll try it on your patient."

"If, and only if, it's shown to work."

"Agreed."

Scrivener walked to the far end of the room, almost out of sight. Zielinski heard the groan of a metal door being opened, and could just about make out Scrivener climbing into a big white suit. An oxygen tank swung on his back as he pulled down a heavy visor over his face.

"God speed, sir." Armstrong offered a jesting salute before returning to his workbench.

Scrivener's eyes weren't visible beneath the visor, but Zielinski guessed they were boring a hole in Armstrong's back. With an inaudible retort, Scrivener strode down the corridor.

"You weren't serious, right?"

Armstrong shook his head, clearly unwilling to start another debate, but Zielinski persisted.

"Do you think he's really got a cure?"

"Of course not," Armstrong scoffed. "I can't believe he kept a sample of T-14, let alone be willing to use it."

"What is it?"

"He had the audacity to say *I'm* obsessed with reptilian splicing." Armstrong rummaged through his notes, speaking more to himself than Zielinski. "I tried to perfect a bioweapon. *He* created monsters."

"Monsters?"

"Indeed. He tried to argue the case, of course, but it was fruitless. He told our superiors the claws and teeth would make them better killers, and the scutes replacing skin would serve as a natural armour."

"Scutes?"

"The plate that makes up the skin of crocodiles, alligators, or the shell of a turtle. Naturally, his argument was dismissed. Even if he did create an antidote, T-14 was too volatile. His research was axed, and we moved on to other bio-weapons."

"So the mice will turn into monsters?"

Armstrong lowered his paperwork and strode over to the monitors. "See for yourself."

He entered the same command as last time, but the screen didn't change, instead offering an error message and a dull sound effect.

"Odd," he murmured. He typed the command again, which prompted the same error. "The power cut must've disrupted the stream."

A metallic clang sounded down the corridor, followed by rapid footfalls.

"Lock it down!" Scrivener ordered. He ran into view, prising off his visor and throwing it aside. "Now!"

"What?" Armstrong jumped aside, allowing Scrivener to tap furiously at the keyboard.

He gasped. "The mice! They're gone."

A hydraulic hiss from the end of the corridor accompanied an automated voice: "Test area lockdown initiated."

"What do you mean, they're gone?"

"How else do you want me to say it?" Scrivener disrobed, throwing the white hazmat suit aside. "They've disappeared, departed, deserted, flown the coop!"

"But how?"

"How should I know? They're your subjects, Armstrong."

"It must've been the power cut." The doctor held a hand over his mouth.

Infected mice were the last straw for Zielinski. "Let me out," he spat. "Untie me, now!"

The doctors paid him no heed, only stoking the fire burning within. If the mice were free, there was no telling what part of the lab they were in. One bite and that would be it. Even if he were lucky enough to avoid rodent incisors, if either of the doctors were to become infected, he'd be a ready meal for the walking corpse they'd inevitably turn into.

He thrashed against his bindings again, trying to ignore the painful friction.

"Well, it's over, isn't it?" Armstrong groaned, retreating to his workbench. "Half of my work was in there."

"We don't need your work." Scrivener produced the crimson vial once more. "*This* is the solution."

"One we can't even test."

"Yes. We can."

Scrivener's cold eyes fixed on Zielinski, freezing him in place.

"You're not testing it on our only living subject," Armstrong insisted. "I won't say it again."

"What other choice do we have?"

"If it doesn't work, it'll kill him."

"And if it does, it'll save the world—or what's left of it."

Armstrong dashed over and stood between Scrivener and Zielinski once again.

"I can't let you do it, Martin."

"Sacrifices need to be made in the name of science."

"Not like this."

Zielinski had seen countless fights in his time, more than enough to detect a flash point. Whether it was the clenched fists, the tight jaw, or the aggressive stance, Zielinski had never really been able to pinpoint it. Perhaps a combination? But he could always detect an imminent brawl, and this was no exception. It started when Scrivener tried to push Armstrong aside, only to be met with a vicious shove and a subsequent right hook. The clenched fist flailed through the air, missing its target. But Armstrong didn't stop. He threw another, years of pent-up frustration being showcased in his frenzied attack. He continued to advance, his punches dodged or blocked by Scrivener, who stumbled back from the onslaught.

Zielinski longed to cheer the doctor on, assuming his life would be in the balance of the victor. But, for that very reason, he kept quiet, not wanting to distract Armstrong, whose initial burst of energy had begun to wane. Sensing the same, Scrivener lunged forward, grabbing the doctor's overcoat and slamming him into the workbench. The pair fell into a heap on the ground, both scrambling to gain the upper hand.

Zielinski slid a cuff into the middle of the bedframe and yanked as hard as he could. His wrists screamed with every jerk, but it was a welcome alternative to being experimented on. Ignoring the burning rash on his skin, he clenched his fist and continued.

His arm grew weak, the pain unbearable, but what caught his attention was the smash and clatter of the grappling men. Scrivener had squirmed his way on top of Armstrong, hands clasped either side of the doctor's head as he smashed it into the floor. A dull thud echoed around the lab. Armstrong's arms shot up, vying for Scrivener's neck until he smashed his head back again. The crack resounded. This time Armstrong went limp, his hands dropping to his side.

Scrivener staggered to his feet, steadying himself on the workbench. His slicked hair stood on end, with a trickle of blood escaping his nose, running down to a swollen lip. Scrivener wiped it away and fixed his hair, composing himself with a single deep breath.

"Now then," he said. "Where were we?"

18

The pressing silence set Amy on edge. Once again, she longed to be out of the cottage, fighting wave after wave of the undead. Anything other than being cooped up in the silent room with Donna. How long had it been since Ben and Kev had left? Thirty seconds? Forty? She couldn't hear the rumble of their engine anymore, so maybe a minute had passed. Each second brought with it a mounting tension. The skin-shredding awkwardness became unbearable until Donna split the atmosphere like a hot knife through butter.

"I know you're mad."

Amy blinked. This wasn't how she'd imagined the conversation would start.

"I should've reloaded when you said," Donna continued. "I don't know what happened, I just… froze."

"What are you talking about? I'm not mad."

"You don't have to spare my feelings. I don't blame you, I'd be angry too."

Amy took a step closer. "Donna, I promise I'm not mad. I'm glad we survived."

"Then why did you want to speak to me?"

The awkward feeling returned, this time with a hint of annoyance. *Is that what he said to her? For fuck's sake, Kev!* Amy massaged the bridge of her nose. She didn't know how to play the policeman's game. He had thrown her in with limited information, no rules, and a loaded dice. Now it was her turn to roll.

"Kev asked me to speak to you." Her mum had always told her that honesty was the best policy. And if the truth got Kev into trouble, so be it. At least Amy wouldn't have to play a game of deceit, one in which he was proving more and more proficient. "He's worried about you."

"Worried? Why?"

Amy tried to ignore the uncomfortable direction of the conversation.

"Well... you lost your son. No mother should ever experience that. I can't even begin to imagine what you're going through."

Amy expected the words to evoke a wave of tears, like punching holes in a dam. But Donna seemed unmoved. There was a slight wariness, perhaps, but she was still emotionless.

"No," Donna uttered after a few agonising seconds had passed. "You don't know what it's like. When I gave birth to Riley, when I saw him for the first time, I knew right then I would always be there for him. Nothing would ever hurt him. I would protect him, and nurture him, until he could fend for himself. And even after that, I knew I would always watch over him. Then he was... taken from us."

Amy waited for her to continue. But instead, Donna retrieved a bottle of whisky and glasses from the cabinet.

"Drink?" Donna shook the bottle before placing it down on the table and taking up one of the chairs.

"Sure."

Amy couldn't remember the last time she'd had whisky. Hell, she could barely remember the last time she had consumed *any* alcohol. It had most likely been on a girls' night out before she moved to Cranston, or a glass of wine with her mum, unaware at the time that it would be the last. She felt tears form and downed the dram Donna had poured.

The burning in her oesophagus kept the memories at bay and also triggered a sudden cough.

"Not a big drinker?" Donna smiled, refilling both glasses.

"Ugh, it's been a while." Amy laughed, wiping her mouth. She took the next glass slower, this time opting to sip the liquid fire. She knew it was a mistake, but if it helped alleviate Donna of her mental burden, then it would be worth it.

"Yeah, me too. I can't remember the last time, to be honest."

"I guess if there's ever a time, it's now, right?"

"I'd say so. And I think we've earned it after today."

"Absolutely." Amy clinked her glass with Donna's and took another sip.

"I never used to fancy it before," Donna continued. "Kev, on the other hand…"

Amy smirked. "Yeah, I saw his eyes light up when he spotted the bottle the other day."

"Always has been a good drinker. It takes a lot to affect him, though."

"I bet, with the size of him! How long have two been together?"

"Nearly ten years, married for eight."

"Wow, that's a long time."

"You're telling me!" Donna laughed. "No, he's lovely, really. He has a heart of gold. Beneath the whole tough-cop exterior, he's actually quite sensitive."

"Really?"

"Oh yeah, he couldn't even ask me out. He was too nervous. In the end, he got his friend to ask me for him."

Amy snorted. "Really? I can't imagine Kev being nervous about anything."

"Ah, you don't know him like I do. We met at a nightclub. I was with my friends and he was with his. He kept looking over at me. I could see him a mile off. Well, he's hard to miss in a crowd, isn't he?"

Amy downed the last of her drink, the smoky caramel taste lingering on her tongue. She could feel the whisky settling in her empty stomach, promising a hangover should she continue. But before she could say anything, Donna was pouring another measure. She took the glass, intending to raid the food supplies once Donna finished her story. As long as she ate something to soak the alcohol up, she was sure one more glass wouldn't hurt.

"Anyway, after a while, his mate came over and asked me if I'd take Kev off his hands. Apparently, he hadn't shut up about me all night." Donna smiled at the memory. "So I did. We haven't spent a day apart since."

Amy thought back to her time with Ben. They hadn't spent a day apart, either. True, a couple of weeks were incomparable to ten years, but she understood the notion. She couldn't help but wonder if he did, too.

"I know that look," Donna said. "You're thinking about Ben, aren't you?"

Amy felt heat erupt in her cheeks, trying to convince herself it was an effect of the whisky.

"You need to tell him how you feel. It's obvious he feels the same way."

"You think?"

"I *know*. You're all he talks about. You're the first person he looks for in a crisis, and the only one he listens to without question. I'm guessing you spoke to him about going alone with Kev?"

Amy didn't respond, despite the glaringly obvious truth hanging in the air.

"I knew it," Donna said. "If you hadn't, he'd have insisted we all stick together."

"Maybe that wouldn't have been a bad idea." The euphoric buzz of alcohol had started to fade, displaced by a feeling of dread as she thought of Ben and Kev out there against the unknown. Donna was right—it *was* down to her. Ben would never have left otherwise.

"Don't worry, he'll be fine," Donna said, reading her expression once again. She filled the glass higher, despite there being a copious amount already. "Kev is the toughest man I've ever met. He won't let anything happen to him."

"I just feel like it's my fault they've gone."

"They had to go. Ben needs those antibiotics. You said so yourself."

"I know, but what if they don't find any?"

"Then we'll keep searching. There'll be some stashed away someplace. The hospitals will have them."

Amy thought back to Sunnymoor. With how quickly the virus had spread, most of the drugs would likely be untouched. But after narrowly escaping the last time, the prospect of returning was concerning, especially after Kev's confirmation it was teeming with the undead. Amy frowned.

"Did you two go to Sunnymoor?" she asked.

"Huh?"

"Kev, he said it was overrun. Have you been there?"

"It feels like we've been everywhere. We left Sunnymoor before we came across your grandparents' house."

"Did you see much of the hospital?"

"Too much. We were lucky to get out."

"You and me both. Ben and I were lucky we escaped. It's a shame you weren't there a week earlier. We could've used your help."

"Same! It's swarming now."

"I hope we don't have to go back." The prospect sent a chill through Amy's body, despite the warmth of the whisky. She took another drink, easing back in her seat, trying to quell her unease.

"They'll find something. Don't worry."

Amy nodded, bemused. How did a conversation that was supposed to allow Donna to express her grief turn into Amy being comforted? She leaned forward, taken aback by the table seeming to move with her. She blinked hard, clearing the stupor from her vision, and rested an elbow down to support herself.

"Tell me about Riley," she said. "How old is he?"

Donna picked up her glass. "He's eleven, coming up twelve in September."

"I bet you miss him."

What kind of idiotic statement is that? Amy pushed her glass aside in disgust. She wanted to get up and grab a bottle of water, or juice, or anything to flush the alcohol from her system. But she also wanted to find out what kind of wound her words had opened.

"Every second," Donna whispered. Then there they were, the tears Amy had been so fearful of, yet which she had been strangely craving. She was unsure why, but the tears felt like a good sign, a sign she had done what Kev had requested. Therapy involved releasing your emotions, right? But then, hadn't Kev said she was crying regularly, anyway?

Shit.

She considered rushing around the table to console her, but what could she say? 'Don't worry, it'll turn out alright'? 'Everything will be fine'? But it wouldn't, would it? She had lost her son. He wasn't coming back. Every day was another day without him.

"Sorry," Donna said.

"No, I'm sorry, I shouldn't have…"

Shouldn't have what? Deliberately said something to get a response? Amy averted her gaze, unable to find any words. Suddenly, the alcohol didn't seem so bad. She seized the glass and took another swig, her throat numb to the fiery liquid, waiting for the inevitable uncomfortable silence to resume.

"We've all suffered losses," Donna said. "You must miss your family, too?"

"I do. I think about them every day."

"If nothing else, this shit has given us an appreciation for the ones we love."

"Definitely. It's why I'm so anxious about those two going out there alone." The dread returned, prompting Amy to take another swig.

Donna stared at her glass, tracing her finger around the rim. "So let's go to them."

"What?"

"You're right. We shouldn't have let them go alone. We need to make sure they're okay."

"Are you serious?"

Donna shrugged. "Why not? You said yourself there's no room for all that chivalry bullshit. We don't need their help to survive. Hell, they might need *our* help. We work as a team, remember?"

"Right."

"So drink up and let's go and be a team!"

Donna pushed her chair back and rushed out of the room, leaving Amy alone at the table. What had just happened? A rollercoaster of a conversation, with a whirlwind of emotion, culminating in a sudden rescue attempt? Amy rose to her feet, suddenly aware of how inebriated she felt. The room spun with every step, and the ground felt like it was moving, akin to the spinning floors of a funhouse. She held on to the table as Donna came back into the room carrying a rifle and a handgun.

"A bit tipsy?" Donna smirked.

"Just a tad."

"Come on, it's all the Dutch courage we need." She handed Amy the rifle. Its touch felt alien, as if being held by a hand that wasn't hers. Amy tightened her grip, ensuring her numb fingers had a purchase of the grey barrel. She staggered out of the room, following Donna, who seemed a lot more cheerful, almost bordering on excited, as she reached the door and looked through the peephole.

"Okay, we're good."

Before Amy could object, she threw open the door and strode toward—

The police car? Amy thought, *Odd.*

"Why didn't they go in this car?" she asked.

"Probably wanted something quicker in case they needed to make a fast getaway."

Donna jumped into the driver's seat, waiting for Amy to join her.

"Are you okay to drive?" Amy caught herself as she stumbled over the gravel. She pulled the passenger door open and bundled inside. The rifle lodged between the chair and the footwell, obstructing her legs, until she threw it onto the back seat.

"I might be over the limit, but I doubt I'm going to get pulled over." Donna smirked, exuding a confidence Amy hadn't seen before. "Besides, the only copper still alive is our Kev."

Amy didn't have long to consider Donna's behaviour. No sooner had she closed the car door than they were off, racing to the end of the drive before taking a hard left. Amy clung to the handle, the world spinning faster than ever as they sped along the country lane. The car rocked back and forth over the uneven surface, and it was all she could do not to vomit. The trees and foliage whizzing by did little to ease her growing nausea, nor did the ever-increasing speed. She closed her eyes and took a deep breath, praying they would arrive at their destination with her stomach contents intact.

19

"We've been fortunate so far," Mike said, leading Lisa towards the boundary of the camp. "The infected have rarely strayed this deep into the countryside. We've only had three incidents since this all started, and one of them originated from the camp."

"From the camp?" Lisa repeated. "One of your people became infected?"

"A young lady we took in. She didn't disclose she had been bitten, and… well, you can guess what happened."

"How many did you lose?"

"Four." Mike nodded towards a row of circular mounds in the distance, each topped with a makeshift wooden cross. "We buried them away from the camp. At the time, we didn't know what had caused the dead to come back."

"I'm not sure if a couple of feet of dirt is enough to stop them."

"Neither were we. So we tied them in sheets and buried them head-first in a circular grave. If they came back, they wouldn't be able to climb out."

"A dignified Christian burial," Lisa scoffed.

Mike pretended not to notice. "With the church situated on top of a natural elevation, we have lookouts posted at several vantage points." He pointed to a lone figure sat on a large rock, studying the forest below. "If they see anything, we rally the men and eliminate the threat."

"With your hammers and spades?"

"With whatever tools we have at our disposal. We wouldn't use a gun even if we had one. The noise would only attract more."

"A lot safer than having to go toe-to-toe with the fuckers, though." Lisa patted her handgun. "So, is that what you were doing when you found us? 'Eliminating the threat'?"

"No, we were gathering water. Naturally, we're less protected amongst the trees. It's harder to detect enemies, so we set up traps. If any of them are triggered, we're aware of their presence and act accordingly."

"You sound like an organised group. Someone's been getting tips from apocalypse movies."

"It's just good sense." Mike shrugged.

"So what do you lot call yourselves?"

"What?"

"Well, you must have a name."

Mike frowned. "I don't follow."

"You're a group that's banded together during a zombie apocalypse. You must've come up with a corny name. Let me guess, The Redeemers? The Salvation? Christ's Combatants?"

Mike smiled and shook his head. "No. We're a community. That's all."

"Well FYI, 'The Community' sounds boring as fuck. You gotta get creative, Mike."

"And what were you? The Three Musketeers?"

Lisa scoffed. "That prick Jay isn't with us. You're welcome to him."

"So it's only you and Frank?"

Lisa felt as if her stomach had been thrown off the hilltop.

Shit, Kara's still alone.

"That's right," she said. "Out of curiosity, how are you fixed for transport?"

"How do you mean?"

"How many vehicles do you have? I've counted three so far. Do you have any more?"

Mike studied her carefully. "We have more. There are a couple of patrols out for supplies. Why do you ask?"

"Why so suspicious, Mike?" Lisa asked, emphasising her alarm. "I'm only asking."

"For what reason?"

"I was wondering if we can borrow some wheels once Frank's better."

Mike stared at her, twisting his mouth in contemplation.

"And by borrow, I mean take without giving back," Lisa added. "It would be the Christian thing to do. Give generously without a grudging heart, and all that jazz."

"We rely on our vehicles. I'll have to think about it. Now, if I recall, you said you would divulge some tales."

"I'm afraid your recollection is skewed. I told you I have tales to tell, not that I would divulge them. But," Lisa said, before he could protest, "since I'm sure you're going to provide us with a vehicle, I'll spill the beans. What do you want to know?"

"How many are out there?"

"Survivors? A few. Zombies? As many as you'd expect. I assume you already know to avoid the chompers?"

Mike nodded.

"And the only way to kill them is trauma to the brain?"

"We suspected as much."

"Then you know as much as me."

Mike shook his head. "I'm not convinced. Is that all you know?"

"Oh, I know way more, but nothing that would benefit you."

"Try me."

"Okay, if you're sure you're ready to hear it?"

"Shoot."

"Well, it's a genetically engineered bioweapon that's transmitted via fluids. A viral agent. It's designed to kill the host then reanimate them after death, effectively turning them into a hungry leper. They're not corpses per se, as their vital organs, respiratory and circulatory systems will continue to work if they're still intact. This keeps the brain alive longer and allows the virus to continue manipulating its host. If not, the virus keeps the brain animated for a period of time, but eventually it will die."

Mike stopped and stared at her, as if assessing her sincerity.

"In a nutshell: avoid the chompers, kill the brain."

"How do you know all this?"

"We found some documents at the old army base on the way to Doxley. That's where the virus was developed."

Lisa started walking again, with Mike skipping to catch up.

"That's a few miles north of here," he said.

"Yeah? Well, don't get your hopes up, we ransacked it."

They stopped beside a gazebo, where a couple of men were discussing means of securing the camp perimeter.

"What about survivors?" Mike asked. "What's your experience with them?"

The prisoners of HMP Harrodale flashed through her mind like an intrusive presentation.

"We've encountered a few, and not all of them are friendly."

"I gathered. I'm guessing Frank's gunshot wasn't an accident?"

"You guessed right."

"These survivors have guns, then?"

"You're quite the sleuth, aren't you, Mike?"

"How do they get guns?" Mike asked, ignoring the jibe. "This is England, for Pete's sake. Rifles and shotguns I understand, every farmer within a hundred miles will have had one. But your handgun is illegal."

"Yeah, because we don't have *anything* illegal in this country. Maybe you should call the police and turn me in."

"What kind of guns do they have?"

159

"Does it matter? A gun's a gun. If there's one pointed at you, duck." Lisa tried to suppress a smirk at the exasperation on the man's face. "The ones we saw had rifles and shotguns. Some were pellet guns, but others had a decent calibre. My advice to you is to start screening these folk before you let them in. It's not just the zombies you need to worry about. Like you said, it only takes one bad apple."

"Mike!"

A middle-aged woman approached.

"Lisa, this is my wife, Marie," he said. The woman flashed a quick smile and nodded toward Lisa, but didn't exchange any further pleasantries.

"Peter has brought two survivors back: a man and a woman. Do you want to come and greet them?"

"Yes, of course. Lisa, are you coming, or…?"

"I'll have a nosey round, thanks."

With that, Mike and Marie walked away, exchanging hushed words. *Probably relaying what I've told him*, Lisa thought. They stopped talking when they reached a silver Ford Mondeo and greeted a couple: the biggest mismatch Lisa had ever seen. The woman was young, early twenties at most. Her head darted back and forth, taking in every inch of the camp, like a hamster being introduced to a new cage. The man had to be in his late forties. Thick, greying hair circled his head, with a gleaming bald spot resting at the top. He wore a stained shirt which was much too small, exposing the base of his bulbous gut. One hand held a rucksack, while the other pushed his glasses up the bridge of his nose. Behind those glasses were the darkest eyes

Lisa had ever seen. They looked as though they belonged to a shark.

"More lambs to the slaughter."

A strong American accent caught Lisa by surprise. It had come from a lone figure in a nearby deck chair. He stroked his beard thoughtfully, a cigarette balanced between his lips, watching the exchange between Mike and the newcomers through his dark aviators.

"Lambs to the slaughter?"

"Yes, ma'am," he replied, in a southern drawl. "He gonna sacrifice those two beneath the full moon tonight. I hope you like bonfires."

"It depends. Will there be marshmallows? Sorry, *smores*."

The man laughed and pulled another deck chair closer. "Sit down, take a load off."

"Thanks, but I'm good. So what's really gonna happen to them?"

"They'll be assigned jobs, same as the rest of us."

"Really? I think I prefer the bonfire idea. So what brings you to these parts, cowboy?"

The man leaned back in his chair. "Well, I was on vacation in your fine country when the shit hit the fan. I doubt there's a return flight home anytime soon, so I guess that makes me a British citizen now, huh?"

"I guess. Welcome to England."

"Thank you. Although, I gotta say, you strutting about this place looking like G.I. Jane is making me kinda homesick."

"You don't like guns?"

He sucked on the cigarette, blowing smoke aside before offering it to Lisa. She raised a hand to decline.

"I'm American," he said. "What do you think?"

"Well, you're not getting one," Lisa said in a sing-song tone. "These are mine."

"Don't worry. You won't be getting no trouble from me."

Mike had finished greeting the newcomers and strode back over, leaving Marie to show them around.

"Sorry about that," he said. "I like to greet all newcomers to this camp. Isn't that right, Jack?"

"Yes, sir," the American replied. "The most gracious host there is."

"Thank you. How come you're not fixing the bike?"

"I've fixed it, boss. Got it purring like a kitten on catnip."

"Already? How?"

"I used those parts I salvaged in Bealsdon. They don't call me Chop Shop for nothing."

"You've been to Bealsdon?" Lisa asked.

"Yes, ma'am. Biggest mistake we made, huh, Mike?"

Mike didn't reply, instead he motioned towards the large outbuilding.

"They're serving up food in the canteen. Go and help yourself, Jack, then speak to Luke for another job."

"Yes, sir."

The American heaved himself to his feet, and with a final drag of his cigarette, strode over to the building.

"If you've been to Bealsdon, you know how bad it is out there," Lisa said, turning on Mike. "So why the questions?"

"I wanted to hear other perspectives."

Lisa rested her hand on the holstered handgun. "I dunno, Mike. You're coming across shady as fuck right now, and I don't like it."

"What are you gonna do? Shoot me for asking questions?"

"No, but I'll shoot you if you have an ulterior motive."

"What ulterior motive could I have?"

"You tell me."

"I don't."

"Prove it."

The man rubbed his chin in exasperation.

"Yes, we've been to Bealsdon, and yes, we got into trouble. It wasn't as bad as Jack makes out. In fact, I was surprised there weren't *more* infected. I started to wonder if there were more survivors, and if there was an evacuation we'd missed out on. Maybe even a safe place we could hide. Somewhere safer than here."

Lisa shook her head. "So all your positivity is just a façade? In reality, you're as scared as everyone else."

"Of course I am. Fear is not a sin. But I still trust in the Lord to keep us safe and guide us."

"Yeah, like he did for the other eight billion people on the planet." Lisa turned away and walked toward the outbuilding. "So what's for lunch?" she called over her shoulder.

"Mash and beans."

"Oh, the council estate special, my favourite."

"I can't tell if you're being sarcastic or not."

"Get used to it, Mikey. I'm fluent in sarcasm. But for the record, I grew up on a council estate, so this will be like home."

Lisa hoped she was wrong, but the mere mention of her upbringing evoked even more memories. She pushed open the door, at once distracted by the number of people inside. It was a stark contrast from when she was in there earlier. She counted at least eight people—men, women and children—either sat at the table eating, or queuing for their portion of mash and beans. Jay was at the front, graciously accepting his food. When he spotted Lisa, he waved and walked over, carefully balancing his paper plate, despite the meagre portion.

"They have hot food!"

"For me?" Lisa gasped. She took the plate with a gracious smile and sat down at the nearest table. "Thank you, Jay."

"Don't mention it," he muttered, trudging to the back of the line.

"No utensils?" Lisa asked.

"I'm afraid not," said Mike. "You'll have to use your hands."

"Don't be silly, you just need to be creative."

She pushed the food to the edge of the plate before ripping it down the middle. Using the severed piece like a giant spoon, she scooped up the mash and beans.

"See?"

"How innovative," Mike said. "We really could use your forward thinking around here."

"You've got me for as long as Frank needs. How is he, by the way?"

"He's still asleep, as far as I know. But he's in good hands. Theresa is increasing his fluid intake and has administered antibiotics, just in case."

"I'm grateful. Thank you."

"We—uh, we don't have much in the way of medical supplies. In fact, she's used the only antibiotics we've been able to get hold of."

"Then I'm *very* grateful," she said, through a mouthful of beans.

"If you're feeling generous, perhaps you could accompany us to Bealsdon tomorrow?"

Lisa threw him a perplexed scowl. "You said you ran into trouble the last time you went."

"We did." Mike looked over the group of people. Most chatted quietly whilst queuing, others ate in silence. "But we're running low on supplies, and Bealsdon is the closest town. With your help, we're more likely to get out in one piece."

"I dunno, Mike—"

"Think it about it. Please?"

Lisa nodded reluctantly, which prompted a smile from Mike. He walked away, leaving her to her thoughts. She wanted to help, but heading into Bealsdon with very few bullets was never the best idea when it was only she and Frank. Include more unarmed people, and it sounded like a recipe for disaster.

She shovelled the food into her mouth. There was no seasoning, the mash had thick lumps, and the beans were lukewarm—an accurate representation of her childhood nutrition.

"Damn, girl, how'd you get yours so fast?"

American Jack plonked himself down at her table, grinning from ear to ear.

"You gotta know the right people," she replied. Jack grabbed a handful of mash and ran it over the beans.

"Mm-hmm. Man, this is some damn good bangers and mash. I ain't never had this shit before."

"It's not bangers and mash."

"Huh?"

"Bangers are sausages."

"Well, I'll be damned." Jack laughed. "My country ass thought bangers were beans, y'know, cause they make you fart."

Lisa smirked, discarding her empty plate towards the end of the table.

"You learn something new every day," he continued.

"You do indeed."

She scanned the room, settling on the newcomers she had seen earlier. Despite being at the same table, they were worlds apart. The young woman ate in silence, twisted away from the man. His eyes met Lisa's, and he offered her a warm smile. Lisa didn't return the gesture. She turned her attention to Mike, who was deep in conversation. She wanted to help, but there was no way she was heading back to Bealsdon. Not while Frank was incapacitated.

"Say, Jack. Where is that bike you fixed up?"

Jack swallowed, dabbing bean juice from his beard and moustache. "Parked up beside the big ol' church."

"Do you have the keys?"

"Yes, ma'am." He produced a key chain from his trouser pocket. "Why do you ask?"

"Mike promised me a ride outta here. It's why he asked you about the bike earlier."

"Really? I thought we were going to use it for supply runs?"

Lisa shook her head. "Change of plan. Mike said it would be too noisy and attract attention."

"Man, he's dumber than a sack o'hammers. These zombies got supersonic hearing now? I can put up with all the Bible-bashing bullshit, but he wouldn't even let me play the guitar I found! Can you believe that? We're in the middle of nowhere, dude. Let me get my Elvis on!"

With a hefty sigh, he dropped the keys in Lisa's palm.

"Well, for the record, if this was my camp, I'd let you play guitar every night." Lisa grinned as she pocketed the keys.

As soon as Frank was up, they'd be out of there. Although she wasn't entirely sure where *there* was. They had been walking in the forest for so long, any orientation she'd started with had long since faded. But if the army base was nearby, and Bealsdon was the closest town, they'd be able to find their way from one of those.

Her thoughts were interrupted when the door behind her flew open. A man dashed into the room.

"Mike?" he gasped.

"What is it?" Mike leapt up from behind the table.

"We've got infected heading this way."

"How many?"

The man took a deep breath, holding the wall for support.

"Dozens."

20

He could feel it flowing through his veins. Poison, killing each and every cell it came into contact with. T-19, they called it. Meaning there were eighteen other variants. Eighteen test subjects who had to endure the same thing as he. Eighteen dead.

Soon to be nineteen, Zielinski told himself.

The crook of his elbow pulsed angrily where Scrivener had injected him. A cotton ball had been taped over the site—a derisive practice, given the lethal shot that had been administered. Like using tape to reattach a severed limb. He clenched his fist, unsure if the fire in his veins was an effect of the virus, or a phantom pain concocted by his imagination. He could feel his heart racing—a conflicting function, one which kept him alive, but which was bringing him even closer to his demise.

"You need to relax," Scrivener said, studying the bedside monitor. At least that's what it looked like he was doing. It was hard to see his face beneath the biohazard suit, which he had donned prior to administering the virus.

"Fuck you."

"You're going to be fine."

"Fine? You've infected me with the virus, you fucking prick!"

"In the name of science. You're about to do way more for mankind than your pitiful existence was ever destined for. If this works, I can save the world."

"And if it doesn't, I'm dead."

Scrivener shrugged. "We all have to die sometime, Mr Zielinski. Poor Armstrong found out the hard way."

A dark trickle of blood had escaped Armstrong's ruptured head, and was creeping across the floor. He had promised Zielinski no harm would come to him. Now Armstrong was dead, with Zielinski not far behind. It wasn't far off the way he had predicted he would die. With every come-down from the smack, Zielinski had always imagined the next hit would kill him. He'd be found slumped in a back alley—a hypodermic dangling from his arm, caked in vomit and shit. His self-appointed prophecy was kind of true, but for now, his bowels and stomach remained intact.

"What's gonna happen to me?" he whispered. He squeezed his eyes shut, as if the verbal response would serve as a physical blow.

"Right now, the genome is multiplying. Every cell it comes into contact with, it attacks. It hijacks the cell's function and replicates. Over. And over. Spreading all the way through your body."

Zielinski could almost feel the infected blood flowing through his veins.

THE MUTATION

"During this stage of gestation," Scrivener continued, "your white blood cells are trying to fight, and failing. Your body doesn't know how to combat this virus. It's never encountered it before. Which is how vaccinations work. That's what I was developing, until Armstrong, rest his soul, made his little discovery."

"How long will it take?"

"Until you die? Hard to say. It depends on the body's resilience. When Justin—our lab assistant—became infected, it took hours for the virus to take hold. But then again, he took it orally, whereas you've had it injected directly into your bloodstream."

"He drank it?"

"Yes. Not willingly, of course. I had to mix it into his drink."

"*You* infected him?" Zielinski found himself wishing Armstrong was alive to hear the confession. "Why?"

"Science." Scrivener grinned, a wide toothy grin which made his moustache appear even smaller.

"My experiment failed, but I have a feeling you're going to be the breakthrough. Don't worry, it won't take long. Right now, the virus is working its way up to the pituitary gland, which is the final stage. In some cases, this causes the brain to malfunction. The host might vomit, convulse, develop a high temperature or a relentless itching of the skin—all defence mechanisms the human body implements to try to stay alive."

Zielinski knew it. Vomiting and bowel eruptions incoming. The thought of itching sent pinpricks across his newly shaved head, as if spiders were scuttling across his scalp, squeezing under the sensors that had been taped to his dome. He twisted against his confines in a pitiful attempt to scratch.

"That might not happen to you, though," Scrivener said, reading his look of despair. "Other subjects merely devolved into a semi-autonomous state—autopilot, if you will. They remained capable of menial tasks like cleaning, washing, even reading, although they were unlikely to comprehend what the words meant."

Zielinski shuddered. He tried to ignore the throbbing in his ears, his heart pumping the poison through his body. The gnawing ache in his midriff grew. He wanted to believe it was nausea, but he had experienced hunger far too many times throughout his life to convince himself.

He needed food. Meat. Juicy steaks streaked with marble fat and oozing blood. He had never been a fan of raw meat, yet now it was all he desired. Pregnancy cravings, borne not from a foetus, but from the developing virion coursing through his body. While one brought new life into the world, the other brought death.

No, he thought. *He's going to cure me. He wouldn't inject me unless he was certain.*

Yet, despite his attempt at reassurance, the cold, calculated look behind Scrivener's visor proved otherwise.

"So when I turn into a zombie, how do you bring me back?" Zielinski asked, desperate to find an ounce of compassion behind the doctor's deadpan face.

"I inject you with T-14, or I suppose T-20 should be the new name, given the degree of alterations I've made to its genetic makeup. It will destroy the virus and take over the host."

"By host, you mean me?"

"Precisely. As soon as this happens, I administer the antidote, effectively purging the virion from your system, and bringing you back from the dead."

"I don't understand. How do you know when to inject the antidote?"

Scrivener swung the monitor around to face Zielinski. It showed a monochrome image of his brain gently rippling in a psychedelic motion.

"I'm monitoring your cerebral activity. Those sensors attached to your head are showing everything going on inside. As soon as there's a spike in stimulus, I'll know to administer the antidote."

"I still don't understand."

"Nor do I expect you to."

"Why not create an antidote for T-19, or whatever it's called?"

Scrivener scoffed. "Do you want me to create a cure for cancer whilst I'm at it?" He swung the monitor back toward him before settling on a tall metal stool. "Science is complex, Mr Zielinski. I don't expect somebody of your intellect to grasp any scientific explanation I could provide, so I'll give you the simple answer: no."

Zielinski wanted to argue more, but the itching was bordering on unbearable. Every hair follicle seemed to be ablaze with burning maggots writhing around on his flesh. He clenched his fists, digging his fingernails into his palms. The skin punctured, leaking warm blood onto the armrest, but Zielinski didn't care; it took his mind off the urge to scratch. Then a fresh wave of hunger started. How long had it been since he had last eaten? A day? Two? How long could a human go without food?

Scrivener was a psychopath. A mad professor playing God. Yet, despite his raging ego, he was nothing more than a man. *No.* Not a man. He was merely a sack of meat and bones living in an egotistical bubble. A bubble Zielinski longed to burst. The same type of bubble that formed in sausages when there wasn't enough meat. He used to love them when he was at school. The way the warm, meaty fluid oozed out of the ruptured casing and filled his mouth when he bit into them—yeah, that was something else.

Zielinski swallowed the puddle of saliva that had formed in his mouth, contemplating how Scrivener resembled a sausage. The white biohazard suit was merely an outer casing for the meat that lay within. True, there was more substance on the late Dr Armstrong—chunky arms and thighs, and a rotund belly—but he was dead. There was something tantalising about living flesh that Zielinski couldn't put his finger on.

He watched Scrivener examine the different monitors, fantasising about tearing into his skin and muscle. There wasn't much on him, but it would be warm, and free from infection, unlike his own flesh. Zielinski clenched his jaw. It was becoming too much. The thought of clamping down, tearing flesh from bone, feeling the warm, meaty fluid fill his mouth—

"Hungry?" Scrivener stood over him, regarding him curiously through his visor.

"Yessss." A stream of saliva spilled down the sides of his mouth, pooling in his neck. "Nee… Foo."

Zielinski squeezed his eyes shut, trying to free himself from the torturous cravings for a brief moment of clarity.

"Food," he said. "Give me food."

"I don't have anything which would satisfy *that* kind of hunger," Scrivener said, his delight evident. "I could get the mice, but with their being infected, I'm guessing they won't appeal to you."

"Mice?" The word was familiar, yet he couldn't make sense of it. It had a coldness to it, but had Scrivener said it was food? He remembered the rodents scurrying around the pen. Infected. Not tasty. Not tasty at all.

"Yes, they're still there. They never left. But it was the only way I could convince Armstrong to let me test the sample on you."

Zielinski felt a wave of anger surge within him. He didn't know why, but he felt it all the same. The adrenaline flowed through his body and he found his teeth clamping together—an act he was unaware of until one of his incisors snapped under the pressure.

"My, my. You *are* hungry, aren't you?" Scrivener stepped toward the body of Dr Armstrong. "I'm not an unreasonable man. I'll allow you to satiate your appetite if you wish."

He grabbed the arm of his motionless colleague, dragging him closer to the bed. Zielinski stared, repulsed by his urges, but desperate to fulfil them, nonetheless.

"Here we are." Scrivener hoisted the body up to the bedside, clutching his wrist above Zielinski's face, the doctor's limp fingers dangling tantalisingly over his mouth. Zielinski clenched his jaw as tightly as he could, using his last thread of morality. But when the fingers brushed against his lips, that thread snapped.

He lurched forward and clamped down on the suspended digits. Blood filled his mouth, propelled by a faint pulse. He pulled back, the flesh unravelling down the bone, rolling into a pulpy mass. It was tasteless, but Zielinski chewed the rubbery morsel with vigour, while Scrivener watched him with morbid curiosity. Zielinski swallowed the meat and leaned back up for more, crying out as Scrivener hurled the body aside.

"I think you've had your fill," he said.

Zielinski shrieked in anguish, thrashing against his bindings, no longer aware of the friction burns on his wrists and torso. Indifferent to the frantic beeping of the machines. Determined to reach Scrivener, who now held a syringe filled with red liquid.

"It seems stage one is almost complete. Time to commence stage two."

21

Ben stared at the wad of bandages wrapped around his hand. The wound pulsed, a dull ache bursting across his raw knuckles. The notion of infection tormented him. After spending weeks trying to avoid the zombie virus, it would be a cruel irony if he were to succumb to a regular infection. He exhaled a scornful laugh.

"What's up?" Kev asked from his hunched position at the steering wheel. Despite pushing the driver's seat as far back as it would go, his hefty physique was never intended for a sports car.

"Nothing, it'd just be ironic if I ended up dying of natural causes as opposed to zombies ripping me to shreds."

"There's nothing natural about gunshot wounds. Guns were invented for one purpose: to kill."

"Yeah, and death is natural."

"Premature death isn't."

Ben frowned, surprised by the reversal of opinions. "You don't seem to have a problem using them."

"No. It's what I'm trained to do. But it's not always the best option. Sometimes we have to do things we don't like."

What the hell is that supposed to mean?

"Are you on about those blokes you killed?" Ben asked. "We've already talked about this. It's water under the bridge."

Kev said nothing. He eased off the accelerator, giving a wide berth to a corpse in the road. The crushed limbs, warped torso, and strewn innards indicated a car had hit it on more than one occasion. It was impossible to tell if it had once been a zombie, given the flattened remnants of its head, but Ben suspected as much.

The road continued to weave through the trees—a single lane with the occasional passing place on either side. The speed at which they were travelling would have normally put Ben on edge. If a car topped one of the banks, or veered around the sharp turns, there'd be no way they could stop in time. But aside from the roadkill cadaver, there was no evidence of anybody else travelling along the route.

"Sometimes you have no choice," Kev said. Ben looked over at him, expecting to see a prompt or justification for his peculiar dialogue, but he remained focused ahead.

"What do you mean? There's always a choice. You don't have to kill everyone we come into contact with."

"Sometimes that's the only option."

"Unless they've got a gun pointed at you, I'd respectfully disagree."

Another corpse loomed into view, this one topless, suspended on a low-hanging branch. The way the woman was positioned, it appeared as though she was relaxing in the shade. The giveaway was the entrails dangling from her stomach, drooping below the branch like crimson vines. Red patches on the road showed blood had dripped down. This time Kev slowed to a crawl, studying the scene in a mystified silence.

"What is it?" Ben asked.

"This isn't right." They stopped next to the tree, Kev's gaze roaming high and low before he got out of the car.

"What are you doing?"

Ben jumped out and followed him towards the elevated corpse. As they neared, he realised the dead woman's hands were clasped behind her head, exhibiting the most laid-back death pose he had ever seen.

Kev ran his fingers over the bloodstains on the road.

"Dry," he muttered.

"We best not hang around, then," Ben said. "She could turn into one of them any second."

He started walking back to the car, but Kev stayed crouched next to the bloodstains.

"Zombies didn't do this." His voice was little more than a whisper. He rose to his feet, automatically resting his hand on the grip of his weapon.

"What do you mean? Her guts are hanging out."

Kev made for the base of the tree and hoisted himself up beside the corpse.

What the fuck is he doing? Ben froze, expecting a group of zombies to come ploughing through the undergrowth at any second. But the forest was still. The only sound came from Kev, who eased the dead woman forward. Her hands remained clasped behind her head until he pried away the scalpel that had been keeping them embedded. At once, the limp arms fell to the side, and the dead woman's head slumped to her chest.

"Holy shit," Kev murmured. He released the corpse, allowing it to slide sideways off the branch. It hit the road with a dull thud, intestines splayed either side.

"Zombies didn't do this," he repeated, jumping down from the branch and landing next to Ben.

"She was killed by survivors?"

Kev shook his head. "Only one."

The scalpel glistened in the sun as he examined both sides. Not finding anything of note, he hurled it into the bushes.

"Albert Crosswell."

Ben shrugged.

"You must remember him. The Skin Flayer? Killed all those people a couple of years back."

"Oh, yeah," Ben said. He recalled the extensive manhunt for the serial killer, who had claimed seven victims before being caught. More notable were the graphic details of the victims' demise. One newspaper was reprimanded at the time for publishing a photo—albeit pixelated—of one of the murder scenes.

"But he was in London. Why would he be here?"

"They moved him away from the area. He transported to Moorside, you know, the nuthouse near Charbridge?"

Ben nodded curtly, his mind drifting back to his conversation with Amy. *Didn't she say her brother was in Moorside?*

"I was on the armed convoy transporting him. They handed him over to us just outside Sheffield. We took him the rest of the way."

"How do you know it's him?"

Kev bent down and flipped the woman over, revealing a swathe of raw muscle down her back.

"He skinned his victims. Used to take tattoos as trophies. His favourite cuts were the back and thighs, which he made into leather. When the cops found him, he had tried to make a lampshade out of them. Must have thought of himself as a British Ed Gein."

An uneasy silence formed as Kev got back to his feet.

"Are you sure it's him?"

"Oh, I'm sure. There's not many people who would go around skinning folk. And leaving her up there with a scalpel in the back of her head? It's gotta be him."

"As if we haven't got enough to worry about," Ben said.

"Like I said earlier, sometimes you don't have a choice. When it comes to the likes of Albert Crosswell, you shoot on sight, and then shoot him again to make sure he's dead."

With a final scan of their surroundings, they returned to the car and resumed their journey towards Bealsdon.

"So where do you think this guy is now?" Ben asked. The notion of a psychopath roaming the forest was one he'd never imagined he'd have to endure.

"It looks like the body's been there a day or two. He could be anywhere by now."

"Comforting."

"Don't worry about him. He'll be long gone. Let's stay focused."

Yet, despite Kev's reassurances, all Ben could think about was the fugitive Moorside patient. If he had escaped from the facility, that meant Amy's brother could be out there too. Hell, *he* could be Amy's brother for all he knew. She'd said he was older than her and had developed mental conditions. Murdering folk for their skin was a pretty big mental condition.

A chill ran down Ben's arms. It dawned on him how little he knew of Amy. Her accent was pretty nondescript, which in itself was a rarity in Yorkshire. What if she was originally from London? She and her mother could have moved away for a fresh start after Albert's incarceration. Or perhaps they had moved north to be closer to him? What if he was looking for her? She had given him her address, and their mother's. What if he was working his way through different towns in search of her?

"What's up?" Kev asked.

"Nothing."

The pieces of the puzzle were starting to come together, and Ben didn't like the picture being revealed. He didn't even know Amy's last name. Amy Crosswell sure had a ring to it.

"Come on, something's bothering you. Spill the beans."

"Nothing's bothering me. I'm just wondering how someone like that could escape from a mental institute," Ben muttered. He needed answers, but didn't want Kev to guess his reasoning.

"Who? Crosswell?"

"Yeah. He would've needed help, wouldn't he?"

"I guess. It'd be hard getting out of there on your lonesome."

"Does he have any family up here? A brother or sister, perhaps?"

"Nah, he's an only child. Thank fuck, eh? It's bad enough with one nutter out there."

All at once, the pressure on Ben's chest lifted, replaced with a feeling of elation. "Are you sure?"

"One hundred per cent. He was your stereotypical psychopath. An only child from a broken home. Mother was a smackhead who abused him. She ended up OD'ing and he wound up in the care system. Fuck knows where he got his skin fetish from, but that's a job for the psychiatrists. Or was, at least."

Ben eased back in his chair. "How do you know so much?"

"We had to sit through a two-hour brief before the escort. Back then, I could've told you his favourite football team and his shoe size." Kev chuckled.

"So you think he was working with somebody on the inside?"

"Your guess is as good as mine. It's not the easiest place to get out of. But like I say, he'll be long gone by now. I wouldn't worry about it."

He still felt a tug of apprehension, but Ben's major worries had been alleviated now he knew Amy wasn't Albert Crosswell's sister. It didn't mean he wasn't out there, too. But at least he wasn't on a psychotic skinning spree. As far as Ben could tell.

They reached the town without any further grisly sights, courtesy of zombies or otherwise. But as they passed the 'Welcome to Bealsdon' sign, it was obvious that luxury had run its course. Waves of destruction had crashed over the streets, leaving behind limbs, organs, and bloodstained pavements. None of the motionless corpses were intact, and the mobile few at the end of the street didn't look any better. They roamed aimlessly—as far as their mutilations allowed—but none had seen their car as it rolled to a stop.

"Damn, I'm starting to wish we took my car," Kev said. "We won't be ploughing through them in this thing."

"I still don't know why we didn't." Ben sat up, rifle gripped firmly in his working hand. "You said this car was fast, but your police car is pretty nippy, too."

"Yeah, but we couldn't risk it. That lad escaped us, remember? There could be an entire gang out here baying for revenge, and what will they be looking for?"

"The police car," they said in unison.

"Gotta be on the safe side," Kev added.

The zombies appraised the nearby buildings and cars with a languid curiosity, like captive animals apathetically eyeing a gawking audience. Except there was nobody in the vehicles or the houses, as far as Ben and Kev could see. If there were, the zombies would be a lot more agile, and far more vocal.

There was, however, quick movement close to the feet of the walking corpses. Ben glimpsed it only for a second, but it was definitely there. The motion was akin to dogs snaking through a crowd of people, looking for scraps on the floor. Only this wasn't an animal. The movement came again as a young child bounded onto an upturned bus, head snapping back and forth. It crouched down on all fours, legs splayed either side like a spatchcock chicken.

It had to have been run over. That was the only explanation Ben could think of to warrant such deformity. But then, a second child joined it on the bus. This one was barely a toddler, but dashed around with a dexterity beyond its years. It, too, moved around on hands and splayed legs.

"What the fuck happened to them?" Kev muttered.

"I don't know. Looks like they've been crushed."

"Poor bastards."

The two undead children continued to scan the desolate street until one of them clapped eyes on the red sports car. It leaned forward, emitting a nerve-shredding screech which alerted the rest of the horde.

"Those 'poor bastards' are going to kill us," Ben said. Kev floored the accelerator, racing towards the undead gathering which was now running towards them. The car ploughed through the mass, smashing aside those at the front of the procession. Rapid thuds pounded the bonnet and the roof. Bodies flew in all directions, some jumping back to their feet upon impact with the pavement, others succumbing to the blunt trauma. When their car drew parallel with the upturned bus, the zombie children leapt for them.

Twin thuds resonated from the roof of the car, but the children weren't hurled aside like the others. The banging continued, this time from tiny fists.

"What the fuck?" Kev crashed through the last pair of zombies. Both hurled high into the air before striking the tarmac, but the thuds above them continued.

"How are they still on the roof?"

Kev slammed on the brakes, this time sending one of the zombie children soaring into the air. It crashed against the road, rolling a dozen or more times, until it lay dormant. The other child slid down onto the windshield, splayed palms and webbed fingers holding it in place. Kev floored the accelerator, but the zombie remained fixed to the glass, its deformed legs holding it steady while it punched the window.

A sick thud sounded beneath the car. Ben guessed it was the other child being crushed beneath the wheels, but the obstructed windscreen made it impossible to tell. The deformed zombie slammed itself forward, striking the glass with its fists, head, and elbows. A spiderweb cracked through the windscreen before Kev slammed on the brakes again. This time, the child lost its bond with the glass and soared backwards.

"Go, go!" Ben snapped.

Kev veered down a side street and raced to the end of the road. Parked cars on either side concealed any would-be attackers, but there were no forthcoming threats.

"What the fuck was that?" Ben gasped.

"I don't know. I've never seen that before."

Kev sighed heavily, unable to mask his astonishment—the first signs of alarm Ben had seen him exhibit.

"Paraplegics, perhaps?"

"What? Both of them?" Ben scoffed. "What are the chances?"

"I don't know."

"And how did they stick to the car like that?"

"I *don't know!*" Kev held a hand over his mouth, breathing deeply. "We need to stay focused," he said after a few moments of silence. "Antibiotics, remember?"

"Yeah."

Although medication seemed trivial now. Everything he thought he knew about the undead creatures had turned on its head. If a pair of undead children could demonstrate such acrobatic prowess, what else could the zombies do?

The possibilities were endless.

22

Lisa jogged outside as the first scream sounded in the distance. Grunts and roars drifted up from the woodland below, but even from her elevated position on the hill, she couldn't see much within the thick canopy of trees. All she could do was listen as the men in the woods were ripped apart.

Mike and some others reached her side.

"How many people have you got down there?" she asked.

"Three, maybe four."

Another scream punctured the foliage. One less survivor.

"What's your plan?"

Mike faltered. "I don't know. We've only ever had one or two to deal with. If there's dozens in there, we—we're going to have to hide."

"Hide? Where?"

"The church. Everyone, get into the church!" He ushered the spectators towards the holy building, like a farmer herding sheep. The community whimpered and scurried, some rushing to collect weapons, others racing inside. Lisa remained in place, examining the edge of the woodland for any sign of movement. The yearning cries and the rustle of foliage sounded closer. She propped the rifle against her shoulder and stared down the sight, anticipating a break through the trees at any second.

"What are you doing?" Mike yanked the rifle aside, but Lisa shoved him back.

"Touch me again and I'll blow your fucking head off!"

The foliage parted, and a lone man sprinted out of the forest, racing towards the bottom of the hill. Lisa aimed her rifle again.

"Don't shoot him, he's one of us!" Despite the urgency in Mike's voice, he didn't encroach on Lisa's space again.

"I'm not going to shoot him. It's his pals I'm after."

"Don't shoot them either. You'll attract them to us!"

The foliage lining the forest disappeared beneath a swarm of trampling feet. A linear procession of zombies emerged from the trees before forming an arrow-head as they sprinted after the man.

"He's doing a pretty good job of that himself."

Lisa fired. The first shot whizzed past her target. When she tried again, the rifle clicked empty.

"Shit!"

She hurled the weapon aside and drew her handgun, firing in rapid succession. Some bullets brought the zombies to ground, others zipped past. Despite her best efforts, it wasn't enough. The man slowed as he ascended the bank, with his pursuers closing the gap. One zombie lunged forward, clipping the man's ankle, causing him to stumble.

"No!" Mike whirled away as the man's screams topped the hill.

"We need to go," Lisa said. "Get inside, quick!"

She ran with Mike towards the church, unsure of how many bullets she had left, but more than aware they wouldn't be enough. Marie ushered the last of the people through the doors as they approached.

"Get inside, Marie!" Mike snapped. They bounded up the stone steps, pursued by the zombies scaling the hill.

The heavy doors slammed shut, with those manning it working in unison, heaving the heavy pews up against it, one on top of the other.

"Mike!" a woman yelled within the anxious murmurs of the group.

"We need another pew up against this door," Mike told those around him, oblivious to the woman's call.

"No, Mike!"

"Luke, secure the vestry." Mike clapped a man on the shoulder as the frantic woman pushed herself to the front.

"Mike! He's out there. Peter's still outside!" she cried.

"What?"

"He went to make sure there was nobody left out. We need to let him in."

The woman reached for the barricade, but Mike's grasp on her elbow thwarted her attempts to leave.

"If we open the door, we're all dead."

"But we—" The woman stopped protesting when a cry of agony rang outside the church. "Peter!" she screamed, lunging for the stacked benches. "Peter!"

Mike and another man held her back.

"He's dead, Belinda," Mike said, but his words vanished beneath the woman's sobs and the ravenous moans of the undead outside.

Lisa felt a firm grip on her shoulder.

"What the fuck's happening?" Frank grumbled. He stood hunched to the side, a hand pressed against his wound.

Lisa gasped. "You're awake!"

"How can I not be with all this shit going on?" He propped himself up on one of the pews.

"How are you feeling?"

"Confused." He nodded to the barricaded doors. "Zombies or guns?"

"Zombies. At least a dozen, maybe more."

"Shit." He looked around at the rows of stained-glass windows. "Where the fuck are we?"

A thunderous crash reverberated around the church. The zombies slammed against the huge wooden doors, but their assault left the barricade untouched. Unperturbed, the pounding continued, thundering through the hall. The children bawled, clinging to their parents, who tried to maintain their resolve.

"We're in a brothel," Lisa said. "Where do you think we are?"

"I think we're in deep shit if we don't get these windows secured."

"They're at least ten feet high," Jay piped up from beside them. "We'll be fine."

Frank cast him a scornful glance. "You're still alive, then?"

Jay grinned awkwardly, pulling his machete close to his body. Perhaps a subconscious effort to stop it being taken from him again.

"Alive and kicking," he said.

"For now."

Frank looked to the windows again, trying to ignore the slamming of flesh and muscle against the oak doors. "If those things start to climb they'll smash through here in seconds."

"How can they climb?"

"I've told you already!" Frank snapped, earning a glance from those who stood nearby. "We had one running and jumping to get at us. It climbed up onto the roof we were on."

"Wait, are you saying they can break these here windows?" American Jack stepped closer, removing his aviators.

"Yes."

"Well, shit, we gotta get the hell outta here."

"What do you suggest?" Lisa asked.

"I suggest you go out there and blast those suckers to smithereens."

"That'd be a good idea, except we're almost out of bullets."

"How many do we have?" Frank asked.

Lisa released the handgun magazine. "Three. And this still has one in the chamber." She handed him his shotgun, flexing her rotator cuff. It felt good not to have the gun draping over her shoulder.

"Fuck. That's not enough. We need to find somewhere more secure."

"What about through there?" Jay asked, motioning towards the vestry.

"Can they get in?"

"I doubt it," Lisa said. "It's all boarded up in there."

"Sounds good to me. Let's go." Frank heaved himself away from the bench.

"What about them?" Jay asked, motioning to the survivors.

"Fuck them."

The majority of men stood around the door, keeping the stacked benches in place. The two newcomers were nearby, the young woman on her knees, sobbing, and the shark-eyed man standing with his back to the wall. He watched the group with disinterest, apparently unfazed by the surge of undead monsters trying to break in. Theresa the vet consoled two children, while a couple in the corner comforted a third.

"There's kids, Frank," Lisa chided. "We can't leave them."

"*Crying* kids. And as long as they're crying, those fuckers out there won't be going anywhere."

Despite the ongoing assault, the benches blocking the door remained unmoved. But so did the dogged determination of the zombies. Their efforts continued, striking inharmonious thuds throughout the church.

"Even if they stop crying, the zombies might not leave," Lisa said. "Especially if they *are* getting smarter. What's stopping them from just waiting it out? We have to come out sometime, right?"

Frank let out an agitated sigh. The prospect was one that had troubled him since they had discovered the traps in the woods—a nagging idea that continued to prod the back of his mind. What if they were capable of planning? The church was under siege, after all. All the zombies had to do was wait.

"I got an idea," the American said. "It might be stupid, and it's gonna take balls of steel. No offence," he added, glancing at Lisa.

"None taken." She shrugged. "While you're all weighing your balls, tell me the plan and I'll go and do it."

Jack smirked. "Right. You still got those bike keys I gave you?"

Lisa reached into her back pocket and produced the key chain.

"Good. She's parked on the other side of the wall. I say we create a distraction—a whole ruckus up against the door—and with those deadheads preoccupied, we break the window. You jump down to the bike, then use it to lure them away."

"Break the window?" Lisa repeated. "What if they hear?"

"They won't if we're loud enough."

"So you want us to climb out, jump on the motorbike and have the zombies chase us?"

"Yes, ma'am. I told ya you'd need balls of steel. But the bike's got a full tank of gas, so no chance of her running dry."

"It's not a bad idea."

"What?" Frank snapped. "You wanna go out there with only three bullets?"

"Any other suggestions?"

"To get yourself killed? Plenty. But if you want to stay alive, going out there isn't the solution."

"Nor is waiting in here to die. It's going to be dark soon. If we're going to do this, we need to do it now."

"Great. I'll go tell Mike." Jack strode away.

"It means we can get the fuck out of this place, too," Lisa said, her voice lowered. "We need to get back to Kara."

"You're not staying?" Jay gasped.

"No."

"But how the hell are we meant to survive with no guns?"

"That's not my problem. We'll lead them away from here, but after that, you're on your own."

Jay chewed his fingernails in contemplation.

"And I meant what I said, Jay," Lisa continued. "You tell these guys about our hotel and I swear I'll kill you."

Jay nodded, staring into the distance. Frank kept quiet. He had so much to say, yet his minimal energy was being used staving off the lethargy weighing down his eyelids.

He readjusted his position against the bench, wincing at the stab of pain.

"Will you be alright to climb up there?" Lisa asked.

"Yeah. Will you be alright getting us out of here?"

"After all the times I've saved your arse, you still doubt me?"

Frank smirked. "Not at all."

They turned towards hurried footsteps.

"Absolutely not!" Mike snapped. "Going out there would be suicide and leave us at even greater risk."

Jack shuffled up beside him, shaking his head in wonderment. "Mike, give the lady some credit. She's got some snap in her garters."

"No! I'm sorry, but I won't allow it."

Frank clenched his jaw, ready to rip the man's head off. But Lisa beat him to it.

"What makes you think you have a choice?" she growled, stepping forward, her face inches from Mike's. "You think you can tell *me* what to do?"

"I don't want—"

"I don't give a fuck what you want or don't want!" She cocked her head, her eyes piercing his. "This is what's gonna happen, Mike. Your people are going to create a distraction over by the door. Hell, move those screaming kids closer as well. With the zombies distracted, Frank and I are leaving through that window, there." She pointed her handgun at the stained glass, but kept her unblinking gaze fixed on Mike.

"And then what? Leave us here to die while you run?"

"No. We're going to use the motorbike."

Mike glanced questioningly at Jack.

"That's what I tried to say before you went stormin' off," Jack muttered. "They're gonna lead the zombies away."

"Or at least we *were*," Lisa added, "until you came over swinging your dick about."

Mike closed his eyes. "Please, you don't need to be so vulgar."

Frank snorted. "Vulgar? I bet the sex is magic in your gaff. C'mon, Lise, let's get this done."

Frank went over to the window, estimating at least seven feet up to the ledge. There would be no way he could jump, not with his debilitating injury. Apparently, Jack and Jay were thinking the same. They heaved one of the pews up against the wall before going for another.

"Last chance, Mike," Lisa said. "Do you want our help or not?"

He looked past her towards the men constructing the platform, then over his shoulder at the others: his community. The group he had promised to safeguard.

"Okay," he said, his voice barely audible over the encompassing clamour. "Please, don't let us down."

"You said you had faith in me, remember?"

The corners of Mike's mouth twitched as he left to address the others.

"Right then," Lisa said, joining the trio beneath the window. "Are we ready to roll?"

"You want me to ride?" Frank asked.

"No, I want you to hold on to me and not fall off. Think you can do that?"

Frank grinned, stepping aside, allowing Lisa space to climb onto the stacked benches. She hoisted herself up and crouched on the ledge.

"Over to you, Mike!" she called.

"Okay, everyone!" Mike called. "Now!"

The congregation erupted, banging the door, stamping their feet and jeering at the top of their voices. The children covered their ears, cowering at the feet of their parents, who hollered as loud as they could.

The huge, heavy doors shook more than ever, the countering roar from the zombies matching the volume inside the church. Lisa could almost feel the echoes rushing past her as she swung the handgun into the window. It shattered, the multi-coloured pane smashing in all directions, sending jagged sheets falling outside.

The diminishing auburn light still offered a clear view of the landscape. A rusty tint shrouded the fields below the hill and the forest beyond. More importantly, it showed no signs of movement along the side of the church. The black motorbike stood propped against the wall a few metres from her elevated position. It gleamed in the sun—an impatient shimmer endorsed by the diminishing sounds from the door. The zombies were losing interest.

After scraping the last of the jagged glass from its frame, Lisa lowered herself out of the window and dropped to the ground. She stared at the end of the building, expecting a zombie to leer around the corner. With hesitant steps, she approached the bike as Frank scrambled down after her.

"Please tell me you've still got the keys?" he whispered.

Lisa nodded, easing the bike away from the wall. The zombies were going to rear around the corner. She knew it.

Swinging her leg over, she straddled the bike and put the key in the ignition. Frank climbed on behind her, shuffling tentatively. She could feel his hand pressed against his wound as he moved closer. The thudding and roaring continued at the door, but was diminishing as each second passed. She was sure they'd be able to hear the engine burst to life.

With an intake of breath, she turned the key, squeezed the clutch, and pressed the start button with her thumb. The engine grumbled, ticked over, and fell silent.

Shit!

She pressed it again, listening to the bike trying to start, only to fall dead.

"You gotta be kidding me," Frank growled.

Lisa ignored him, checking the kill switch and the clutch before firing the bike up for a third time. It tried to start and failed.

"Shit."

She was contemplating a fourth attempt when movement at the end of the church snared her attention. A familiar man stumbled around the corner. Fresh blood soaked his tattered white t-shirt, still spilling from the gaping wounds in his chest. A ruptured eyeball lay blind in its socket like a deflated balloon. The other darted left and right until it fixed on the pair straddling the unresponsive bike. A wide grin exposed broken teeth. Its head flew back, and the zombie emitted a feral roar before sprinting toward them.

23

The car trundled through the back streets of Bealsdon. Throughout their ongoing search, they had found two newsagents, three Chinese takeaways, and a house which had been converted into a chip shop. But still, no pharmacy. Ben suspected they would have better luck if they searched the high street, but was in two minds about voicing his opinion. Since their encounter with the deformed children, Kev seemed rattled—a contradiction to his usually composed disposition. His furrowed brows had become a permanent fixture, and the only time he spoke was to express disgruntled mutterings whenever a passing shop didn't display a 'Pharmacy' sign.

Despite the fruitless offerings of the side streets, they did benefit from a lack of zombies. After nearly five minutes of roaming, the only corpses they encountered were motionless ones. Every street harboured grisly remains, with none untouched by the zombies' wrath, but the threat had long since moved on.

"Seems the side streets are safer," Kev muttered. "No pharmacies, though."

"What do you think? Is it worth going back on the main roads?"

"Yeah, if you want to be attacked again. And I'm not sure these windows will withstand much more."

Ben followed the crack across the windshield to where it spiderwebbed out—the impact of the deformed child's head. Or was it his elbow? Or his fist? Ben couldn't remember. The assault was so quick. So sudden. And besides, it didn't matter how the glass had broken, what was more concerning was how the child had stayed attached for so long.

"We're gonna have to do something, though," Kev continued. "There's fuck all down these back alleys."

They stopped at a T-junction. One way led to an open high street, whereas the other ran past rows of terraced houses.

"If the shit hits the fan, do you think you'll be alright shooting?" Kev asked.

"It's hit the fan twice already, and it's only..." Ben glanced at his wristwatch, forgetting about the deep crack and the stationary hands. Any other time, he would've disposed of the watch and got another one that worked. But sentiment kept it strapped to his wrist—his old life, a reminder of a time that would never again come to pass.

"You wanna add a new watch to our shopping list?" Kev chuckled.

"No, I'm good. And I think we'll be alright. Let's go down the street and see what we're dealing with."

201

"You're the boss."

The statement couldn't have been further from the truth. Despite Amy and Kev's reassurance, Ben knew he was still a burden to the group. He was using up food, water, medical supplies, and if his hand *was* infected, he'd require even more care and resources. And what could he offer? He couldn't cook, struggled to drive, and now he could hardly shoot. A one-handed survivor was no good to anybody, even if his impediment was only temporary.

Ben tried to eliminate the intrusive thoughts, but he could only discard them to the back of his mind. There they lingered, festering like his oozing finger stubs.

"Looks promising," Kev announced.

Ben snapped out of his reverie, focusing on the main road. High street stores lined both sides and stretched all the way to a defunct water feature which divided the road in two. Beyond this, the stores turned into office blocks which extended to the end of the road.

There were milling figures in the distance, but none close enough to pose an immediate threat.

"I don't see a pharmacy, though," Ben said.

"We haven't even started looking yet. Come on, let's get out and have a walk."

"Get *out*?" Ben stared at Kev, waiting for the punchline.

"Yeah, this engine's louder than skinheads at an EDL march. It'll be less conspicuous if we're on foot."

"I don't know…"

"I'm not saying ditch the car entirely. I'm on about walking to the fountain."

Kev cut the ignition and swung his door wide. There was no more discussion to be had.

You're the boss, Benny Boy.

Ben held the rifle in his good hand as he climbed out of the car, head darting back and forth. Aside from the distant figures, there was nobody in sight. The dilapidated storefronts showed no sign of life, or stock. It dawned on him that even if they *found* a pharmacy, chances were there'd be nothing left.

"Locked and loaded?" Kev asked.

Ben nodded, raising the rifle into view.

"Here, let's swap. You'll be better off with this." Kev offered him the handgun. "Remember, use your deformed hand as a platform."

"Fuck off," Ben snorted, as they exchanged guns. "I remember."

"Good, then you can lead."

"Me?"

"Yeah, you look one way, I'll look the other, stops us from being blitzed."

Ben frowned. With the racket the zombies made, he doubted they could 'blitz' anyone. But he strode on without dispute, the bigger adversary being his paranoia. *If anything comes out, it'll get me first*, he thought. *A human shield—it's my biggest use right now.*

He glanced back at Kev, who stayed close behind him, the barrel of his rifle swinging left and right as he scanned the storefronts.

"Keep your eyes on those zombies up there," Kev warned.

The wandering corpses were still a way off. Ben wondered if they'd be able to see from that distance. They certainly hadn't reacted; their movements were slow and lethargic. He wouldn't be needed as a human shield just yet. He examined the shops as they passed: bakeries, pawn shops, banks, gambling establishments—not a single pharmacy in view.

What if there isn't one? What if Kev isn't even looking for a pharmacy? What if he wants me out of the car so he can leave me here?

Ben checked Kev in his periphery. He was still close behind, gun still held aloft.

No. He would've run back by now… Unless he's gonna shoot me.

Ben dismissed the idea, shaking it from his head. He was being stupid. The intrusive thoughts had taken on a new level of absurdity. Kev had no reason to kill him.

He snapped his head forward, realising he had moved almost two metres without keeping tabs on the zombies ahead.

Keep looking at the rabbits, Benny.

He stopped, anticipating a bullet tearing through his body. Would it be his head, or his torso? He didn't have to wait long. He felt the impact on his back as Kev collided with him.

"What the hell are you doing?" Kev gasped.

Air whooshed out of Ben's lungs, but it was caused more by shock than the impact. His legs felt weak, and he inhaled a ragged breath, trying to compose himself. It worked. A wave of elation washed over him when he spotted a green cross embedded in the O of 'Bealsdon Pharmacy.'

"There!" His voice came out hoarse, but he didn't care. He was alive, he was useful, and after they'd found some antibiotics, he'd be beneficial to the team once again.

"Nice one." Kev clapped him on the back as they approached the shattered windows. All of the window display was strewn across the pavement. A banner depicting a beaming woman advertising a box of allergy relief tablets was shredded and soiled. The boxes in question littered the street. Nobody had taken them.

There's still hope left, he thought, as they entered the store.

***

Amy was gripping the door handle so hard her hand was shaking. She had closed her eyes soon after leaving the cottage, and had kept them squeezed shut. She breathed in deep, heavy breaths, trying to distract herself from the jolting car and her somersaulting belly. Donna was driving as though her life depended on it, yet the glee in her voice was akin to that of a child at a theme park. She had talked incessantly at the start of the journey, but when Amy could offer only one-word answers for fear of vomiting, the conversation had trailed off.

Amy sucked air through her teeth, savouring the clean—although slightly humid—air streaming through the open window. She had originally breathed through her nose, but the cheap pine air freshener in the police cruiser knocked her sick. Although, despite the neutral air coming in from outside, she knew it was only a matter of time. She could feel the thick saliva fill her mouth—her body's preparation for the vomitus onslaught.

"You need me to stop?" Donna asked.

Amy shook her head. She wanted to tell her that slowing down would be a good start, but even the thought of saying those words—any words—caused her to gag. The whisky had been a bad idea. She had predicted as much back at the cottage. Now all she could do was wait for it to settle, or for her body to expel it, whichever came first.

"Oh, God," Donna said.

Amy opened her eyes as the car veered towards the encompassing trees, breezing past an undead teenager standing in the middle of the road. The zombie tried to give chase, but its broken shinbone thwarted its efforts and it crumpled to the ground.

"Starting to see more of them out here," Donna said. "Must be from Cranston. We need to prepare."

Amy took a deep breath. *C'mon, breathe,* she told herself. *We'll be there soon. We must be getting close.* But then Donna's words registered. They didn't make sense, but she had definitely heard them.

"Cranston?" Amy repeated.

She knew as soon as the word had left her lips that the vomit would soon follow. She clapped a hand to her mouth, her body heaving.

"Stop the car," she urged. Donna pulled over to the treeline, the car lurching to a stop. Amy pushed open the door just as the spurt of vomit erupted from her mouth. She fell to her hands and knees, showering the undergrowth in whisky and bile. Each wave brought a stronger geyser, showering more of the forest shrubs farther back.

Amy's arms and legs trembled and the incessant jet continued to flow. It felt as though somebody was squeezing her stomach, like a Scottish piper playing a shrill tune. Finally, the vomit subsided, leaving her feeling physically and emotionally drained. She wiped her mouth and rose unsteadily to her feet.

"Feel better?" Donna asked, leaning against the bonnet.

"You said Cranston," Amy wheezed.

"What?"

"That zombie… You said she must be from Cranston."

"I'm only guessing," Donna said. "Why, do you know her?"

"No, but…" Amy wiped her mouth again, catching a trickle on her chin. "Why would we be near Cranston? Cranston's south. Ben and Kev went up to Bealsdon."

Donna didn't answer, her eyes searching Amy's while she considered a response.

"Oh, is it?" she said. "I've never been good at geography."

"But you know where we're going, right?"

"Oh yeah, we'll be there soon. We need to get back in the car, though. We're a bit exposed out here."

The woods were still, but Amy knew she was right. They were vulnerable, especially since she had left her gun in the car.

"Okay." She got back in the passenger side, another surge of nausea churning as soon as she smelled the pine air freshener. But this time she kept her eyes open as they set off again down the snaking road. It's not that she thought Donna was lost; she seemed to know exactly where she was going. Amy's sudden concern was that it wasn't where they had originally set out for.

The passing trees dwindled, replaced by a long field of rapeseed. Beyond it stood a farmhouse. It wasn't one she recognised, but the sense of familiarity was palpable.

What is it? She wondered. Was it the road, or the fields? Or the name Cranston still floating in the air? She hadn't lived there long, but she was sure she'd recognise some landmarks if they *were* getting closer.

Why would we be near Cranston? We're heading to Bealsdon.

Yet, try as she might, the road didn't appear to lead to Bealsdon. Not at all. But that wasn't the only thing bothering her.

'Did you know her?' Why would she think that?

It seemed like a bizarre question for Donna to ask. Out of every zombie they had encountered, why would she ask now? Why that specific one? There was nothing notable about the dead woman. No distinguishing features, or identifiable traits—aside, of course, from Donna's theory that she came from Cranston.

But I never told her I lived there.

She side-eyed Donna, who still wore a subtle smile, exuding a happiness Amy had not witnessed at all in the few days of knowing her. For someone who was supposedly depressed, she was coming across awfully chipper.

"Something wrong?" Donna asked.

"No."

But there *was* something wrong. So many variables were not adding up, and the more she thought about it, the stronger the feeling of dread.

24

"We're gonna have to ditch the bike," Frank said, as the mutilated man rushed toward them.

Lisa tried the start switch again, but Frank had already jumped off. He levelled the shotgun at the zombie, waiting. When it was within range, he fired. The reverberating boom joined a roar from the motorbike as it burst to life.

"Yes!" Lisa shouted, "Get on!"

Frank didn't need to question the urgency in her voice. He knew the blast would attract more zombies, and the shrieks from the front of the church corroborated that fact. He swung his leg over the bike, wincing in pain, as the zombies sprinted into view.

"Hold on!"

The words came after Lisa took off, and it was all Frank could do not to fall off the back. He swung his arm around her chest, the shotgun swinging precariously by its strap in his other hand. He expected Lisa to give the zombies a wide berth as they made a beeline for the bike, but she turned slightly, narrowly avoiding the first corpse that leapt toward them.

"Lise!"

Despite being so close, he knew she couldn't hear him over the roar of the engine and the zombies as the bike cut past. Some tried to lunge for them, others turned and pursued. They had passed the majority when Frank felt a jerk on the shotgun. The sudden jolt was almost enough to knock him off the bike. He didn't see the zombie grabbing it. All he could do was release the strap, surrendering the weapon to the undead horde.

They made their way around the church, dodging the few remaining zombies, with the roaring group behind them. The sun had started to fade, leaving the brightest light coming from the single headlamp on the bike. The forest at the foot of the hill grew dark, the space beyond the first couple of trees nothing more than an eerie void.

"Shit."

Lisa heaved the bike to the side to dodge a lumbering figure. Frank pulled his leg in, his knee inches from the ground. The bike righted, and they raced to the end, turning onto the other side of the church.

"Fuck. That was close."

Lisa didn't reply. They rode back to the front, where the zombies rejoined the pursuit.

"There, that should be all of them. Now we need to lead them away." She eased off the throttle, slowing enough to maintain the zombie's interest.

"Great."

"Enjoying yourself?" she called back.

"Immensely."

"Thought as much. Although, I'd rather you not cop a feel while we're facing peril."

Frank realised he was firmly gripping Lisa's left breast. But rather than take his hand away, he squeezed harder.

"Prick," she hissed through clenched teeth.

Some of the zombies were emerging from the back of the church, continuing their pursuit. But others were closer, deducing that it would be quicker to approach from the front of the building, rather than continue the cat-and-mouse chase around it.

Frank's fear set in again. *They're getting smarter. What if they realise what we're doing? What if they don't follow?* He decided not to voice his concerns to Lisa as she accelerated once more. The sooner they were away from the church, the better. His tongue felt dry, his stomach empty. Eden was calling him, and he couldn't wait to answer.

He draped his left arm over her, freeing up his right so he could apply pressure to the wound, which pulsed fire up and down his side. It felt like it was radiating into his ribs, spreading through the bone until it diminished into a dull ache deep inside. He was relieved to feel the soft, dry fabric beneath his palm. Whoever had bandaged him had done a pretty good job.

Should be grateful Gus didn't have a shotgun.

The thoughts were of little comfort, inciting ire rather than relief. He hoped Gus had died a long, agonising death, with Henderson's corpse for company. But then, he'd survived a similar wound, so perhaps Gus had, too?

THE MUTATION

If I see him again, it won't be a handgun I shoot him with.

But that's all they had left. The rifle had vanished, and the shotgun was in the possession of the zombies, who didn't know their arses from their elbows, let alone how to use a gun. Or did they? If their development was anything to go by, was it really so implausible that they might learn how to use it?

The shotgun was empty. They don't have bullets.

That idea did offer some comfort, if only a temporary reprieve. The jolt and judder of the motorbike was still enough to fray his anxiety. He gripped Lisa harder as the bike rolled over the uneven country road. How bikers survived on the narrow, pothole-laden death-traps was beyond him. Behind them, the zombies were still pursuing, but the encroaching darkness shrouded how many there were.

"I'd say we're far enough from the church now!" Frank called. "How about you pick up speed and get us home?"

"Gladly, if I knew where home was."

It dawned on Frank that he didn't know where the Eden hotel was, either. They drove into a shroud of shadow, the last remnants of light eclipsed by the tall, imposing trees of the forest trail. The headlight's beam cut through the darkness, but the woodland on either side remained concealed. Frank felt trepidation rear up in his chest.

All it takes is for one of them to jump out from behind those trees, and we're dead.

The rumble of the bike and the zig-zagging headlight conjured tricks and illusions. Everywhere Frank looked, the shadows seemed to encroach, darting towards the bike, only to withdraw when the light skimmed across them. Tree limbs reached out, wooden fingers grasping, echoes conversing. The forest was alive with phantom movement and reverberating sound.

"Get us back on the main road," Frank said, his words coming out harsher than he'd intended.

"What do you think I'm doing? Looking for a picnic spot?"

A crossroads loomed ahead, offering three different paths, each as bleak as the other. The bike slowed to a crawl as Lisa appraised the options.

"Left, right, or straight ahead?"

The right turn went deeper into the forest. The number of trees increased, and the road devolved into more of a dirt track. The left was a mystery, the road only stretching so far before dipping down a slight incline.

"Keep going straight," Frank said. "The road's wider."

"Peculiar logic, given we're on two wheels," Lisa said, with a laugh. "But okay."

Frank held on as the bike sped up again. "If it's a wider road, it's more likely to lead out of here."

"Let's hope so."

"How much fuel have we got?"

"Full tank."

That was one positive, at least. The last thing they needed was to break down again, especially at dusk. The surrounding trees dwindled, allowing patches of light onto the road. The shadows were clearing. But Frank knew, with darkness at their back, it wouldn't be long until they returned. And with no guarantee they were even travelling in the right direction, their problems were far from over. What they needed was a map, or a signpost; anything to help guide them. But the only map Frank had seen was on—

"Do you still have that leaflet?"

"What?" Lisa called over her shoulder.

"The hotel leaflet. Do you still have it? It had a map on the back."

"No. I haven't seen it since we went back to the army base."

"You left it?"

"I dunno. Maybe."

Back to square one. Yet, he felt a pang of relief when the road emerged from the forest. The customary hills and fields surrounded them once more, showing no sign of movement as far as the diminishing light allowed.

"Is that a sign?" Lisa asked.

In the gloom, it looked like a rigid figure. A sentinel with its arms outstretched, pointing toward their two available routes. As they pulled up to a stop, the rustic sign became clearer.

"Bealsdon's left," Lisa said. "Which means the hotel is probably right."

Frank didn't answer. He stared at the wheat fields beside them, tilting his head, trying to pick up the sound which had drifted by only a moment ago. It was a clicking noise. Wet and audible, like somebody clicking their tongue. There was no movement within the crops, but he was sure he'd heard it.

The chance to hear any further sounds dissipated when Lisa revved the engine and turned at the junction. Frank looked back, expecting something, or someone, to dart out of the field after them. But all he saw were the same immobile crops, eaten up by the darkness as they faded in the distance.

The bike continued on, splitting the silent countryside with its shrill engine, announcing their presence to anything within half a mile. For all they knew, they were attracting any number of undead creatures, leading them straight to the hotel. And with only three bullets left, defending it would prove an impossible task. Little did Frank know, the Eden hotel was already entertaining visitors. Three, to be precise. All wearing black. All armed. All searching for Kara.

***

Kara lay beneath the bed in room 17, listening for any sounds in the rest of the hotel. She knew they were inside. They had to be. She had left the front doors unlocked, expecting Frank and Lisa to return within an hour or so of leaving. After several hours had passed, she had grown concerned. Not so much for their fate, more for herself, and how she could defend the hotel on her own, armed with only an empty handgun and a prayer.

As darkness beckoned, the prospect of venturing down to the ground floor became harder and harder to comprehend. She could imagine stepping through the gloom, toward the heavy glass doors of the foyer, turning the lock, only for a zombie to smash through anyway. *No.* The foyer doors were the least of her worries. If a zombie wanted to get inside, they would smash their way in.

But now she regretted her decision. If the people who had arrived in the dark estate car had faced a locked door, perhaps they would've left.

Yeah, right, she thought. Two of them held metal bars of some description, and the tallest one held a rifle. They wanted to get inside, and they damn sure wouldn't let a locked door stop them. She had observed their approach from her vantage point on the rooftop. The sun had set, leaving a navy sky in its wake. She had watched it grow darker, like ink slowly spreading over dark blue parchment. Then, headlights—tiny white pinpricks—growing larger as the car came closer.

Kara had assumed it was Frank and Lisa. Then she realised how low the headlights were. They didn't belong to the prison van they had left in. The first pang of fear seized her, but she didn't run. She stared curiously as the car trundled along the track, through the opening in the construction fence, and rolled to a stop outside. Three doors opened. Three people stepped out.

Kara dashed across the roof, back inside the hotel, and down to her designated room. She wasn't entirely sure why. All the rooms had the same layout, aside from a few of the luxury suites on the top floor. But something about the familiarity of her own personal space seemed comforting.

I'd better make the most of it before they take me away.

She thought back to the black-clad men who had smashed their way into the house. So little time had passed, yet it already felt like an age. They had taken Leanne and Sam by force and they—

Kara felt a tear run down the side of her face. They had murdered Dan—the only one who'd put up a fight. Would the same fate befall her if she tried to fight back? She released her grip on the handgun.

Fight back with what? An empty gun?

At that moment, she hated Frank and Lisa more than ever. It was their fault she was defenceless. They had left, taking every means of protection she'd had. An empty gun would be useless against people swinging metal poles, not to mention the guy with the rifle.

Maybe that's empty, too. The thought was shot down as soon as it surfaced. The gunmen in the house had bullets. And they weren't reluctant to use them. Even gunning down their own.

What was his name? Tito? Timo? Whoever he was, he seemed to be in charge. Perhaps it was him leading the assault on the hotel. He was the one who had ordered Leanne and Sam to be taken away. *Perhaps he'll let me live?*

But then she remembered Abigail. So sweet, so innocent, brutally murdered at the hands of cold-blooded killers. She had succumbed to the depths of human depravity. There were no laws. No morals. There were only men living out their darkest desires in a dystopian hell. She wasn't going to be another victim. She would sooner die than grant them any sort of sick gratification. And if she was going to die, she'd take as many of the bastards along with her as she could.

Kara grabbed the handgun and shuffled out from under the bed. Her room was dark, but she could still make out the assortment of furniture—her unkempt bed, the desk and chair, the wall-mounted TV, and a tall standard lamp. She tucked the handgun into her waistband and grabbed the lamp. The chrome bar felt cool and solid beneath her touch as she eased off the lampshade. She eyed the two-pronged, energy-saving bulb, trying to think of the most effective weapon.

A distant clang outside caused her to tense. It seemed to have come from the ground floor, but she knew it wouldn't be long until they ascended the stairs, searching the rest of the rooms. If they were to split up, she would stand a better chance of survival. Her only hope was to dispatch the gunman first.

She draped the lamp over her bed, scrambling for her pillow, which she then placed on top of the bulb. With both fists clenched, she pressed down hard until a soft pop emanated from beneath the fabric. She picked the lamp back up, now a makeshift spear with the jagged edges of the broken bulb. She was about to remove the circular base of the lamp when she heard another noise.

This one was close. Somebody had reached her floor.

Kara held her breath, retreating to the wall behind the door. The plush carpet in the hallway disguised the intruder's steps. All she could hear was the relentless hammering in her eardrums. Would they check every room? Or see which doors were unlocked?

The silence in the corridor began to feel overwhelming. Had the intruder walked away from her room, or were they standing outside the door? The peephole would provide an insight, but the prospect of moving was a no-go; she would give away her position. A second passed. Then another. With no further sound from the corridor. Each second brought with it a mounting frustration, brimming over the edge of her sanity. She couldn't take it any longer. She had to find out.

Readjusting the spear in her hand, she shuffled into place behind the door, eyes fixed on the handle, waiting for it to move. When she was in line with the peephole, she peered through.

The corridor beyond was dim, the tiny window offering nothing more than a distorted spectrum of dark shades. She guessed the black strip at the bottom was the carpet, the rectangle in the centre was the door opposite hers, and the creeping shape moving in from the right was the intruder. The figure moved slowly, finding balance with each step before taking another. Eventually, it stopped in line with the two doors.

This was it. Show time. Whichever door the intruder chose, Kara would be ready. She held the spear in both hands, reaffirming its weight as she watched. The figure's head turned between the two doors, agonisingly slow.

Eventually, it chose the door opposite hers.

Kara released her breath in a slow, steady stream. She watched through the peephole as the door opened, revealing nothing more than a dark void. The intruder remained fixed to the spot, peering into the unoccupied room. Now was her chance.

Kara threw open the door and charged into the corridor, brandishing the lamp pole, the jagged edge slicing through the air. The figure whirled around, but didn't have time to respond as Kara lunged forward.

The spear hit its mark, slicing through flesh and artery, triggering a strangled grunt. The astounded eyes were those of a woman. She opened and closed her mouth, like a fish out of water, soundless words forming on her lips. For an instant, the two women were frozen in time, neither moving nor speaking. No sound at all, aside from the staccato gagging noises coming from the victim.

She dropped her weapon, trembling hands reaching up to the spear. Kara pried it out, bringing with it an arc of blood flowing onto the carpet. She lunged again, impaling another part of the intruder's neck. The gagging sound grew stronger as the woman tried to cough up the blood filling her lungs. She fell to her knees, temporarily kneeling upright, until Kara yanked the spear out of her throat again. The woman fell to the side as the blood gushed out of her body.

Kara retrieved the intruder's weapon, assessing it in the dwindling light of the corridor. It was curved like a crowbar, but the end had a hollow insert. *Maybe a tool, or something off a car?* Kara thought. Whatever it was, it felt solid. She slid the weapon into her waistband, replacing the handgun, which she now held with renewed determination.

One down, two to go.

She didn't know where the other two were, but the odds of her surviving had instantly improved. With the spear and the handgun held aloft, she made for the staircase, tilting her head around the side. There was nobody there, but she heard a rummaging sound coming from the ground floor. With slow, steady progress—mimicking the stealth-like movements of the recently departed woman—Kara descended the stairs.

As soon as the foyer came into view, she froze. The glass doors at the entrance were ajar. They had parked the dark estate car beyond, its engine still running, its headlights on full beam, illuminating the entire reception area. It was a peculiar tactic. Anyone within view of the hotel could see inside, as if it were a giant fish bowl. If any zombies were in the area, they'd be easy pickings. But it also meant she could see the intruders as well.

Kara glided down the rest of the stairs. At the reception desk, a figure dressed all in black was hunched down and delving through the cupboards. His head, encased in a dark balaclava, darted back and forth, frantically searching through the contents. He had placed his weapon—a long, rusted wrench—on top of the counter. He was unarmed.

Gotcha.

But where was the third one? The man with the gun—he was the one she needed to kill. A quick sweep of the rest of the floor told her he wasn't there. A thousand approaches suggestively crossed her mind. She could kill the unarmed man in the same way as she had the woman. Or she could strike him over the head while he was hunched over. She didn't know how much force it would take, but she was sure she could muster it. Hell, she could kill him with his own weapon—a divine form of justice, especially if he was involved in the abduction of Leanne and Sam.

The man closed the cupboard and shuffled along to the next. She was running out of time. With a deep, calming breath, Kara cleared the rest of the stairs, and silently advanced toward the reception desk. The man remained hunched over, oblivious to her presence, and was now further away from the wrench. Kara raised her spear, hesitant only to find the best target. The way the man was crouched, she couldn't get a clear shot of his neck.

Her deliberation would prove to be her undoing.

Out of the corner of her eye, she detected movement. The gunman entered, the rifle aimed directly at her. In a split second, she vaulted the counter. He fired, and the stooped figure flinched before she was on top of him. She jammed the handgun against the back of his head and dragged the whimpering man to his feet.

"Put it down!" she bellowed. The gunman remained still, his rifle trained, moving ever so slightly as he tried to find a clear shot.

"Drop it!" she screamed again, digging the muzzle of her gun into the man's head, prompting him to cry out.

"Please don't kill me!"

The muffled voice beneath the balaclava sounded familiar.

The gunman opposite sneered. "Go ahead, shoot him."

Kara felt her world fall apart around her. She had played her hand, and now there were no aces left up her sleeve.

Shit.

25

"Look at the state of this place." Kev stepped over an upturned metal rack, its contents strewn over the pharmacy floor. Ben walked around it, glass and scattered pills crunching beneath his shoes.

"I wonder why they left all this," he muttered, kicking aside some of the stray boxes. "I thought it would've been cleared out by now."

"There's nobody left *to* clear it out." Kev bent down and picked up a pack of children's vitamins. "Zombies don't have any use for these."

He pocketed the box and made for the fridge. Most of the shelves were empty, but there were still some soft drinks left. He grabbed a bottle of Dr Pepper and began to chug.

Shutters secured two sections of the counter, but only partially covered a third. Someone, or something, had stopped it going all the way. Ben clutched the handgun as he leaned through the gap, peering over the other side of the counter. There was nobody there, dead or otherwise.

But what he did find was an array of pre-bagged medication—prescriptions waiting to be picked up, the intended recipients probably long-dead.

"Jackpot."

Kev let out a bellowing burp, hurling the empty bottle as he approached the counter.

"What've ya found?"

Ben moved aside, allowing Kev to lean over the counter.

"Huh, I guess we got lucky after all."

He heaved the shutters higher for his bulk to fit through.

"You look for the antibiotics," said Kev. "I'm gonna check the back."

"Do you want me to come with you?"

"Nah, we need to be quick. Those zombies were a fair distance away, but they could be here in no time if they wanted to be. Let's not hang around."

With that, Kev disappeared into the back room. Ben busied himself tearing open the bags of medication, muttering under his breath.

"Steroid cream, inhaler, co-codamol." He pocketed the last box, but some of the others were not as clear. He started reading the longer names, struggling to pronounce them: "Cip—ramil, gly—ceryl trinitrate, flu—clox—acillin, amitriptyline…"

Wait. Amy said anything ending in 'illin', or 'ycin'.

He picked up another box of flucloxacillin and began forming a pile of medication for them to take.

Five boxes later, he realised he was still alone behind the counter.

"Kev?"

There was no response.

He left the boxes behind, brandishing his handgun as he cautiously approached the back room. He eased the door open, peering into the dimly-lit area lounge. A coffee table stood in the middle of the room, two leather couches flush against either wall, and a vending machine perched beside the doorframe. The room was windowless; the fleeting light came from the main store and through small rectangles of frosted glass in the ceiling. Yet, despite the minimal light, he could see Kev wasn't there. A solid metal door at the back of the room appeared to lead outside, whilst a pine door to his left seemed to lead into a cloakroom, or a small bathroom.

Ben took another step into the lounge, Kev's name on the tip of his tongue. But before he could call out again, the pine door swung open. Kev recoiled, his hand darting for his rifle until he realised it was Ben.

"Shit, what you doing sneaking about? I almost blew your head off!" Kev allowed the rifle to swing by its strap as he closed the door behind him.

"I'm checking you're alive. What were you doing in there?"

"Tactical piss." Kev chuckled. "You don't wanna be caught short, right?"

"Right." *So much for being quick…* "Is there anything in here?"

"Nah, locked doors, no key," Kev replied, ushering Ben back into the main store. "Did you find anything?"

"Yeah, there's boxes of flucloxy-something here. I think this is what we need." Ben reached down for the next bag. "Naproxen's a painkiller, right?"

"Sure is."

Ben held the bag up for Kev, but found him staring intensely at the street beyond.

"What's up?"

Kev shook his head, flashing his signature grin. Whether it was an attempt at reassurance, or just part of his usual cheerful demeanour, Ben couldn't tell. He watched Kev heave himself back over the counter. This time, his gaze flitted back and forth across the shutters.

"You sure you're okay?" Ben asked.

"Yeah. We need to get moving."

"What about all this?" Ben laughed, motioning to the boxes at his feet. "I can't carry all this on my own. I've only got one hand, remember?"

"You can't get the staff these days," Kev said, rolling his eyes. "Go on then, pass it all over."

Ben passed the bags to Kev, clutching the tops with the thumb and forefinger of his injured hand. Kev grabbed each one and placed it at his feet, waiting patiently—if not a little disinterestedly—for the next.

The change in his temperament had become clear as day. Something was bothering him. Perhaps something he didn't want Ben to concern himself with? Or maybe a recollection or something from the past? Whatever it was, it didn't feel like an appropriate time to question him. He was right: they needed to get moving.

Ben passed another prescription across the counter, only this time, Kev didn't grab the bag. He closed his hand around Ben's, his fingers digging into the stumps. Ben groaned, ready to admonish Kev for his clumsiness, and tried to pull his hand back. But Kev didn't let go.

Ben let out a subdued cry as Kev dug his fingers deeper into the bandage. He pulled him closer until he was leaning over the counter.

"Kev—What're you—?"

A fist slammed into Ben's nose, the impact throwing him back into the shelves behind him. The remaining boxes rained down as he fell into a heap. He heard the rattle of the metal shutters, but the source of the noise didn't register. His vision blurred through a stream of tears. His nose throbbed, pumping blood down his face at the same rate as it was flowing from the stumps beneath the bandage, which had since turned a glistening shade of crimson.

"I'm sorry, mate. I really am."

Ben managed to look up from his twisted position on the ground. Kev had pulled the shutters all the way down, and stood peering through them like a guard watching a convict.

"You—fuck."

"I had no choice. We need Amy, and—well, this is the only way."

Amy?

Mention of her name spurred Ben into action. He staggered to his feet, handgun clenched in his fist. He propped the gun on his injured hand as Kev had shown him, only this time, pointing at his mentor.

"Need her? For what?"

"Put the gun down," Kev said. "It didn't have to be this way. I could've killed you. But I'm giving you a chance."

Ben closed his finger over the trigger.

"Kev, open these shutters, or I swear I'll shoot you."

"I'm a good guy, I promise. I didn't want any of this. It's just—sometimes good guys don't always get a good deal."

"Open the shutters, now!"

"I'd keep your voice down if I were you. I'm giving you *life*, Ben. Don't throw it away by inviting zombies in here."

"Giving me life?"

"I'm going to report back and say you're dead. I'd rather that not be the case, though. Please, stay alive. And please don't come after her."

"Last chance!" Ben stepped closer until the gun was only inches from the metal cage and less than a metre from Kev's face.

"Goodbye," Kev said, stooping down to collect some boxes. When he rose to his feet, Ben pulled the trigger.

Click.

He pulled the trigger again. And again. Yet no bullets left the chamber.

"I'm sorry," Kev said. He strode out of the pharmacy, leaving Ben alone with his empty gun, his swollen nose, and his tortured psyche lashing him with feelings of guilt and betrayal.

***

With growing alarm, Amy stared out of the window. Nothing looked familiar. Not the landscape, the stone walls bordering the fields, or the zig-zagging road. There had been no signs for miles, intensifying her sense of dread. The evidence that was stacking up did little to help, either.

Evidence of what? She knows I'm from Cranston? Big deal.

But she knew there was more to it than that. More conversations resurfaced. More unsettling factors.

Donna had suggested they go to Sunnymoor for antibiotics. *"You'd know where they're stored, so we wouldn't have to be there long."* It was true. When Amy was being shown around the hospital as part of her induction, she had spent a good portion of time in the pharmacy. *But how would Donna know that?*

Donna's smile had wavered. She chewed her bottom lip, eyes darting left and right as she and Amy continued down a seemingly endless road.

Maybe she didn't? Maybe she assumed I'd know because I'm a nurse. Hospitals don't exactly have the same layouts, but perhaps she didn't realise.

But try as she might, Amy still wasn't convinced. She hadn't even told them she was a nurse, as far as she could recall. With her handling of Ben's injuries, they might've guessed, but she had never openly discussed it. Nor had she put much thought into it—until now.

"So where else have you and Kev been?" Amy tried to keep the suspicion out of her voice.

"Ugh, where haven't we been?"

"Cranston?"

Donna nodded. "Yeah, that's where we went first. The whole town was *filled* with black smoke. There was a massive fire in the centre and it was still spreading after we left. I'd be surprised if there's anything still standing."

Fire? There wasn't any smoke when me and Ben were there.

"Was it that bad?" Amy asked.

"Oh god, yeah. Black as night. You couldn't see anything, even with the headlights on. I'm surprised we can't see the smoke from here—or anywhere else, for that matter."

Amy frowned. "And that's the *first* place you went?"

"Yep."

"When the virus first started to spread?"

Donna glanced at her. It was a fleeting glance, but enough for Amy to register the alarm in her eyes.

"Well... we survived at home for the first few days. But it kept getting worse. Kev decided to get guns from the armoury—we only live a five-minute drive from it. He got back, but told us it wasn't safe to stay."

"So you went to Cranston?"

"No... we—we were looking for somewhere more isolated. Somewhere easier to defend."

"And did you find it?"

Donna didn't answer. All signs of joviality had passed; her lips formed a thin line.

Is that how Riley died? With her sudden change of demeanour, Amy could only assume Donna was holding back, or reminiscing about the loss of her son. *Or both.*

But she needed to know. With her heightened suspicions, she craved an answer. A resolution. Anything to satiate the stony trepidation that had formed in her gut, displacing—or exacerbating—the nauseating churning.

"Can I ask you something?"

Donna attempted a half-hearted smile. "Sure."

"How did Riley die?"

Amy studied her face, waiting for the façade to fall, unsure of what was hidden behind. Would it be sorrow? A wave of uncontrollable tears that would put them at risk of crashing the car? Or would anger be the dominant emotion? A spewed torrent of vitriol and abuse at her nosy, intrusive passenger? She had expected one or the other, but what she saw was a range of expressions flashing across Donna's face like the changing reel of a stereoscope: shock, grief, anger, then concern.

"I—uh. Can we—can we talk about something else?"

Amy continued to appraise her, searching for answers in her eyes.

"He's somewhere else." "He was taken from us." Not once had she or Kev said he'd died.

"He *is* dead, isn't he?"

Donna didn't need to say anything; her face said it all. She could spin any yarn, paint any picture, tell any story, but there was no escaping the superstitions of motherhood. She couldn't tempt fate by lying and saying he was. All she could do was smile wanly.

Amy raised a hand to her temple, trying to process her evolving theory. *They lied about their son. But why? And where* is *he? And,* she thought, glancing around, *where the hell are we?*

The countryside suddenly looked more industrial, something which certainly didn't belong to the Bealsdon region. Derelict factories and obsolete refineries loomed ahead, where the narrow road ran straight into an industrial estate. A huge wire fence stretched as far as the eye could see, wrapping the disused buildings in a protective metal barrier. Twin makeshift watchtowers flanked the road, and Amy was sure she could see people standing at the top. A large metal-plated sign read: Longhill Steelworks.

"I'm sorry."

Donna's words felt like an icy fist clenched around Amy's heart. Her blood ran cold, and she could feel the heat drain from her face. They passed two vehicles, both falling into formation, trailing them as they neared the industrial estate.

"Sorry for what?" the words trembled from Amy's throat, dry and coarse. Her rifle was on the back seat, but she wouldn't be able to reach it without drawing Donna's attention. And even then, they were being followed by a pair of vehicles carrying an unknown number of people, wielding any number of weapons. Then she noticed the handgun. Donna held it against her thigh, pointed straight at Amy.

They slowed to a halt at the barrier leading into the industrial estate. The cars shadowing them stopped, expelling their occupants quickly. Most wore black, almost uniformly aside from a few minor discrepancies. One of them approached the driver's side of their police cruiser while the others stood nearby. Some carried shotguns, others held melee weapons.

"Fucking hell, Kev. When did you get so hot?"

"Let us in."

The man looked past Donna. "This her?"

Donna nodded.

Amy tried to plan her escape. Even if she could grab the rifle, there were too many people to take on alone, with goodness knows how many more inside. Beyond the chain-link barrier, she could see people milling back and forth, striding with purpose. Men, women, and children, all occupied with various tasks.

"Where's Kev?" asked the man at the window.

"He'll be here soon."

Another knot twisted in her already-contorted stomach. *Ben!*

"He's gonna be in bother, killed two of our lads this morning. George only just escaped."

Donna sought to hide the tremor in her voice. "Can you let us in? Death's waiting."

Amy had heard enough. If she was going to die, she'd take as many of them with her as possible. She lunged, grabbing the gun with one hand, the other clamping around Donna's throat. But the man at the window was quick. Before Amy could get hold of the gun, he leaned in, grabbed her by the hair, and punched her in the face.

Amy reeled back, balancing against the passenger door before she felt it give way. A man on the other side of the car swung the door wide, seizing her by the arms after she hit the floor.

"No!" Donna cried. "Leave her!"

Amy thought she could feel herself being dragged to her feet, but with the world still spinning, it was hard to tell. Her vision blurred, and the surrounding sounds seemed to muffle. Then she heard the unmistakable click of a handgun.

"I said leave her."

Donna aimed the gun at Amy's captor.

"Fucking hell, where'd you get a set of balls from?" the man sneered. "Fair enough."

He shoved Amy into the passenger seat.

"You got any more guns?" he asked.

"There's a rifle in the back."

Amy placed a trembling hand on her forehead. There was no blood, but she could already feel a lump starting to form. The man retrieved the rifle out of the back—her last means of escape. Gone.

The metal gates slowly started to open.

Once there was enough room to pass, Donna started the engine and rolled through into the steelworks.

"I'm sorry," Donna said. "I didn't want you to get hurt. I didn't want any of this."

Amy didn't reply. Her seething gaze skimmed over the workers going about their different tasks. There were people ploughing the ground, others fashioning piping and drainage. Even the children were helping, carrying boxes and tools back and forth.

"You'll be safe here, I promise."

Donna's words meant nothing to her. Her betrayal had tarnished any assurances she could possibly have made.

"It's a real community. Everyone helps each other, and nobody's left to fend for themselves." The false optimism in her voice was almost transparent.

"We've got a community. There's just over seventy of us, with more survivors joining every day. We've got a ready supply of food, water, and electricity."

More pieces of the puzzle. More hazy confusion.

"I didn't want to do it." A sob racked Donna's body, tears rolling down her cheeks. Real tears. Or at least they looked real enough. Amy wasn't sure what to believe anymore. She turned away, dismissing the woman's actions like everything else, until—

"He took Riley."

Amy's gaze snapped back to Donna.

"He said he'd kill him if we didn't find you."

"Who?"

Donna dabbed her eyes as they pulled alongside a factory. The men and women stopped what they were doing and stared at the newcomers.

"We had to do it. We had no choice."

"Who told you to find me?!"

The factory doors opened, but before he'd even stepped into view, Amy knew who he was. The only person left who might seek her audience. The only person deranged enough to hold a child to ransom. She locked eyes with the man, not even hearing Donna's answer.

"Your brother."

26

Martin Scrivener stared into the cold, eager eyes of his undead patient. Zielinski leered at him, spilling a cocktail of blood and spit over his cracked teeth. He leaned as far forward as his restraints would allow, his head twisting.

"You look like shit," Scrivener said.

The zombie growled back. Whether it was a primal utterance, or an acknowledgement of comprehension, Scrivener could not tell. Their tests had always proved inconclusive when assessing the infected subject's mental capacity. Whilst the majority reacted to normal stimuli—sight, sound, smell—there were others who had shown basic cognitive abilities. Through limited research, he hadn't ascertained the true cause of the anomalies, but an educated guess suggested it was down to the differences in genetic makeup.

The longer he observed Zielinski, the more convinced he was that he fell into the former category. The body was active, but there was no intellectual capacity.

Wasn't much to begin with, Scrivener mused.

The monitors to his side reported an elevated heart rate and irregular brain activity—a familiar indication the virus had taken control of the host.

"Fear not, Mr Zielinski. We'll have you back to normal in no time."

The zombie continued snarling, oblivious to the sarcastic remark. Scrivener's expression soured. His facetious comments were wasted if there was nobody alive to hear them. He glanced down at Armstrong's corpse. It was a shame the man didn't live to see his aspirations realised, but at the same time, he was a moralistic thorn in Scrivener's side. A small pool of blood had formed beneath his arm, originating from the gaping wound, no doubt.

He sure was hungry.

Zielinski's bared teeth still had gooey, off-white flesh dangling between them. Scrivener smiled. He wondered how much more the zombie might eat if given the chance. Would he consume the rest of Armstrong, or had he been dead too long? He knew the undead preferred warm, living flesh, but at what point did it become unappetising? It was an intriguing notion, but he had more important things to consider.

After stepping over the doctor's corpse, Scrivener marched over to the workbench where he had stored the modified T-14 virus. He grabbed the vial, the red liquid sloshing around inside as he held it up to the light. One thing he admired most about genetic engineering was how destructive a single molecule could be. It necessitated—no, *demanded*—respect. After all, he was altering things which were never meant to be altered. Playing God, in a way.

THE MUTATION

Who am I kidding? I am *God.*

With a hypodermic needle, he pierced the vial, decanting the crimson formula into the syringe. T-14: his greatest creation, something he'd known as soon as he'd witnessed the first mutation in his rodent test subjects.

First, they'd lost their fur. It had fallen out sporadically, but the shedding had accelerated when the mice began to tear large tufts from their coat. At first, he mistook their acts as cannibalism, but soon realised the blood was coming from the surface of the skin—skin that began to change. Small platelets formed. The raw hue of the flesh darkened into a blackish-green. Then, those platelets had begun to harden. Before he knew it, the mice didn't have skin anymore; they had scales.

Zielinski growled in excitement as Scrivener came closer.

"My, my. Eager, aren't we? I suspect you're waiting for me to save you."

Zielinski heaved against his bindings.

"I'm guessing you don't want any more of this meat," Scrivener said, nudging Armstrong's body. "Not without all the warm blood running through his veins."

Scrivener's smiled dropped. Once again, his remarks were incomprehensible to his audience. He was alone, and if his antidote didn't work, he would stay that way. Although, weighing up the options of surviving in isolation, or in the company of an uncouth lout, he'd take isolation any day.

The things I have to do to save the world, he thought.

Zielinski's head pressed against the leather strap across his forehead—an additional restraint Scrivener had added during the man's lucid state. He couldn't risk being bitten. Not when he was so close to making a breakthrough. True, the gloves were reinforced, but the rest of the biohazard suit was not. If he accidentally strayed too close to the zombie, it would be Goodnight Vienna. Still, Scrivener was glad the Kevlar fabric didn't extend to the rest of the suit. A film of sweat was already sticking fabric to flesh, and his visor was beginning to cloud.

Soon, he told himself. *Inject T-14. Wait for it to take hold. Administer the antidote. Get the hell out of this suit.*

He leaned forward and twisted the zombie's head to the side, careful to avoid its snapping teeth.

"Come now, Mr Zielinski. Don't put up a fight. This is the quickest way for the virus to reach your brain."

He jabbed the needle into the zombie's neck, watching the red liquid gradually disappear as he lowered the plunger.

"See, it wasn't so bad. In a couple of minutes, it should take effect. Then we wait for it to do its job."

Zielinski thrashed against his restraints, his yearning screech adopting a frenzied pitch.

"Don't use that tone with me," Scrivener chuckled. "I don't have to administer the antidote. I can let you turn into… well, I'm not entirely sure what. Something between a gorilla and an alligator, I suppose. A *gorilligator*, perhaps."

People would've paid for this kind of comedy.

"No. A specimen so perfect has to be credited to its creator. You can be a *Scrivesaurus Rex*! No—no, a *Scrivenator*... Or maybe a *Scriva*."

Zielinski arched his back as far as the restraints would allow. His body shuddered, hands and feet flapping against the bed.

Dejected, Scrivener sighed. "Not that it matters. The antidote will stop any mutation occurring. Unless, of course, I don't administer it in time. Perhaps I should wait? Then bring you back to life with claws and fangs, like the abomination you are."

Zielinski's eyes rolled back in his head, leaving white orbs speckled with blood. He shuddered violently. If past experiments were anything to go by, Scrivener knew T-14 had taken hold. He had a few minutes before the mutations were due to begin.

He gave another sigh as he retrieved the antidote. He had never seen a complete human metamorphosis in the T-14 test subjects. The first—and only—corpse he had tested on, Armstrong had destroyed before the full extent of its potential could be realised.

Pathetic, he thought. *Reported the trial with tales of woe. 'Making monsters of men'. Coward.*

He kicked the doctor's corpse—a gesture intended only to satisfy his burdening frustration. He wasn't expecting Armstrong to seize his leg and sink his teeth into the white biohazard suit.

Scrivener screamed. With a yank of its head, the zombie tore the flesh away. Scrivener stumbled back, reaching for the workbench, for the gurney, for anything to stop him from falling. But his fingers found nothing but air. He slammed against the ground, immediately set upon by Armstrong's reanimated corpse, leering at him with wide, ravenous eyes, pincer-like fingers seizing his arms, nicotine-stained teeth snapping against his visor.

He shoved the zombie aside, rising to his knees, long enough to see Zielinski mutate into a creature befitting Hell itself. Its eyes became eternal black voids with a spherical glaze. A new, irregular structure formed beneath its taut skin. Its hands trembled, gripping the metal runners either side of it, which bent under the exertion.

Armstrong lunged for Scrivener and the pair hurtled across the floor, Scrivener's visor clattering away in the process. He could feel the warm blood running into his shoe, pooling over the sides, smearing across the lab floor as he wrestled with his former colleague. The zombie squirmed on top of him, streams of saliva running down its chin. It saw Scrivener's exposed face and darted forward.

"No!"

Scrivener threw his hand up, blocking the dead man's teeth, which clamped down on the Kevlar glove. He reached out and grabbed the metal leg of a lab stool, swinging it with the remnants of his ebbing strength. The zombie reeled aside, crying out as Scrivener brought the stool down again. The plastic seat snapped, part of it embedded in Armstrong's head. The zombie's protests faded when the stool came down again, crashing against its temple. It stopped moving, but Scrivener wasn't taking any chances.

THE MUTATION

He flipped the stool, exposing the metal prongs which had once held the seat in place, and pushed it into Armstrong's eye socket. The stool lowered steadily until a pop from the eyeball allowed it the rest of the way. Scrivener pressed all his weight over the metal rungs, which eventually reached the back of Armstrong's skull.

Scrivener pushed the corpse away. He grabbed his leg, drenched in blood, and wept. He was dead—or as good as. It was only a matter of time before the virus consumed him, providing he didn't bleed to death first. His legacy would die with him. Nobody would ever know of his greatness, or his efforts to save the world.

Fuck them, he thought. A world without him wasn't worth saving, anyway. His attention drifted over to the test subject. The rapid onset of mutation was astounding. A thin smile stretched across his face. At least he would live to see a full transformation.

He grabbed the stool again and hoisted himself up to his knees. His leg burned with the pain, spewing more blood onto the floor, but he focused on the spectacle before him.

The skin on the restrained man's arms had adopted a peculiar sheen, wet and glistening, until it tore right before his eyes. A squelching sound mingled with the zombie's groans as the flesh parted.

Scrivener felt saliva pool in his mouth. He licked his lips, watching a chunk of meat fall from the creature's arm. It hit the floor with a wet slap, followed by more meaty droplets. The flesh slid away from its body, exposing dark, bloody scales. Amongst the squelching, tearing, and groaning, there came a new sound. A snapping. Cracking, as Zielinski's skeletal structure altered.

Scrivener heaved himself higher, watching the creature's fingers snap back, jolt forward, and extend beyond the capabilities of the flesh and muscle that had been encasing them. Blood spattered the floor, which began to resemble that of an abattoir. Redundant bone, muscle, and fingernails fell next, forced aside by long, sharp talons. He was so fixated on the claws, Scrivener hadn't even noticed the vast disfiguration of Zielinski's face.

Incredible.

The monster's black eyes stretched farther apart, its nose nothing more than a pulpy mass, and its mouth... Scrivener gasped. Long, jagged barbs had replaced every incisor, canine and molar, and sat in a wide, elongated maw.

A tear trickled down Scrivener's cheek. He had created new life. His magnum opus. The ultimate weapon. Suddenly, with the masterpiece before him, death seemed trivial. His demise would not save the world, true. But it would definitely end it; he was God, after all. And without him, the world would be over. He'd make sure of it.

Scrivener tried to clamber forward, but his weakened state allowed only a trembling step before his leg gave way. He crumpled to the foot of the gurney, despair clouding his thoughts. What good was the ultimate weapon restrained to a bed? Then the bindings snapped and the absurdity of his thoughts registered.

The creature rose from its confinement. Nothing could hold it back. Not a leather-strapped bed, not a sealed room, not even the locked-down medical facility.

It would find its way out of the laboratory, like every living being escaping the womb. But first, it would eat. An honour Scrivener openly welcomed.

The dark scales enveloping the monster's hulking frame shimmered. Its razor sharp talons flexed in anticipation, the rows of jagged teeth catching the light as the creature advanced towards him.

Perfection.

Part Two

THE MUTATION

1

Gus Razor leaned back in his chair, one foot up on the desk, his body tilting to the left, where the bullet wound throbbed mercilessly. He maintained his stoic expression, offering no sign of pain to the two prisoners stood before him. Both held shotguns by their side, moving from one foot to the other—the agitated movements of men ready for confrontation. Gus licked his lips, savouring the uncomfortable silence.

"Well?" the older of the two men asked, his hair flopping in his face. His piercing glare flitted between Gus and the anxious doctor sitting in the corner, who kept her head bowed, not daring to look up at the tense exchange.

"Well, what?" Gus said. "You seek an audience with me under the pretext that you have some vital information. Then you come strutting in with your boyfriend, telling me you wanna take over this place."

"It's not just us," the man said. "We've all voted."

"Voted? Fuck off. Those boys couldn't hold a piss-up in a brewery. You're trying to tell me there's a democratic union down there?"

"The majority rules," the other man said.

"Nobody asked you, sweetheart. Put Mop Head's cock back in your mouth and shut the fuck up."

The man snarled and went to raise his gun until his companion held up an arm to stop him.

"Hold on, Riggsy. There's no sense in shooting an unarmed man. Not unless we have to, of course."

Gus sneered. "You think I'm unarmed?"

He retrieved the barbershop razor from his pocket, admiring the mirror sheen as he placed it down on the desk.

"Is that it?" Mop Head scoffed.

"No." Gus reached into his other pocket and produced a long, taped shiv. It resembled an ice-pick, its tip pointed to almost a hypodermic finish. He placed the weapon neatly beside the other.

"You're fucked in the head, Razor. Or do you think your little ankle biter will protect you?"

T-Bird Kennedy glared from his position beside the door, his tiny stature compensated by the bulging muscles stretching his shirt to the limit. Huge trunk-like arms hung by his sides, fists opening and closing as if he were crushing walnuts between his fingers.

"If you think I need protection, *you're* the one fucked in the head. In fact," Gus said, turning to T-Bird, "Terrance, show yourself the door, son."

The man's snarl faded. On command, he strode out of the office, closing the door behind him.

"See, that's why you should never put a good dog down. He's loyal, he's—"

"Last chance, Razor!" Mop Head interrupted, stepping toward the desk. "Get the fuck out or I'll rip you to pieces."

"Oh, don't give me that patter, sweetheart. Rip me to pieces? You can barely rip his arsehole with that tiny cock of yours."

"That's it!" Riggsy shouted. He brought the gun up again, and for a second time, Mop Head brought him back in line.

"Hang on, Riggsy." Mop Head planted a palm on the desk and leaned closer to Gus. "I don't think you understand the situation. Y'see, the boys down there don't think you're fit to lead. Not only that, but you've been—" his gaze drifted to the doctor, "—stashing away the best resources. They want change. So now it's—"

Gus whipped the razor across the man's throat in one quick motion, his eyes bulging as the yawning wound spurted blood all over the office. He whirled around, clasping both hands to his neck, but not before showering Riggsy in a wave of red.

"Fuck!"

Riggsy lifted the rifle, but Gus was too quick. He threw the ice-pick with lightning precision, piercing the convict below his Adam's apple.

"Why don't you boys ever learn?!" Gus bellowed, striding round his desk into the spurting blood. "Never bring a gun to a knife fight. Especially if you're up against Gus *fucking* Razor!"

He swung a boot into Mop Head's abdomen, but it landed unnoticed. His final breath had long since passed. A wet, guttural sound came from the younger man's vicinity, his body flopping around desperately.

Gus turned to Doctor Miller, hiding her tear-stained face behind trembling hands.

"What the fuck are you sitting there for? Get up and help."

A confused frown creased her face. She studied Gus and the blood on his clothes, assuming it all belonged to the men he had killed. But when he clasped his side, she guessed otherwise. She jumped to her feet, rushing over just as the door flew open.

"Everything all right?" T-Bird asked.

"Yep. Peachy, Terrance," Gus muttered, propping himself against the table. "Now go and get Harper and Chomping Charlie."

"What do you want doing with these guys?" T-Bird kicked the nearest bloody corpse.

"They're part of the furniture. Now fuck off."

Gus waited until the man had left before rounding on the woman beside him.

"C'mon, Doc. Sort this shit out. We're bleeding everywhere over here."

Doctor Miller nodded, easing his hand away from the day-old bullet wound.

Gus had released her from the cupboard soon after taking Henderson's top lip as a trophy. She had dressed the injury, assessing it to be a flesh wound, one he should survive providing infection didn't set in. After that, he ensured she remained by his side, declaring to the rest of the inmates that she was under his protection. The vast majority had seemed unperturbed until now.

"We need to get this cleaned up," she told him. "This isn't the best environment for recovery."

"Well, it's the only environment, so we need to make do."

"I don't have the necessary equipment."

"Like?"

"Like sterile water, bandages..."

Gus leaned over the desk and retrieved a bottle of vodka stashed in one of the drawers. He placed it on the table, along with a wad of toilet paper and a roll of duct tape.

"Just pour some of this over it and wrap the cunt up."

The doctor stammered, as if trying to find a way to advise against his methods whilst not coming across as reproachful. In the end, she settled for a slight nod and set to work. Gus didn't make a sound while she dressed the wound. He stared unblinking at the door, waiting for the inevitable knock. It came sooner than he thought.

"Enter."

The door swung open, and Dan Harper walked in. His tentative steps stopped altogether when he saw the bodies in the middle of the room. He opened his mouth to speak, but couldn't find the words to vocalise the mixture of alarm, terror, and anger flashing across his face. He brought a hand up to his shaved head, running his palm over the ginger bristles as he processed the scene.

"Sit down, Harper."

Gus nodded to the blood-spattered seat in front of his desk. The man hesitated, looking from the chair to the bodies and then back to Gus.

"I won't tell you again!"

Harper moved in front of the chair and eased himself down, grimacing as the blood soaked through his tracksuit bottoms.

"Fuck me. It's not like you to be so quiet, Harper. What's the matter? Never seen a bunch of dead guys before?"

Harper shrugged. "Plenty. I just didn't expect to see two in your office."

"Really? What did you expect to happen? These two came in here telling me I'm not fit to lead. At the very least, they'd be losing their kneecaps. But to come in armed…" Gus sucked air through his teeth. "It was never gonna end well, was it?"

"I didn't know anything about it."

"No? They reckon they had support, and there's no bigger gobshite down there than you. You sure you didn't hear anything? Maybe twisted a few ears?"

Harper gasped. "No! Honestly, I didn't say anything."

"Honesty is a fable amongst thieves. And rapists and murderers, for that matter. So forgive me if I question your sincerity."

Gus picked up the barbershop razor and perched on the edge of the desk.

"Here's what's gonna happen. You're gonna go back down there, and you're gonna sing like a canary. Tell them what you've seen here and remind each and every one of them what happens when they fuck with Gus Razor."

The man nodded.

"I mean it, Harper. I want you to belt out those numbers, like Whitney Houston after two lines of Charlie."

A knock at the door halted their conversation.

"Speak of the devil," Gus said. "Come in, Charlie."

Chomping Charlie stepped in, T-Bird at his heel.

"Here he is," Gus said, beaming. "How you doing, son?"

"G-g-g-good," Charlie stammered. He chewed on his cuticles, staring in wonder at the pair of corpses.

"Harper, you have your orders. Put your tongue to use. If not, I'm cutting it out."

He snapped the barbershop razor shut as Harper jumped to his feet. He nodded hurriedly, stepping over the corpses and heading for the corridor.

"How's Henderson going down? Gus asked Charlie once the door had closed. "Any of the boys complained?"

"G-g-g-good. Some of them found h-h-h-hairs in the soup, but…"

Gus shrugged. "It's to be expected. He was a hairy man."

He patted his breast pocket, where the severed lip had started to dry out.

"Any of them cottoned on yet?"

Charlie shook his head.

"Good. Let's keep it that way for as long as we can. They're not daft. They'll click on eventually, but hopefully by then we'll have more supplies."

"W-w-w-we don't have m-m-m-much left," Charlie said. "Only half his arm, and a l-l-l-leg."

"That's why I summoned you." Gus grinned. "I've got more meat for you. Reckon you can knock up more culinary delights with these two?"

Charlie chewed his lip, staring at Mop Head's body. "Smackhead," he said. "No good."

"It doesn't have to be Michelin-star grub. Just keep them fed and quiet."

"Not much meat." Charlie stooped down and lifted Mop Head's limp arm.

"Fuck me, you'd think you were Gordon Ramsey the way you're carrying on. Can you use them or not?"

Charlie nodded. "W-w-w-we'll make it work."

"Good, I'll have Terrance bring them down to you. Oh, and Charlie," he added, as the man turned to leave, "how much *actual* food do we have?"

"N-n-n-not much."

"Great." He rolled his eyes as Charlie left the room, and directed his attention towards T-Bird. "Looks like we're gonna have to mobilise the troops. There's no way I'm eating that shit."

"Where do you want us to target?"

"Drive south. Ransack Sunnymoor, and use your loaf— we need food and water over anything else. Weapons, if you find any. Guns and ammo: definitely. But rations are top of the list. Now repeat it back to me."

"Food and water. Guns and ammo, and maybe weapons. Got it."

"Good. And don't you dare come back without another van. We've only got one, so make sure you bring more wheels back with you."

T-Bird nodded. "Do you want me to move the bodies first?"

"I think that's a good idea, don't you?" Gus whispered. "Go and get the tarp you used to wrap Henderson up. And don't let the boys see you take these pricks to the kitchen. We don't want them clicking on, do we?"

T-Bird agreed and left the room, closing the door quietly.

"You shouldn't do that," Doctor Miller said, keeping her head bowed.

"Do what?"

"Trick them into cannibalism."

Gus shrugged. "They'll have eaten worse at one of those grotty kebab houses."

"But, Charlie. He's—"

"Special?"

"—Not exactly a chef. And he uses every part of the corpse. I read his file before he was admitted here."

Gus shrugged again. "Waste not, want not."

"He eats the brain, Gus! Don't you know the health risks it can cause?"

"Who cares? *We've* been eating normal food. And when those boys get back, we'll have more."

"That's the thing. We might be okay, but if they become ill, or worse, you won't have anybody to do your bidding."

Gus twisted his mouth in contemplation.

"And you should really put first-aid supplies on the list of things you want them to get," she continued. "Your wound needs treating properly."

Gus held a hand to his side. "Don't worry about it. There's a first-aid kit at the army base."

"What army base?"

"The one we're going to once those boys get back."

"Why?"

"Because that's where Frank will be. And that's where he's gonna die."

2

The handgun shuddered in Kara's hand. She tried to convince herself the trembling human shield was causing it, but she knew better. She was terrified. The gunman stood opposite them, his rifle poised ready to kill her the second she stepped outside the protective outline of her captive. A tense, noxious silence enveloped them, broken only by the man's soft whimpers.

"Go on, do it." The gunman laughed.

Kara looked past her human shield. The man before her was also dressed in black, with a balaclava concealing his features. All she could make out were his eyes, which glistened with delight as he relished in her torment.

"I tell you what, I'll give you a chance. Put the gun down, and we'll let you live. Nobody has to die. How about that?"

"I've got a better idea." Kara snarled. "How about you put *your* gun down, run as fast as you can, and maybe *I'll* let *you* live?"

The man sniggered. "Yeah, I don't think so, darling. We've got the upper hand."

"Is that right? You'd have to be a pretty good shot to hit me from there. What's stopping me from shooting you, then your little friend here?"

She jabbed the gun harder against her captive's temple, prompting another whimper.

"I'm wearing body armour for a start. You'd need a headshot. And the second that gun moves away from Sammy's head, he'll be all over you. Won't you, Sam?"

The man didn't reply. His breath hitched, his body continuing to tremble in Kara's grasp.

Sam? That's where she recognised the voice! When he and Leanne had been taken, she thought she'd never see him again. What the hell was he doing with these guys?

"Bullshit." She tried to maintain her composure, but couldn't keep the tremble from her voice. The gunman sneered, interpreting her hesitation as fear.

Does Sam know it's me? she wondered. *Evidently not, given his terror. Or maybe he does? Perhaps his fear is genuine because he thinks I'll do it. Because he intended to kill me?*

Kara pushed the thoughts aside. *No. He can't know it's me.*

"Last chance." The man tapped his rifle.

"You're the ones who broke into the house on Mainsforth Street in Doxley."

Kara felt Sam tense in her grip. *It is him!*

"You killed one of my friends and took the others away."

The gunman shrugged. "We've broke into a *lot* of houses. And there's more than us out there. *Way* more. We're part of a community. One you can join if you put the gun down in the next three seconds."

He repositioned his rifle, adopting a firmer stance as he aimed directly at them.

"Three!"

"Kara, it's me, Sam," her captive whispered.

"I know," she whispered, her face beside his ear.

"Two!"

"Put it down. He'll kill us both."

Kara's hand shook. She eased raggedy breaths out of her mouth, trying—and failing—to maintain her composure. But then she heard something. Below the rumble of the car outside, there was another sound. A similar rumble. One that started to grow louder.

"One!"

"Okay!" she shouted. "Okay, I'll put it down."

She held Sam in front of her and stooped behind him. The gunman watched her, but he was listening to the thundering engine, which sounded louder than ever.

Kara released the gun and got back to her feet.

"You stupid—"

The assailant's words were cut off as he finally gave in to the luring roar of the motorbike outside. Another beam added to the radiance of the car's headlights, before the huge hotel window exploded. The motorbike burst into the foyer, accompanied by the crack of a handgun. The rifleman fired back, but a bullet lodged in his shoulder, sending the shot wide. He cried out before the motorbike slammed into him. The impact displaced the rider and their passenger, who both crashed to the floor, rolling over the smooth tiles until the far wall stopped their trajectory.

Time seemed to stop, as everything in the foyer froze. The two riders lay motionless. The mangled remains of the gunman were still, with only the pop and splutter of the motorbike engine signalling the passage of time. Kara held a hand to her mouth, staring blankly at the carnage, completely forgetting the man standing beside her. Sam appeared equally entranced, his eyes wide beneath the balaclava.

After an eternity had passed, one of the riders moved.

Frank sat up, groaning. He clutched his side with one hand, the other clasping the side of his head, as if he were keeping it from falling off.

"Holy shit." Kara dashed forward, dropping to her knees beside Lisa, who also began to stir.

"That was some fine driving, Lise," Frank muttered. He stretched his legs out, scattering glass particles aside.

"You *ride* a bike, dickhead," Lisa retorted. "Not *drive*."

She held her ribs, shuffling into an upright position.

"Can I do anything?" Kara asked, placing a hand on Lisa's shoulder.

"A *thank you* would be nice," Frank grunted. He dragged himself to his feet, propping himself up against the reception desk. "Where's my gun?"

He saw the discarded handgun in the middle of the floor. Then his roaming gaze fell on Sam.

"Shit!"

He lunged forward, seized the gun off the ground, and aimed it at the startled man.

"No, wait!" Kara cried.

Click.

Frank hurled the empty handgun aside and staggered to his feet.

"That's the gun you left me," Kara snarled. "This one is yours." She stooped down beside the motorbike and retrieved the other handgun. "But don't hurt him. He's my friend."

"Friend?" Frank said.

The man in black pulled off his balaclava.

"Sam." Kara rushed forward and wrapped her arms around him. They hadn't been close prior to the abduction, but after so much loss, the sense of familiarity was almost overwhelming.

"You know this guy?" Frank asked.

"Yeah, he was part of my group. They took him and—oh my god, Leanne!"

"She's fine." Sam sniffed, wiping his eyes and running a hand over his nose. "They took us to an industrial estate and gave us all jobs. It's like a concentration camp! I'm so glad you and Abi escaped. Where—?"

His expectation as he scanned the room brought Kara to tears. She fought to keep them at bay until his sudden recognition sent her over the edge.

"Oh no," Sam whispered. "Kara, I'm—I'm so sorry."

She clung to him again, burying her face against his shoulder. It was a pain she could never imagine getting over, and she probably never would.

Frank went to help Lisa. She clung onto his neck as he hoisted her to her feet.

"You still in one piece?" he asked.

"Pretty much."

"Are there any more of you?" Frank called to Sam.

"There were three of us. He was in charge." Sam motioned to the disjointed body. "And there was a woman who went upstairs."

"Is she—"

"I killed her," Kara said, cutting Frank off. "She's on the first floor."

"You killed her without a gun?"

"Yes," she snarled.

A look of admiration replaced Frank's confusion. "I guess you *can* take care of yourself. And what about your little friend?" He nodded to Sam. "What can you bring to the table?"

"I—uh."

"He's good with electronics—radios and the like," Kara said.

"Bit useless when we haven't got electronics or a radio," Frank muttered. "What did they have you doing at this *concentration camp*?"

"Well… this." Sam gestured around him. "They have teams that go out. Sometimes it's to get supplies, other times it's for fuel. And sometimes… it's to get people."

That's what they were doing when they broke into the house, Kara thought. She had been right to hide. But then… that's what had led to Abigail's death. She blinked her tears aside.

"So Leanne's safe?"

"As safe as she can be, given the circumstances."

"Where is this place?" Frank asked.

"Longhill Steelworks. It's about thirty miles south of here."

"Thirty miles? You're a long way from home."

"It's not my home. We're forced to work there. Anyone who tries to leave gets punished."

"Punished? How?"

Sam shook his head. "You don't wanna know."

"Oh, believe me, I do."

A feral shriek echoed in the distance. It seemed to have come from the rear of the hotel, but the group stared at the smashed, unsecured entryway.

"We don't have time for this," Lisa said. "We need to find a way to barricade the entrance."

"We won't be able to barricade it tonight," Frank replied. "Our best bet would be to secure the upper floors."

"And what if they get in?"

"We wait for them to leave."

"But what if they send another *team* to come looking for him?"

"Will they?" Frank asked.

"More than likely," Sam said. "They've got a guy—an ex-cop, I think—he gets sent out to track people down. And if he's not available, they send out a bigger group."

Frank and Lisa exchanged a look of astonishment. Kara knew exactly what they were thinking. *Kev. But he was with us for days,* she told herself. *It can't be him. Can it?*

The screech came again, closer this time.

"We need to move," Frank said. He limped over to the rifle, which had landed next to the wall after their destructive entrance. "Lise, check the body for bullets." He hurled the weapon to her before rounding on Sam. "And you, do you have any weapons?"

"Only this." Sam reached over the counter and grabbed the wrench.

"You best give it to Kara. She'll manage a lot better than you."

She knew Frank didn't mean it in a literal sense, but she was grateful for the recognition. Yet, the sarcasm seemed to go unnoticed by Sam, who held the wrench out toward her.

"Keep it," she said, retrieving her makeshift spear from the ground. "I've got this."

She caught sight of the metal bar she had taken from the dead woman and felt a flicker of guilt. If Sam had been enlisted against his will, what if the woman had, too? Had she murdered an innocent person? Someone merely following the orders of a tyrannical dictator?

She had a weapon, Kara told herself. *It was her or me. If I hadn't have killed her, she would've smashed my head in.*

But the contradictory thoughts continued to plague her. What if she'd been a wife, a mother, or a sister? What if there was somebody back at the camp waiting for her to come home? Waiting for something that would never happen.

They'll never see her again. I murdered her.

Or had she?

A sudden thud from above caught everyone's attention. They stared at the ceiling. Nobody moved, listening for the sound, which quickly came again. And again.

"I thought you said you killed the other one?" Lisa whispered.

"I did."

The thud came again.

"Only three of us came in the car," Sam said.

Another thud, this time rapid footfalls running back and forth on the floor above.

"Well, it sounds like we've got company."

3

The pharmacy had grown dark, but Ben hadn't noticed. Lost in a pain-induced reverie, he stared blankly at the ground from his seated position against the wall. Kev's betrayal danced through his mind, tormenting him like a crane fly always beyond reach. How had he been so foolish? Taken in by the kindness and warmth of the couple, oblivious to their ulterior motive.

What is *their motive?* He wondered. *"We need Amy." But for what? What could they possibly want with her?* He pondered the possibilities, but came up blank every time. *She's a nurse, so maybe they mean from a medical standpoint?* But why would they need him out of the picture? He rubbed his forehead, as if the probing, circular motions could massage an answer out of him.

Maybe it's sexual? They're swingers and want to engage in a sordid threesome?

He shook his head. The theories became more outlandish the more he considered them. Instead, he pushed aside the 'what' and focused on the 'who'.

THE MUTATION

"I'm going to report back and say you're dead." Report back to who? Who are they working for?

A noise outside hurled Ben back into the pharmacy. He looked around the gloomy space behind the counter, then up to the shutters. He had tried pushing them up, but a padlock was securing each one. All except that which Kev had dragged down. He had slid a toothbrush—of all things—through the latch; a seemingly futile resource to secure the shutters, but one which would give him ample time to leave the scene whilst also allowing Ben to escape. Only, this proved more difficult than expected. The thin, rectangular gaps in the shutters were too small for Ben to slip his fingers through, and the toothbrush was wedged tight. No matter how hard he yanked the shutters—an act which proved cumbersome given his incapacitated hand—the toothbrush wouldn't budge.

The sound came again, but didn't seem to be coming from inside the store. Ben shuffled to his knees, easing himself up until he could see over the counter. The pharmacy was still empty, but there was movement beyond the window. Slow, steady movement from a dark figure. The dwindling light offered no more than an outline, but it was nearing the front door.

Crouching, Ben silently retreated into the room beyond the counter.

He reached out, his hand skimming back and forth as he shuffled further in. He knew there was no way the zombies could be in there with him. The only ways in were via the main pharmacy or the heavy door at the far end of the room. He had tried to open it earlier, but found it locked, with no sign of a key. *I bet Kev took it.*

Despite this, he still felt the caress of groundless fear run up his spine. There was nobody else in there. There couldn't be. But what if—

His fingers brushed against the coffee table and he recoiled, catching the gasp that threatened to escape. He felt along the smooth wooden surface, guiding him in the couch's direction. After a few seconds of crawling on his hands and knees, he reached out and felt the cool leather beneath his fingertips. The couch groaned under his weight as he heaved himself up, his sense of trepidation fading until his arm knocked a magazine off the arm of the chair. What would ordinarily have been an unnoticed slap amidst the din of a working pharmacy now betrayed his presence to the creature outside.

An outburst sounded from the front entrance. Then came footsteps shuffling through the cluttered store. Ben listened to the crunch of boxes and the pop of broken glass. The zombie seemed to be checking every inch of the pharmacy. Its shambling steps grew closer until a gentle rattle came from the shutters.

Ben held his breath, picturing the walking corpse pressed up against the metal barrier, searching the other side for any sign of living flesh. Seconds passed. The shutters clattered again. The zombie's search had not ended. It moved along the counter, knocking bottles and boxes aside in a bid to see more of the obstructed space. Ben remained still. Waiting for it to leave. *Hoping* it would leave. If it got in, he'd be defenceless. The handgun lay discarded near the counter—not that it would be much use without any bullets.

He chastised himself again for taking the gun from Kev without checking the ammo first. He had assumed it would be full. Thinking back, he couldn't work out when Kev had removed the bullets. He had been deceived right from the start. He trawled back through their interactions over the past few days. From the moment they had encountered Kev and Donna at Amy's grandparents' house, they had seemed kind and sincere.

A discontented grunt came from within the store, and he heard the zombie finally move away from the counter. It pushed through the scattered stock, heading back toward the entrance.

Ben dropped his tensed-up shoulders, relaxing into the couch, reminiscing about their first meeting with the couple.

"We mean you no harm. We only want to talk." Ben scoffed, cringing at how loud it sounded in the empty room. The zombie could still be within earshot, but he couldn't help it. *Even their opening line had been a lie. They'd wanted Amy all along. And they had stumbled across the right place.*

Before Ben could even process those recollections, his brain fired more.

"Sometimes we have to do things we don't like. Sometimes you have no choice."

That one felt more ominous, and he could only wonder what fate Amy had in store. He clenched both fists, ignoring the fire from his missing digits. The pain was his penance. He should have been more cautious; should never have left Amy alone, despite it being her idea. *No, it wasn't Amy's. Kev asked her to stay behind. He said Donna was depressed.* They had planned it all along. But so many things didn't add up.

If they wanted Amy, why didn't they kill me when we first met? Why did they storm the prison with us? It didn't make sense, and the more he thought about it, the more perplexing it became.

Another sound stole his thoughts, this one from behind the heavy door at the end of the room. He heard a grunt first, then a less audible scuffle. He stared towards the door, his eyes unable to penetrate the blanket of darkness. The sound continued—a scrape along the wall, then a soft rattle of the metal door, as though somebody was pressed against it, holding themselves up. It reminded Ben of his time working the doors in York, way back in the '90s. He and his friends had often joked about the similarities between the stumbling drunks and Romero's undead. The swaying stance. The shambling walk. The putrid odour: they were all the same, only with different desires. Whilst Romero's zombies sought flesh, Yorkshire's drunks pursued kebabs, drugs, sex, or more alcohol.

They shared the same vacant expressions, emitted the same noises, and—for those lucky enough to score a few lines of blow—made the same gurning faces.

Only this was real life. And these weren't Romero's walking corpses. These zombies were fast. They were determined. And—like the one on the other side of the door—they were inquisitive.

The zombie continued to press against the metal obstruction. It couldn't get in, just as Ben couldn't get out, yet he still took a step back when the handle began to turn.

What the…?

It was trying to open the door.

But how? They didn't have the mental capacity to do that. Did they? They couldn't open the lift doors in the hospital, or the car doors when he and Amy were escaping. They didn't think that way. All they knew was physical force, and a primal urge to satiate their illicit desire.

Yet, the handle continued to rise and fall, the door clattering.

It wasn't a zombie. It couldn't be.

Then who?

Who would be brazen enough to roam the streets at night, yet foolish enough to continue trying the door when faced with resistance? Ben had realised the door was locked as soon as he tried the handle. Admittedly, he had given it an extra yank to be sure, but he understood immediately it wouldn't open. The person on the other side of the door didn't seem to comprehend that.

They continued to pull, the door rattling in its frame.

Maybe they have a key? He hadn't heard one slide into the lock, but what if it had? What if it was a temperamental mechanism, and the door was about to swing open at any moment?

Ben rose from the couch, a mixture of intrigue and terror compelling him towards the door. There was a spyhole at eye-level, showing the street beyond. Earlier, it had shown nothing but a gloomy alleyway, and he doubted he would see anything now in the dark. Yet he continued to step blindly through the room, rounding where he assumed the coffee table was, and approached the door.

Now he could hear deep breathing, and what sounded like a distant grumbling. Footsteps. A bottle rolling across the floor, as if knocked aside by wandering feet. Then a guttural groan, tinged with a high-pitched wheeze.

Zombies.

The door handle stopped moving, but the person on the other side didn't flee, despite the zombies drawing closer. Then, with the echoing footfalls, came another sound.

Clicking. It reminded Ben of the tongue clack a dog owner might use when calling their four-legged companion. It was fast and repetitive, growing louder. Getting closer.

Ben swallowed a gasp when the thing outside the door clicked its tongue in response.

He took a step back, as if the staccato clacks were piercing the door.

They were communicating.

No. They can't be.

The noise continued. A shrill chirp, this time with intermittent growls. They were closer now, gathered around the secure metal door.

Did they know he was inside?

No. How could they?

But then, how could they turn the handle?

So many questions, so few answers.

He remained frozen, staring through the darkness, waiting for something beyond his comprehension.

THE MUTATION

Even after the zombies had moved on, searching for more convenient prey, Ben remained still, trapped in the nightmarish trance.

Everything he thought he knew had been turned on its head. He could no longer rely on the limitations of the primitive zombie brain. They *were* capable of thought and processing, and who knows what else? Were they learning? Building their problem-solving skills like infants? If not confined to primal thinking, what were their limitations? Or, more worrying, *were* there any limitations?

The facts were about as clear as the room he was in. And as he stood, and stared, and waited, he accepted that some questions would always remain unanswered. The confines of the pharmacy could offer him sanctuary from the enigmatic creatures, but that was it. He would find no answers tonight.

Finally, his knees released their hold, and he staggered back to the couch. He needed rest, and the opportunity to process everything. Hoping daylight would renew his cognitive function, and perhaps bring with it the chance to escape, Ben closed his eyes.

Daylight didn't resolve his turmoil. But what the new day *did* bring was a distraction. After what felt like only a couple of minutes, his eyes snapped open and he glanced around the staff area, listening to the clatter of boxes in the pharmacy. Footsteps. At least three or four people. Then he heard a voice.

4

Gus sat behind his desk while T-Bird rolled the first corpse in the tarpaulin. He sneered at the man's efforts. Whilst it had been years since Gus had disposed of a body, he remembered his routine as if it were yesterday. The tarp had always been an anti-forensic measure, if anything. And never used to transport a whole corpse.

He would start by laying the body on the sheet and removing the head. Then, with chains around the ankles— or better yet, meat hooks behind the Achilles tendon—he would hoist the corpse high, suspending it from a beam or other structural support. A container would catch the blood spilling from the neck stump, and he would leave the body elevated for several hours, allowing gravity to do its thing.

Next, he would dismember. He'd start his ritualistic process by removing the hands at the wrist, the forearms at the elbow, and the upper arms at the shoulder. The legs would follow—in the same meticulous manner—until all he had left was an assortment of parts.

Disposal would depend on timing, location, and whether or not he wanted to send a message. Fire was the usual failsafe, but was nowhere near as satisfying as leaving a head at the door of the deceased's loved one, or genitals nailed to a post in rival territory. Good times. Times he missed now more than ever, watching T-Bird's haphazard attempt at rolling up the corpse.

"What did you get banged up for, Terrance?"

T-Bird looked up from his perch beside the human burrito. "What?"

"You know I don't repeat myself."

"Drugs, robbery, and attempted murder."

"Attempted? Didn't have the balls to finish the job?"

T-Bird's dumbfounded expression prompted Gus further.

"If you're gonna work for me, you need to be mustard. Understand?"

"Erm… No, not really."

Gus grimaced. "What is it about the queen's fucking English you boys don't get? I don't need a maid cleaning up after me. I need a soldier making the mess *for* me. You need to be ruthless, ready to kill without notice, not just getting the mop and bucket out when you're told."

Confusion contorted T-Bird's face. "So… do you want me to leave them?"

"Do you think I'm gonna clean this shit up?"

"No."

"You're damn fucking right I'm not. Carry on, son."

Shaking his head, T-Bird pulled the second sheet over the next body. Gus leaned back and ran a hand through his hair—an action that triggered an intense agony in his side. He stifled a wince, careful not to show vulnerability to his newly-appointed henchman. T-Bird remained focused on his task, though, quickly working to wrap Riggsy's corpse.

But as seconds passed, his urgency devolved into agitation. The dead man's arms refused to stay within the plastic sheet, displaying an insolence not usually reserved for corpses.

"Are you really letting a dead man get the better of you?" Gus asked.

"He's still alive."

"So? Remedy it."

Riggsy's pale face emerged from the tarp. His wide eyes flicked between them, his mouth sucking slivers of air past the shiv lodged in his throat. He twisted his lips to form words, but all he could manage was a weak gurgle.

"Kill him."

T-Bird faltered, lowering himself beside the dying man. He batted away Riggsy's hand and pried the shiv free. A spurt of blood arced out of the neck, intensifying as he plunged the blade in again. He continued puncturing Riggsy's throat over and over in a blind rage. Blood showered the room, spattering metrically in time with T-Bird's hammer-fisted strikes. Finally, he hurled the shiv aside and rose on unsteady legs.

"Looks like the pocket rocket has blown a fuse." Gus laughed, wiping one of the wayward blood drops from his cheek. "How does it feel to join the big leagues?"

T-Bird nodded, rubbing his face clean with an unsoiled part of his shirt. "Good," he panted.

"I'm glad. Now, get a mop and bucket. You've shit all over my office."

T-Bird blew out a gust of air and nodded again, heading towards the door.

"Take one of the bodies with you! For fuck's sake."

T-Bird hesitated before stooping down, grabbing the wrapped corpse, and hoisting it onto his back. He shuffled out of the room, hooking his foot around the door to close it behind him.

He's about as much use as tits on a fish.

"Don't you fucking start!"

Gus cradled his head, rubbing his eyes with the palms of his hands.

"I—I didn't say anything."

He gasped. "Doctor Miller. I almost forgot you were there. You do a grand job blending in with the furniture."

"It's back, isn't it?"

"It? What's *it*?" Gus snorted in agitation.

"The voice. You aren't taking your meds, are you?"

"Excellent detective work, Doctor. Ever thought of hanging up the stethoscope and becoming a nark?"

Doctor Miller leaned forward, cautious about choosing her next words. "We talked about this, Gus. The violence, the psychopathy, it's exacerbated by *him*."

"Oh, it's a *him* now, is it? I thought you said we shouldn't personify it?"

Doctor Miller sighed. "I'm sorry. These are trying times; I used the wrong terminology."

"No. You didn't... I am he, and he is me. Together for—will you stop that shit!"

Gus clutched his head and leaned into the table.

Ha, ha. What's wrong, Gus? I thought we loved poetry?

Stop. Now.

Enough of the chitchat. Tell her to mind her fucking business, or we'll cut her head off.

"Gus?"

Have you forgotten about the hole in our side? We need her to keep us alive. For now, at least.

Pfft, 'tis but a flesh wound.

We're not killing her.

Fine. Then we'll cut out her tongue. She doesn't need that to heal us.

We're not cutting anything.

"Gus?"

You better answer her. Sounds like she's getting impatient.

"What?" he snarled.

Pussy.

"This is the worst I've seen you. If it's displacing your core identity, you…" She averted her gaze, searching the ceiling for a solution. "We need to start you on the Solenian again. Right away."

"I hate to tell you this, Doc, but it's the end of the world. You'll be lucky to find any meds out there."

"But the violence—"

"—Is a necessity. In a world of rabid dogs, you need to be a gun." He retrieved his handgun from the desk. "But a gun is only useful with bullets. Understand?"

The doctor didn't respond.

"No, of course you don't. I bet you couldn't imagine harming another human being, could you?"

The continued silence stoked a fire in his chest. He shoved his chair back and bore down on the startled woman.

"The rules have changed. There's no law. There's no order. And in a house full of convicts, you need to be prepared to pull the trigger!"

Miller whimpered as he shoved the handgun into her palm.

"There." He took a step back and pointed to Riggsy's corpse. "Put a bullet in his forehead."

"Why?"

"Because I told you to."

The doctor shook her head, casting tears either side of her face.

"C'mon, Doc. You know the drill. You've just watched the same routine with little Terrance. Kill or be killed."

"H-he's already dead," Miller stammered.

"Then it should be easy. Take the shot."

"I'm not a soldier; I'm a doctor."

"You were a fucking detective a minute ago. Things change."

The gun trembled in her grasp. "I can't."

"Let me remind you of something. Right now, you're in *my* office and under *my* protection. If you can't shoot a dead man, I see no point in keeping you here. Take the shot."

The doctor's silence continued to fuel the blaze in his chest. With an indignant grunt, Gus marched to the door and pried it open.

"Go on, then, off you go. Let's see how long it takes to pull the trigger out there."

Miller gasped and brought the gun up to Gus' face.

"Oh, now we're taking a step up."

He slammed the door and took a step closer.

"Go on then, pull the trigger. Although, you've watched *this* routine as well. Remember how it ended?"

He kicked Riggsy's corpse.

"You've seen what happens when someone—"

Click.

The doctor pulled the trigger, prompting shocked expressions from both of them.

"You saucy mare!" Gus Razor gasped.

Miller whimpered, trying to pull the trigger again, but it was no longer cocked. She flipped the gun over and found a rectangular hole in the base of the grip.

"Looking for this?" With a sneer, Gus raised the magazine into view.

The doctor hurled the gun onto the desk and slumped back into her chair with an exasperated groan.

"You keep tickling my turnip like that, sweetheart, and we're gonna get on well." Gus stepped over the corpse at his feet and returned to the desk. "I'm curious. What did you intend to do next?"

"In a house full of convicts, you need to pull the trigger, right?"

Gus grinned. "You learn quick. But you forgot a gun is only useful with bullets." He slid the magazine back into the handgun. "And there aren't enough in here to kill them all. Remember that next time."

He handed the gun back to the doctor, who studied him, searching for a hidden motive. Finding nothing more than a black, heartless void, she tentatively picked it up.

"You're giving me another chance to kill you?"

"No. I'm giving you a chance to redeem yourself."

"How?"

"When the time's right, pull the trigger."

She looked curiously at the gun. "When?"

"You'll know when."

"What's to stop me from killing you now?"

"Nothing. But you need to consider which is the lesser evil."

Miller grew rigid in her seat. "I've been a doctor here for ten years. I've analysed rapists and murderers... and you."

"And?"

"And you're the worst. All the others have reasons for their behaviour: motives or past trauma. And whilst it's never justifiable, it can at least be understood. But not you. There's no reason for your cruelty, no limit to your malice. Sure, I operated on the hypothesis that your auditory hallucinations exacerbate your violent behaviour. But that's not really true, is it? Even whilst on Solenian you still committed grave atrocities to your fellow inmates. And even years before your... diagnosis."

"How else do you keep people in line?" Gus shrugged.

"Exactly. And it's that mindset which leads me to realise there is no hope for you. That you are the greater evil, and without you, the world will be a lot safer."

Her grip on the handgun tightened as Gus chuckled.

"I'm the only reason you're still alive, Doc. Do you think those boys care about your medical knowledge? Your experience? No. Without me, you'd be bent over this desk. Every orifice filled with stagnant pork. Those creeps thrusting and grunting. Slobbering and spaffing all over this fucking room."

He kept his glare fixed on the doctor.

"They wouldn't care if you're breathing, bleeding, crying, or dead. In fact, some of them would insist on it. But, you're right: I *am* the greater evil. The things I've done lie well beyond the realm of nightmares, and when I reach hell, I guarantee it won't be as a servant. Anyone in close proximity to me is dicing with death. Yet, the delicious irony is you need to stay glued to me if you want to survive."

Doctor Miller stared at him, processing his words, her acceptance displayed by the single tear trickling down her cheek. She made to give him the gun back, but Gus raised his hand.

"Keep it. We both know I'm on borrowed time. After that, you're on your own."

The door burst open as T-Bird rushed into the room. "We've got a problem."

"No, *you've* got a problem… with knocking, apparently."

"You need to get down there."

"I don't need to do shit, Terrance. Who the fuck do you think you are, coming in here like that? Turn around and let's try again."

"But it's—"

"I don't give a monkey's cock what it is. Fuck off outside and try again."

They watched T-Bird scurry out into the corridor. No sooner had the door clicked shut than a hurried knock rapped against the wooden pane.

"Enter. Ah, Terrance. What a surprise," Gus said, as T-Bird re-entered. "I don't see a mop and bucket in your hands. I'm going to assume you have good reason?"

T-Bird nodded.

"What's the problem?"

"Rats."

"Rats? Are we talking rodent, or grass?"

"Zombie rats."

5

The sporadic thuds continued—frantic footsteps belonging to innumerable feet. Frank stood at the foot of the stairs, staring up into the darkness. If anybody were to come around the corner, they'd be on him well before he saw them. Moonlight shrouded the dilapidated foyer, casting his shadow over the first few steps of the staircase. Lisa joined him and stood at his side with the dead man's rifle.

"How many bullets did he have?" Frank asked.

"Enough," Lisa said, almost inaudible against the banging above them.

Frank smirked. "How many?"

"Three."

He shook his head. The ruckus implied there were more than three people on the next floor. Even if they neutralised the threat, they were still vulnerable to further attacks.

"Well," said Frank, raising the gun, "let's hope you don't miss."

"Ditto."

He moved forward, taking one step at a time. One bullet. It's all he had left. After that, his life was in Lisa's hands. She cradled the rifle against her chest, one hand positioned over the trigger, the other gripping the barrel. He knew that if anything appeared, she'd be ready. Hell, even Kara had shown her worth. Taking out an intruder with a makeshift spear was an admirable feat. Even if it hadn't worked.

Frank stopped as the footsteps sounded closer, nearing the top of the stairs before fading again. Whoever was up there clearly had no perception of the hotel floor. Either that, or they were indecisive. *A zombie? But how?* Perhaps the woman was infected. Maybe Kara *had* killed her, and her reanimated corpse was running about. But then, who did the other footsteps belong to?

Frank resumed his ascent, desperately trying to pierce the black veil. He knew that when they got to the top of the stairs, the moonlight should offer some aid. The window at the far end of the corridor might not have light streaming in, but it would hopefully be enough to allow him to see something.

Five stairs from the top, and the gloom began to thin. A different shade of black occupied the corridor to the left, at least as far as he could see. The dull thuds sounded distant, their rhythmic beats coming from the other end of the hotel. But they didn't sound as numerous as before. Had they split up? Some exploring one side of the hotel, and the others... silent? He didn't know what to think anymore. The zombies were unpredictable now—an enigma. For all he knew, they were standing just out of view, waiting for him to reach the top.

"Let me go beside you," Lisa whispered, exhibiting her uncanny ability to read his mind. "I'll look one way, you look the other."

Frank nodded, but doubted she'd be able to see anything in the pitch black. Still, he held his tongue. They were two steps from the top now, and if the zombies were waiting, he didn't want to alert them to their presence.

The rapid thuds still sounded distant. He guessed there were at least three of them. And they were running in unison. Now he could hear the growls.

Zombies.

No doubt about it now. They had found a way inside. Somehow.

With a deep intake of breath, he dashed to the top of the stairs and aimed the handgun down the corridor.

He was right.

Not about the zombies—the corridor was empty, as far as he could tell. But the meagre light from the window at the far end helped him see some of the space ahead.

"It's clear," Lisa whispered.

"Okay, so now what?"

Splitting up didn't seem like a sensible option, but neither did waiting around. He heard Lisa respond, but didn't comprehend her words. His attention became fixed on the space ahead, and the rhythmic thuds that were getting closer: two pairs of feet, pounding along the floor, getting louder and louder. Only, something wasn't quite right. The corridor in front of him was twenty metres long at most. Anything sprinting would have reached him in seconds. Yet the thuds grew louder. Then came a pitched, eager wheeze.

He tightened his grip, pointing toward the noise.

"Frank?" Lisa kept her back to his, whispering over her shoulder.

The noise grew closer. Two distinct sounds. One wheeze. *Something on all fours?* His aim instinctively drifted down, expecting to see something scuttling towards him. Something on hands and knees, or crab-walking.

"Frank?" Lisa dropped the whisper. Whatever was coming knew they were there. And it was almost on them.

A yearning gasp brought Frank's gun back to eye level. It was in front of him. It had to be. But where? The banging continued. Then he saw the darkness change shape against the wall. Another shriek.

Bang.

His one and only shot rang out, illuminating the corridor and the zombie child leaping at him from its perch on the wall. The bullet slowed its momentum, but it still clattered against Frank's legs, causing him to stumble back.

"Fuck!"

He fell past Lisa and crashed to the floor. The zombie child reared its head, grinning with broken teeth, and staring with wide eyes. It made to lunge forward, but Kara's strike forced its head into the carpet. She struck again, swinging the metal bar into the back of its skull. Frank scrambled aside as Lisa opened fire.

"They're on the fucking walls!" she shouted, taking a step back and almost tripping over the dead zombie. More growls split the corridor as the second rifle round hit its target. Frank staggered to his feet, holding himself up against the wall, trying to process the scene that briefly flashed before him. It was instantaneous, but the small children dashing across the walls burned into his mind's eye.

"Get back!" He ushered Kara and Sam to the top of the stairs. Lisa's third shot rang out, usurping one of the zombies from the wall. The burst of light revealed another, preparing to leap. Frank grabbed Lisa by the arm and heaved her back, pursued by an eager cry. The zombie blindly collided with them both, shoving them into Kara and Sam, who stumbled down the staircase.

Frank grabbed the balustrade, crying out at the pain in his side. He caught Lisa, listening to the thumps and thuds of the others stumbling to the foot of the stairs. They hit the ground with a grunt and a screech—the latter coming from the undead child landing beside them. The headlights illuminating the foyer showcased the zombie infant in all its hideous glory. Its lower limbs seemed to be inverted, the insides of its legs flush with the tiles, and its knees level with its pelvis. Despite the disfigurement, it moved with an unnatural sprightliness, prancing across the floor towards its prey.

"Sam!" Kara stooped down and retrieved the metal wrench that had landed beside them. In an instant, she swung at the diminutive creature, connecting with the side of its head. The zombie faltered before another blow caused it to collapse.

Sam shuffled away, gasping as Kara continued striking the zombie.

Frank released his grip on Lisa when another thud came from above.

"How many are there?" she groaned.

"I don't know." He could see her standing up through the gloom, searching for the discarded rifle.

The persistent thuds ceased, and Kara dropped the wrench. She tried to rise, but cried out as her foot gave way.

"Are you hurt?" Sam asked.

"I think I've sprained my ankle."

He rushed to her side, wrapping an arm around her to hold her up.

"We can't hold them off," Frank said, "we're going to have to barricade a room."

"What good will that do?" Lisa replied. "They'll still be here when we come out."

"Yeah, but at least we'd be able to see them if we wait till daytime. Come on. Let's go."

He climbed back up the stairs, listening for any further racket from the floor above.

"Come on," Lisa whispered to the others, "we need to get into a room."

"Can you manage the stairs?" Sam asked Kara, tentatively releasing her as she scooped up the weapons.

"Yeah."

Frank listened to the pair climb the stairs below him, but he couldn't hear any noise from the hotel. In the corridor, the shape of the motionless child stood out in the darkness.

There was no sound aside from Frank's ragged breaths and the whisper of fibres as he walked over the plush carpet.

Stepping over the corpse, he reached for the closest door and stopped.

What if there are more in this room? What if they are in every room? He told himself the idea was ridiculous, but until then, so too had been the notion of dead children running across the walls. They had to have got in somewhere, and the prospect of their having merely materialised within the confines of the hotel didn't seem so far-fetched any more.

"What's up?" Lisa whispered, stopping beside him.

"Hoping this room is empty," Frank replied. "You ready?"

She nodded, as Kara and Sam regrouped behind her.

"Okay, let's go."

Frank eased the door open, appreciative of the dim light in the room. He could see the outlines of the furniture. Or at least, it looked like furniture. None of it moved as he entered, which was a bonus.

He peered through the bathroom doorway: nothing.

He released his breath in a long, slow stream as he reached the bed.

A soft click from the door told him they were safe. For now.

"Are we good?" Lisa whispered, reaching his side.

"Looks like it." Frank stepped over to the window as she busied herself moving the chairs.

"Let's get these up against the door," she told the others. "The more weight we can put behind it, the better."

THE MUTATION

Frank listened to the quiet sounds of displacement as they moved the bedroom furniture up against the door. It seemed almost trivial, when there could be a million other ways the zombies were getting inside the hotel. Reanimated corpses were one thing, but gravity-defying zombies that could leap as if propelled by a springboard were something else entirely.

How did *they get in?*

Any doors left unlocked were on the ground floor, and they'd have to have gone through the foyer in order to get to the higher levels. That could only mean they had entered before 'the community' arrived. But how had they gone unnoticed by Kara? And how was she still alive?

No. It didn't make sense.

He pressed his forehead against the window. There didn't appear to be a horde gathering outside, but the blanket of gloom would be the best cover if there was. All he could see was what the moon allowed, and at present, it was being exceedingly generous. He thought back to the illuminated foyer. The twin headlights disintegrated every shadow in the large reception area, but at the same time, showcased the hotel from miles away.

No wonder we have visitors, Frank thought. *It's a spotlight for an all-you-can-eat buffet.*

A flicker of anger developed. The trio had stopped barricading the door, and now Sam helped Kara over to the bed, oblivious to Frank's venomous glare.

His party caused all this. He's the reason we're stuck in here.

Lisa blocked his view as she moved closer.

"What's up?"

"Nothing," Frank muttered. "Just trying to work out how those things got inside."

"Maybe a fire door?"

Frank shook his head. "We secured them all, remember?"

"Well, the only other way would be the window on the second floor."

It made sense now. They were using the same open window he and Lisa had first used to access the hotel. But while he had hoisted Lisa up from atop the van, the zombies didn't need such acrobatics. Not when they could climb walls.

He lurched away from the window, stumbling against the bed as more thuds reverberated through the building.

Lisa gasped. "What is it?"

The rapid thumps grew louder, reminiscent of a giant rat scurrying over the floor. Except this was coming from the walls.

"It's not the door we should be barricading," Frank said, as the scuttling sound reached its peak on the other side of the wall. "It's the window."

6

"Hoowee, this place is a mess!" The voice belonged to an American man somewhere near the front of the pharmacy. "Y'all sure we're gonna find something in here?"

"Look around, Jack. These boxes are full."

"Yeah, fulla nothin'. What the hell do we want with diapers and shampoo?"

Ben lurched upright when he heard a rattle from the shutters. Had Kev sent the men for him, or to make sure he had got away?

"All the good stuff is gonna be back there," said one of the other men. "Doubt we'll be able to get in, though."

"Wanna bet?" The American chuckled. "Lookee here. They must have run out of padlocks."

No, they can't be linked to Kev. So who the hell are they?

A metallic rattle split through the store as they pushed the shutters high. Ben snapped his gaze around the room in search of a weapon. Nothing substantial, and certainly nothing within reach. Crossing the room would almost certainly result in his being spotted. He briefly contemplated the handgun until he remembered where he had left it.

"Are you going over or what?" the American asked.

"Why me? You go."

"What happened to that famous English resolve I've heard so much about? Don't tell me you boys are yella."

"Says the guy who got forced to come on this little expedition."

"Hey, somebody's gotta protect the folk back there. Old man Mike doesn't know his ass from a hole in the ground."

"He took you in. Have some respect."

"I do have respect. But you gotta admit, if his brain was dynamite, he still couldn't blow his nose."

Ben eased himself to his feet, grimacing at the low groan of the couch. He tiptoed to the wall beside the door, listening as one of the men climbed onto the counter.

"I'll go if it stops you girls bickering."

He dropped to the other side with a thud, kicking aside the strewn paper bags.

"This is looking promising," he said. "These bags are full."

Ben pressed himself into the wall as the man drew closer. In a second, he'd be level with the doorway, able to peer into the lounge area. As soon as he stepped through, Ben knew he had to act.

"Shit, there's a gun here."

"You boys wouldn't know a gun if it hit you in the face." The American laughed. A second thump sounded as he vaulted the counter.

"Look. See."

"Oh shit, that *is* a gun. Damn, your drug stores are packin'! Y'all got a problem with meth-heads too, huh?"

"Not like this. Someone's been here."

The snap of metal filled the air. "Yeah, and they ran dry," the American said.

"No chance of finding any bullets round here. Hell, I'm surprised someone found a gun."

"Maybe it was that woman," came another voice. "Louise, or whatever she was called."

"Lisa," the American corrected. "How can you forget a goddess like her?"

Ben almost gasped in disbelief. It was a small world, smaller still when most of its inhabitants were dead. He knew which Lisa they were referring to. It had to be her. It had only been a couple of days since they had parted ways, and if anybody could help him save Amy, it was her. Frank would be reluctant, but after the lengths they had gone to in order to save Lisa, it would be the least he could do.

Ben needed to find them, and fast—

"Do you think there's anything out the back?"

—But first, he would have to deal with the men who were about to discover his hiding place.

"I'll go."

The first thing through the doorway was the business end of a machete, followed by the man wielding it. He strode into the room, oblivious to Ben hiding flush against the wall until it was too late. In an instant, Ben lunged forward, grabbing the hand holding the machete and wrapping his arm around the man's throat.

"Move and I'll break your neck," Ben growled. He kept their bodies flush together, whirling to face the doorway. He expected the others to come bounding in, but they were unaware of the confrontation.

"Now, give up the machete."

He manipulated the man's fingers into submission and prised the handle off him. He readjusted his stance, bringing the blade up to his captive's throat before the next man entered.

"Holy shit!"

The American stood before him, the handgun in one hand, a bag of medication in the other. He sported a black bandana, which ran tight over his smooth dome. A medium-length goatee beard reached the crest of his faded *Metallica* t-shirt.

"Get back!" Ben snapped.

"Look dude, we don't want no trouble." The man raised his hands, taking a retreating step towards the door. Another face appeared behind him, alarm registering on the weathered features.

"Nor do I," Ben said. He nudged his trembling captive forward into the main pharmacy area. There, he a saw third man, the same etchings of terror marked on his face.

"Are there only four of you?"

"Yes, sir," the American replied. "We're looking for supplies, is all."

"You mentioned Lisa," Ben said. "Blonde hair, about five-foot-seven, hanging around with a guy called Frank?"

The man's eyes widened. "You know her?"

"Yeah, she's a friend of mine."

The American smiled. "Well, any friend of Lisa's is a friend of ours. Why don't you let poor Jay go, and we can talk about it?"

None of the men appeared confrontational. Those at the back held the melee weapons at their side, ensuring they kept their distance. After seconds of deliberation, Ben released his grip, allowing his captive to stagger forward.

"Shit, you know how to make a first impression," Jay grumbled, dabbing his neck, checking if the machete had drawn blood.

"Where is she?"

"Who?"

"Lisa."

"The hell if we know," the American muttered. "She took off last night with a whole horde on her tail. She got us out of lumber, though."

Ben groaned, leaning against the doorframe. "And you don't know where she went?"

The man shook his head. "Sorry, dude. But I'll tell you what: I bet Mike knows. She was speaking with him before she left."

"Who's Mike?"

"The leader of the group," Jay said, still massaging his neck. "If you give us a hand loading all this stuff, we'll take you back with us."

"Your group? How many are there?"

Jay shrugged. "Ten, maybe? Help us get this stuff in the truck and you can count them yourself."

"That might have to wait," Ben said, looking past the men and through the window beyond. A pickup truck—a new addition since the previous day—blocked most of the view. But what he could see was a huddle of bodies scrambling to check the contents of the vehicle.

He initially mistook them for more looters until he saw swathes of flesh dangling from one woman's face.

The men inside recoiled when they spotted the undead creatures.

"Goddammit," Jack muttered.

"That's your ride out of here?" Ben asked.

"Yeah. We gotta find another way out. Is the back door open?"

"Why do you think I was still back there?" Ben threw a condescending scowl in Jack's direction.

"I don't know. This could've been your safehouse or something."

"There's nothing safe about it."

Outside, more bodies came into view. No longer interested in the vacant truck, the zombies started looking elsewhere. Their first port of call: the pharmacy window.

"Oh, shit!"

The glass erupted as the mass of bodies slammed against the window, the corpses spilling into the pharmacy. The two men sprinted to the counter. One managed to vault it, but the other stumbled amongst the boxes.

"No... No!" he screamed, as the wave of zombies engulfed him. His cries quickly died, replaced by tearing, squelching, and squeals of glee. Jack yanked the shutters down, seconds before more of the undead slammed against it. The quartet backed away, slipping into the lounge area and slamming the door behind them.

"Let's block the door," Ben said. "The vending machine. Go!"

He ran to the side and pushed against the bulky machine. It started to move, more so when the others joined him. With their combined strength, the machine fell across the door with an almighty smash. The glass viewing compartment shattered, spilling its contents over the floor.

"Well, at least we won't starve to death for a while."

Jay crouched, scooping up the bags of crisps and chocolate.

"Forget that," Ben snapped. "Get the couch up there as well."

He rushed to the other side of the room and dragged the couch away from the wall. The movement sent fire through his finger stumps, but he masked it with the exertion of moving the furniture. Together, the men lifted it up and atop the vending machine. Only the top quarter of the door remained on show. But Ben wasn't sure if it would be enough.

"I take it you've tried this?" Jack asked, striding over to the metal door on the other side of the room. Ben stayed quiet, waiting for the man to answer his own question. He tugged the handle, but the door remained shut.

"Well, boys, looks like we might be here a while." Jay slumped onto the remaining couch, unwrapping a Snickers bar and resting his feet on the coffee table. "Best make ourselves at home."

"Will your group send more people when you don't return?" Ben asked.

"I doubt it," Jack said. "We're not soldiers. We don't have guns or weapons. We're just trying to survive."

"And survive we will!" Jay called. "Let's chill here for a while, wait for the chompers to leave, and then we'll be on our way."

"What makes you think they're gonna go?" Jack asked.

"Oh, c'mon. You know what they're like. They'll get bored within the hour and bugger off somewhere else."

Jack removed his bandana, wiping his face in exasperation. "Have you forgotten what Lisa and Frank told us yesterday? Hell, and the reason they had to lead those zombies away? They aren't going to leave. Not on their own."

"Wait. What?" said Ben.

"They said the zombies are getting smarter. They're jumping and climbing."

"You don't know that," Jay protested.

"The hell I don't! You heard Frank as well as I did. He saw it."

"The man was delirious through blood loss! He probably saw them *riverdancing*, as well."

"Well, I know what *I* saw. Those zombies had us under siege."

"Bullshit," Jay said, hurling the chocolate wrapper aside. "We were only in there ten minutes. They could've wandered off any time."

Ben listened to the exchange, but all he could think about was his own encounter the previous night. The clicking noise. The communicating.

They are *getting smarter.*

The realisation started to sink in like a lead weight in the pit of his stomach. He wasn't being paranoid. Others had seen it, too. And if the undead were getting smarter, how the hell was he going to survive? A metallic jolt came from the next room, followed by a clamour of bodies breaching the counter. Next came the slam against the lounge door.

The quartet stared. Three inches of wood and a faltering barricade were all that was keeping them in the realm of the living. Each jolt against the door caused the couch to sway, and if it toppled, then what?

Their adversaries were strong, they were relentless. And with an increased mental capacity, they would never give up.

7

"I swear to god, Terrance, if you're tugging my todger, I'm going to beat you over the head with it."

Gus dashed down the stairs with T-Bird at his heel.

"I promise. There's at least four of them. They're running all over the canteen."

"That's what rats do, dickhead. How do you know they're zombie rats?"

They reached the bottom and rounded the corner, a distant quarrel drifting down the corridor.

"They're running round with their guts hanging out, huge chunks missing, and they're... biting."

Gus lurched to a stop, shoving T-Bird aside to avoid them colliding. "Have the lads been bitten?"

"I don't know. When it all kicked off, I came to get you."

"For fuck's sake, can't you use your loaf for once in your life?" Gus took off down the corridor once more. "Do I look like a fucking rat catcher? What do you want me to do?"

T-Bird continued walking in silence until they reached the hall beyond the canteen. A group of inmates huddled around the door, some pressed up against it, others arguing back and forth. They stopped when Gus arrived, the din lowering enough to hear the rabid squeaks on the other side of the door. The rats slammed against the metal pane, their efforts echoing around the canteen.

"Right, first off, why are you lot cowering out here like a bunch of girls? They're rats, not fucking Dobermans."

"They're infected," Harper replied.

"You don't know that," snapped another.

"They're dead, Gibbo. Just like you!"

"I'm not dead!"

"You're as good as."

"Put the gun down and we'll see who's dead."

"Oy!" Gus snapped. "I'm the only one who shouts in here, and I'm the only one giving orders."

He looked from Harper to Gibbo, who cradled his balled fist.

"Have you been bitten?"

Alarm flashed across Gibbo's eyes. "They're not infected. They're not."

Gus yanked the shotgun out of Harper's grasp and blasted the cowering prisoner with both barrels. Gibbo jolted back, his body rolling twice before settling in the corridor.

"I'm not having a rat man running round my prison. Anyone else bitten?"

The others shook their heads.

"Thought as much. Make sure you stay that way when you go in there."

"What?" Harper took a step back.

"We can't have rats in the canteen. It's unhygienic, isn't it, Charlie?"

The chef nodded, chewing his cuticles.

"See? You don't want rat shit in your amuse-bouche, do you? Get your arse in there and sort it out."

"The minute we open the door, they're going to be on us."

"You're not too savvy, are you, Harper? You boys go round the other side, blast the fuckers to pieces, and we'll come in this way. Is your thick ginger cranium able to process that?"

Harper nodded, glancing at the others, who all showed wistful compliance.

"Good, here's your shooter. Now fuck off."

Harper took his shotgun back and followed the others down the corridor. They stepped over Gibbo's body, nobody making a sound as they reached the corner and disappeared from sight.

"If that boy had a brain, he'd be deadly. What do you think, Charlie?"

The man giggled, continuing to chew his fingers.

"You like that one, don't you, son?" He ruffled the man's hair. "Heard you like a good brain. Is that true?"

Chomping Charlie nodded furtively as he moved onto another digit.

"Doc Miller says it's dangerous. We don't want these boys dying out, do we?"

"They won't d-d-d-die," Charlie replied, shaking his head. "They could do with b-b-brain food."

"We can't really have parts left over," T-Bird added. "We'll get—"

"—rats?" Gus sneered. He strode over to the door and slammed a palm against it, the noise barely audible over the din from the other side. "Eating every scrap hasn't kept them away, has it? I bet it was that scruffy cunt Carver, and his pile of corpses. Took us bloody ages to get rid of them!"

A booming shotgun rang out from the canteen, ending the uproar at the door. A second and third shot sounded in quick succession, the reverb gradually settling throughout the room.

"Where's the rest of them?" a panicked voice cried out. "Harper, where's—"

The voice turned into a scream, which cut off in the wake of two further gun shots.

"Sounds like our cue," Gus muttered. He pushed the doors wide and entered the canteen.

"Do you want the shooter?" T-Bird asked.

"Do I look like a fucking pussy, Terrance?"

Gus counted two dead rats nearby, and another beside the body of one of the inmates.

"It bit him," Harper said, matter-of-factly.

"I gathered. Where's the rest of them?"

The men scanned the floor uncertainly, peering under tables, not daring to tread too close.

"We only counted four," Harper said. "There's one missing."

"I can see that, you soppy twat. I asked *where* it is."

The man shrugged.

"You're not much use to me alive, are you, Harper? Get on your hands and knees and find the little bastard."

He made to turn away until a darting movement caught his eye.

"There!" one man yelled. He fired his rifle, the clap echoing around the room. The bullet struck a table as the rat darted under the next one.

"There it is," shouted another. He leapt on top of a table as the rat darted towards his legs. Failing to reach its prey, it scurried towards Gus, its black eyes bulging amidst blood-matted fur.

"Have it!" Gus booted the rat high and wide, sending it sailing across the canteen and into the kitchen area beyond. It landed with a clatter amidst the pots and pans.

"Don't just stand there, you fucking pricks. Kill it!"

The men trod gingerly over to the kitchen.

"That's tonight's special sorted, Charlie."

Gus clapped the man on the back.

"Don't worry, son, the health inspector isn't due."

A clash of pots and pans radiated out of the kitchen. The men stood beside the entryway, motioning for each other to step inside.

"What the fuck are they doing?" Gus grabbed the handgun from T-Bird and aimed it in their direction. "Every last one of you better be in there by the time I count to three. Anyone stood outside is going to be shot!"

The men shoved each other, motioning hurriedly for the others to step in.

"One!"

They darted inside, the noise escalating as pans skittered across the floor.

"Two!" It was an unnecessary call, given that all of them had disappeared. Gus handed the gun back to T-Bird, tapping his foot patiently.

"There's a rat in me kitchen, what am I gonna do?" Gus sang, rocking on the balls of his feet. "C'mon, Charlie. You know the words."

The man offered a wan smile, but he continued to stare at the kitchen, chewing the pad of his thumb.

"There!" The exclamation preceded a rhythmic clamour—a dull, gong-like sound—which Gus imagined was a pan being brought down on the undead rat. After a few more strikes, the kitchen fell silent.

"Sounds like the coast is clear," he muttered. "Charlie, go and put the kettle on. I could do with a brew."

But the man remained still, watching the kitchen, almost in anticipation.

"Oy, are you listening? What's the matter with you?"

Gus didn't need to wait long to find out. The prisoners in the kitchen emerged, one carrying a severed arm, which dripped clear fluid.

"What the fuck is this?" Harper spat, hurling the limb towards them. It skidded across the floor, reams of flesh falling away until it settled at Charlie's feet.

"It's clearly a boiled arm," Gus replied nonchalantly. "You need to get your peepers tested, Harper."

"*Why* is there a boiled arm in the kitchen?"

"Where else are you going to boil it? In the fucking khazi?"

Harper took a step forward, glowering at Charlie, who drew back. "Have you been feeding us body parts?"

"So what if he has?" Gus snarled, stepping between the two men. "It would be me who authorised it. Nothing happens around here without my say-so. What are you gonna do about it?"

The tension in Harper's face eased, showing a conflict of emotion instead. He retreated to the other prisoners.

"For the record," Gus continued, "he's been cooking it for himself. You boys have been enjoying the finest gruel, while Charlie has been chowing down on human tender cuts. You ought to show a bit more gratitude."

"I didn't see any other food in there," Harper murmured, careful not to antagonise Gus Razor any further.

"No, you wouldn't. That's because you greedy bastards have finished it all! Which leads me nicely on to my next point: you boys are going down to Sunnymoor."

"Sunnymoor?"

"There's a bit of an echo in here, isn't there? Yes, Sunnymoor. You, T-Bird and those other twats back there are going on a supply run."

"What kind of supply run?" Harper pressed, keeping his tone level.

"What do you think? Food, water, guns, anything that will keep us alive in this shithole a bit longer!"

"When you get there, split into two groups," he told T-Bird. "Make sure you get another set of wheels before you load up on the other shit."

T-Bird nodded, motioning for the men to follow him.

"Hold up, little man," Harper said. "Who put you in charge?"

"*I* did!" Gus growled. "And if I hear any reports of insolence while you're out there, I'll slice those freckles right off your ginger face! Do you understand?"

Harper clenched his jaw and nodded.

"Good, now fuck off!"

With that, he strode out of the canteen, listening for any sign of discord in his absence. There was none, only the clunk of his boots as he entered the corridor and proceeded to make his way back to his office.

Those boys can't be trusted.

Yeah? Tell me something I don't know.

Our circle is getting smaller, Gustav.

I know that as well. Seriously, why pipe up if you've got nothing to say?

Just to remind you, I'm still here.

Gus clasped his head, breathing deeply as the searing pain throbbed in his ears again. He leaned against the wall, resisting the urge to slump to the ground.

Trust me, I know you're there. I can feel it.

That's the tumour, not me.

Same thing.

He pushed himself away and continued towards the staircase. His vision felt blurred, but it was hard to tell in the confines of the gloomy corridor. What he did know was the symptoms were getting worse. Glioblastoma, they called it, and boy was it a mind-fuck.

How long did the quack give us?

Which one?
The one with the pelican beak we wanted to slice off.
Three months.

Gus turned up the stairs, fighting off the nausea which threatened to overpower him.

Meaning we've got a month to get our affairs in order.

If you believe that shit. I'll *decide when I die, not a fucking cancerous tumour.*

That's the spirit.

He reached the top floor, where the queasiness began to fade. A flicker of relief formed, extinguished only when he saw his office door ajar.

8

A miniature spotlight shone in the corner of Frank's eyelid. He twisted uncomfortably until memories flashed back, causing him to jolt awake. The small rectangle of light streamed through a gap in the barricaded window. He looked around the room, able to make out more than the previous night due to the dim light. Two motionless figures—Kara and Sam—occupied one of the twin beds and the floor, respectively. Beside him, Lisa sat with her back to the wall.

"Good morning," she said, keeping her voice low so as not to disturb the others.

Frank groaned and clambered to his feet. "How long was I out?"

"A few hours. I know you wanted to keep watch, but I figured you still needed to regain your strength."

"Were there any issues?"

Lisa shook her head.

"Well, that's one thing. Have you heard any more of them in the corridors?"

"Not a peep. There hasn't been a sound for hours."

"Maybe they've got their head down in one of the beds." Frank scooped up the empty rifle, rapping the stock against his palm.

"What's your plan?" Lisa asked.

"We assume the role of the Three Bears and beat them to death." He turned to the stacked armchairs and table covering the window. "Give me a hand with these, will you?"

Lisa heaved herself up and seized one side of a chair while Frank grabbed the other. They felt lighter when they were being stacked. But Frank assumed that adrenaline, and the impending threat of wall-crawling zombies, were contributing factors. Now, his muscles ached, he was fatigued, and the exertion of removing the chairs was almost too much.

He dropped the chair sooner than planned, jolting Kara awake. She pushed herself up against the headboard, wincing and clutching her ankle.

"What's going on?" she asked, shielding her eyes as sunlight flooded the room.

Frank dropped the second chair before slumping into it.

"It's morning. Time to hunt some zombie children."

"You wanna leave the room?" Sam asked.

"Well, I don't plan on dying in here with you lot. What's it like out there?" he asked Lisa, who stood facing the window.

"Desolate."

"Do you have any bullets left?" Kara asked, eyeing the rifle in Frank's hands.

"Nope."

"So, how do you hope to fight them?"

"The way I told you yesterday."

Kara looked at him blankly.

"Learn to use a bat, remember?"

"Oh, yeah. How could I forget? When you left me alone with no means to protect myself."

"You're still alive, aren't you?"

"Yeah, just about."

"And you're welcome. So what weapons do we have?"

Kara leaned over and retrieved her makeshift spear, propped up against the side of the bed. "Well, since you left me to fend for myself, I had to improvise."

"Good work, MacGyver." Frank climbed to his feet. "I would've thought these were hollow."

He lifted the lamp, assessing the weight, before dropping it with a satisfied grunt.

"Nope. They make a good spear, too. It's how I killed that woman."

"Okay, you can take care of yourself. I can take a hint."

"Yet still too arrogant to apologise."

"Fine. But I'm only sorry for doubting you; I'm not apologising for leaving you here. If you had come with us, we wouldn't have returned so quickly, and these pricks would've taken over."

He pointed at Sam, who flinched away from the accusation.

"Quickly?" Kara sneered. "You were gone all day!"

"Yeah, well. Something came up. Trust me, we came back as soon as we could."

"He's right," Lisa added. "We only intended to be a couple of hours at most. But we got caught up with some religious nuts, and—"

"And what?"

"And we haven't got time to chat," Frank said. "The building is still unsecure. The longer we wait, the more zombies we're likely to face."

He flipped the lamp over and unscrewed the base.

"So, weapons," he continued. "What else do we have?"

"I've got this." Sam retrieved the large wrench from the floor beside him.

"Have you used it before?"

"I... uh."

"Well?"

"No. I haven't."

"Have you killed *any* of those things?" Frank hurled the base aside before flipping the lamp over and unscrewing the shade. The man's silence told him everything he needed to hear.

"We need to stick together, then," Lisa said. "We'll clear this floor, then work our way up to the next. If we're lucky, there won't be many."

"If we're lucky, there won't be any at all," Frank said. He dropped the shade and tested the durability of the lamp pole. It felt firm, the solid weight reassuring in his grip.

"Right, c'mon. Let's get this over with. Can you walk?" he asked Kara.

"Yeah, I'm fine."

"Use that thing as a walking stick if need be. But don't be clinging on to him. We need everyone to—"

"I said I'm fine." Kara swung her legs off the bed and steadily applied weight to her ankle. If it still hurt, she didn't show it.

"Good. Lise, you want this, or you good with the rifle?" Frank offered the pole, but Lisa shook her head.

"I'm all right."

"Okay, then, shall we?"

Frank led the way over to the door. Despite his jibe at Kara, he felt a reliance of his own on the metal pole. His legs had adopted a slight rubber quality, and the ever-present pain in his side was a constant reminder of his vulnerability. For a moment, he considered if he had the strength to tackle a zombie child. Pushing aside his concerns—and the furniture barricading the door—he peered through the spyhole.

Distorted light shone down a warped corridor. While it was hard to make out anything substantial, there was no sign of movement at all. He eased open the door, treading softly out of the room. The corridor was empty, except for a motionless body towards the end.

"That's the woman I killed," Kara whispered.

"And she's definitely dead?"

"I stabbed her twice in the throat. What do you think?"

"I don't know what to think anymore," Frank muttered, cautiously heading down the corridor. "You're hard as nails."

He checked each door as he passed, pulling them to, ensuring they were fully closed.

Not that it matters, he thought. *If they can run, jump, and climb, what's stopping them from opening a door?*

The concerning prospect remained with him until he reached the dead woman in front of an open doorway. She remained still, face-down on the plush carpet, which sported a darker red in all the places it had absorbed her blood. Frank held the metal bar above her head, expecting her to jump up at any second. When she didn't, he shoved a boot into her side, rolling her onto her back. The woman's half-open eyes stared through the ceiling, her mouth agape, as if she had died trying to draw in a final breath. Her bloodied throat sported a pair of deep lacerations, with fragments of glass jutting skyward.

In the open bedroom, sunlight shone through the partly drawn curtains, revealing the same table and chairs as in all the other rooms. After a quick scan inside, it was clear nobody had been there. The bed was made, the generic hotel gratuities lined the desk in uniform fashion, and the sterile bathroom appeared untouched.

"Next floor?" Lisa asked.

Frank nodded, leading the way to the stairs. He was tempted to venture down to the ground floor, to assess the carnage of the foyer in the light of day, but he knew they had to secure the rest of the hotel first.

Up the staircase, there was nothing untoward, at least as far as he could see. Yet, adrenaline coursed through his body, and his breath seemed to be flowing at a faster rate. The metal pole felt slick in his hand as he ascended the stairs. This was the floor he had been fearing. It was where the zombies had to have been gaining entry, and, most likely, where they still remained. He trod carefully, sensing the others at his back.

Frank stayed close to the wall as he made his way to the next level, straining to see as much as he could. There was nobody there.

They tip-toed up to the second floor, pausing once they reached the top. Despite it appearing exactly the same as the previous corridor, Frank couldn't shift his sense of unease. The pressing silence had a more eerie quality, as if there was a degree of anticipation. Something there, waiting for them to emerge.

With a deep, inaudible breath, he edged forward into the corridor.

Unlike the first floor, the light fixtures on the walls were bent and broken. Glass and gold fittings lay amongst the carpet, which also sported trails of mud and debris. They weren't footprints. They were long drag-marks across the floor, progressively fading until the mud had rubbed off whatever appendage had been used. Frank didn't get chance to consider the cause.

Down the other side of the corridor, no more than ten feet away, was one of the zombie children. It had its back to them, swaying ever so slightly, staring off to the end of the corridor. Its back legs splayed, distorted in an unnatural position. With its lower half flush with the ground, it arched its torso, both palms on the ground, holding itself upright.

Frank held a finger to his lips and motioned for the others to join him, scanning the doors running the length of the hallway. Some stood ajar, including the one with the open window. Unlike the first floor, he had a feeling some of the rooms would be occupied. He adjusted the pole, adopting a two-handed stance.

Lisa clutched his shoulder. They couldn't get closer to the creature without passing the open rooms.

Frank signalled for Sam and Kara to target a door each. He then nodded to the zombie, which remained unmoved. Was it dead? Sleeping? Waiting? Frank couldn't tell, each premise more terrifying than the last.

With another deep intake of breath, he led the group forward. Each step he took brought with it the crippling fear that the zombie would whirl around. But the carpet absorbed the sound of each step. When they neared the opposing open doors, Sam and Kara branched out. They tip-toed alongside the wall, stopping only once they reached the doorframe.

Frank—still in the middle of the corridor—saw more of each room as he progressed. Both were well-lit, and despite exhibiting a chaotic mess, neither appeared occupied. He stopped only a few feet from the undead child, waiting for Sam and Kara to close the doors. Sam eased around first, carefully gripping the door handle and pulling it closed. Kara, on the other side, disappeared into the room.

Shit.

The sudden commotion inside filled the entire corridor. Kara cried out, prompting the zombie in front of Frank to whirl around. Its wide, bloodshot eyes fixed on him. Its mouth opened as it made to roar, revealing cracked and broken baby teeth. Frank brought the pole down, striking its head. He didn't let up; he brought it down again, splitting the thin flesh above its brow. Only when the undead child stopped moving did he acknowledge the chaotic sounds around him.

Sam clung to the door handle, whimpering as he fought to maintain control. A zombie on the other side roared in anger, but it was the clash in the opposite room that concerned Frank. He rushed inside, finding Kara grappling with one zombie whilst Lisa bludgeoned another. The creature suffering Lisa's assault grew still, but Kara's assailant was more determined than ever, lunging against the horizontal pole she was using to keep it at bay. In an instant, Frank swung a boot into the undead child. It reeled away, scrambling underneath the bed.

"Get out!" Frank roared. He shoved Kara back as Lisa vaulted the bed to stand beside him. The zombie remained beneath it, its agitated growls lost in the noise from the corridor.

"There's more out there," Frank said. "Let's go."

Lisa rushed into the corridor with Kara, but Frank only took a couple of backsteps, his eyes fixed on the bed. As soon as it thought the threat was over, the zombie emerged.

"Gotcha." Frank lunged forward, swinging the pole down with both hands. The zombie lurched aside, darting away from its haven beneath the bed, and instead jumping to the desk. Frank swung again, the pole striking only air, after the zombie leapt onto the wall. It scuttled along like a humanoid arachnid, before leaping at him. Frank brought the pole up in time, deflecting the zombie onto the bed. It rolled away, seeking its previous refuge beneath the bed, but this time Frank was ready. He drove the pole down into the creature's lower back. The weapon pierced its skin, impaling it above the pelvis. It roared in anger, clawing at the ground, trying to clamber away.

"Frank!" Lisa ran into the room, her rifle swapped for the rusted wrench Sam had previously been holding.

"Kill it!" Frank snapped, pushing all his weight onto the pole while the zombie tried to pull away. Lisa rushed beside him and swung the wrench down. An audible crack came from the skull, and another when she struck again. The zombie went limp, but Lisa hit it again for good measure.

"C'mon." She seized his arm and dragged him back into the corridor. The door Sam had been jostling for control of now stood ajar, and both he and Kara stood in the room over a motionless corpse. But their attention wasn't fixed on the child. They were staring outside. Lisa led him over, past the zombie with its skull caved in, and over to the window. Kara and Sam moved aside, allowing them a better view.

"What is it?" Frank asked.

"Look."

Between the endless fields, the distant dirt road, and the buildings beyond, he couldn't see anything, at least nothing out of place. Beyond all that, he could make out a heat mirage churning in the distance. Seconds passed, and he gradually came to the realisation that it wasn't an illusion at all. The mirages he had seen in the past were always close to the ground and floated like water ripples. This one lumbered along, breaking and reforming in varying rates, but all continuing in the same direction.

Shaking, Frank took a step back, transfixed on the trundling train of zombies.

"That's the biggest horde I've ever seen," Kara whispered.

Frank swallowed his fear in one gulp, trying to compose himself, trying to muster a response to the impossible sight.

"That's no horde," he said. "It's an army."

9

The rhythmic pounding still thudded through Ben's head, even though the zombies had ceased their assault over five minutes earlier. He knew they were still there. Their growls continued to emanate through the pharmacy, which felt more like a prison now they were trapped inside. He leaned against the wall, observing his fellow inmates. Jack and his companion sat on one of the leather sofas, while Jay stooped beside the vending machine, carefully retrieving bags of crisps through the broken glass.

"Dude, knock it off," Jack said. "We've got enough. Let's stay quiet for a bit."

"Why? It's not like they're going anywhere, right?"

Jay added more crisps to his ever-growing pile.

"No, but giving them a constant reminder isn't going to help none, either."

Jay lowered himself onto his stomach, reaching back into the machine.

"C'mon, Dave. Back me up here." Jack clapped the man beside him on the shoulder, spurring him into an awkward exchange.

"Jay, stop."

Jack looked at him in disgust. "Some help you are." He rose from the couch and tapped one of Jay's skewed legs.

"Alright, alright." Jay started shuffling back, before jolting in discomfort, catching his arm on jagged glass. The clatter of the vending machine and Jay's outburst prompted another assault on the door. The zombies roared, slamming themselves against the other side once again. Ben massaged his temple, ran a hand over his face, and shoved himself away from the wall.

"Where are you going?" Jack asked.

"For a piss."

He strode into the small bathroom and shut the door behind him. He welcomed the additional sound barrier, but it wasn't enough to silence the onslaught from the next room. The zombies raged on, lunging at the storeroom door. The chances of them getting in were relatively slim, especially with the added bulk of the barrier. But Ben knew there was always a chance. He leaned against the door, staring at the small squares of light beaming in through the ceiling.

"I need a bandage," Jay snapped. "My arm's cut to shit."

"You'll be lucky," Jack said.

"Lucky? We're in a pharmacy."

"No, we're in the staffroom of a pharmacy. There's a difference."

"But my arm—"

Ben groaned and snatched up a toilet roll when a glint caught his eye. He stared into the toilet bowl at the key beneath the water.

What the hell?

It didn't make sense. Nothing did. The more he thought about it, the more it seemed he was taking part in a twisted game. Why would somebody drop a key into a toilet? Were they trying to flush it? Or had they left it there to be found?

Ben reached in, snatching the key out of the water. As far as he could tell, there was only one key missing from the store—the same one he had accused Kev of stealing. While he had only been partially right, he couldn't help but feel an even greater rage towards the policeman. Kev was meticulous. Precise. He had never intended for Ben to die in the pharmacy, and he had taken every step to ensure that didn't happen. Yet, with the length of time he had been stuck inside, Kev could've taken Amy anywhere by now.

He marched back into the room, hurling the toilet roll at Jay, immediately quashing his incomprehensible remonstrations.

"What are you doing?"

Ben ignored Jack's query as he made his way to the heavy door. He pressed himself against the spyhole, peering out into the shadowy alleyway. It was empty—the motionless shapes he attributed to bins and an upturned cardboard box. He wiped the key on his trousers and slid it into the lock.

"Holy shit," Jack said. "I thought you said it was locked?"

Ben turned the key, relishing the satisfying click. "It was."

"What are we waiting for?" Dave said. "Let's get the hell out of here."

"And do what?" Ben asked. "Run as fast as we can?"

"We need to get out."

"No, what we need is a distraction. You saw how many were out there. If they're still sniffing around your truck, we're not going anywhere."

"He's right," Jay said. He held a wad of toilet paper against his arm, winding the rest of it around to hold it in place. "If they see us before we get in, we're dead."

"So what are you thinking?"

"Hold on." Ben ushered the men away from the door and gently turned the handle. The zombies in the pharmacy had ceased their assault, allowing the shrill creak of the door to pierce the room as Ben eased it open. At first, he questioned his initial assessment of it being unoccupied. The bins appeared larger, and the box seemed closer without the distortion of the spyhole. He glanced both ways, confirming his initial deduction.

"Okay." He eased the door shut, stepping back into the pharmacy. "The alley is clear. The left side is the quickest way to the front of the shop. Let's head out there and see what we're dealing with."

"All of us?" Jay asked.

"Strength in numbers."

"No. No. No. Not when you're going for stealth. The fewer of us, the better."

"Okay, do you wanna go?"

325

"Me?" Jay stepped back in alarm. "Hell, no. It's your plan. You go."

"I'm the only one without a weapon."

Jay thrust his machete forward. "Not anymore."

Ben hung his head. How the hell did he get lumbered with such a rag-tag group? He took the weapon and eased the door open once more. The alley felt warm—not terribly clammy, but enough to form a bead of perspiration down the back of his neck. Then again, it could have been trepidation. He couldn't tell.

He walked down the alley, each step taking him further away from his refuge and exacerbating his sense of dread. There was no sound from the end of the street, but he couldn't help but imagine a horde of the undead lurching around the corner. If they did, what would he do? *Run back* was the obvious answer, but what if the others locked the door behind him? He turned back and saw them watching him around the open door. Their heads aligned like traffic lights. The Three Stooges of the apocalypse.

"Bloody hell."

The prospect of abandoning them suddenly became a desirable one. He could check the coast was clear and then run. It would be easy enough to find another vehicle, and as long as he stuck to the back alleys and side roads, he was sure he'd survive. But then he remembered Amy. He'd never be able to find her on his own, and even if he did, he'd need help to save her.

No. He needed Lisa and Frank. They had the firepower, and they owed him.

He reached the edge of the alley and looked out onto the street beyond. There was nobody on either side. The back of the pickup truck jutted out into the road. It was close. They could run, climb into the back, and drive away in no time. Their only hurdle would be the zombies he envisaged congregating around the front. Satisfied he had seen enough, he headed back.

"What's it like out there?" Jay asked, once Ben was safely back inside.

"Clear. They're all at the front of the building."

"So what do we do?"

Ben shook his head.

"Why don't we do the same thing we did last night?" Jack suggested. "Make a big noise, and when the zombies come a-knocking, we haul ass out the back?"

"That only worked because the bike was round the side of the church," said Jay. "Our truck is at the front. No. We need to do more than that."

"I've got it!" Jack clicked his fingers. "We let them in."

"What?"

"Think about it. We move the barricade, let them think they're making progress, and run out the back. When they break through, they're going to flood this room, which should free up the truck. It's foolproof."

"Not when a fool comes up with it," Jay said.

"Do you have any better ideas?"

Jay scrunched up his face.

"I didn't think so. C'mon. This is gonna work."

Jack dragged the couch off the vending machine. The disturbance was enough to reignite the fury on the other side of the door. Jay rushed over and helped Jack hurl the couch to the ground.

"Okay, you boys move the machine," Jack said. "We'll watch the alley."

Dave chewed his lip in contemplation. Despite his unease, he nodded and started to help. The wooden doorframe splintered under the relentless assault, and Ben wondered if they even needed to remove the last barrier. He looked back at the metal door, where Jack stood holding it open. It was now or never. Ben reached down and hooked his fingers beneath the dented metal, his injured hand resting on the side.

"Ready?" he called over the ruckus.

Dave nodded.

"Three. Two. One. Move!"

They heaved the vending machine aside, freeing up a small space behind the door. It was enough for the zombies to gain entry, but not enough to allow the torrent of bodies Jack had suggested. Ben stooped down again, Dave mimicking his movement, clearly on the same wavelength.

"Three. Two—"

The door burst open, slamming against the vending machine, as countless arms sprung through the gap. Dave squealed as three of the grasping hands clamped around his arm. A surge against the door pushed the vending machine aside, and all at once, the bodies spilled into the room.

"Shit!" Ben vaulted over the coffee table and raced through the open door, joining Jay and Jack in the alleyway. He slammed it shut behind him, instantly met with a thud as body after body slammed against it.

"Move!"

He shoved the dumbstruck men down the alley, and they sprinted into the street. It was still empty, but the racket from the pharmacy drifted behind them. If there were any zombies nearby, the noise would definitely attract them.

"Oh shit, Dave," Jack said.

"He's dead," said Ben. "Mourn him later, or we'll be next."

Staying close to the wall, he dashed to the end of the building, slowing only when he neared the bed of the pickup truck.

A lone zombie stood in the pharmacy doorway, watching the frenzy within, shuffling its feet as if debating whether to join the others or remain standing outside.

Ben turned back to the two men, gesturing to the front of the truck. Jack reached into his pocket and produced a key fob.

'Go on,' Ben mouthed.

Jack shook his head, shoving the keys towards Ben.

For fuck's sake. He snatched them from his grasp, shaking his head in disapproval. The zombie at the entrance had taken a step back, still observing the carnage within.

What the hell's it waiting for?

Ben didn't have time to contemplate. Any second, those at the rear of the procession could venture back outside. He crouched down, scrambling along the back of the truck until he could see around the side. The lone zombie remained, its beady eyes fixed on its brethren within the store.

Ben started around the side, keeping himself low, his movements measured. He debated whether he could get into the truck without the zombie noticing, but decided against it. The motion of the door would catch its eye, and it would be close enough to make a lunge for him. He had to kill it.

A sound from behind stopped him in his tracks. Jay clambered into the back of the pickup, stumbling over the assortment of tools that lay within.

With a screech, the zombie lunged for Ben, arms outstretched, foam dripping from its mouth. He brought the machete up beneath its chin. The blade sliced upwards, smashing teeth together, stopping only when it reached the top layer of the zombie's skull. Ben pulled the blade free, releasing the corpse as the next zombie rushed out of the pharmacy.

"In!" Ben scrambled into the driver's seat after Jack and shut the door. The undead spilled out of the shop, surrounding the truck as Ben fought to start the engine, something he struggled to do with his slippery, blood-slicked fingers.

"C'mon, move!" Jack gasped.

"I'm trying."

A fist hammered against the back window.

"Hurry up!" Jay cried from behind them.

"I'm trying!" Ben snapped.

Gurning faces surrounded them, and in his side mirror he could see the zombies trying to climb up to Jay.

An eternity passed before the engine roared to life. Forcing the truck into reverse, Ben drove back, crushing any zombies behind them beneath the wheels. He swung the steering wheel and pushed the truck onwards down the road. The ensuing chaos attracted more of the undead from the shadowy storefronts and back streets, but none were quick enough to match the truck.

"We're good. We're good," Jack panted. "Jay, you good?"

"I will be when you stop and let me in!"

Ben watched every alley, doorway and crawlspace as he drove, with more zombies joining those reflected in his mirrors.

"You'll have to stay put for now!" he called back. "Where am I going, anyway?"

"Just get out of here. I'll direct you once we're clear of this hellhole." Jack clasped both hands to his head, massaging his scalp through the flimsy bandana.

The road widened ahead of them, and the looming signs told Ben they were heading north. He breathed deeply, allowing himself to relax a little bit more. He was free. And more importantly, he was alive. All he had to do now was move on to the next part of his plan and hope Mike would be as forthcoming with information as Jack had made out. If not, he'd have to resort to other tactics. He wanted to press Jack further, but noticed he was staring forlornly into the distance.

"Hey, I'm sorry you lost your friends," Ben said.

Jack blinked and shrugged. "They weren't my friends. I'm more worried how Mike's gonna take the news."

"Was he close to them?"

"Close?" Jack scoffed. "Dave was his son."

10

Shit! Shit! Shit!

As soon as he entered the office, Gus knew Doctor Miller wasn't there. He didn't need to check under the desk or in the adjoining bathroom. She was gone.

Good. She was a nightmare, anyway.

We need her.

We don't need shit.

Are you harbouring profound medical knowledge up there? We've got a fucking hole in our gut.

Gus strode over to the window. The prison van trundled away into the distance, loaded with at least five inmates.

That still leaves a handful behind.

They'll be getting more than a handful if they find her.

Gus stormed out of the room, listening for any screams or cries within the prison walls. It was a vast structure, but with only a few inmates left, sounds travelled a lot farther. Yet as he listened, he could hear nothing more than silence. A persistent, pressing silence.

Perhaps she's in the van.

No, Terrance would have told me.

Not if they were in cahoots.

Gus marched down the corridor, considering the plausibility. The pair had never been alone together; it would be impossible to orchestrate that kind of escape. He lurched to a halt when he passed the door that granted access to the roof. It stood ajar.

Ohh, I wonder if she's jumped.

If she wanted to kill herself, she's got a gun.

Gus ascended the stairway leading to the rooftop, his footsteps echoing around the enclosed space.

With one bullet. What if she missed?

How could she miss?

I don't know. How could she get through medical school without learning the symptoms of glioblastoma?

Gus clenched his jaw as he reached the top of the stairs. He didn't blame Doctor Miller for not picking up on his symptoms, but her fixation on his mental health had certainly resulted in a delayed diagnosis. He threw open the fire door to the roof and stepped out onto the loose gravel.

Doctor Miller stared out at the moors, lost in a completely different world. Despite the blazing heat, she hugged her arms across her chest, the handgun held close.

Gus stopped beside her, kicking a bunch of pebbles over the edge. "Decided to go for a wander?"

"Yes," she replied. "I felt like a captive."

"Prisons tend to have that effect."

"I needed some fresh air."

Gus smirked. "The stench of BO and testosterone too much for you?"

"Actually, I was thinking about the stench of death in your office."

"Yeah, you can't get the help these days. I'll have Terrance sort it when he gets back."

He guessed they'd be at least an hour. Possibly longer, depending on what resources they found. Then, once they had returned, it would be on to the army base. He didn't know what kind of opposition they would face or how much firepower they had. Their biggest threat would likely be the sniper, but Gus had already come up with a plan to get past him.

Snipers are long distance. Once we're up close and personal, he'll be ours for the taking.

Providing he doesn't shoot us before we get there.

That's why we're not going in the prison van. He won't fire at an unmarked car.

You have too much faith in the Old Bill.

He's not a cop anymore.

Precisely.

Gus massaged his temple, resisting the urge to vocalise his inner conflict.

"Something the matter, Doc?" he asked, sensing Doctor Miller's studious gaze.

"Gus, why won't you let me help you? We can find more medication; we could start the project again."

"And what good would it do? I'm living on borrowed time, remember?"

"We could at least make your final days more comfortable."

Gus scoffed. "Comfortable, in here? You must be joking."

"Then why stay?"

"Doc, I don't know if you've clicked on yet, but if you direct your peepers over yonder, you'll see why we're staying put."

A distant, solitary figure limped towards the prison, its fractured leg jutting out at an odd angle. The remnants of its upper body jiggled and swayed as it continued on.

"In these trying times, you need safety and security. Otherwise, you'll end up like that mangled Herbert."

They watched the zombie for some time. It continued through the ploughed field, occasionally disappearing from view. But every time, it re-emerged, determined to reach the secure building.

"So, why are you pursuing this vendetta against Frank?"

Gus frowned. "What?"

"If safety and security are important, why throw it away just to get back at him?"

"Because debts have to be paid. Favours returned. Call it my unfinished business, if you will."

"You shot him. He shot you. You're even."

"No," Gus sneered. "I get the last word. Every time."

"So, you're going to leave the safety and security of this building to kill him? What's to say you don't die on the way?"

"Because I'm Gus fucking Razor. I bow out on *my* terms. Nobody else's. The bullet in your shooter was intended for me."

Doctor Miller smiled thoughtfully. "Maybe it still is."

Gus sneered again, but his humour faded when he looked back out at the bordering field. The zombie had gained ground, but its attention was now fixed on a convoy of SUVs heading their way. Three Land Rovers drove with purpose, none of them straying from their linear formation. The zombie reached out to the nearest vehicle, only to be met with a hail of gunfire.

"Seems our little rendezvous has come early. Look alive, Doc, you might not be that way for long."

He shoved Doctor Miller towards the door and bounded down the stairs after her. Together, they dashed along the corridor, retracing the route to the office.

Check out the balls on Frank Lee. Gathered a few mates, and now he's back to finish the job.

He never was smart, that boy.

He'll be smart when we put a bullet in his head.

Maybe.

What do you mean 'maybe'?

I mean, that was an automatic rifle they fired there.

And?

And if they've got that kind of firepower, with our reduced numbers, we're gonna struggle.

We're Gus fucking *Razor. We never struggle.*

They made it to the office as an almighty clatter sounded outside.

"That's the gate gone," Gus said. "You wait in here, and don't go for any more wanders."

He didn't hear Doctor Miller's protests as he slammed the door. He dashed down the hallway as a series of engines roared outside.

336

What the fuck are they doing?

He bounded down the stairs and reached the rec room before he spotted any of the prisoners.

"You two, where the fuck are the others?" he demanded, storming towards the startled pair.

"Five of them have gone out. I dunno where the others are," one man answered.

"Maybe the canteen," piped up another.

"How many bullets do you have?" Gus nodded to the rifles the men were holding.

"A few."

"Good, get to the front of the building, and fire at whoever's coming through those doors."

"What?"

"Move!" Gus shoved the men towards the end of the room, kicking one of them when he didn't move fast enough. The pair disappeared through the door as Gus rushed to the canteen.

Those boys aren't going to survive.

Like I give a shit.

You ought to keep one to hand to use as a shield if things get tasty.

I'll *decide what we're doing.*

A tremendous crash came from the prison entrance. The roar of engines grew louder, echoing through the corridors.

They knew about the barricade. They've gone straight through.

I can fucking hear that.

Gus reached the canteen where several cons sat with bewildered expressions.

"What the fuck are you gawping at? Get off your arses and kill the cunts!"

The men scrambled to their feet, some loading their weapons, others staring in horror as the first gunshots rang out.

"Charlie! Give me a weapon," Gus demanded. Chomping Charlie dashed out of the kitchen wielding twin meat cleavers. Gus took one of them before rounding on a prisoner, loading his rifle.

"Here, swap." He snatched the gun out of the man's hands, replacing it with a cleaver. "Now fuck off."

Gus shoved the man toward the door, where the other inmates were rushing to intercept the unknown threat.

"Charlie, you should never bring a knife to a gunfight. But since you did, stay covered and hack them to death when they're within range. Understand?"

"Y-y-y—"

Gus didn't wait for him to finish. He shoved Charlie towards the door before making his way down another corridor. The gunfire continued. Pops and cracks he attributed to rifles, with the occasional boom of a shotgun. Next came a return volley of automatic fire.

Machine guns, Gustav. That's the military.

The military are dead. Frank's obviously found a stash in the fucking base.

We checked the base.

Clearly not enough.

He reached the stairs and bounded up them two at a time. Despite being encased by the thick walls of the stairway, the ensuing commotion grew louder. Now he could hear a bout of indecipherable yelling interspersed with the gunfire. The intruders were drawing close.

No sound of a sniper yet. Perhaps he's waiting outside.

Or switched to an MP5.

Gus reached the top of the stairs and dashed across the metal walkway. The hall below was empty, but the gunfire was louder than ever. The barking orders he could hear didn't belong to his men. Whoever it was, was telling the invaders to spread out.

Unusual tactic. We can pick them off one at a time.

It can't be the cop. He'd know better than that.

Then who the fuck is it?

The gunfire had all but ceased when Gus spotted movement from a doorway. He aimed the rifle, finding three men within his line of sight as they dashed into the hall. They managed a quick scan of the area before he shot the first in the chest.

The remaining two hunched down, before he dispatched the second. The last man aimed his rifle at Gus, but didn't have time to pull the trigger before a section of his head exploded.

Definitely not military.

No automatics between them, either.

So where—

More movement from the doorway. A tall man wielding a submachine gun spotted Gus. He arced the gun up, spraying a torrent of bullets before he even had the sights trained. Gus dived behind the cover of the wall, bringing his knees up as bullets ricocheted off the metal walkway beside him.

These aren't soldiers. They're not even trained.

The machine gun stopped when a shotgun reverberated in response. A second blast came, and then a third, before a yelp sounded through the hall. Gus leaned out from behind the cover and saw the tall man lying prone. One of the convicts scooped up the MP5.

"How many's left?" Gus called down.

"I don't know. We've blocked the exit, but I don't know if any got past us."

"Then find out!"

Gus rushed back down the stairs. He had run out of ammo. If there were any more intruders in the prison, he needed to be wary. He could hear distant shouts, and what sounded like a clatter, but no further gunshots.

He reached the bottom of the stairs, where he slammed into a fleeing figure.

"No, please," the man whimpered, cowering to his knees before Gus could react. He held both trembling hands aloft, his head bowed. "Don't hurt me."

"Hurt you?" Gus stepped forward, looming over the intruder. "You come into *my* house. You kill *my* men, and you plead for *mercy*?"

"I didn't kill anyone."

"No? So those were fireworks I heard earlier? Where's your gun?"

"I didn't have a gun."

Gus swung a boot into the man's midriff, sending him sprawling into the ground.

"I didn't, I swear! They gave me a machete."

"And where's it at?"

"I dropped it."

"Convenient."

A single gunshot echoed from somewhere within the prison.

"How many of you are there?"

"Eight," the man wheezed. He tried to rise, but Gus stepped on his upper back, pinning him to the ground.

"And how many are left?"

"I don't know. Really, I don't. As soon as the shooting started, I ran."

"How noble of you. I bet your friends were thrilled."

"They're—they're not my friends."

Gus dragged the captive to his feet when a flurry of footfalls sounded at the end of the corridor. He positioned himself behind the man, half expecting to see more of the black-clad intruders. But the men who came into view were from the prison.

"There's another!" one shouted. He raised his rifle, stopping only once Gus emerged from the behind the man.

"Put your dicks away. I've got this one!" he growled. "How many are dead?"

"Four of ours, seven of theirs."

"That means they're all accounted for, if this speck of shit is telling the truth."

"I swear I am," the man whimpered, twisting in Gus' grasp. The two prisoners approached, eyeing the captive in disgust. "Five men, two women."

"That only makes seven."

"And me as well."

"And what are you?" The man jabbed his rifle into the captive's genitals, prompting a pained squeak.

"Oy, less of the foreplay," Gus snarled. "Have you searched the bodies?"

"Yeah." The man's face brightened in recollection. "One of them had this."

He reached into his pocket and produced a grenade.

"Where the fuck did they get that?" Gus snatched it out of his grasp.

Looks legit.

"Better ask him," the prisoner snarled at the cowering man.

"Oh, we'll find out soon enough," Gus sneered. "I'm taking him into the interview room. Make sure this prison is secure and do *not* interrupt us. Clear?"

"Crystal," the man muttered. He gestured for his companion to follow, and they walked back down the corridor.

"Please don't kill me," the captive whimpered. "I'll tell you everything."

"Kill you? Where's the fun in that? You tell me what I want to know, and I certainly won't kill you. Fair?"

The man nodded hurriedly.

"Good. Then let's find out what you know."

11

A sharp rap from the rear window preceded an outburst from Jay.

"I think we're far enough away now!" he hollered. "Stop the truck and let me in!"

Ben eased off the accelerator and slowed to a stop at the side of the road. They were at least a couple of miles from Bealsdon, and hadn't seen a single zombie since. The surrounding fields remained barren, the only obstruction a quaint cottage.

"It's about time," Jay grumbled, swinging open the door. He waited for Jack to shuffle into the next seat before climbing in. "Did you forget about me?"

"Not at all," Ben said. "I needed to make sure we were safe."

"Yeah, those suckers are fast!" Jack added.

"And smart, too." Jay scoffed as they took off once more. "They'll be chasing us in cars next."

"You never know."

"Oh, come on, Jack. Is that a bandana or a tinfoil hat? You're hanging on to the words of a delirious bloke and his trigger-happy missus. We haven't seen any sign of intelligence."

"I have," said Ben.

"You've seen them climbing and scheming?" Jay asked.

"No. Communicating."

Jay burst out laughing, craning his head back for effect. "Communicating? What were they doing, sharing recipes?"

"No. They were clicking."

"Clicking? Like castanets?"

"No."

"What? Are we facing flamenco dancers as well, now?"

His laughter was cut short when Ben slammed on the brakes. They lurched forward as the truck squealed to a halt.

"You want to get out and walk, or are you going to shut up and listen?" Ben growled.

"I—uh."

"They click with their *tongue*. Different rhythms, different pitches, and they seem to understand each other. I know what I saw, and I won't be ridiculed by a little scumbag like you. Got it?"

"Now, hold on—"

"No, *you* hold on! I've known you for less than an hour and you're already grating on me. Use less of this, and more of these." Ben pointed to his mouth and ears, to Jay's bemusement.

"Guys, can we talk and drive?" Jack asked, staring ahead of them. "I don't think that raccoon cares much for our chatter."

He gestured at the creature shuffling out of the woodland towards them. Its black-and-white face seemed to be the only part intact. The rest of its body was a crimson pulp, dragging behind as it drew closer to the truck.

"That's a badger, you tit," Jay murmured. "We don't have raccoons here."

"Either way, he don't look friendly. Shall we go?"

Ben put the truck in gear and sped forward. When they neared the undead creature, he veered into it, crushing the remains beneath the vehicle's hefty wheels. The badger's distorted remains reminded Ben of the splayed children he and Kev had encountered the previous day.

"There's something else," he said.

"Huh?" Jack turned to face him.

"It's not just the clicking. Some of them look... different."

"Different?" Jay repeated. "How?"

Ben glanced across at him, searching for a mocking smirk or derisive glimmer in his eyes, but finding only a vague flicker of curiosity. Whether it was authentic, Ben couldn't tell, but it appeared that Jay had taken his warning on board.

"We came across a couple of zombie kids the other day. Their bottom half was warped. Their legs were spread side-on, as if they had been crushed. But they were quick. They were jumping on cars and leaping high in the air, like they had been that way their whole life. They jumped on top of our car, and could we fuck get rid of them."

"Even when you braked?" Jay asked.

"We braked, accelerated, twisted and turned. They stuck themselves on. We eventually managed to throw them off, but it didn't make sense."

"Sorry, who's *we*?"

Ben chewed his lip. He had nothing to lose and needed to trust the men if he was going to find Frank and Lisa.

"There were four of us hiding out in a cottage. Well, first it was me and... my friend. Then a cop and his wife showed up, asking if they could stay. We let them, and everything was fine until yesterday. The cop suggested we visit Bealsdon, just me and him. When we arrive, he attacks me and locks me in the pharmacy."

"Holy shit," Jack gasped.

"Why?" Jay added.

Ben rubbed his forehead, struggling to vocalise any of the countless theories darting in and out of his mind. "I don't know," he said after a while. "They wanted Amy. From what I gather, somebody sent them, but I don't know who, or why."

"You think Lisa's involved?" Jack asked.

"No. But she and Frank owe me a favour. It's a long story, really."

"Good luck getting them out of their love nest," Jay scoffed.

"Love nest? What love nest?"

Jay's grin dropped. "They—uh—just seem all over each other. I'm guessing they'll have a little hideaway somewhere."

"The only place I can think of is the army base up near Doxley. We were there before, but they said they weren't staying."

"It's a good lead. If Mike can't help you, that'd be a good place to start."

"So, where is your group hiding out?"

"An old church on top of a hill," Jack said.

"A church?"

"There's other buildings as well, a community hall and stuff. It's run by Mike and his wife, Marie."

"How long have you been there?"

"Pretty much since this shit started. I was on a tour bus which got ambushed by those things. Me and some of the other tourists hauled ass across the fields until we found Mike. Now, let me tell you, we were as welcome as a porcupine in a nudist ranch. He'd just killed the priest and his nerves were frazzled."

"He killed the priest?"

"Yes, sir. The old man was infected. Tried to bite Marie and wouldn't let up. In the end, Mike and Dave gave him the wire-brush treatment, and... you can guess the rest."

"Now there's twelve of you?"

"Give or take. Jay, Lisa and Frank joined us yesterday, and then two others soon after. I haven't learnt their names yet. Seems as soon as you get to know folk, they end up dying."

"You came with Lisa and Frank?" Ben asked. Jay shook himself from his daze.

"Uh—yeah. I stumbled across them in the woods. They gave me quite the welcome. Similar to the one you offered, as it happens."

"You can't be too careful," Ben said.

"Yeah, that's their feelings, too. I must have a dishonest face. Anyway, Frank ended up collapsing, and that's when Mike and the rest of them found us."

"He collapsed?"

"Yeah, there's a massive hole in his side. They brought us back to their camp and Theresa patched him up."

"Theresa?"

"She's our medic," Jack said. "She was an animal doctor before this, but I guess we're all animals, right? Besides, she's as bright as a penny. The rest of us don't know our asses from our elbows."

"Speak for yourself," Jay said.

"Dude, you told Mike you're an energy consultant. That fancy pants title don't mean shit in an apocalypse. Now me, I'm a mechanic. Cut me open and I bleed oil. That's where my skill set lies."

"What about you?" Jay asked Ben.

"I worked in security."

"Oh well, at least I'm not the only one with a useless profession."

Jack rapped his knuckles against Jay's knee. "You leave that man be. Without him, we'd still be stuck in the pharmacy listening to you complaining."

Ben slowed as a crossroads loomed ahead. The road sign stated Doxley was twenty miles left, and Sunnymoor thirty miles right.

"It's the left turn," Jack told him. "We drive through a forest for a couple of miles and then it's a dirt track on the right. Don't drive too fast; blink and you'll miss it."

Ben followed the directions, veering around an abandoned car. The exposed engine didn't appear intact, with worn parts strewn around the front of the vehicle.

"That's one we did last week," Jack said. "Mike had us scouring for vehicles. If it wasn't up to scratch, I'd strip any useful parts and move on."

"Vehicles? Is he wanting to leave? I got the impression you lot were settled there."

Jack shrugged. "Always good to have a set of wheels handy if things go south. Besides, he sends out groups for different things."

"Does he ever leave?"

"Yeah, from time to time. Although, since we've had more people join us, he's spent more time at the camp. Wanting to make sure everyone's pulling their weight, I guess."

Ben nodded, but his attention had drifted as soon as they entered the woodland. The sun penetrated the overhead foliage in places, casting light and shadow at varying angles. The rapid flashes were easily mistaken for movement, and it was all Ben could do not to speed up through the woodland passage.

"How far to this turn off?" he asked.

"A couple more miles. It's not a dense forest for the most part, you can see through a lot of it."

Jack's words held a reassuring tone, but Ben wasn't convinced. Every glimmer of light or shadow-masked bush felt like a threat. He recalled the woodland where he and Kev had practiced shooting. And the scourge of zombies attracted to the subsequent sound.

It was a stupid idea. But it had equipped him with a better technique for accuracy, and built his confidence as a result—which was the main reason Kev had suggested the outing. The only question was, why? Why did Kev go through all that if he was planning to leave him for dead?

Because he didn't. He left me to fend for myself.

It was an enigma, becoming all the more puzzling the longer he thought about it. He didn't even realise Jack was still talking until he saw him staring.

"What?"

"I asked what happened to your hand."

Ben flexed his fingers, which he instantly regretted as he felt the sting. "I got shot."

"Dang, and I thought you guys were all tea and crumpets over here. Y'all popping more than us!"

"I didn't realise there were that many guns round here," Jay added, leaning over to see Ben's injury. "Who shot you?"

"There are loads of bad people still around. Some are more dangerous than the zombies."

"Well, isn't that cheery," Jay muttered.

"I mean it. You need to be careful, especially if your group don't have any decent weapons."

"We're in the middle of nowhere," Jack said. "We should be fine. It's the zombies I'm worried about. If they're getting smarter, we're not going to survive much longer."

"Is it secure, at least?"

"As secure as an old church can be. But the windows aren't boarded and the doors have taken a beating."

"You'll need to secure them."

"Hell, yeah. But what worries me more is if those zombies are getting smarter, what's stopping them from coming back? Sure, Lisa led them away, but what if they remember? What if they come right back and attack us while we're unawares?"

Ben didn't have an answer. The weight of Jack's concerns hung in the air, pressing the silence all around them. The sense of foreboding was almost too much to bear until finally Jay broke the silence.

"So, two zombies are eating a dead guy, right. One starts at the feet, the other at the head, and they agree to meet in the middle. After a while, the first zombie notices his mate hasn't said much, so he asks 'are you alright?' His mate says: 'Yeah, I'm having a ball.' First zombie says 'Whoa, slow down, you're eating too fast.'"

Silence again. Only this time it was short-lived, split by Jay's infectious cackle. He slapped his knees, wiping a stray tear from his eye, doubled over from his own hilarity. Ben shook his head, aghast. The joke wasn't even funny, and the subject matter was highly inappropriate. But as soon as Jack snorted, he knew it was no use. The urge to laugh became too overpowering, and he couldn't hold back.

The trio cackled heartily, all their problems, concerns, and fears dissipated by the mirth that stole their breath. Ben's body ached, but he couldn't stop, nor did he want to. After enduring so much, physically and mentally, it felt good to release the tension. He could almost feel the serotonin shooting through his body. He wiped the blur of tears from his eyes as Jack tapped his knee.

"Here—here," he chortled, motioning towards a turn off. "Don't miss it."

Ben eased the truck down the narrow trail, listening to the final remnants of laughter die out. He wondered what the rest of the camp would think when they arrived, all three beaming like idiots.

They'll wonder why only three have returned. And who the new guy is in place of Mike's son.

The humour was over, and reality dragged the corners of his mouth back to their neutral state. All they faced were shock and heartbreak. Mike and Marie would find their son was dead, and if the other guy had a family, they'd learn about his fate, too. They'd blame Ben, wondering why he was there instead of their kin. And then he'd have the audacity to ask them for help.

They emerged from the shroud and ascended a large hill. He could already see the top of the church, could already hear the contemptuous interrogation he was bound to be subjected to. He tried to envisage what he'd be asked, what their reactions would be, what awaited them atop the hill.

THE MUTATION

Although what he actually saw was the last thing he'd expected. He stepped on the brakes, a unanimous gasp escaping all three of the men as they lurched to a halt. Ben stared, open-mouthed. He had expected to see the church, and the outbuilding, and a handful of people waiting for them. He'd expected them to be standing up and intact. But never in his wildest imagination had he expected to see so much blood.

12

The quartet stood in the hotel room, frozen in silence, watching the distant ripple of bodies trundling in the same direction. The zombies moved with purpose, order, and discipline. Whether it was instinctual or motive-driven, Frank couldn't tell. But it was happening, nonetheless. Hundreds, if not thousands, of flesh-hungry corpses marching to an unknown destination.

Frank had never put much thought into how they would survive the apocalypse. Taking one day at a time was enough to keep him going. They'd have to face a few zombies here and there, sure. But as long as they avoided the major towns and cities, there'd be no reason they couldn't stay alive. Now, seeing the army of undead mobilising, he wondered how long they would actually survive.

The hotel wasn't secure. That much was certain. And it was too late to find somewhere else. With no efficient weapons, they'd be sitting ducks. He took a step back, stumbling over the outstretched arm of the dead child. He caught himself on the edge of the bed, finally taking in the deformed creature in the light of day.

Its skin had a waxy sheen that looked pallid against the plush red carpet. Its arms were bare, but had lost some of their natural shape, flattening out where the palms met the wrists. The deformities in its legs were far more apparent. They resembled chicken wings that had been plucked of their plumage. Its knees—or what used to be its knees— now sat alongside its hips. Scaly legs jutted outward, flush against the floor. The sides of its feet were now flat, its toes nothing more than a web of flesh.

"What the fuck," Frank said. He prodded one of the legs with the metal pole, noting the tightly-bound flesh and muscle.

"It's like a nightmare," Lisa muttered, crouching beside him. "They're more monster than human."

"That's an understatement."

"The question is, did the virus cause them to change, or something else?"

"What do you mean?"

Lisa rose back to her feet. "This outbreak started after those bastards in the military base tried to create a weapon. What if these things were part of the tests?"

"Then why would they be here?"

"I don't know. But the base isn't far. It just seems funny, don't you think?"

"Whatever it is, we're not equipped to deal with it, especially if they're all joining together. We need to secure this place."

"How? It's all windows. If those things attack, they're getting inside."

"I know, I know. But we need to do something."

"We could secure this floor," Kara suggested, tearing herself away from the window. "Block the stairs, disable the lift. It'll keep us safe for the time being."

"What about food?"

"I'm not saying it's a permanent solution. But it'll tide us over. Especially if those zombies keep moving away from here."

Frank shook his head. "It'll have to be the top floor. We can't secure the middle."

"We don't even know if the top floor is clear," Lisa said.

"Well, it's about time we found out. You two, are you still good for weapons?" He looked from Kara's dented metal pole to Sam's empty hands. Before he could ask anything else, Lisa stepped forward, handing him back the wrench.

"Make sure you use it this time," she warned, retrieving her rifle off the bed. Sam's face turned scarlet and he nodded.

"We stick together, and this time, we *close* the doors." Frank focused his attention on Kara, who mirrored Sam's crimson shade. "We can check the rooms after we secure the corridor. Deal?"

With a unanimous nod from the group, Frank stepped back into the corridor and led them over to the staircase. Four of the undead creatures had occupied their current floor. There was no telling how many they would face on the next. Yet, he felt cautiously optimistic. Given the zombies had gained entry on the second floor, it was less likely they would have ventured up to the third. He approached the foot of the stairs, trying to keep riding the wave of positive thinking.

"Did you lock the door leading to the roof?" Lisa asked Kara.

"I'm not sure. I can't remember."

And there it was: wipeout. The positivity turned to dread, and all Frank could imagine was a swarm of the creatures traversing the side of the building, reaching the rooftop, and spilling down the stairs. He tried to take a calming breath as he began his ascent to the next floor.

He tiptoed up as he had done before, listening to the suspense-filled silence, praying there wouldn't be more of the undead to greet them at the top. When he rounded the corner, though, the corridor appeared untouched. Every door was closed, every painting still hung, with no marks along the carpet or the walls. The door leading up to the roof appeared to be shut, but that didn't mean much. It was a heavy door, one which would close over of its own accord.

"You two, make sure all those doors are closed." He gestured for Kara and Sam to head down the corridor. "We'll go and check the roof."

Kara and Sam walked away without question, but Lisa gripped his arm.

"Are you sure? We could barricade the door and stop them getting in."

"We will. I just want a better view of what's out there, first."

Frank eased open the door to the dark stairway. The door at the top was shut, quashing any light along with it. With his staff held aloft, Frank made his way up the stairs, contemplating whether a zombie could be hiding in the shadows. With each passing second, and each progressive step, he knew if there was anything else in there, it would have attacked.

They reached the top of the stairs without incident and pushed the heavy door open. The groan of metal stirred a zombie child out of its reverie. It whirled around, screeching at Frank and Lisa, who had emerged on the opposite side of it.

"One," Frank said. The child bounded towards them on all fours. "You see any others?"

The child drew close, bursts of gravel shooting up around its warped limbs as it went.

"No," Lisa said. "Unless there are others climbing up."

At a couple of metres away, the zombie child leaped towards them. With its burst of speed and altitude, one could mistake it for having bounced off a springboard. Frank barely managed to raise his staff before the zombie collided. With a jerk, he heaved it up to his right, sending the child soaring over the safety railings and plummeting to the ground. The action evoked a wave of pain in his side, and he felt the wound tear. He clutched the bandage, blood already seeping through and warming his fingers.

Lisa gasped. "Are you hurt?"

"I'll be fine." He clasped a palm against his side, hobbling over to the railings. The zombie lay motionless alongside the dark saloon.

"That was close," he said.

"I'll say. It could've bitten you!"

Frank shook his head. "I meant where it landed. It could've totalled our new ride."

"You're planning on using it?"

"We lost the prison van, the bike is in pieces, and the other van has a flat tyre. It's our only means of transport."

"Who cares about transport when you're faced with them?" Lisa pointed to the surging mass in the distance. The zombies had cleared one field and were entering the next, which was bordered by forest. "Unless we find a helicopter, I think most transport is redundant now, don't you?"

"I don't know. They're not heading in our direction, so that's one thing. And it means wherever they're leaving is safe… theoretically."

"What do you mean?"

"Well, think about it. They're grouping together and they're moving. Why would they do that?"

"Showing signs of pack mentality?"

"Exactly. And packs go wherever the food is."

"So they're actively seeking us out, now? Well, that makes me feel so much better."

"But think about what they're leaving behind."

"Zombie shit?"

Frank smirked. "Empty towns. I reckon we could drive west, find the nearest town, and ransack without issue."

"But what if they come back?"

"I doubt it. They'll either find another food source, or keep heading east. Hopefully, they reach the sea and fuck off for good, but I doubt we're that lucky."

Frank's smile faded when he saw the look on Lisa's face. She held a hand to her mouth, staring out at the diminishing crowd.

"What's wrong?"

"They're heading straight for that community."

"What?"

"The religious nuts. Their church is over that way, remember?"

Lisa made for the door, but stopped when Frank seized her wrist.

"What are you doing?"

"We have to warn them!"

"Warn them? Are you mad?"

"Frank, they have kids there! We can't leave them!"

"And what do you suggest they do? Barricade their little church and start praying?"

"No. We bring them here."

Frank dashed ahead, blocking the doorway. "Wait. What? You want to bring them here?"

"Why not?"

"For fuck's sake, Lise. I know it's a hotel, but we don't have to treat it like one. We've already taken in two strays. The last thing we need is more."

"So you're going to let them die?"

"I—I don't know. But let's not act rashly. With the speed they're walking, it'll take them hours to reach the church. We can get there in fifteen, twenty minutes, easy. So let's stop and think."

"What's there to think about?"

"How we hope to feed them all, for one."

"Everyone can chip in. They can bring their cars, we can go on scavenger hunts, and if you're right about the empty towns, we should be able to stockpile loads."

"We're meant to be securing this place, remember?"

"And with more people, we can do it faster."

Frank groaned. He knew she had a point, but the prospect of adding to their party only fuelled the antisocial furnace raging in his core. With a reluctant groan, he stepped aside and followed Lisa back down the stairs.

"Is everything secure?" she asked Kara and Sam, who stood either side of the doorway.

"Yeah, what were you two arguing about?" Kara asked.

"We weren't arguing, we were discussing."

Kara scoffed. "That's what my mum used to tell me when she argued with my dad."

"Well, I'm not your mum," Lisa said firmly. "And we *were* having a discussion."

"About what?"

Frank leaned back against the wall, his hand still pressed over his wound.

"The horde is heading towards a group not too far from here," Lisa continued. "We need to warn them and bring them here."

"I thought we were securing this place?"

"Those zombies are moving away from here. We should still have plenty of time to do both."

"But what about The Apostles?" Sam asked, unable to keep the tremor from his voice.

"Who?"

"The people who abducted me."

"The Apostles?" Frank snorted, pushing himself from the wall. "Why do they call themselves that?"

"He makes them."

"Who does?"

"Death."

13

"Deaf?" Gus repeated, eyeing his captive with disdain. "What is he, mutton or something?"

"No, 'Death' with a 't-h'. It's what he calls himself." The man glanced around the interview room. Carver's corpse and scattered organs were no longer there, but the blood spatter remained, as did the noxious smell of burnt flesh and hair. Gus clicked his fingers, regaining the man's attention.

"And he has you lot calling yourselves The Apostles? What does he think he is, some kind of god?"

The man flipped his hands over and shrugged.

"Keep your hands on the table or you lose them." Gus growled.

"I don't know," the man whimpered. "It's been that way since I got there."

"Which was when?"

"About eight days ago."

"And how did you stumble across these apostles? Were they praying in a church?"

"No. I was hiding in a house in Cranston. They had sent a group out to round up survivors. They took me back to—"

"To where?" Gus sat up, mindful of the man's sudden change in body language. Deceit was afoot.

"I—uh."

The man's hesitancy turned into a scream when Gus slammed a shiv through the back of his hand. It pierced flesh, muscle and bone, pinning his palm to the table. The man made to reach for it, but Gus grabbed his other hand, bending his fingers back to breaking point.

"What do you think you're doing, boy? When I stick your hand to the fucking desk, I want it keeping there. *I'll* choose whether to remove it, not you." He bent the man's fingers further back, causing him to crumble in his chair. "Understand?"

"Please!" the man cried.

"That's not answering my question."

He wiggled the handle of the shiv, prompting another scream.

"Yes. Yes, I understand," the man whimpered.

"Good. Now say 'Thank you, Mr Razor.'"

"Th—thank you, Mr Razor."

"Now put your hand on your head."

Gus released his grip on the man's fingers. He raised his trembling hand, placing it atop his head.

"Very good. Now, you lie to me, mumble, or give me anything other than a straight answer, I'm putting a shiv through that hand while it's on your fucking bonce."

The man nodded, tears streaming down his cheeks.

"So we're going to start again, and this time we'll ease you in. First of all, what's your name?"

"Greg."

"Gregory, you seem like a man who doesn't like extra holes being added to his body. If you'd like to prevent that from happening again, tell me where they're based."

"Longhill Steelworks."

"See, that wasn't so hard, was it? Do they operate anywhere else?"

"There's a farm a few miles south. They have people working there, too."

"Farming, perchance?"

Gregory nodded. "Yes."

"Good. Now let's talk numbers. How many *apostles* are there?"

"I really don't know."

"An estimate will do."

"Sixty, seventy. They bring in more every day."

Gus rose from his seat.

Seventy fuckers working for him. He's outdone us, Gustav.

We've already killed eight of them.

Not yet. This guy's still breathing.

He won't be for long.

"Let's talk weapons. What kind of guns does he have?"

"Quite a few. Some of the raids focused on the hunting shops. They've got rifles and shotguns—"

"That was an MP5 out there!" Gus snapped. "You don't find those in *shops*."

"He has a cop working for him. He had access to the police armoury and brought all the guns to the steelworks."

Holy shit, the cop's with them.

"This cop, big bastard? Bald head, beard?"

"Yeah."

Maybe Frank's an Apostle.

Nah, Frankie wouldn't sign up for that bullshit.

You never know.

"Have you seen him recently?"

"Yeah, he came back yesterday."

"Was he alone?"

"Yeah, but his wife brought someone back."

Gus stopped pacing and went over to the table. "Who?"

"I dunno. Some lass. I only saw her in passing."

Okay, so where the hell is Frank now?

I think we've got bigger fish to fry, Gustav.

I'll be the judge of that.

You can't deny this Death geezer has done well for himself. He's got a highly skilled cop under his thumb, shitloads of firepower and slave labour. Admirable, really.

"And what about this?" Gus asked, setting the grenade on the table.

"I don't know. I promise. I've never seen any of them with grenades before."

Gus pressed his palms against the table, looming over the man. "How many are willing to fight for him?"

"Willing? Not many; most are forced to work for him."

"And what happens if you refuse?"

Gus returned to his seat, boredom starting to displace the previous buds of admiration.

"You're put in The Box."

His interest was piqued. "Box?"

"It's like a small cage hanging over a pit. He uses it as zombie bait."

"Zombie bait?" Gus leaned forward, willing Gregory to continue.

"Yeah, he puts people in it and has a loud music player attached to attract the zombies. When they try to grab the person inside, they fall into this big pit."

"And I'm guessing this pit is full of spikes or something?" Gus sneered, more angry with himself for being lured into the fantastical tale. He pocketed the grenade, waiting for a response.

"I don't know. I've not been close enough."

"Right."

Gus pried the shiv out of the man's hand and hammered it into his forearm. Gregory's wails hit a higher pitch. Instinctively, he reached for the handle again.

"You want more?"

Gus yanked the makeshift ice-pick free and grabbed Gregory's other hand. He slammed it against the table and brought the shiv down on top. The man cried out again, sliding so far down his chair he was almost on the floor.

"And voilà, we have stigmata! Wait till Death sees that! He'll piss his pants."

Gregory held an arm to his face, weeping into the bloodied fabric.

"What's wrong? I'm doing you a favour. You'll be well ahead of the other apostles when he catches sight of those drum rolls on your hands."

A sharp knock at the door cut through the man's wailing.

"Enter."

T-Bird strode into the room with Harper and another man at his heel.

"It's about fucking time. Where the hell have you been?"

"Sunnymoor," T-Bird said.

"It was a rhetorical question, dipshit. While we've been defending the prison from Gregory here, you've been having a Jolly Boys' Outing."

The men stared at the captive, who continued to weep into his arm, his hand still skewered on the table.

"He caused all that?" T-Bird asked, gesturing over his shoulder.

"Him and his little crew, yeah. We lost four men while you were gone, so it better have been a success."

"Yeah, I'd say it was. We got a new van, a car, turned over a corner shop, and got more food supplies and a few cases of bottled water."

"Weapons?"

T-Bird's face dropped. He looked to the others for support, but both withdrew.

"It's a good job Gregory has gifted us in that regard." Gus turned to his captive. "What were you boys carrying?"

"Some had rifles. One had a machine gun, the rest of us had machetes and bats."

"Why didn't he send the big guns?"

"We were told it was empty. Possibly a few zombies, but that was it."

"Lucky you cowards went into hiding when Carver bit the big one," Gus said to the others. "They might've sent more guns otherwise."

"Who?" T-Bird asked.

"Just some outfit down at the steelworks. We'll be paying them a visit soon."

"You won't need to," Gregory said. "When we don't return, he'll send more."

"A rescue party? Isn't that nice. We'll be sure to lay out the red carpet." He turned back to the men in the doorway. "Harper, get the others to round up his dead mates and bring them out front. I want the heads lopping off all of them. After that, await my instructions."

"Okay."

"Oh, and kill him, too."

"What?" cried Gregory. "You said if I told you everything, you wouldn't kill me!"

"And I stand by that. Gus Razor is nothing if not a man of his word... Which is why Harper's gonna kill you. Toodle-oo."

Gus strode out of the room with T-Bird at his side. He slammed the door, drowning out Gregory's pleas for mercy.

"I wonder how he'll kill him?" Gus said as they strode down the corridor. "Do you reckon he'll use the blade, or shoot him like a pussy?"

"I don't know."

"I wasn't talking to you, Terrance."

He'll put him down like a sick dog. Rifle to the back of the head.

And waste a fucking bullet in the process. He better not—

A gunshot sounded down the corridor behind them.

The stupid prick.

I'll punish him later.

"So, what's the plan?" T-Bird asked.

Gus stopped and stared at him. "Come again?"

"I'm just wondering what the plan is?"

"You've been doing too much thinking recently, my little pocket rocket. Any more of that and I'll send you back to Snow White with the other dwarfs."

They turned up a flight of stairs, their echoing footsteps drowning out Harper's barking orders to the others.

"The plan is we show them how we treat our guests. When they arrive, they're going to think Vlad the fucking Impaler lives here. But before that happens, we're going to visit the army base."

"We're going after Frank, still?"

"Yes. But I'm going to give him a chance to survive. At least for a while longer. Better the devil you know, if you catch my drift?"

T-Bird scratched his chin. "Not really."

"This is a serious outfit we're up against. So, we'll give Frank and his tart the chance to join us. We deal with this threat first, and then deal with Frank after."

"Okay. But what if they say no?"

"Then we kill them and be back in time for tea. Speaking of, did you get any teabags?"

T-Bird nodded. "And biscuits."

He retrieved a packet of custard creams from his pocket.

"Hmm. Maybe you're not as daft as I first thought."

They stopped beside the office door, where Gus took the biscuits from him.

"Right, I want you to go up to the roof and throw down all those scaffolding poles that are up there. Then, you go down and wait for me. Got it?"

"Got it."

He entered the office once T-Bird strode down the corridor. At first it appeared empty, until Doctor Miller emerged from behind the door.

"What happened?" she asked.

"We died. What do you think happened?"

"There were a lot of gunshots."

"There's a lot of bodies."

"Who was it?"

Gus strode over to the desk and pried the top off a bottle of whisky. "Just some feral youths. I told you, it's dangerous out there."

"Bullshit. Youths don't run round with guns."

"They do now. That's the new norm. Get used to it."

"How many died?"

"Four of ours, eight of theirs."

Doctor Miller groaned, slumping into one of the chairs.

"You don't have to mourn them," Gus sneered. "They were scum."

"I'm not mourning *them*. I'm mourning the state of the world. As if zombies weren't bad enough, we have to survive all-out conflict."

"Could be worse."

"How could it be worse?"

"At least you've got biscuits." He threw the packet of custard creams to her, before taking another swig of whisky.

Stop being nice to this quack. You're going to give the impression we have a heart.

Sweetening the deal. I'd prefer she still be here when we come back.

Then take her with us.

We need a show of strength when we hit the base, not a bunch of rapists slobbering over fresh meat. She'll be safer here.

He set the whisky down and made for the window overlooking the front of the prison. A pile of headless bodies lay outside the double doors, with more being decapitated as he looked on. He tried to count them, but the amalgamation of limbs proved difficult. Gregory's was the only corpse he recognised. The shiv jutted out of his dangling hand. The top half of his scalp had become a bloody pulp. His head bobbed as Chomping Charlie seized a handful of hair. Cleaver in hand, he lopped the head clean off, and threw it in a pile with the others.

"What are they doing out there?" Doctor Miller asked.

"Sending a message before we leave."

"You're still going to kill Frank? Would it not be wise to stay put?"

"There is no wisdom without experience. And experience tells me to right any and all wrongs done to me."

"Then your wisdom is flawed."

Gus grinned. "We're all flawed, doctor. But those who understand that have one less flaw than those who don't."

A sudden clatter echoed outside.

"Look out, dickhead!" one of the men yelled, as metal poles rained down from the rooftop.

"That's my cue," Gus said. "Take care of this place while we're gone, won't you?"

"What makes you think I'm staying?"

Gus offered the doctor a wry smile. "You can leave, but remember, you only have one bullet in the gun; make it count."

He closed the door behind him and went down to the front of the prison.

The scaffolding lay all over the entrance, with some propped up against the mountain of corpses.

"Right then, I want eight heads stuck on top of eight poles. Get them evenly distributed up against the front of the building."

He looked around at the pile of corpses.

"Why am I only counting six bodies?"

Harper stepped forward, his boots scuffing the ground uneasily.

"Well—uh. There were two women, and the boys thought—"

"There'll be no necrophilia while I'm in charge, you dirty little cunt. Get them bodies out here with the rest of them. Now."

Two of the prisoners begrudgingly went back inside, while the rest set to work, sticking the heads on the end of the poles.

"When you've done that, we're going to impale the bodies and get them up there as well."

"How?" T-Bird asked.

"Stick the pole up their arse and out through the neck. How else do you think?"

"They're round poles. If they had spikes on the end, maybe. But these aren't going to go all the way through."

"Are these only for show, then?" Gus flicked T-Bird's bulging upper arm. "Put some of your roid-rage to use and skewer me some human kebabs."

"But how do we keep them upright? The weight will tip them over."

"Use your loaf, Terrance. Get some of the other poles to prop them up. Fuck knows there's enough of them."

The two prisoners returned, each dragging a dead body.

"Take the heads off and put them with the others," Gus ordered. "And—oy!" He snatched the MP5 that one of the men had slung over his back. "I'll be having that."

Gus stepped back, monitoring the work from the doorway. When Death and his apostles showed up, they'd be greeted by the macabre display and an all-out war—one which he was starting to hope would involve an alliance with Frank and his group.

14

"Oh my god."

Jack was the only one able to muster the words, but all three men were thinking the same. Everywhere they looked, they saw death, mutilation, and destruction. Bodies lay strewn all over the hill, their bones, muscles, and organs exposed in equal measure. Long trails of blood and intestines ran over the grass leading up to where each eviscerated individual had fallen.

"What are we gonna do?"

"We need to get out of here," Jay replied. "The zombies might still be around."

"Is this everyone?" Ben asked, counting the number of corpses.

"Most of them."

"I don't see any kids."

"There's one!" Jay prodded the window beside him, pointing at a distant figure lying face-down.

"Oh, shit." Jack pressed his palms into his eyes, resting his elbows on the dashboard.

"Is Mike one of them?" Ben said.

Jay skimmed over the open area, leaning forward to see the space beyond the church.

"No."

Ben killed the ignition.

Jay gasped. "What the hell are you doing?"

"Checking they're all dead." Ben swung open his door and jumped down from the truck.

"I think it's pretty obvious, don't you?"

"Not really. Some might've escaped." He walked around the front of the truck to the passenger side, but Jay held the door closed.

"Escaped?" he called from behind the window. "How do you figure that?"

Ben pulled the door open, causing Jay to stumble out of his seat.

"Because you said there were about ten people here, including women and children. I only see one child, and you said Mike isn't one of the dead."

"So?"

"So let's find them."

"What if the zombies are still hanging around?"

"Then we'll be careful."

Ben reached inside the truck and grabbed the machete from the footwell.

"Jack, are you coming?"

The American ran a hand over his beard before shuffling across to the door. "Yeah, I guess. Y'all ain't leaving me out here on my own."

He jumped down and grabbed an iron bar from the rear of the pickup before joining the others.

"Wait a minute," Jay said. "That's my machete."

"Are you gonna use it?" Ben asked.

"I sure hope not, but I'd rather have it, just in case."

"Fair enough." Ben handed the weapon over before setting off towards the large community building. He tried his best to avoid the blood spatter over the grass, but as he neared the first corpse, it became an insurmountable task.

"That's Charles," Jack said as Ben stooped beside the corpse. "Guy was pushing seventy. He ain't outrunning nobody."

"Didn't even try," said Jay. "There's the chair he used to sit in."

Ben ignored the exchange, perplexed by the raw rectangle of muscle shimmering on his forearm. The man's mouth hung wide, as if his final scream had been captured in time. The gaping maw in his neck resembled a larger, grisly mouth.

This isn't right.

Ben stood up and strode over to the next corpse: a young woman lying face-down in the grass.

"Whoa, hold up," Jack snapped, fear altering the pitch of his voice. "We don't know how long they've been dead. They could come back at any time."

Jay gasped. "Shit, he's right. We can't stay here."

Ben rolled the woman onto her back. The first thing he noticed was the long crimson trail across her neck, running from ear to ear. Next was the thin incision across her abdomen. Her internal organs bulged against the deep cut, but hadn't spilled out of her body.

"This wasn't zombies."

All the corpses had had their throats cut. Some had large strips of flesh missing from exposed body parts, meticulously cut by something with a sharp edge, as opposed to having been torn apart by teeth.

"Did you have someone here called Albert Crosswell?"

"Not that I know of," Jack replied.

"Who the hell's Albert Crosswell?" Jay added, opting to stay close to the truck in case the corpses started to move.

"The serial killer. Do you remember the Skin Flayer?"

Jay's mouth dropped. "The one who skinned those people?"

"Yes. He's here."

"What—but—how?"

"When we were driving up to Bealsdon yesterday, we found a body which had been skinned. Kev—uh, the cop—told me about him. Apparently, they transferred him to Moorside a few years ago. This is his signature."

"Shit, yeah. He takes tattoos, right?" Jay asked.

"Yeah."

"Goddammit," Jack gasped. "Charles was a Navy vet. He had the sigil tattooed on his arm right there. He told me all about it."

"We can't stay here."

"Pull yourself together!" Ben snapped. "We need to stay focused."

"I don't know who y'all are talking about, but there weren't nobody called Albert in this camp," Jack said.

"Did you know them all?"

"Yeah, most of them. I like to introduce myself. Southern hospitality, y'know? Except…" Jack's words trailed off as he regarded the woman in front of them. "I didn't get to meet her, or the guy she came with."

"What did he look like?"

"He was a fat guy with glasses. Forties, fifties, maybe? Had one of those monk-cuts: y'know: the big ol' bald head with hair round the side?"

"Sounds like him."

"Ah, mate, I can't hang round here," Jay whined. "He's a fucking serial killer, for Christ's sake."

"Yes, we need to be careful, but we're *not* leaving. It's one man. There's three of us. We can take him."

When it comes to the likes of Albert Crosswell, you shoot on sight, and then shoot him again to make sure he's dead. Kev's warning taunted him. It held a lot more weight now Ben was in close proximity to the psychopath, and without his gun.

"Look at them all!" Jay snapped. "They've been sliced to pieces."

"Some could be still alive, and if it's not a zombie bite, we might be able to help them."

Ben walked over to the community centre. The doors stood open, offering a clear view inside before they drew near. A mismatch of tables and chairs filled the open space, with an empty serving station at the far end. Strips of light shone through the barricaded windows, coupling with the burst through the main entrance. The trio stepped inside, the deathly silence split by their footsteps on the laminate floor.

"It's clear," Jack murmured. He lowered himself to the ground, peering under the array of tables to confirm. "Maybe the others got away?"

"Hopefully," Ben replied. "Is there no food or water here?"

"There was."

"Has he taken it?"

"Looks like it. But hey, he's left my guitar." Jack retrieved the instrument from one of the tables.

Ben frowned. "Great, at least we've got some firewood."

He led them back outside, scanning the area for any sign of movement. The corpses remained motionless—a sight he was no longer accustomed to in the post-apocalyptic world.

The pathway leading up to the church was slick with blood, right up to the heavy wooden doors, which hung wide. Like the community centre, the scene inside became clear as Ben approached. Several pews lay upturned either side of the aisle. Those closest to the altar remained in place, where a lone figure sat hunched over. Ben froze in the doorway, taking in the rest of the scene. The white altar was smeared red, with an indecipherable message daubed by a bloody hand. Beyond it, a man stood against the wall, his pose mimicking the crucified messiah hanging above him.

"Holy shit," Jack whispered. "That's Mike."

With a subdued groan, Ben led the way towards the altar. The machete trembled in his hand, but he didn't attempt to steady it. He fixed his attention on the lone woman hunched down on the first bench. As he neared, he realised she was on her knees. Her hands were clasped as if in prayer. But as he came closer still, he saw that a wrought iron spike impaled them together, pinning them to the woman's bowed head.

"That's Marie," Jack stammered. "Mike's wife."

Ben continued, staring at the elderly man's contorted body. His arms were stretched out wide, held in position by nails embedded in his palms. A huge chunk was missing from his right forearm, with long trails of blood running down his torso. A deep incision in his side housed a metal rod wedged into the ground, holding him in place. Jack stood beside Ben, shaking his head solemnly.

"He didn't deserve this," he muttered flatly. "None of them did. They were good people."

"They always are."

A frown creased Jack's face when he saw the chunk of missing flesh.

"Did Mike have any tattoos?" he asked Jay.

"Not that I remember."

"Then why would he take his skin?"

"He didn't." Ben motioned to the altar. A pale, bloody lump of flesh sat in a golden chalice. A second goblet stood on the other side holding a red liquid.

"The body and blood of Christ."

"The sick fuck!" Jack knocked the chalice off the altar, sending it clattering down the aisle, echoing around the church. And another sound, a quiet sob, accompanied it.

Ben held up a finger to silence the men, trying to identify the source of the noise. It had come from his left, that much he was certain of, but where? The twin doors of the confessional booth were a plausible option, and he signalled for the others to follow him.

"What—"

Ben raised his hand. In his other was the machete, held aloft as he walked towards the first door. When he was within a couple of feet, it burst open. A woman leapt out into the open, crying and swinging a candlestick. Ben staggered back, losing his footing against the others, and stumbled into the pews. The woman advanced, the makeshift weapon held high above her head.

"Theresa, stop!" Jack called. "It's us."

The woman froze. "Jack?"

"It's us. Put it down."

The woman crumbled, tears spilling down her cheeks as she allowed the candlestick to clatter aside. She crawled back to the confessional booth, where two children cowered, their teary eyes fixed on Ben. The woman wrapped her arms around them, pinning them close to her sides.

"It was the bloke who arrived yesterday," Theresa cried. "He killed them all."

"Not everyone." Jack knelt down, placing a comforting hand on her shoulder. "You and your kids are safe."

"Where is he now?" Ben asked.

382

"I don't know." Theresa rubbed her eyes against her upper arm, unwilling to let go of her children. "It all happened so fast. We heard screams, so we hid. Then he dragged Mike inside. I could hear Marie begging. Then there was a thump, and she stopped. Mike was alive when he did—did that." She pointed to the suspended body. "He kept running out to kill others, but he always came back in to finish what he was doing. Then he left."

"How long ago?" Ben asked.

"I don't know. An hour, two, maybe?"

"Then let's hope he's gone for good."

"We can't guarantee it," Jack said. "What if he comes back? We need to barricade this place."

"I'm not staying here. I told you, I need to find Lisa and Frank."

Jack groaned indignantly. "The only guy who could've helped you has been stuck like a pig."

"Then I'm going to have to find them on my own."

"C'mon, dude. There's kids here. At least help us secure it first."

"You can't secure this place. You need to find somewhere safer."

"Like where?"

Jay stepped forward.

"I—uh—I know a place."

15

Sam shifted under Frank's interrogating glare.

"Is that everything?" Frank finally asked.

"Everything. That's all I know, I swear."

"So, let's recap. I want to make sure I've understood this correctly: A guy who calls himself Death has set up a cult called The Apostles, which goes out and abducts survivors, bringing them back to said cult and forcing them to work for him. I'm guessing they're the same ones we found siphoning fuel in Doxley."

Lisa nodded, lost in a sea of thought.

"Most likely," Sam said. "Fuel's high on his list. There's loads of diesel generators at the steelworks that keep everything running."

"And he's got about seventy people, all doing his bidding?"

"At least."

"And none of them have tried anything?"

"I told you, anyone who steps out of line gets put in—"

"—I know, I know, *The Box*," Frank said impatiently, still perplexed by the farcical tale.

"And when you're on these little expeditions, that's what stops you from running?"

"That, and his lieutenants."

Frank shook his head in disbelief. "He fancies himself as a military man now?"

"It's what he calls them. There's always one on every outing. They keep us in check."

"The bloke downstairs?"

Sam nodded. "And if we were to get away, he'd send more people out to catch us."

"What would the punishment be if you killed another Apostle?"

Sam shrugged, shaking his head. "I don't know. I wouldn't like to find out. The Box is bad enough."

"We don't need to find out because we'll be ready," Lisa insisted.

"No, I'm not thinking about us. When we were in Doxley the other day, we came across two people who were spouting shite about a community. Do you remember, Kara?"

"Oh yeah, the ones the cop killed?"

Lisa gasped. "Wait, what?"

"Exactly." Frank moved away from the wall, hiding his pain as he sought a more comfortable stance. "Why would he kill them if he's one of them?"

"It doesn't make sense."

"Maybe we'll be able to ask him. How long will this Death bloke give you before sending more people here?" he asked Sam.

"If we don't return? A few hours? A day, maybe?"

"Did he send you here specifically?"

Sam shook his head. "We were supposed to be heading for Witton Village. But the guy downstairs saw the signpost and brought us here first."

"They might not know where we were, but I think we're still on borrowed time," Frank told Lisa. "If we warn the Bible-bashers, that'll leave these two to defend the place on their own. If we all go, they might have taken it over by the time we get back."

"They'll die if we don't warn them."

"*We'll* die if we don't fortify this place."

"It doesn't look like we've got time for either," Kara said, from the window. "They're here."

"What?!" Frank dashed to her side. Sure enough, a pickup truck sidled towards the hotel. He couldn't see the driver or any passengers in the cab, but there were a couple of men in the cargo bed, swaying as the truck rolled over the uneven track.

"How many?" Lisa asked.

"Five, if there's three in the front."

"What do we do?"

"We get away from the windows for a start," Frank said. Kev's sniper skills were impeccable, and if he was one of the five, he'd be able to pick them off no problem. They needed a blitz attack. It was the only way.

"The roof," he said. "We need to get up to the roof."

The single stairway leading up would allow them to engage the intruders in close confines. If Kev was with them, their infiltration would be tactical and precise, similar to their assault on the prison. They would stay close, compact, and clear one room at a time. If anything, it would give Frank plenty of time to come up with another plan.

They emerged onto the roof, where the faint rumble of the truck's engine floated up to them. Frank closed the door after Sam, frantically searching for a means of barricading it. But the roof was empty. To his left was a barren stretch of gravel, and to his right—

"Kara!" Frank snapped. The young woman was leaning over the protective barrier, observing the vehicle below. He raced over and dragged her back. "What are you doing?"

"Checking who it is."

"We *know* who it is. They could've blown your head off. Do you want to die?"

"I'm not bothered," she murmured.

Frank scoffed. "Well, if you check again, you might not have a choice."

"It's not them," Lisa said.

Frank turned to find her leaning over the railing as well.

"Are you fucking mad?"

"It's not *them*, Frank."

"Then who is it?"

He heard a number of doors slam as he made his way to Lisa. Two men hopped down, joining another man, a woman, and two children at the front of the truck. Frank scowled when he saw Jay was with them.

"The little bastard," he growled. "Wait till I get hold of him."

"We were going to bring them here, anyway."

"He doesn't know that. Where's the rest of them?"

"Maybe the zombies were faster than we thought."

Frank exhaled deeply. "Hopefully, they've brought some good stuff with them at least... Is that—is that a *guitar*?!"

The man with the bandana retrieved the instrument from the rear of the pickup, slinging it over his back.

"Why would he bring a guitar?"

Lisa clapped a hand to her mouth, suppressing a nervous giggle.

"Oh no, what did you do?" Frank groaned.

"I may have... mentioned that if he was at my camp, he could play as much guitar as he wants."

"Oh, you dick. He needn't think he's bringing that shit in here. I'm not having—"

"Is that Ben?" Lisa interrupted.

The security guard spoke to the woman and her children, seemingly advising them to stay beside the truck.

"Yeah, it is," Frank said. "What the fuck's he doing here?"

"And without Amy."

The three men strode to the entrance of the hotel, each carrying a melee weapon.

"We better get down there."

Frank led the way back down through the hotel. When they descended the last staircase, the trio were inside, assessing the mangled corpse from the previous night.

"That's what we do to uninvited guests," Frank said, startling the men.

"There. See," Jay said, beaming, displaying an enthusiasm not matched by his actions as he retreated behind Ben. "I told you they were here."

Ben stepped forward, exposing Jay to Frank's venomous glare.

"I'll deal with you in a minute," he warned Jay. "And what do *you* want?"

"Help," Ben said. There was no animosity in his eyes, only a fledgling of hope.

"Help? With what?"

"Amy," Lisa offered, striding to Frank's side.

"Yes," Ben murmured.

"What happened?"

"Kev took her. He attacked me, locked me in a pharmacy, and—I don't know why."

"Do you know where he took her?"

Ben shook his head. His resolve remained firm, but Frank knew how he was feeling. It was the same loss he had felt when Lisa was being held captive in the prison.

"And what about this lot?" Frank motioned to the other two men, then to the woman with the children.

"We had nowhere else to go," Jay said. "The camp, it was—"

"—we know. It was attacked."

"Yeah. How did—"

"—We saw the zombies."

"Zombies?" Jay scowled.

"Yeah. There was an entire army of them heading your way," Lisa said. "We were going to warn you and bring you back here, but didn't think they'd have reached you so soon."

Jay looked at the others, perplexed. "No... It wasn't zombies. It was Albert Crosswell."

"Who?"

"The Skin Flayer. He was in the camp."

"Bullshit," Frank sneered. "Crosswell was a cockney villain. Why would he be up here?"

"They transferred him up here a few years ago," Ben said. "Kev told me. And the bodies we found... it was his MO, and same description. It has to be him."

"Wait. Description?"

"Yeah," Jay replied. "Theresa witnessed the whole thing."

He waved a hand, motioning for her to come over. She nodded, tentatively leading the children into the dilapidated entryway. Glass popped and crunched beneath their feet. The two kids stared at Frank with unease, clinging to their mother's arm. Theresa cast a strained smile towards him.

"Hello, again."

Frank frowned. "Have we met?"

"Theresa's the one who looked after you," Lisa said. "She's got medical knowledge."

"We can all contribute," Jay added.

"Whoa, hold up." Frank stepped forward, raising both hands to silence the newcomers. "Nobody said anything about you staying here."

"But—you said..." Jay looked at Lisa in confusion.

"We *did* say you could stay," Lisa said. "But only if you pull your weight. We all need to chip in if we're going to make this work. That means the kids, too," she added.

Theresa nodded meekly in return.

"Fine," Frank said. "You can stay. But you needn't think you're playing that guitar."

"But…" Jack looked back at Lisa, who mouthed 'I'll speak to him' reassuringly.

Frank pretended not to notice. The foundations of control were quickly crumbling around him. He leaned against his staff, partly through exasperation, but more from the weak feeling in his legs. He pressed a hand to the slick bandage on his side, the warm blood seeping through his fingers.

"That's kind of you," Ben said. "But what about Amy? I was hoping you'd help me find her."

Frank considered an answer, but his brain refused to play ball.

"Have you tried Longhill Steelworks?" Lisa asked.

"What?"

"We think Kev is part of a group called the Apostles. Have you heard of them?"

Ben shook his head.

"They operate out of the Steelworks. It's about thirty miles south of here."

"How do you know that?"

"It's a long story. When was she taken?"

"Yesterday."

"And do you think they'll harm her?"

"I—I don't know. I hope not. He said they… need her. But didn't say why."

Probably because she's a nurse, Frank mused. *Hell, I think I need her.*

He pushed harder onto the sodden bandage, trying to prevent any further blood loss. Fire shot down his leg, almost causing his knees to buckle. He held onto the metal pole, trying to keep himself from swaying.

"What do you—" Frank blinked hard and cleared his throat "—want us to do?"

"The same thing we did for you when they took Lisa. I want you to help me get her back."

"Can't. We don't have guns."

"Do you not have—"

"We don't have vehicles," Frank continued, oblivious to Ben's retort. "We don't have numbers. We have nothing."

"He's right," Lisa said, though she kept her eyes glued to Frank. "We don't have much. We could drive down there, scope the place out?"

Frank snorted. "If you want to be in the *scope* of a sniper. Sure."

"So you won't help?" Ben asked.

"Before I do anything, I need help from you." Frank turned to the woman with the kids. "Theresa, was it?"

Theresa nodded.

"I'm gonna need you to patch me up again."

As the words left his lips, Frank surrendered the losing battle with his legs. He dropped to his knee, pulling his shirt up and exposing the sodden bandage.

"Oh, shit," Lisa said.

Frank closed his eyes, allowing himself to be lowered to the ground.

"Is he going to be alright?" came Lisa's panicked voice.

"I think so," Theresa replied. "A combination of blood loss, dehydration and exhaustion. He needs rest and fluids."

"If he's been shot, won't you need to extract the bullet?" Jay asked.

"I've already checked. There's an exit wound. It went straight through, there's no internal organs there, just tissue and muscle. He was lucky."

Lucky. Ha. Frank thought back to what Lisa had said. How Gus had never intended to kill him, and how the shot was exactly where he had intended it. *Well, the joke's on him. I shot him in the same place.* He thought back to Gus and Henderson lying in the office, both trying to stave off death as long as they could. Henderson only had a matter of minutes left, and without medical attention, he was sure Gus would have succumbed to his wound, too. Yet, he couldn't help but wonder if the gangland boss was still alive. And if he was, what kind of revenge did he have in mind?

16

"Take it all in, boys," Gus said, standing back to admire the row of impaled corpses. "Now *that* is art. I wish Carver was still alive to see this."

The group of bloodied men gathered around their grisly efforts. The scaffolds holding the bodies up were slick with blood, shimmering in the sunlight. It had been a tremendous effort, but after a while, they had skewered all eight corpses and raised them high. One or two had slid down, but they remedied that by adding more poles.

"This geezer might be deaf, but let's hope his peepers are up to scratch. I want him to take all this in. Nobody fucks with Gus Razor. Nobody."

"How long do you think it'll be before he gets here?" T-Bird asked.

"Do I look like Mystic fucking Meg? How am I supposed to know? But I can tell you one thing, if this doesn't strike the fear of god into him, I dunno what will."

He clicked his fingers, gathering the attention of the men.

"Listen up. We're heading north to the old army base. I want your guns loaded, your blades sharpened, and your mouths shut. Let me do the talking. If any of you sacks of shit step out of line, you'll be joining these bastards up here. Understand?"

The men nodded.

"Good. Now I don't know what kind of reception we're going to get. Frankie's notorious for his short temper, and I don't know what firepower they've got, so be on your toes. But *nobody* shoots without my command. Got it?"

Another series of nods.

"This is a show of strength. We're convincing them to join us, so I don't want any of you running your mouth."

Harper raised his hand. "What happens if they don't cooperate?"

"We kill them. Any more stupid questions?"

Silence fell, with each man averting his gaze when he fell under Razor's interrogating glare.

"Okay, follow me and stay in the convoy. Let's move out."

Gus strode over to the prison van and hopped into the passenger seat, hurling his gun on the dashboard. "Terrance, you're driving."

A collection of doors opened and slammed shut as the men got into the recovered vans and cars. T-Bird clambered into the driver's seat beside Gus.

"You gonna need a booster seat or what?" Gus chortled, watching him adjust the steering wheel. T-Bird held his tongue, pulled the seat forward, and started the engine.

The vehicles behind them grumbled to life as he drove forward, leading the procession out of the prison and onto the main road. Gus estimated it would take them twenty minutes to get to the base, providing there were no hiccups along the way.

What if we run into these apostles en route?

Then we kill them.

And Frank?

Afterward, yeah. But we'll still need his group to help us take on the others.

They came across an abandoned motorbike which sat alongside the remains of an indistinguishable animal. Then the body of a deer further down the road. Gus tried to think back to when he escaped the prison. There was no motorbike then, or dead animals. There was the woman with the missing tits, but she seemed to have got up and disappeared. For such a remote stretch of land, there was an awful lot happening.

Eventually, they arrived at a junction.

T-Bird read the nearby sign. "Left to Sunnymoor. Right to Doxley."

Gus stared at the broken wall ahead of them: the route Frank had opted to take when they first fled. It felt like a lifetime ago.

I wonder what he found.

We know what he found: that blonde tart and the other misfits.

But where did he go?

The field stretched way beyond his line of sight, the tyre tracks still clear in the ploughed earth. A harsh beeping sound brought him back to the van.

"Who the fuck was that?!" Gus snapped.

The beep came again from the car directly behind them.

"Give me the shooter, I'm gonna—"

Gus flinched when a dirty palm slapped the passenger window. Next came the snarling face of an old woman, pressing her forehead against the glass.

"It's right, you tit," Gus snapped. "Turn right."

The woman stumbled to the ground as T-Bird obeyed the orders. Gus watched in the side mirror as the following car veered around her. She tried to rise, but the van at the rear of the procession ploughed straight through, bounding over her mangled corpse.

"I didn't think you needed directions, you soppy twat," he snarled. "Keep following this road until you reach the sign for the base."

T-Bird didn't reply, instead focusing on the winding trail through the thickening woodland.

The rest of their drive proved uneventful. Yet with every blind turn, Gus imagined a horde of zombies or a busload of apostles racing into view. He knew the chances were slim. The steelworks were south of the base, and they were heading north. They were more likely to encounter zombies than hostility from other survivors. That attitude quickly changed when they reached the military base.

"Here it is," Gus said. "Slow down."

They crawled along until they were level with the destroyed barricade. There were no vehicles parked out front, and no sign of anybody in the upper windows. If anyone was looking out, they would clock the approaching motorcade for sure. Yet, there were no shots fired.

So far, so good.

"Okay, take us in there."

Gus monitored the upper floor windows as they drove through the open gateway. He could feel the same trepidation as the first time he had approached the building. The same feeling of being watched. The same fear of being peppered with machine gun rounds. But like the first time, they pulled up to the front doors without incident.

Gus grabbed the MP5 off the dashboard and hopped out of the van. Aside from the occasional sound of doors opening and closing, the base was silent. The windows, despite being boarded, showed no signs of movement through the gaps.

"This it?" Harper asked.

Gus ignored him and approached the double doors. He made for the handle but stopped short.

That cop is a tricky bastard. He might've rigged it.

There was no sign of interference, but Gus knew better than to make assumptions. He beckoned for T-Bird to approach.

"Oy, muscle. Break this door down."

He took a step back, allowing the stocky man to get into position. The others gathered round, aiming their guns at the door as T-Bird took a slight run and slammed into the wood panelling. The door flew open with ease, causing him to stumble onto the threshold. He hit the tiles hard, his body sliding with a high-pitched squeak.

Gus walked in, stepping over the downed man, to find the hallway exactly the same as he had left it. The doors leading into different parts of the base were all shut, and the stairway was clear. The barrels they had used to barricade the door lined the wall.

"Close the door and block it with those barrels," he ordered. "I don't want anyone following us in, or getting out."

T-Bird clambered to his feet and went over to help the others barricade the door. Despite the grunts from the men and the clang of metal, there was no response from anybody else in the base.

I don't like this. It feels like an ambush.

But how did he know we were coming?

If he saw us approaching, he could've got the message out quick enough.

But why would they hide?

Maybe they don't have the firepower we thought.

"Doesn't look like anybody's home," Harper said. He finished stacking the barrels and approached Gus, careful not to stand within striking distance.

"I bet you were shit-hot at hide and seek," Gus grumbled, turning to the others. "We're gonna flush them out. Turn this place upside down and round them up. Do *not* kill anybody until I say so."

With that, he made for the stairs, the men behind him splitting into groups of two and three, each heading towards different doors. He sensed T-Bird falling in beside him, not that it mattered. The MP5 would be enough protection.

Once he reached the top of the stairs, the base had fallen silent, the different rooms below offering substantial soundproofing. If any of the men had found someone, they weren't making it known. Gus strode through the corridor until he reached the windows overlooking the front of the building.

Where the fuck are they?

Next floor. Let's see what weapons are left.

Gus walked back to the staircase, peering into the open rooms as he passed. They were all empty—void of people, furniture, or anything—just as they had been the last time he was there.

The next floor was the same, every room untouched and uninhabited. It wasn't until he reached the front windows again that he found something out of place. The guns and ammo, which used to be housed at the lookout point, were gone. In their place lay a dark green leaflet.

"Eden Spa Hotel," Gus read aloud, stooping down and retrieving the document. "Natural spring, solar power, infinity pool, sounds right up my street that, Terrance."

He stuffed the leaflet into his pocket and strode back through the corridor.

"Round the boys up, there's nothing here."

"Are you sure?"

"You can bet your little Hampton I am. Our little lovebirds have found themselves a nest."

Gus stopped short when he heard the first sounds of commotion coming from outside. It sounded like shouting, but he couldn't be sure. He strode into one of the empty rooms that overlooked the rear airfield. The fighter jets were all still accounted for, and the dead bodies they had disposed of still lay in the same distorted state. The large dome remained untouched, with the men crowded round, cupping their hands to the glass, trying to see inside. Gus knew it was a fruitless endeavour. The tinted glass offered the slightest glimpse of what lay below. A steep drop, plunging into unknown depths. Gus had expected there was another entrance to the lab, but during his inspection of the base, he hadn't found it.

"C'mon, let's get down there before those pricks fall through."

The words had hardly left his lips when an explosion of glass sent the men hurtling in all directions. Some landed hard, some rolled, all dazed and confused. Then, when they saw the creature bearing down upon them, they screamed.

Gus watched in stunned silence as the monster ripped apart the men with ease, its long claws slicing through their flesh like butter. When the men tried to flee, it bounded towards them on all fours. Gunfire erupted on the airfield as some of the men retrieved their weapons. But the bullets only served to draw attention. The creature's scaly flesh seemed to deflect each shot.

Gus backed away from the window when the monster pounced on another gunman, crushing him beneath its bulk and ripping his head clean off with its maw of razor-sharp fangs.

"Fucking run!" Gus whimpered. He bounded down the stairs three at a time, almost stumbling as he reached the bottom of the stairwell. He rounded the corner, arriving at the final set of stairs when the commotion spilled into the base. The doors slammed shut, the sounds of gasping and panting echoing around the hall.

"L-l-l-lock!" Charlie started.

"With what?" Harper interrupted. His voice broke as he held back a sob. "Forget it, run!"

Gus heard the two men dashing across the tiled floor as he bounded down the last set of stairs. The gunfire outside had stopped, along with the screams. He met Harper and Charlie in the hall. Neither held a weapon, both covered in blood spatter.

"Gus, it's—"

Gus knew what Harper was going to say despite not getting the chance to finish his sentence. The doors behind them smashed open, swinging on their hinges as the scaled beast bounded into the room after them. The four men ran to the front door, Harper in front until Gus clipped the back of his heel. The man smacked the ground, and with his breath blasted from his lungs, he couldn't muster a scream when the creature landed on top of him.

Gus didn't look back as he hefted the barrels away from the door, but he could hear the squelching sounds of Harper being dismembered. He heaved one barrel aside, allowing it to roll towards Charlie, who was still struggling to move any of them. The sounds of evisceration ceased and Harper's remains lay in a crimson pool as the beast set its claws on the ground, emitting an ear-splitting roar towards the trio.

"This way! Move!" Gus dragged T-Bird with him over to the nearby room—a convenient human shield. The monster's claws clacked against the tiles and it leapt through the air. It struck Charlie, colliding with bone-crushing force. A short yelp escaped the man before the creature clamped its jaw around his face.

Gus slammed the door, and looked around urgently for something to barricade it. The only object of note was the empty vending machine at the back of the room, but he knew they wouldn't be able to move it in time. Instead, he picked up a nearby chair, jamming the backrest beneath the handle. Another inimitable roar echoed around the hall. Gus dragged the heavy oak table to the far end of the room, tipping it onto its side next to the vending machine.

You better hope this works.

When he heard the snarl right outside, Gus pulled the pin from the grenade and lobbed it towards the door. It hit the wood panelling and settled into the nearby corner. A moment of calm followed. No clashes against the door, no roaring from the creature beyond. Just the ring of metal still hanging in the air.

Next came the explosion.

Despite the protection of the vending machine and the heavy table, the shockwave still blasted Gus into the wall. His ears rang, his vision blurred, and the air whooshed out of his lungs. He couldn't breathe. He couldn't see. But he could hear the walls crumble around them, bringing the floors above crashing down. One other thing he heard—something he was certain of—was an agonised, inhuman roar. He'd got the bastard. Whatever the fuck it was, he had sent it back to hell. And as darkness consumed him, he knew he'd be joining it soon.

Epilogue

Amy readjusted her position in the cheap plastic chair, moving away from the sun's dazzling beams. The rectangle of light shining through the metal slats over the windows now warmed her chest. It was an uncomfortable feeling, especially when coupled with the overpowering urge to vomit. She was unsure if there was anything left in her stomach, but if the wave of nausea didn't let up, she'd be sure to find out. She rested an arm against the table, finally looking up and returning the unblinking gaze of her brother, who sat opposite.

"It's good to see you," he said. "It's been too long."

It had been years since he was incarcerated, since he had committed those horrific crimes. She had been told he'd never taste freedom again, and she'd never be able to see him without a screen partition and hospital staff in attendance. Yet here he was, sitting less than two metres away, with no security or barriers between them.

"C'mon, aren't you happy to see me?"

"Happy?" The word scraped against her throat, but she didn't allow the discomfort to replace her angry scowl. "You had me brought here against my will. For what?"

"Protection."

"I *was* protected, Alex. I was doing fine."

"You invited two strangers into your company who could've killed you any time they liked. How is that fine?"

Amy looked away as her rage-induced tears threatened to surface. The betrayal was still raw, and the manifestation of grief, anger and regret still threatened to overwhelm her. It had all become clear: Donna's tears, Kev's desire to head south for gas canisters, their quiet plotting. Clear, but it still didn't make sense.

"You took their child from them," Amy said, locking eyes with her brother once more. "You threatened to kill him."

He stretched out his arms. "It's what I'm good at: finding weaknesses and exploiting them. You should know that by now."

"Why send them in the first place? Why didn't you look for me yourself?"

Alex rose from his seat, sauntering over to the metal slats which looked out on to the steelworks below. "Tell me. What's out there?"

"Survivors," she said, after a prolonged silence, during which her brother continued to stare outside.

"Not just survivors. It's a group of people going about their delegated tasks. Like cogs in a well-oiled machine. What you see out there is my kingdom. Quite an impressive feat in only a few weeks, wouldn't you say?"

"You didn't answer my question."

Silence descended again. There was a distant clang and muffled shouting from the people below, but he didn't seem interested.

"I rule with an iron fist," he said after a while. "If I left this place to find you, the structure, the order, the entire kingdom would collapse. Kev and Donna came here looking for sanctuary. And they found it. They generously offered all of their weapons and supplies and were happy to join us. Once I discovered Kev's background. I knew he was the man for the job."

"So you took their child?"

"Collateral." Alex shrugged. "I gave them our family's addresses, and off they went."

"They didn't have to trick me."

"Oh?" Alex cast Amy a derisive smirk. "You would've come of your own accord? I somehow doubt that, given your reluctance to even acknowledge me."

Amy held a hand to her face, an unconscious gesture to hide the guilt.

"Yes," Alex continued. "Donna told me everything. And I suspect that when Kev gets here, he'll corroborate it."

Amy felt the sickness churn again. Ever since she'd arrived, she'd been wondering what would happen to Ben. Would Kev convince him to follow her? Or would he abandon him in Bealsdon? Abandonment was the most extreme outcome she allowed herself to consider.

"So tell me about Ben." Alex leaned against the metal slats, enjoying the interrogation.

"What about him?"

"Well, it sounds like you two are close. You've been with him from the start, right?"

Amy kept quiet. Anything she had to say would only fuel her brother's spite.

"I bet mum would've liked him. Shame she didn't get to meet him."

The sob escaped before Amy could quash it.

Alex grinned. "Oh, right, that's not exactly true, is it? Tell me, sis, was it your beloved Ben who drove a garden fan through her skull?"

Amy's body racked with uncontrollable sobs.

"Was it?"

"No," she snivelled. "It was me."

"Bullshit."

"It was me!" Amy jumped to her feet, shoving the chair aside. "She was already dead when we got there. She attacked me! It wasn't our mum."

"And what of our dear grandparents?"

Amy wiped her eyes with the back of her hand, her body trembling as anger coursed through her veins.

"Did he kill them?"

"They were already dead when we got there."

"Too late to save them, as well? That must be weighing hard on your conscience."

"At least I tried. Unlike you." Amy rested her palms on the table, ready to engage in the verbal duel her brother so desperately desired. "So tell me. How many more people have you killed, Alex?"

"Death," he replied.

"What?"

"Call me Death."

Amy frowned. It wasn't the direction she had expected the conversation to go. "Why?"

"Those aren't people down there. It's a collection of souls. Young and old. My collection. You see, Death doesn't discriminate. I decide how long each of them survives. When their time is up, I send them to the afterlife. Do you know how that feels?"

Amy shook her head, biting back the riposte she wanted to hurl his way.

"No. How could you? You *save* lives. You cure. You heal. Constantly prising people out of Death's grasp."

"I guess we're complete opposites."

"Exactly!" Alex slapped a palm against the wall. "The world has changed. Right now, *I* rule, with imbalance, disorder, and chaos. Those people out there are yearning for direction, for some structure in their lives. And it can't stay this way. It needs to be balanced. Darkness and light, winter and summer, Yin and Yang. I am Death. You are Life. Together, we can rebuild this world."

He watched Amy for a response. But she maintained an indifferent expression, refusing to give him any satisfaction. She knew he was insane. She may have been the last to acknowledge it—despite the trial, the evidence, and his ultimate confession—but she knew. His eyes told her everything. There was no more light, happiness, humour—all the things that had once made Alex the brother she loved. Only a black void.

After hearing what he had done to their neighbours, seeing evidence of the mutilations in court exhibits, and listening to his rambling justification of higher powers and supreme beings, Amy had broken down. She had lost her brother that day, and with him, every happy memory they had shared.

Now, hearing the familiar narrative, staring into the same dark, soulless eyes, the grief resurfaced. But she couldn't let it overwhelm her like the first time. She choked it back and cleared her throat.

"So… you want me to stop you killing people, is that it?"

Her brother sneered. "I'm not the monster you think I am."

"People don't butcher their neighbours, Alex! They don't hold children as *collateral*. Monsters do that."

"I had no intention of harming the child. And it worked. You're here. Donna and her child are reunited, and from the looks of it, Kev is about to be reunited with them, too."

This time, Amy took the bait. If Kev had returned, had he brought Ben with him? She jumped to her feet and strode to one of the other windows, peering through the metal slats. The red sports car trundled over the dirt path, driving with an urgency that caused some of those nearby to jump out of its path. It lurched to a stop when Donna came into view with a young boy who she clung to her side.

Kev scrambled out of the car and ran to his wife and son. He swung his huge arms around them, gripping them in a fierce embrace. Amy watched the car, waiting for the passenger door to open and for Ben to appear. But she knew he wouldn't. Why would Kev have brought him back? Those weren't his orders.

Seconds passed. The car door remained closed, and Kev finally tore himself away from his family. He exchanged a few words with Donna, who nodded in response, then he strode with purpose to their building.

"Isn't that nice?" Alex grinned. "Another family reunited. Think how many more we could save. My kingdom is thriving. My army is growing. We're winning the war against the undead. With you by my side, those people out there will have hope. They will have Life."

Amy didn't register his words. She continued to stare blankly at the car, her brain working overtime. If she could convince Alex that Ben would be helpful, perhaps he'd let him in. Or could she escape? Play along with his fantasies and find a way of orchestrating a way out? But then, what would happen to all the survivors? What if he murdered them out of spite? It wasn't outside his realm of madness, that was for sure.

A knock at the door stopped her thoughts in their tracks. A man strode in, armed with an assault rifle, Kev at his heel.

"Kev's here," the gunman said.

"Thank you, Timo." Alex strode to greet them. "Kev, I trust everything is in order?"

The policeman's glance flitted to Amy before he nodded.

"Good. I've already spoken to your wife, but I want your full account. Walk with me, we're going to—"

"Kev!" Amy blurted as the men approached the doorway. "Where is Ben?"

Kev's tortured gaze caused her world to crumble.

"Go ahead." Alex grinned.

Kev paused, delaying the inevitable heartbreak Amy knew was coming. She could feel her legs tremble, ready to give way.

"He's dead."

Amy screamed, defying her own expectations as she charged for him. Kev took a step back, but Timo lunged forward, barging her with the side of his rifle. Amy fell to the floor, but she wasn't done. With another growl, she clambered to her feet, stopping only once Timo aimed the rifle at her.

Alex stepped forward, beaming from ear to ear. "I'd take a deep breath if I were you, Life. You don't want your name to be an ironic contradiction. There's nothing for you out there. Sit down. Take stock of what you have, and together we'll rebuild this world."

Amy remained still, fists clenched, hyperventilating as she sucked air through her gritted teeth. She watched the trio leave, listening to their footsteps fade after they closed the door. Only once they were gone did she give in to her initial reaction. She fell to her hands and knees, silent tears falling onto the linoleum beneath her. The tightness in her chest caused her to retch, but nothing came up.

She breathed deeply, allowing tears to flow whilst holding at bay the sob she so desperately wanted to release. She pushed the heartache aside. Curling her fingers into fists, she focused on the hatred and vengeance raging deep in her core.

You save lives. You cure. You heal. You are Life… An ironic contradiction. Alex had no idea what was coming. What she was capable of. *She* would be the chaos he spoke of. *She* would be the change. And as soon as she had expelled the rest of her grief, she'd be coming for him.

EXCLUSIVE CONTENT

Want to be the first to find out about news, deals and upcoming releases?

Sign up to my newsletter at www.damienlee.co.uk_and you can get a free novelette!

You can unsubscribe at any time, but there will be plenty of bonus content, giveaways and freebies for all who remain signed up.

Also, if you're on Facebook, come and join us at the Damien Lee Fan Club. We have games, books, discussions, an array of memes, and exclusive news and giveaways, too

Printed in Great Britain
by Amazon